SOULCATCHER

J.Q. DAVIS

Published: J.Q. Davis 2020

jq.davis@yahoo.com

Editing: Precy Larkins

Cover Design: Murphy Rae, www.murphyrae.net

Formatting: Elaine York, www.allusiongraphics.com

SOULCATCHER

*To my body, for disappointing me
and making me proud all at the same time.*

CHAPTER ONE

It Hurts Like Hell

I pulled up to the swanky loft two hours away from my crappy downtown apartment. After retrieving my bag out of the passenger seat of my beater, I glanced up at the tall building and rolled my eyes. The owner of this place probably thought it was so ironic and cool to make it look all industrial and rundown, but I assumed they had no idea what it was like to live in a real dilapidated shithole.

A man and a woman strode past me. A scarf dangled from the guy's neck, his long, curly beard partially tucked into it. The strap of a guitar case was slung over his shoulder as he casually walked with both hands in the pockets of his skinny jeans. The woman was wearing a fedora; one hand clutched a coffee cup while the other held a flowerpot with a single green plant shooting out of it. Typical hipsters. I didn't have to talk to them to know that they were pretentious little pricks who thought they were better than everyone else because they chose to walk or ride their retro bikes around the city instead of poisoning the air with smog from a car.

My client's apartment number was sixty-six. One more six and it would have been a warped coincidence. I knocked on the gray door, a hollow echo reverberating from my knuckles meeting the metal. It opened, and my client greeted me. "Oh, you must be Frankie. I'm Kenneth. Please come in."

I stepped inside.

"You can have a seat on the couch. Can I get you something to drink?" he asked.

"No, thank you." I usually never accepted a client's offer of food or drinks, unless it came in the form of an alcoholic beverage. I sat down on the edge of the sofa and pulled out my paperwork. This part was annoying, but it had to be done.

After going over the necessary information, we agreed on the right location in his home to proceed with the transaction. Preferably someplace with a door to close to muffle the screams.

"Is this going to hurt?" he asked.

"No," I lied. It was going to hurt like hell. Well, maybe not as much as things did in the Red Realm, but close.

"What does it feel like?"

"A mosquito bite," I lied again, pulling out my instruments. *It will feel like the air in your lungs*

2

have been sucked right out for longer than you can stand. For those few minutes, you will feel helpless as the pain shoots through your body, ping-ponging off each and every bundle of nerves inside of you.

Kenneth took a deep breath in and stared out in front of him. He clenched his jaw and sucked in his lips, a telltale sign that he was rethinking his decision. I set up my tools and restrained his wrists to the armrests of the chair, and then I dropped down to his level. I was careful not to get too close to him. I didn't want him to recognize the smell of alcohol on my breath.

"Kenneth," I said softly, laying a hand on his while he gripped tightly onto the wooden chair. "You're scared, aren't you?"

Anyone with two eyes could clearly see by the sweat beading on his forehead that he was frightened. His perfectly parted and patted-down hair was beginning to come undone, and his black thick-framed glasses were sliding down the bridge of his nose. He nodded eagerly.

"Do you think you can do me a favor?"

He nodded again. I stroked his hand and spoke with more sincerity while keeping focused on my balance. That was kind of hard to do. Probably should have saved those last few swigs from my flask until *after* the appointment. "Think about what will happen when we're all done. Think about what it will mean from this day forward. You'll finally have everything you've always wanted. You have worked so hard to get to this point. You deserve this, Kenneth. You deserve to be happy."

He furrowed his brow and tilted his head. He was hanging on to my words, but I could tell by the swift movement of his chest that he was still hesitant. His heart was still racing. I had to go just a little bit further. "Think about seeing your work in those bookstore windows. Everyone will finally know who you are. Everyone will read your stories, the ones that you put your heart and soul into." Literally. "You chose to do this because you believe in yourself. And it's so good to believe in yourself, Kenneth. You believe in yourself, don't you?"

"Yes..." His eyes locked onto mine. His breathing began to slow down. I focused on calming him with my words and my touch, and I could feel that he was giving in.

"You chose to do this because you want to be known, and you deserve to be known, Kenneth."

"I do. I deserve it."

I stared deeper into his eyes and concentrated on creating a slideshow in my mind of what his upcoming life would look like. He didn't blink, and I knew I had him. He became lost in the exciting future my eyes were showing him. He could see friends and traveling and awards and money. He could see pleasure and business and success. But right as I was certain that he'd become convinced, I lost my balance and stumbled backward a bit, which forced my eyes to drift away from his. Shit!

Kenneth attempted to turn away from me, but I grabbed hold of his chin and held his face in place before he could. I blinked a few times and concentrated again on generating a slideshow of his future. When I opened my eyes wide and captured his gaze again, something was wrong. He gasped and winced. There was panic in his face, and he frantically tried to wriggle his wrists out of the restraints. "No! No!" he cried out. "Please!"

It was happening again. My eyes were revealing the complete opposite of what they were supposed to be showing him.

I slammed my eyes shut. "Kenneth, it's okay! Calm down!" I yelled back. I kept my head down and changed my tone, trying to soothe his panic through my words. "Shhh...relax. It's okay." I rubbed his arms and his hands until the tension subsided. "It's okay. It's going to be okay." Shaking my head, I took a few deep breaths in and out. When I felt like I had regained my composure, I lifted my gaze back up to his. He hesitated, averting his eyes away from mine. But when I began to speak again, he found his way back.

"Kenneth, you are going to submit your manuscript, your life's work, to an agent who will decide to represent you. You will become a published author whose books will become bestsellers. Those books will turn into movies, and you will eventually become famous."

His breathing slowed down, and I could feel his guard begin to fall. The right visions were there, and I had him again.

"Kenneth, do you still want to do this?"

He didn't hesitate. He didn't stutter. He did not turn away. "Yes. I want this."

I stood up quickly and glanced at my watch. "Good. I've got another appointment in a few, so let's get started."

The tools I needed consisted of two main things: a sterile wipe and the Seal. A bite block and restraints were also available to clients upon request, or if I felt it was necessary. Kenneth was a bigger guy. He could accidentally hurt me as a result of his reflexes, so I made him wear the restraints. I offered the bite block to him with a gesturing look, but he refused. It was normal. Not many people felt comfortable with it. It reminded them of the dentist or the fact that they didn't have control over what might happen next.

"Do you have a preference?" I asked, waving my hand over his bare chest. I preferred to allow the client to choose his or her location.

"It doesn't matter," he stated without emotion. I lifted the iron rod and it instantaneously illuminated. The amber glow radiated off us both as I approached his awaiting skin. This part was never my favorite. Some of my colleagues enjoyed it, but I never did.

It was an unwanted reminder of the moment it happened to me.

I wiped his dark skin, took a deep breath in, and pushed the scalding brand against his chest. His body immediately stiffened, and his fingers curled into the arms of the chair. I gave him credit for trying his hardest to stifle a scream, but it only lasted thirty seconds before the agony got the best of him. I fought to hold in a sarcastic chuckle. He wasn't going to be different than anyone else, no matter his gender or size. The pain was too great, and they all eventually gave in to it.

The veins in his neck protruded as he howled, until finally, he was able to close his mouth and clench his teeth. I quietly hoped he was careful. I had a few clients grit so hard, a tooth or two broke—hence the option to use a bite block.

Spit shot out of his mouth with every exhale, and the guilt seeped into me. The same guilt as usual.

His burning flesh began to smoke, and I was thankful that I remembered my nose plugs this time. If only I could drown out the sound of the sizzle on the surface of his body. The worst part of it all was happening internally at that very moment. His insides would be set ablaze. Every ounce of emotion, every thought, every feeling he had ever felt would be detaching, breaking apart, fiber by fiber. He would be yanked away from his memories, his love for life, his passions. His hopes and dreams ripping away from the depths of all that made him who he was. It was excruciating for him but tugged on every bit of morality I owned. Even with the liquor flowing through me.

The radiance of the rod began to dim, and I knew it was finally ending. I pulled the heavy iron shaft away from his chest, revealing the Seal of the Red Realm imprinted on his skin.

It was done. His soul was no longer his own.

CHAPTER TWO

My So-Called Life

Two long hours of driving later and I was finally home. I threw my keys into the bowl and closed the apartment door behind me. The day had just dragged on and all I wanted was to shower and relax. But first, I needed a damn drink.

"Long day at work?" Alex, my sister, asked over her shoulder as she stood near the sink, drying dishes.

I poured tonic over vodka and ice. "Yeah."

"It's been three years and you still let it get to you?"

"It'll always get to me, Alex," I mumbled under my breath before swallowing a big sip of my drink.

"You would think by now you'd be used to it. This is what we do," she pointed out. I rolled my eyes and tried to drown her out. I swear I'd heard this same mantra from her thousands of times.

"I know you don't like what we do. I know you've heard me say this a thousand times," she repeated my thoughts. "But it's the way it is. If you don't accept it, you'll just be miserable for the rest of your life. Do you want that? Mom and Dad would not have wanted that for either of us."

I squeezed the bridge of my nose and wished for a tornado to ram straight through our building. She continued to ramble. "Being unhappy is only gonna make your life harder. And then you'll never meet a guy. Men don't like unhappy girls. They like girls who smile. I mean, all you ever seem to do is mope around. Maybe it's because you drink too much. You shouldn't even be drinking at your age. Technically, you're not even allow—"

I slammed my glass down on the table. "Alexandra!" My sister jumped at my outburst and turned to give me a look of disbelief. "Please!"

"Frankie, I'm just trying to—"

I stood up from the kitchen table. "No! I've been listening to you say the same shit to me over and over again for a very long time. I am not happy. I don't like what I do. I had three clients today, and three times I had to watch as their insides were ripped away from them. I had to watch them suffer. I have to watch them suffer over and over again every day."

Alex stepped away from the sink to stand next to me and stroke my hair. "But it's what they want. And it only lasts fifteen minutes at the most. They get it all back," she reassured me.

Sure, they got it all back, everything they lost in those fifteen minutes, but the memories and the lingering pain of losing it all would stick around for the rest of their lives. After what we refer to as The Breakdown happened, they would have nightmares and the thoughts of what awaited them in the afterlife would find a place to live in the back of their minds, even if they believed in it or not.

I ignored her sincerity and recoiled from her hand, swatting away her arm. "I don't care. I don't like that I'm the one who's causing their pain. I know this is my life, but you know as well as I do that I didn't ask for this. You made that choice for me. So, I would really appreciate it if you would just shut the hell up from now on about my happiness or lack thereof, since you took that option away from me."

Her eyes widened and defeat washed over her. The tears in her eyes began to form, but I quickly turned away and rushed to my room before I could see the first drop fall down her cheek. I hoped that she wouldn't follow, but Alex was a follower. She followed and spoke until everything was right in the world.

I didn't want to talk. I wanted to just have my alcohol, take a bath, and nap before I was due back at the office.

I finished the vodka cocktail and slid my clothes off while the tub filled. Taking a peek into the mirror at my naked body, I briefly wondered if Alex was right. Was I drinking too much? Was I too unhappy with my life? And while we were at it, was I too skinny? Through a slightly off-kilter, dizzy perspective—a result of all the alcohol consumed throughout the day—my eyes wandered up and down my bare body, from my feet to my legs to my stomach and my breasts to the mark on my neck. I wasn't a fan of maintaining long hair. I was a roll-out-of-bed-and-barely-even-brush-it kind of girl. But I tried to keep my darkly dyed locks long enough to hide my Seal since I didn't have the option of choosing where it went in the first place.

I tilted my head and traced the tattoo with my fingertips. The two intricately detailed black serpents intertwined and connected at their heads, meeting each other's open mouths and pointy fangs to form an infinity symbol. It still appeared freshly engraved into my skin, and it was a constant reminder of my ill-fated destiny.

Yes, I was unhappy. Yes, I needed another fucking drink.

I found the vodka hidden in the linen closet in the bathroom and poured a little more into my glass, more than what was left of the soda. I took a sip and climbed into the tub, resting back onto the porcelain and allowing my skin to soak in the warm water. I wanted to erase what my clients' faces looked like from my memory. Forget that I was the reason their eternity was going to consist of pain and torture. I wanted to forget about my own eternity.

The alcohol helped to forget.

When I finally felt like I was drifting away into a land of nothingness, there was a knock on my bathroom door. "Frankie?"

It took her longer than usual, but she followed. This called for another sip.

"Can we talk?" Alex asked quietly from the other side of the door. I brought the glass up to my mouth again. "You can give me the silent treatment if you want, just let me say something."

I stayed silent.

"I'm coming in." Did I mention Alex was a nagger? A follower and a nagger. She came in and knelt down next to the tub. "Ugh...look at you."

I scoffed and peeked down at my naked body submerged in bubble-less water. "What?"

"You're so skinny, Frankie."

"Someone's jealous," I said smugly.

"Someone's worried," she shot back.

I exhaled in aggravation. "What do you want, Alex? Are you just going to sit here and point out all my flaws?"

"No. I came in to tell you that I'm sorry."

That took me by surprise. "You're sorry? For what? For basically calling me an alcoholic?"

"For everything. For that, for your life, for this," she said, pointing to my Seal. My reaction was to quickly cover it. "I know how much you hate what it means." She reached behind to her shoulder as if to scratch an itch, but I knew she was touching her own Seal.

"Alex, I don't want to get into this again. It was so long ago and there's nothing we can do about it now."

"You're right," she agreed. "There's nothing we can do about it. But I can tell you how much I wish I could change it. I can tell you that and try to finally make you understand why I did it."

"I know why. We were sick...blah, blah, blah," I mocked. I knew why my sister had to sell my soul and hers to the devil three years ago. We were sick. Really sick. Like, we were going-to-die type of sick.

See, the maternal side of my family inherited a gene mutation that increased a person's risk of getting cancer in various parts of their body. There was a fifty-percent chance of passing it on to other family members. But in my family, there was a one-hundred-percent chance because everyone became heir to the gene, and everyone developed cancer, and everyone died. Our aunts, uncles, and cousins, including our mom, succumbed to the disease. It was a horrible, horrible curse.

My only sister, Alexandra, and I were tested after our father passed away (unrelated to the curse) and we found out, to no surprise, that we each had the gene. It was as if taking the test jinxed me, because ten seconds later I was diagnosed with stomach cancer and lying in my death bed. Alex was diagnosed soon after, and we were both given a grim prognosis. She was much older than me and technically my guardian since I had just missed the mark of adulthood at seventeen. So, Alex was designated to make medical decisions for me. And what does a person do when they are dealt the cards of doom? They go see a man about some souls, of course.

Apparently, my sister knew a guy who knew a guy who would take two souls for the price of not dying from cancer. The only catch, huge catch, was that we must work for the complex counsel of devils that controlled the depths of the underworld, otherwise known as the Red Realm—A.K.A. Hell. And yes, devils with an *s*, meaning multiple.

Before we knew it, we were miraculously healed, moving into an old, dingy apartment building in an unknown city and working day and night at some company that dealt with...dealing souls. It was hard to believe at first, but when the doctors couldn't explain how aggressive stage four cancer somehow "disappeared without a trace," it was hard *not* to believe there was some kind of divine, or ungodly, intervention at play.

"Please don't do that, Frankie. Don't be that way. You know why I did it. It wasn't just because we were sick. And you know I didn't realize the consequences."

I rolled my eyes. "Oh, did they not tell you we'd be working for Hell?"

"No. I mean, you know I didn't truly understand it all at the time," Alex clarified.

There was a bigger market for soul-selling than you would think. It was a no-shit business, complete with execs and bosses and paperwork. Alex and I became Afterlife Sales Representatives, otherwise known as ASRs. That was our official job title. We were also known as Soul Sealers, or simply Sealers. Our job wasn't necessarily in sales. Once a person verbally agreed to sell their soul with a more qualified sales agent virtually or over the phone, another representative was sent to the client to continue the transaction, obtain the necessary documents, and apply the Seal of the Red Realm, which was needed to enter Hell. Cue Alexandra and me, the Sealers.

This wasn't true for all people who sold their souls, but only for those who traded to avoid mortality. Souls sold for other reasons were just normal. Those people lived until it was time for them to die. Once their time had expired on Earth, their bodies remained for the purpose of burial and such, and all of who they were transitioned into soul form. The souls were then sent to spend eternity under the thumbs of the kings and queens who ruled the Red Realm. People who didn't sell their souls and had nothing to do with soul-selling were still on the radar when they died. If they did bad shit, they could still go to Hell. Soul-selling was just another way to increase volume, in a very deceitful and manipulative manner.

Working for the Red Realm meant that my sister and I were immortal. Our souls stayed in our bodies... forever. It was the consequence of selling our souls in exchange for a prolonged life. If we weren't going to breathe our last breath when we should, then our bodies, our souls, our whole selves just worked endlessly for the devils. We didn't go anywhere. Some of my co-workers believed it was a gift, but I didn't. I wasn't a fan of my job, and I certainly didn't want to live an eternity doing it. This life fucking sucked.

On the other hand, I would much rather live a life I didn't like on Earth than end up in a fiery Hell.

Alex continued her pleading. "I just wanted you to live, Frankie. I wanted you to experience life. You were too young to die." There was a sadness in her eyes, as if she missed the old me.

"You think this is living? Experiencing life?" I took another swig, then burped loudly in Alex's direction. "And I'm not young anymore. I'm technically twenty years old." It was sometimes hard to believe that I was three years older now. When I looked in the mirror, I still resembled the seventeen-year-old me. The immortality clause slowed the aging process down to practically nothing.

"Why can't you just accept this?" she asked impatiently. "We have the opportunity to live a normal life."

"Normal?" I snorted. "If you mean that living forever and not being allowed to have kids is normal, you must be delusional!"

There weren't too many company rules to follow, believe it or not. But the one that bothered me the most, and the one that certainly prevented us from having a "normal" life, was the non-procreation clause. Bearing children was no longer an option for the Sealers or any ASRs. I didn't know the specifics, but we were told in orientation that having kids just didn't work for us anymore, biologically, because of the immortality and aging process. Even dating or having relationships was frowned upon. Not a hard no, but the bosses preferred their employees to be married to their jobs. Besides, it would be difficult to carry on a serious relationship with someone and not be able to tell them what we really were. And it wasn't that I wanted to have a million children or anything, but it would have been nice to have the option. I had aspirations, even though I was only twenty. I had dreams and ideas of how I wanted my life to go long before I became a Sealer.

"It's so easy for you to say we can be normal, right? You've already lived your life," I said.

Alex wasn't missing out on much. She was older than me by twenty-three years. Sounds crazy, I know, but Mom tried to get pregnant several times after giving birth to Alex and couldn't. The doctors told her she had developed an ovulation disorder. It seemed like my poor mother had more medical issues than she deserved. But then, twenty-three years later, I was born. Yup. I was a miracle baby.

Since my sister was much older, she'd already experienced life much more than I had. She got married to a man named David, someone who was once the love of her life. Unfortunately, that love couldn't stop David from gambling their marriage into the shitter. They ended up getting divorced right before our sickness and soul-selling, but regardless, she already had the beautiful wedding and the whole shebang. She and David didn't have children because, ironically, Alex couldn't conceive children either. She was told that her womb was not hospitable enough to carry them. As a result, Alex chose to become a schoolteacher, which proved to make her very content. She was able to be close to children even though she could never have any of her own.

I stood up hastily, splashing water all over my sister, and stepped out of the tub. This took some hard concentration of my footing. The floor was looking a little unleveled and threatened to make me fall over. The alcohol wasn't mixing well with this stupid conversation. I wrapped my robe around my wet body before stomping into the bedroom.

Alex followed. "Frankie, you choose to be miserable. I know we can't have kids and our job might be crappy sometimes, but we can still be normal."

I pulled out the travel-sized bottle of vodka hidden in my underwear drawer, and without even pouring it into my glass, took a big gulp. "What is wrong with you? Why do you keep talking about being normal? We haven't been normal for three years. Get the fuck over it!"

She winced at my harsh words. Alex was never one to use curse words. Neither was I, to be honest.

But that was before, when I was the old me and there was no reason to use ugly words.

"There are so many things we can do. We can go back to school, we can have fun together, take some time off to travel. We can do anything," she said, clearly trying desperately to convince me.

"What don't you get? We belong to them! Doesn't that bother you? Doesn't it bother you that we won't ever die?" I hiccupped. "That we have to practically hypnotize people to sell their souls to the devil? Doesn't it bother you that they will go to Hell and be tortured for all eternity because we put them there?"

"They chose to sell their souls. We aren't hypnotizing anyone," Alex corrected, but that was only half true. Our clients did choose to sell their souls, but the Red Realm definitely had some hand in luring and persuading people to do it. And every now and then, some clients, like Kenneth, had hesitations. This was where our supernatural ability came into play.

We were, unfortunately, awarded the gift of showing the client their future through our eyes. This "vision" somehow appeared in our minds when we concentrated and focused on a particular client, revealing the wonderful and rich prospect of what was to come in exchange for selling their soul. Imagine watching an old 1950's home movie projected on a white screen. It wasn't a detailed and specific view, but supercuts of the important parts. If the client seemed to be having second thoughts about their final decision, our job was to make sure they didn't change their minds. I guess you could call it some form of psychic power.

My visions, however, had always been a bit glitchy. If I didn't focus enough or correctly, I tended to show my clients a glimpse farther into their future, like after they died and their souls were being tormented in the Red Realm. I'd never mentioned it to anyone else before, fearing that someone would just judge me or say it was a result of my most favorite pastime—drinking delicious vodka—and try to make me quit. Not happening.

I gave Alex the silent treatment while I dried my hair and put on my underwear.

The truth about a client changing their mind was that they couldn't even if they wanted to. Once the deal was done, it was done. If they tried to back out, they immediately met their untimely death. Only, they weren't sent to the Red Realm. They weren't sent anywhere but to a place of complete darkness. A virtual black hole, as I've been told. The Seal was needed to enter the Red Realm, so if a person wasn't given one by the Council of the NonAligned for just being a bad person or by selling their souls, a place of darkness was their eternity and it was called The Nothing.

I'd also heard that The Nothing was home to anyone who disobeyed the devils. A place of punishment, if you will.

These devils weren't big fans of Indian Givers. They were also not fans of honesty either, because the you-back-out-you're-dead clause wasn't written anywhere in the contract and the clients had no idea what was coming to them. If we failed to persuade them with our visions, they were sent to The Nothing, no questions asked. Instead of mentioning anything about The Nothing, clients were told a ruse that involved having to pay a dowry of sorts in order to back out. Sadly, people were too scared to pay large amounts of cash and would rather sell their souls, so most of the time it wasn't a huge issue. The devils really were evil little bastards.

It was time for a cigarette. "I gotta go."

"What?" Alex asked, surprised. "But...I thought we were going to walk to work together."

I picked out a pair of black jeans and a dark hoodie that read CHILL in bold, white letters. "I'll go by myself."

She pouted. "Frankie, please don't be angry with me. I'm just trying to look out for you."

I slipped my boots on and grabbed my leather bomber jacket before heading out the door without a word. I loved my sister. I loved her more than she knew, but I couldn't bear talk about our life anymore. The life that I would just never be happy with. The life that would never be mine again.

I zipped up my jacket and pulled the hood over my head before reaching the exit of our apartment building. There was a chill in the air, the same frigidness that always seemed to be there. After lighting the end of my cigarette, I sucked hard to inhale the toxic fumes. I never smoked before my life changed. And the only alcohol I'd tasted was a stolen sip of wine from my mother when she wasn't looking. I had never done anything remotely harmful to myself or others. But life was different now. Life was darker, and darker meant I didn't care anymore. If anyone who knew me back then could see me now, they wouldn't even recognize me.

CHAPTER THREE

The App

I stepped out of the building and began the lonely walk down the sidewalk. As I passed the store attached to our apartment, my gaze met Reggie's, the tall urban vendor with dreads who sold shoes and repaired cellphones all in the same tiny place. Reggie could be anywhere in his store and always knew exactly when I was passing by. We locked eyes on a daily basis. I'd never actually spoken to him, but our nods seemed to have made us friends of some sort.

The office was about five blocks from where we lived. I'd walked the same path, day and night, for the last three years. And for the last three years, nothing had changed. There was always a large amount of disgusting trash strewn on the sidewalks and streets. At the same times throughout every single day, a subway train zoomed past on the overpass, rattling everything within proximity. And no matter how early or late, homeless freaks covered in shit stains would beg for crack money on the corners.

Alex and I were required to move closer to work when we became wards of the Red Realm, which was very far away from our old home. I'd never been to this city before my soul was sold, a city within a city named affectionately by its locals as Shitsburgh. Not so original, sure, but it accurately described its disconsolate population. Most of the residents consisted of drug dealers, low-income families, and hobos. Tall, aged brick buildings were practically built on top of one another, consistently blocking out any sunlight. They all looked the same for the most part—drab and muddy brown. Except our apartment building.

According to the ten-year-old newsletter taped up in the lobby near the wall of mailboxes, the history of our seven-story building dated back to the early 1800s and was once a pharmacy, a haberdashery, a hotel, a mercantile, a bank, a hotel turned brothel, a department store, and a hotel again before finally becoming the terrible apartment building I called my home. The ceiling leaked, the pipes burst every other month, and it smelled of mold and fried catfish all the time, but it had one thing going for it: the big, red, illuminated letters on the roof that spelled out The Hartley. It was what made our building different than all the others, and I personally thought it was cool and vintage-y.

Shitsburgh was always gloomy, always chilly, and always sad. It seemed this place was built solely to house the degenerates, rejects, and corrupt characters of the world. You would think our business of soul-dealing would be booming in a place like this, but surprisingly, these folks weren't interested. It was as if they had been institutionalized—no hope for making a better life for themselves and living perfectly content with the way they were. Accepting just who they were. Because these people were so caught up in their own screwed-up lives, no one ever seemed to question what we did. I sometimes wondered if maybe we were the reason for the city's downfall. Maybe the devils purposely wanted people around in a constant hazy hell on Earth to successfully obscure the nature of our business.

I was almost done with a second cigarette before reaching the entrance to my place of employment, otherwise known as Centaurus. The Red Realm was divided into regions, and Centaurus was one of its kings, or in other words, the boss of the region. I'd heard stories about Centaurus and his evilness, but it was his wife, Hysteria, who people feared the most. Although Centaurus was the head honcho of this region, Hysteria reigned queen and very much enjoyed sacrifice and torture. She controlled what happened to the souls from this region once they entered the Red Realm, and Centaurus dealt with the above-ground operations. Thankfully, they lived and stayed in the underworld, just as all the devils did.

Boris stood in his usual spot on the opposite side of the entrance. "Good afternoon, Frankie," he greeted brightly in his Scottish accent.

"Hey, Boris." Boris was one of the many brawny security guards, who were also called The Henchmen. Besides wearing sunglasses outdoors *and* indoors (I didn't think I'd ever seen the color of his eyes), he helped fortify the place—not that it truly needed it. The exterior looked like all the other dilapidated buildings that surrounded it. There were no signs, no indication that it housed anything of value or that it was even a business. There was a huge chance that no one was going out of their way to break in. The only trouble we truly had were the homeless people trying to find refuge off the streets, but it only really happened during the unbearably cold times of the year. And if it did happen, the guards were on top of it immediately. What we did at Centaurus wasn't exactly known to anyone, and I was sure the bosses wanted to keep it that way. I never really knew what happened to the trespassers. And I didn't care to find out.

Inside, the building resembled any other office building I'd been to. It had a minimalistic design, a desk with a cute receptionist, and even a waiting area with a coffee station. It never made sense to me, though. No one waited to sell their souls. Our job was to go to the client every time, to ensure we were getting what we agreed to. Since the residents of this crappy city didn't care to mess with soul-selling, the souls we collected were mostly outside of the city limits, in surrounding suburbs and areas nearby. Traveling took up the majority of our time, but after being in the business for a while, you learned to manage it.

The world was filled with other offices like ours, concealed in different locations and sometimes veiled to be something it really wasn't. There were many other regions, many other employees, and many other bosses to answer to.

I made my way to the elevator and pushed the button with the number seven. The building had twelve floors above us, but those weren't used for daily operations. The thirteen floors below us were assigned to many different departments including human resources, payroll, IT, and all the standard areas of business that comprise a company.

The doors slid shut just as an instrumental version of AC/DC's *Highway to Hell* began humming softly through the elevator speakers. I rolled my eyes at the number of times I've had to hear it. This place was just sick.

The elevator opened into a large room filled with cubicles, otherwise known as my office. The sounds of people working and talking were much better than having to listen to another song about Hell. But I really didn't want to hear or see people, either. I wasn't exactly a people person.

I ignored all my co-workers as I strolled past them to get to my desk. This wasn't new behavior or just because I was annoyed with my sister. I did it every day. I had no desire to become chummy with my colleagues, especially when I didn't like my job. It was enough that I had to hear the latest office gossip floating around, even though I didn't want to. I wasn't deaf. I could hear the whispers. We might have worked for the Gods of Evil, but there was just as much scandal here as in any normal office job. People sleeping with people, jealousy over rankings, and just some good old-fashioned shit-talking behind people's backs. I might have fallen victim to some of the high school crap in the beginning but it got old quick, and now I was simply here to do what I had to do. Also, people just knew better than to speak to me. They knew I didn't give a rat's ass about them.

After a little while of catching up with paperwork on my last few clients, a familiar voice filled my tiny space. "Are you still mad at me?"

I didn't turn around. "What do you want, Alex?"

"Do you want to have dinner with me later?" she asked. The inflection in her voice didn't sound like she was too sure of her own question. She was clearly afraid of my answer.

I thought about it as I glanced down at my paperwork. I didn't hate my sister. Sure, she went behind my back and sold my soul to the devil, my actual *soul*, but she did it out of the kindness of her heart. As insane as that sounded, her intentions were innocent. I could only imagine the defeat she must have felt when she learned that we were probably going to suffer very painful deaths from cancer. As the oldest, Alex must have felt it was her obligation and responsibility to care for me—to take over for my parents and guarantee that she could protect me as they would have. And I was sure a lot of her decision had to do with the fact that she herself didn't want to die or end up alone. So, could I really blame her?

If we were getting technical, she hadn't necessarily done the wrong thing. I was only a minor then, therefore, she basically had guardianship over me. But the least she could have done was include me in the negotiations. She didn't tell me our souls had been sold until the transaction was complete and I was getting some crazy-ass tattoo on my neck, the location of which I did not even have a say in at all. I was still very bitter about that.

Under different circumstances, the client must be present and aware at the time of the sale. However, lying in my death bed, unable to move and unaware of what was happening due to illness was a good enough exception to that rule, I'd suppose. Oh, and it didn't hurt that I was a minor. The Red Realm did not mind cutting corners for a gain. So, yes. I should be upset. But the truth was that she was all I had. She was the only family I had. And I loved her. These days my bitchiness seemed full-blown, but I couldn't deny my sister of just trying to be...my sister.

I decided to give in. "Yeah, we can have some dinner. Did you see him yet?"

Alex paused for a moment before answering, "Yes. I did. He should be calling for you soon."

Something didn't seem right in her tone. I swiveled around in my seat. "Is everything okay?"

"Yeah." She smiled, but it appeared nervous. "Everything's fine. I have to get some work done. I'll see you later. Mr. Wong's Kitchen sound good to you?"

I eyed her closely for a moment, searching for anything off about her demeanor. "Sure. I can go for some Chinese."

She smiled again before stepping behind the cubicle wall and out of view.

Alex wasn't the kind of person to get into trouble. She followed the rules and did her job. She was never a part of the office gossip, never one to speak ill of others. Quite honestly, Centaurus was no place for a woman like her. Alex deserved to be working for the other team. In the place opposite Hell. Heaven. She deserved to be an angel. Those guys didn't take your soul. They welcomed it with open arms in a much less painful way. Or so I'd heard. I had never actually seen an angel or heard about the details of Heaven, and no one at Centaurus really talked about any of those things. It was almost like it was intentionally prohibited. As if it didn't even exist around here.

Before I could turn my chair back around to finish my paperwork, another co-worker poked her head over the wall. "Frankie?"

"What?" I knew it was my turn to see him.

"He's ready for you."

I waved her off, and as soon as I was sure she was gone, pulled open the drawer of my desk. Just the sight of the shiny silver flask made my mouth water. I stealthily poured its contents down my dry throat, then headed for the elevator. I pushed the number thirteen and the doors slid closed, leaving me alone with the harmonic instrumental of Meat Loaf's *Bat Out of Hell*. So cliché.

The doors opened and I stepped into the waiting room. I was on floor thirteen once every four weeks, so it was only routine to walk down the blood-colored carpeted aisle that led to the receptionist perched at a large oak desk. It was all so familiar to see the red walls decorated effortlessly with paintings symbolizing demonic belief. Some were pretty straightforward: the devil surrounded by helpless people clearly being tortured or cowering away from his wickedness. But there were some that required more than a glance to understand what you were looking at. Either way, they were all dark and full of malevolence. So much so that you could almost feel the genuine evil presence inside of you as you stared at them.

I often wondered if any of the different portraits of the devils were actually accurate or just designed to conjure up deep, dark emotions. I had never seen any of them for myself and I was always too afraid to ask. I wondered if they looked like normal humans, or men with black wings, or gross lizard-freak things with long, slithery tongues.

A large, gaudy portrait of King Centaurus and Queen Hysteria framed in gold hung in the center of them all. Centaurus was painted as half horse, half man. He had wings and four hoofs, with his muscular chest bare. And a depraved grin. His wife, Hysteria, sat on his back, as if to be taking him for a leisurely horseback ride. She seemed much more human-like, with features resembling a beautiful goddess in a black, sheer gown. Apparently, nudity was no issue in the Red Realm because her nipples and bushy lady bits were clear as day. Her evil was showcased at the top of her head, where bronze horns protruded out in twists high above her.

I took a seat on one of the velvety red chairs and waited to get called in.

"He'll be one moment," Raven, the secretary, informed me. Her stick-straight auburn hair hung below her shoulders and matched the hue of her skin-tight dress. She smiled at me and her crimson lips gleamed.

I hated my job. Deep down, I hated what I had to do, and I hated that this was going to be the rest of my life and then some. But what bugged me more than anything was how unoriginal this place seemed. We've always equated the color red and serpents and goats with Satan. However, for some reason,

I guess I expected all that to be a myth. Before my sister bargained our souls away, I imagined those symbols were merely created to convey a visual effect for something that wasn't truly real. Maybe even something to persuade humans to believe in evil. To convince them not to do bad things or else they'll end up in a bad place. I had no idea who would have thought of such an elaborate scheme, but I didn't rule it out. To be honest, I didn't know that I had believed in Heaven or Hell before my soul was even sold.

But here I was, sitting in a red waiting room surrounded by snakes and goats everywhere, along with sixes and upside-down crosses and the color red on every fucking thing. Either this was real, or I was part of some crazy-ass cult. The verdict was still out. And if Hell was a real place, why wouldn't Heaven be? Complete with all of the generic heavenly features: wispy clouds, magical harps, and streets paved with gold. There just had to be a balance, at least in my opinion.

The phone on Raven's desk dinged. "He's ready for you."

I stood up and walked through the ornately carved wooden doors that led to my boss's office.

Dominic's office was decorated almost exactly like the waiting room with demonic pictures and red everything, only the lighting was dimmer. He sat at his desk; the back of his chair turned toward me. He was looking out of the large window that nearly spanned the entire wall, which revealed no scenery. We were underground, so it made sense that there was nothing to see but darkness. But it did boggle my mind as to why there was even a window to begin with. Was it some kind of third eye? Did he see things through it that no one else could?

I stepped to his desk with a quiet stride and took a seat. After what felt like way too long, he finally swung around. "Franklin."

I restrained myself from rolling my eyes. I hated when anyone said my true name, but Dominic especially. It suavely slid off his tongue, but there was a cold undertone in his odd accent, which was partially English, partially American—like an English actor unsuccessfully portraying an American cowboy.

I took him in for a moment, as I usually did at first glance. Dominic was magnificently handsome. I had no idea how old he was, but the assumption was that his number was in the thousands. I imagined it was the reason for the strange way he spoke. Regardless, he didn't look a day over thirty-five. His hair was cut expertly, long enough to grab a handful. It was jet black and parted, combed neatly to the side with a splice of blond hanging over his forehead. His face was lightly peppered with stubble, a faint shadow of a mustache and beard. There was never a blemish on his skin, and his sharp, square jawline shaped his face as if he were a sculpted masterpiece in Roman times. I had never seen him naked, of course, but could only imagine that the body underneath his expensive tailored suits was just as perfect as everything else. His clothed physique was that of a well-built, vigorous man. It wasn't hard to envision tight arms and six-pack abs underneath it all.

But I quickly derailed those thoughts. I didn't want to see Dominic that way. He was one of the devil's right-hand men. He worked as the middleman between Earth and the Red Realm. Anything that happened at Centaurus or involving Centaurus employees was reported back to King Centaurus himself by Dominic. I had heard that Dominic was never a ruler, but he once worked under the kings and queens of darkness as a facilitator. He led souls into the Red Realm and aided in deciding what would become of them by determining what kind of torment and suffering would be inflicted. And, according to the gossipers around the office, he was an expert at causing unimaginable pain.

Anyone that close to evil could not contain an ounce of good, no matter how suave or charming or fucking hot they may be. Therefore, inappropriate thoughts of Dominic felt...wrong. Even though I often questioned whether or not *I* was a good person myself.

"How are you?" Dominic asked, flashing a brilliantly white smile at me.

"Okay."

"Good." He looked down at the paper in front of him. He wasn't usually too keen on having small talk with his employees, at least not with me. The whole purpose of these monthly meetings was to track our progress and go over any work-related issues we might have. So, he got down to business. "I see you've had three clients so far today. Do you have any more scheduled this evening?"

"Not that I know of, but I have a full schedule for the rest of the week," I informed him. Dominic believed in having a good work ethic. And even though I hated it, I was pretty good at my job. I did have those glitches from time to time, but I always seemed to get a handle on them. It wasn't worth mentioning if it didn't interrupt my job performance.

"Very good. And have you been using the app?" He sounded hopeful but stern.

Ugh...the app.

I wasn't into this new need to catch up with the rest of the world. In the olden days, or just a couple of years ago, word-of-mouth was the way to spread information about how to sell your soul. To this day, it still remained the ideal way to acquire clients. Just like my sister found out, there was always someone who knew someone about who to talk to. Our business was secretive, but there didn't ever seem to be a problem with people finding out how to sell their souls. Quite honestly, if people weren't truly curious or invested in selling their souls to have a better life, most of the time what we did simply sounded unbelievable. Like a joke, even, which seemed to keep higher authorities out of our hair. Not to mention, Dominic pretty much had everyone of importance in the area eating out of his hands. Let's just say some senators and congressmen out there didn't get their titles without giving up something in return.

"Yes, I've been using it," I said.

The sad truth was that our world was now a slave to technology. There wasn't a day that went by when people weren't using the Internet. Whether it was for shopping or working or just having something to do in moments of boredom, our lives revolved around the co-dependency of intelligent, metal machines of all shapes and sizes. Fortunately for Centaurus, this co-dependency also created the slow but certain death of a human's capability to be an extrovert. People have lost touch with the realness of the real world, a world in which you must be social and actually try when it came to meeting another person—in person. There was no more getting dressed up and leaving the house, hoping to make a new friend or find a potential mate. Now, there were dating websites to help the really shy folks or the really lazy ones. A man or a woman could hide behind a computer screen in the comfort of their own homes without wearing makeup or even showering, with the added bonus of being whoever they wanted to be. And if it turned out they weren't interested in someone, all they had to do was block the person out of their lives without so much as an explanation. Buh-bye.

Our newest contribution to the digital age was *SoulCatcher*. "Catch your soulmate before it's too late" was our extremely corny motto, but it seemed to reel people in. Desperate single ladies and gentlemen would download this app on their cellphones, and our very savvy sales team would convince the most hopeless ones to sell their souls for love. Once they had someone hooked, a notification was sent out to a Sealer to complete the transaction in person.

It was actually really sad. Deep down, I felt bad for those poor, lonely people who were just searching for affection, which was why I wasn't a fan of the new app. But I did what I was supposed to do to be a good employee.

Dominic smiled mischievously. "Excellent. You know, it's very important that we find new and advanced ways to connect with the world. Back in my day, it wasn't as easy. People these days are so much more accessible. They are much more naive, much more trusting. They aren't afraid to do anything if they are behind a computer screen. It has made our jobs a bloody breeze."

The phone on Dominic's desk buzzed. "Sir?"

"Excuse me," he said before turning toward the receptionist's voice. "Yes, Raven?" The way he said her name simply dripped sex. I wondered if he and Raven have had or were having sex. As far as I knew, there was no Mrs. Dominic.

"I'm sorry to interrupt, but Mr. Hannigan is here to see you," Raven said.

"Send him in."

I remained quiet. This was definitely a first. Our meetings were never interrupted by a phone call, much less by another person joining us.

"I apologize, Franklin," Dominic said earnestly. "This is a very important matter that must be dealt with immediately. It shouldn't take very long."

I nodded understandably, but inside my curiosity had hit its peak. Dominic was never impolite and he possessed an old worldly-type manner. He would most definitely consider an interruption rude. So this "matter" must have been pretty imperative.

CHAPTER FOUR

No Place for the Weak

The door opened and I instantly recognized Hank Hannigan. His desk was three cubicles away from mine. He looked to be in his forties and had that whole family-man vibe going on. His everyday uniform consisted of Khaki pants, sensible shoes, gold-rimmed glasses, and a collared shirt underneath an argyle sweater vest. I'd never had a real long conversation with him, but I'd eavesdropped around the office enough to know that he has been a Centaurus employee for about five years. I didn't know the backstory on his soul, but I would assume it was something innocent and similar to mine. Maybe he was sick, or maybe he even sold his soul selflessly for his wife or kids to stay alive.

"Hank!" Dominic greeted him with enthusiasm. "Please, come in. Come in."

Hank approached the seat next to mine and sat down. "Dominic," he said in an uneasy tone.

"Hank, you know Franklin."

"Yes. Hello, Frankie."

I smiled slightly at the fact that he called me by what I preferred and nodded, but my eyes remained to the ground. I couldn't help but feel the tension in the room beginning to build.

"How are you, Hank?" Dominic asked.

"I-I'm okay."

"I'm sure you're doing the best you can at the moment. The anniversary of your first day with Centaurus is coming up, which is also the anniversary of the day you left your family. Now, I know that you aren't allowed to see them. Company rules," Dominic said with a roll of his eyes and a shrug of his shoulders, as if he had no control over it. "But I just wanted to let you know that little Isabella is doing really well." He seemed to sympathize with the fact that Hank was no longer able to have contact with his family. It was, indeed, a company rule to leave everything and everyone behind.

Hank smiled wide but nervously. "Oh, that's great. That's just great." He was genuinely thrilled to hear about this Isabella, but he was also clearly trying to stifle his happiness.

"Yes, sir. She is healthy and happy and has even made student of the month! She is definitely living up to the sacrifices you made for her. We don't normally update our employees on their past lives, but I admire you, Hank. I admire your dedication in taking care of your family." I knew nothing about Hank's dedication to his family, but Dominic's words were soothing, even to me. "Choosing to sell your soul and never see your family again in exchange for your daughter to live a full and healthy life is not an easy decision to make."

"Thank you." Hank lowered his head as Dominic expressed these kind words. It seemed Hank Hannigan did trade his soul to save his daughter's life, and I didn't even have to see his face to know how it affected him. I could hear his broken heart beating from where he sat.

Dominic stood up behind his desk. "I just wished that you could be as dedicated to Centaurus. Hank, I have asked to see you in such an impromptu manner because we have a problem. You see, I have gone over your paperwork and it would seem that you haven't met quota."

Hank cleared his throat before stuttering his response. "Y-yes. I do apologize for that. I've been finding it difficult to get clients this quarter and I—"

Dominic interrupted. "You see, it isn't just this quarter, Hank. Your numbers have been dwindling for quite a while, and you and I have had this discussion before."

"Yes, and again, I apologize." There was vigor in Hank's tone, as if he really meant what he was saying.

"Do you understand why it is of the utmost importance to guarantee we are doing our jobs and gathering the specific amount of souls each quarter?"

I knew the answer to this question, and I hoped Hank did too.

"Yes, sir. I do," he replied.

"Well, I will explain it again. Just for the hell of it." Dominic smirked and stuck his hands into his pockets before walking over toward his elaborately large fireplace. "You see, we need souls. Some of those souls are used to build the Red Realm. To help it grow. To physically work day and night in the construction and expansion of our plane. It is constantly in a state of renovation and development. Just as equally, our kings and queens need to fulfill their undeniable desire to bestow evilness upon those souls. If they don't, they could lose their power. They feed on malevolence. They must consume it in order to survive."

So many of us believed that the evil in the world was caused by the devil. But the truth was that we ourselves were the sources of all evil. We made the decisions between good and bad. On judgment day, which consisted of meeting with a counsel of beings neutral to Heaven and Hell called the Counsel of the NonAligned, it was determined which realm a soul would be sent to. I hadn't the slightest clue what it took to end up in either one, but I was assuming the basics were that if you did bad things, you ended up in the underworld. You did good things, you climbed some stairs into the clouds. Pretty simple stuff.

It would make perfect sense to assume that if people stopped doing bad things, they would stop going to the Red Realm, and then the devils would have nothing to feed on and they could lose their mojo. One would hope that they'd just shrivel up and die. But it's virtually impossible to stop people from doing evil and feeding the devils' desires. Therefore, truly eliminating them would never happen as long as people put themselves in the Red Realm. At the very least, limiting the devils' amount of evil consumption could make them less powerful and reduce the amount of torturous activity in the Red Realm.

I had no idea what a weak devil meant, but I did know that the Sealers and ASRs who worked for Centaurus and other regions were certainly puppets on Earth, luring souls into Hell and sealing their fate— souls that might have otherwise ended up in Heaven. So, we were directly contributing to their villainous cravings.

"We have to keep these quotas high, Hank. We have to keep our bosses happy and powerful. Do you understand that?" Dominic asked. His temper was completely under control, but it still felt like he could just crack at any second.

Hank was clearly focused on keeping his nerves at bay. He sat very still with a perfect posture. "Yes, I do understand."

Dominic snapped his fingers and shades of red and orange instantly shot up from the fireplace, filling the room with an amber glow. "You see this fireplace, Hank? You see how easy it was to light this fire?"

"Yes," Hank called out.

"I can put it out just as easily. It's instant. With a snap of a finger, I can have anything I want. I can *do* anything I want. Do you know what else I can do?" It sounded like a rhetorical question, as if Dominic was just going to answer the question immediately himself, but he paused and waited for Hank's response.

But Hank's response wasn't quick enough. Before I could even blink, Dominic flashed over to Hank, picked him up off his chair, and dragged him to the fireplace. He grabbed him by the throat and lifted him up high above him. Hank's reflexes were to grasp at Dominic's arm, but he didn't seem to be fighting out of his grip. Maybe it was because he knew he couldn't match Dominic's strength. All he could do was hang there and gasp for as much air as Dominic would allow him to have.

"I could kill you, Hank. I could fucking kill you," Dominic threatened through clenched teeth.

Hank was weightless in Dominic's grip. There was no indication that he was lifting anything but a mere piece of paper. No quivering in the length of his arm, no protrusion of veins in his neck, no exertion in his voice. "I have given you too many chances to prove that you could be an asset to Centaurus. You are simply a waste of space in our world and we no longer need your services. I could kill you, right here, right now."

The only audible noise coming from Hank was his struggle to breath. But before he even had a chance to plead for his life, Dominic raised him higher and squeezed his neck harder. His large hands tightened more and more, and Hank's ability to inhale and exhale lessened and lessened.

And then, before I could realize what was about to happen and shield my eyes from anything scary, Hank's body fell violently to the ground, with his head following separately and the nauseating sound of blood spilling and splashing over.

I was a Sealer, but the most I had ever seen was the uncomfortable and painful, but short, detachment of a person's soul when I pressed the Seal of the Red Realm into their skin. I have had clients who decided last minute to abandon their deal, but I never had to see what happened to them. I knew they died and were sent off to The Nothing, but I didn't see the actual death. My job was to simply call for the Henchmen and they took care of the dirty work after I was dismissed from the transaction. I wasn't even entirely sure how the whole death part of it all worked, but I doubted it was as brutal as this.

Dominic bent down and retrieved Hank's head. He held it between his hands and stared for moment. "You poor bastard." Then, as if it was a used, balled-up tissue, Dominic tossed Hank's head into the fireplace. He pulled a red handkerchief out of his blazer's front pocket and attempted to wipe Hank's blood off his hands.

"I'm sorry you had to see that, Franklin." He sounded genuinely disappointed in the events that had just taken place, but I didn't know what to say. Dominic walked back and leaned against his desk in front of me. "Unfortunately, I must do these things from time to time. Hank's constant decrease in client numbers cannot be tolerated. We must maintain a company standard, and in order to do that, I must let go of the weak ones. You understand, don't you?"

I wished I didn't have to say anything, but I had to respect my boss. "Yes, I do." My throat felt closed up and my words were strained.

"Good," he said contently. "Now, I believe you are doing a great job. You have really been an excellent and model employee. Keep up the great work and please continue to utilize the *SoulCatcher* app."

"I will." I stood up. Dominic held out his blood-smeared hand, gesturing for me to shake it. My heart thumped in my chest and I swallowed a gag. I looked down at it and back up at him. He was waiting. I had to do it.

I held out my hand, but right before we touched, right before my skin made contact with Hank's body juice, Dominic smiled and chuckled. He recoiled his hand. "Just kidding, Franklin. Go on. Go get some work done, love."

I turned around and headed out of the office thanking God, if there was one. I forced myself not to glance over at Hank's lifeless, headless body.

Before I reached the door, Dominic called out, "Tell your sister I said hello."

I nodded then got myself back down to my cubicle and away from the horror as fast as I could.

CHAPTER FIVE

Follow the Warning Signs

The next couple of hours consisted of finishing my paperwork, but not without taking long swigs from the flask hidden in my desk drawer every ten minutes. And when that was finished, I switched to the flask hidden inside my jacket pocket. I felt like I wanted to tell someone what I'd just seen, but I was too afraid. My stomach began to rumble, and I knew I needed to get some food in me to accompany the vodka—maybe actual potatoes to accompany the potato juice. But I had no idea how I was going to eat after all I'd witnessed.

I slid out of the office as silently and quickly as I could to avoid eye contact with anyone. After exiting the building, I walked down the dark sidewalk to meet my sister for dinner. Mr. Wong's Kitchen was only a block away from our apartment. I decided to take my time to smoke as many cigarettes as I possibly could before reaching my destination. Alex would just have to wait a few more minutes than she wanted to. I was managing to conceal it, but my nerves were still an enormous ball of shock. It was a bit strange that I didn't feel like crying over having a front row seat at Hank Hannigan's execution. I didn't know the man personally, but it should have still been upsetting to watch someone die for the first time—in such a violent way. I didn't feel sad, though.

In some weird kind of way, it was understandable. A part of my brain was replaying it over and over again. Dominic killed him. It was wrong, very wrong. But somehow, it was right. Hank Hannigan wasn't doing his job. He wasn't meeting quota, which was the whole reason for his existence now. His job was to meet quota. It was his reason to live, regardless of what he had in his past life. He made a deal with the devil to keep his daughter alive and he wasn't living up to his part of the bargain. And, apparently, he was given chances to change, to improve his work, but he didn't.

A tic had developed as I walked. I couldn't stop looking over my shoulders. Couldn't stop the feeling of being watched. I was suddenly paranoid. There was an ache in my stomach. My mouth became dry. I needed to wet it. I needed a sip from my flask.

Why was I trying to rationalize what Dominic had done? He murdered a man. There was nothing right about that, right? But it made sense. It was a consequence. It was a fucked-up consequence, but that was what happened in the Red Realm. We worked for the devils. We didn't work for happy unicorns. We didn't walk on rainbows like everything was peachy. Hank knew this. He had to know.

I walked straight into the restaurant and met Alex at our usual table.

"You okay?" She could sense it already.

I took my jacket off and hung it on the back of the chair. "Yeah."

We ordered the same dishes we always did, Moo Shu pork and chicken fried rice with a side of edamame to share. Alex ordered an iced tea. I asked for a vodka tonic. Our meals arrived shortly after our drinks, and I fought back flashes of Hank's head and body and all the blood in order to force the food down my throat.

"What do you miss most about our old lives?" I asked Alex in an attempt to keep my mind off it. This question was out of character for me, but after what I had seen today, memories of my old life began to resurface for some reason.

By the slight grin that appeared across her face, she seemed to be pleased with the direction our conversation was going. She never got to have many like them with me.

"What do I miss? Hmm...well, I miss movie night. I miss coming over on Friday nights after a long week of work to lounge around on the couch with you and

Mom and Dad. I miss wasting an hour just deciding which movie we were going to watch. I miss watching them cuddled on the couch and watching you cover your eyes if there was a sexy scene. You always felt so awkward about that."

"It was weird around Mom and Dad," I confessed shyly.

She took a sip of her tea. "I miss afterward, when we would have a discussion about the movie we watched. They would get so lost in their conversation, especially if it was about politics or something. They were so different, but so alike." She was looking at me, but I could see the recollection deep behind her eyes.

My own memories began to form. My parents were exactly that, different but alike. They were the perfect balance of each other. My mom was free-spirited and funny and honest. Her creative mind sometimes baffled me and inspired me all at the same time. She was an artist, and it was as if it were just yesterday that I'd seen her in the sunroom, surrounded by beautiful, vibrant paintings of the gardens and mountains and water that outlined our lakefront home. In her earlier days, she painted as a hobby, but it was my father who recognized her talent and helped guide her into the direction to dream bigger. With Dad's intelligent thinking and financial planning skills, she was able to open her very own gallery.

My father was the exact opposite. He was a doctor. A man of science. A logical thinker. He was proud of how he had built his life and took pride in the fact that he started with nearly nothing. He took life seriously, but my mother always seemed to bring out his quirky side. He had it in him and when Mom was around, he couldn't help but feel comfortable enough to just let it all go. Free himself. This conjured up a side of him that he never knew existed, and eventually, he was able to write a bestselling series of books about a hilarious, cure-all doctor. A sort of modern-day Patch Adams.

They brought out the best in each other, and they were more in love than I'd ever seen two people be. Truly the definition of soulmates.

"I really miss them." I spoke down to my plate and pushed around some rice.

"I know you do."

It was still hard to believe they were dead, and we were orphans. Mom was the one with the genetic abnormality, and obviously, Alex and I managed to acquire that fucked-up gene. Dad was an only child and didn't have much of a family to begin with. He left an abusive home in his teens to live on his own. He died of a brain aneurysm shortly after Mom passed away, but Alex and I had always suspected it was overwhelming heartbreak that took him.

"Do you miss dancing?" Alex asked, and the question startled me for a minute. It was something I tried not to think about. "I remember sitting in the audience with Mom and Dad at your recitals. Their eyes just lit up when they watched you dance. They were so proud you. Especially Mom. You're more like her than I ever was."

I nodded slowly, remembering how I used to think that I inherited my mother's bohemian nature. We didn't look alike—everyone else in the family had dark hair and brown eyes while I had light, almost blonde hair and blue eyes—but we had similar personalities. I remembered being very positive and happy all the time, having lots of friends and pink sheets on my bed and always wearing flowery dresses. Back then, I cared about shopping and the Homecoming dance and my grades at school.

And if dancing was considered an art form, then I certainly carried that creativity over from my mother. Dancing was my passion.

Alex pointed a fork at me. "And weren't you on the cheerleading team and dance squad, too?" She stared at me as if scrutinizing my appearance. "Seems like a different lifetime ago, doesn't it?" she said quietly.

"That's because it fucking was," I muttered, suddenly self-conscious. I did miss all of it—the dancing, the clothes, the friends—terribly. But dancing the most. It had become part of me, of who I was, and the fact that I didn't do it anymore hurt me deeply.

Alex definitely got the best of both my parents: Mom's airy attitude and Dad's intelligence. She didn't change much after our souls were sold. But I did. I didn't feel right wearing bright colors anymore. It made me feel like a fraud. I started dyeing my hair black not long after we moved to Shitsburgh. I overdid the dark eyeliner and wore heavy combat boots and leather jackets. I was more comfortable with being dark and brooding now. My parents might not have approved, but they were dead. And so was the old me.

Alex took a bite of food before asking, "What else do you miss about our old life?"

This was a heavy question for me. A complicated question. It wasn't because there was so much to miss. I couldn't possibly pick just one thing. It wasn't because there were so many people that I missed. It wasn't because I missed myself and the person I used to be before I became a grumpy, alcoholic chimney.

It was a heavy question because I had buried all of those happy memories, all of those people, and all of what I used to be down into the deepest depths of my mind and my heart, hidden behind all of the hate and unhappiness that I carried every day. The weight of how hopeless I had become guarded it. Caged it. And I had no idea how to find my way back to it.

But Alex's hopeful expression forced me to retrieve something, so I dove in blindly. "I miss Jacob." It was out of my mouth before I could choke it down. I regretted it immediately.

Alex tilted her head at me and lowered her shoulders. "You loved him," she pointed out.

I glared down at my food and suddenly felt too full to have any more. "I did."

Emotions I hadn't felt in a long time began to bubble in the pits of my stomach. They were of longing, a feeling of distance that would never be closed in. An emptiness that threatened to shatter my heart all over again. The truth was that those shattered pieces were never mended. They remained jagged, too broken to ever be replaced. They would never fit back together again.

Jacob was the love of my life, the boy I thought would always be at my side forever. We met in high school, our sophomore year. He was on the football team and I was a cheerleader—the obligatory perfect couple in every high school. We were both smart and wild at the same time and eager for the rest of our lives to begin. It was a whirlwind romance, fast and almost scary in the beginning, slow and steady in the middle, until we finally set our own comfortable pace together.

He proposed to me on a Sunday afternoon, secretly under a weeping willow tree. He wore his football jersey and my hair was tied back with a yellow ribbon. He vowed from that moment on that I was the only girl he ever wanted to watch dream at night. We didn't want people to know about our engagement. We knew we were too young, but we also knew we were all we wanted. We had plans. Big plans. College, careers, children. We both wanted the American dream. We both wanted to experience it all together.

But Mom got sick and died, Dad passed away, and Alex and I became ill. It all happened so fast. Too fast for me to say goodbye before our souls were sold. Too fast to tell Jacob I was sorry. That I would never forget him and that he would always be that one. My one. The one person who would make my heart ache forever.

I was forced to leave my life behind—my past, my present, and my future with Jacob. For months after our parting, there wasn't a day without tears. Alex tried to console me, but I blamed her. She had sold my soul without my knowledge, behind my back, and forced Jacob out of my life. So I had closed her away, and not long after that, everything else that once mattered to me.

I wasn't allowed to revisit my past, ever. The rules were that we had to leave our lives and never look back. But it didn't stop me from searching for fragments of him in every person that I met. And I'd thought about breaking those rules so many times. I'd thought about abandoning this awful life of shadows and gloom to find that light Jacob and I used to bounce off of each other. But I never knew what I would say to him if I found him. I'd deserted him with no explanation, and chances were, he probably hated me. I would never be able to live in both worlds. I would never allow him to know who I was now because I knew he could never love me this way.

There was nothing left to say about Jacob, and Alex knew this. I could tell she never forgave herself for what she'd taken from me. And instead of trying to open me up, but still giving me a chance to get lost in my memories for a moment, she chose to change the subject. "So, how was your meeting with Dominic?"

I was grateful that she didn't push further about Jacob, but I also wished she hadn't asked me about Dominic, either. I didn't want to disclose the gruesome details over dinner. Quite honestly, I didn't think I ever wanted to tell her. "Fine. We just talked about a few of my clients and the *SoulCatcher*."

Alex shook her head. "I know you don't like that app, but you gotta use it if Dominic wants you to. He'll check if you don't, you know that."

"I know. I'm using it." Thoughts of Hank's head popping off his body flooded my brain and took over the sweet ones of Jacob. "How was your meeting?"

"Oh, well...you know...it was fine." She didn't want to tell me, I could feel it. "I mean, I didn't meet quota this week."

She didn't meet quota? This wasn't like Alex. She was a hard worker and aimed to prove she was. More of Hank's blood gushing out of his neck replaced all other thoughts. "What? Well, what did he say?" I asked.

She shrugged innocently. "He just told me to be careful and that I needed to work harder. He said I'm one of his best employees, and he understands that every now and then people just have a slow week. I'm not worried about it."

Something inside me was struggling to make a link. Connect some dots. Hank wasn't an ace employee like Alex. His numbers had been decreasing for weeks. This was Alex's first offense. As much as I wanted to believe Dominic would give her more chances to prove her worth, I just couldn't. He was menacing today. It was the first time I'd truly seen him in the element of where he came from, of who and what he really stood for. Dominic wasn't the devil's right-hand man because he gave people second or third chances. He earned that title for a reason. I could see it in his eyes today, in the way he threw Hank's head into the fire. They were cold and lacked humanity. He would do what he did to Hank to anyone else.

Dominic's words replayed in my head. *Tell your sister I said hello.* He knew I was aware of her meeting today. He called Hank into the office the same time I was there on purpose. He wanted me to see. He wanted to show me what he was capable of.

He wanted to caution me. He wanted to give me a warning about my sister.

CHAPTER SIX

The Rich and the Poor

We abandoned the Dominic conversation and finished our meals. It was obvious neither of us wanted to talk about him. I didn't inform Alex of my revelation over dinner. How could I? It would only make her even more paranoid than it did me. And I really didn't even know how I would explain to her that a part of me was almost agreeing with Dominic's decision to end Hank Hannigan's life. I didn't even understand it myself. Why was I having these thoughts? I was worried that she might judge me and look at me differently, maybe even think I was evil. But I wasn't evil. I hated knowing that I was responsible for sealing a soul's fate to the Red Realm. Maybe it was the alcohol. Maybe I wasn't thinking clearly.

Instead of telling Alex anything about Dominic, I gave her my own warning.

"I'm just saying, you know how Dominic is," I said as Alex signed the credit card receipt for our meal. "He checks everything. He *knows* everything. If he's constantly checking to see if employees are using the *SoulCatcher* app, you better believe he's constantly checking your client numbers."

She folded her copy of the receipt and stuffed it inside her wallet. "It's no big deal. I'll be sure to keep my numbers up, that's all." She was so nonchalant about it. I needed her to know how serious this could get without revealing what I'd seen.

"Well, I heard that someone was recently reprimanded for poor work."

Alex narrowed her eyes at me. It was skepticism. She knew I didn't play into the gossip around the office. "Who?"

"I don't know their name." Believable. She knew I wouldn't care to know.

"What happened?" Her soul was pure, and she didn't want to believe that anything bad happened to said person. Now I had to come up with something that wasn't so terrible, but terrible enough to frighten her.

"They were sent to The Nothing."

I didn't know exactly what happened in The Nothing, but her eyes widened, and her lips formed a hard line as if she might have some ideas. And it wasn't good.

"I promise I will pick up the slack," she said, then smiled sweetly.

Now, I just had to make sure to stay on top of her. Regardless of whether or not I felt Hank Hannigan had it coming, and whether or not I felt Alex was to blame for my unhappiness, I definitely didn't want my sister to die.

We walked back to the apartment in mostly silence. I entered my bedroom and undressed down to my skivvies, then threw myself into bed and shut my eyes, all of the day's drinking finally catching up to me. I prayed sleep would come soon because memories of Jacob threatened to flood my drunken thoughts.

The next few days were busy. I purposely kept it that way in an attempt to fight off old and forgotten feelings, and also the new ones that partially agreed with murder. The weight on my shoulders seemed to have become heavier after the meeting with Dominic and the talk with my sister, which called for heavier drinking. I would do just about anything to keep shredding my old life to pieces. There was no use in remembering. No use in missing what I used to have or what I used to be. It was no longer there and would never be again.

It was the end of the week and my final appointment of the evening. I was due to be in a ritzy suburb about an hour outside the city. As dejected as I had become, there was always a sense of relief when I ventured away from what was my reality. When I left

Shitsburgh, it was almost as if I could breathe again. Seeing all the trees, the greenery, the open space, and the beautiful houses reminded me of my old life. Only now, I felt like a stranger whenever I left the city to visit others. Like an unwanted guest.

I tried not to compare the outside world with my current life too much. If I did, I would yearn for it constantly and I'd only be torturing myself. Instead, whenever I made it out of city limits, I would pull over to the side of the road and lay on the hood of my crappy car. I gave myself ten minutes. Ten minutes to have a cigarette, take a couple of big gulps of vodka, and gaze up at the sky—blue during the day, starry at night. I'd just stare. No thoughts. Inhale the smoke. Exhale the smoke. Stare at the clouds. Stare at the twinkling stars. The only passing thought I'd have was how different it must have been up there, on the other side of evil.

I glanced down at my watch just as I crossed the city line and realized there was no time for stargazing tonight. It was close to the appointment time and Dominic was not a fan of tardiness.

After a long drive in silence, I finally made it. My client sent me a text message with her code, which I used to enter her gated community. I passed the large, bold sign that read *Chateau Villas* in script. The streets were lined with old-timey lamp posts, which gave a nice finishing touch to accentuate the opulence. There was no house smaller than two-stories. Some were even larger with three floors and balconies and bulky, round columns holding everything together. Everyone's lawn was bright green and precisely cut, landscaped with perfectly manicured gardens. It was the type of neighborhood that made you wonder what the homeowners did for a living. Were they doctors? Politicians? Or just inheritors of old money? If my mom and dad didn't love the lake so much, the doctor and the popular local artist would have probably ended up in a place similar to this one.

There was a sense of envy building up inside of me, but I pushed it down quickly. You would think the Sealers made enough money to live an affluent life, considering we sold our souls and all. But we made enough to live and that was pretty much it. I shopped at locally owned bargain bins for clothes and drove a shitty vehicle. There was a strict rule that we were not to draw attention to ourselves. Knowing that some of my co-workers actually really loved their jobs and all the power they held, it made sense. Many of them would not be opposed to living a lavish life. And all that power would manifest into narcissism, which in turn would lead to endless bragging and the possibility of revealing secrets. But even if I was able to accumulate enough cash for a grandiose home and lifestyle, I still wouldn't be happy. It would take much more to make me happy again, if it was even possible.

The client's house wasn't hard to find—just around a bend in a cul-de-sac. I pulled up into the semi-circle driveway and parked my beater directly in front of the door of the three-story home. It took about three rings of the doorbell for Mrs. Swanson to finally answer.

"Hi, darlin'! Come in!" she sang in a southern accent as she walked away. Three tiny toy Yorkies sniffed my legs and yipped for a moment before losing interest to trail behind their owner. I quietly closed the door behind me and followed her into a large den. I wasn't at all surprised by the inside of the home. It was just as extravagant as I'd imagined, maybe even borderline excessive. There were gaudy paintings and statues everywhere. Brass chandeliers hung from the ceiling of each room I could see, and the curtains hanging off the windows were very reminiscent of the *Gone with the Wind* era. The construction seemed nice, as far as the layout and floors and paint colors went. But the decorations were flat-out over the top.

"Come have a seat with me, dear," Mrs. Swanson said. I sat down on the floral couch opposite hers. Her dogs immediately curled up at her feet. "I am so embarrassed! I just got home from the spa and I didn't have any time to put my face on." She tugged on her silk robe. "I mean, look at me. I'm a mess!" She seemed to truly believe she was.

I didn't comment. I was looking at a woman whose hair was done up as if she was going to a cocktail party and a face caked with makeup. Her nose was too small and her lips were too large. The corners of her eyes slanted upwards, as if someone was pulling her hair back too hard. Everything just looked swollen. Her face seemed to have been surgically altered more than once. And judging by the wrinkles in her hands, she was clearly not a spring chicken.

"Would you like anything to drink?" she asked politely.

"Um...no. Thank you."

"You sure? I've got some water, cola, wine—"

"Do you have vodka?" I asked too eagerly. I was running low in my flask, and since she was offering...

She didn't hesitate. "Why, yes. Absolutely. On the rocks?" I nodded, and she stood up and walked toward the wet bar on the opposite side of the room. "I like a girl who knows what she wants and isn't afraid to ask for it," she called out as she poured.

She handed me the drink and I thanked her. "Mrs. Swanson—"

"Please," she interrupted. "Call me Dotty. Everyone calls me Dotty. Mrs. Swanson is for the help. And frankly, my dear, you are helping me more than any of these nitwits around here."

I hadn't read her report thoroughly and wasn't completely sure what she was selling her soul for. I usually knew this information before I met with the client, but it was a busy day and I'd left her profile at the office by accident. Whatever it was, I needed to find out to help guide the glimpses in case she decided to back out. "Dotty, there are a couple of things we need to go over before we begin the process," I explained, opening my bag and retrieving my notepad. "What exactly is this transaction for?"

"Well, I'll give you the short of it," she began. "You see, Tessa Vanderbilt hosts the Chamber of Commerce dinner every year honoring the town's most accomplished philanthropists. You know, the people who have donated the most money to charities and foundations? Well, Tessa has hosted it for the better half of ten years and that self-centered bitch never gives anyone else a chance. She only does it for the attention. She loves to show off her house and hog the spotlight. I mean, the woman is older than me and she's fit as a fiddle, I'll give her that. But she just lollygags all year 'round, not planning anything special for the event. It's always the same boring food and music. And my house is clearly bigger than hers. I take it she'll throw a hissy fit when the Dickens works his magic and the civic association tells her she won't be hosting it anymore, but that's just too bad now, isn't it?"

I knew that I was staring blankly at her, but I couldn't help myself. "So, you're selling your soul to the devil for a dinner party?"

"Sugar, this isn't just a party. It is *the* party. All of the most important people attend and I'm the one who deserves to host it," she demanded, flipping her hair behind her shoulder.

"Do you understand what it means to sell your soul?" I just had to ask.

"Honey, I'm already going to Hell," she admitted nonchalantly. "I've done some questionable things in my day, might as well throw the best party I can before I go!" She didn't seem at all concerned about the fact that this meant she could be tormented or have to work endlessly for the most wicked beings in this universe. I didn't know the details of what souls had to do in the Red Realm, but I'd heard horror stories of heat, shoveling soot, being physically tortured for fun, and reliving the worst day of your life over and over again. If she thought hosting a party was worth any of those things, this woman was seriously nuts.

Then again, I'd had clients sell their souls for some very silly reasons. But I tried not to judge. Maybe this was the most important thing in her life. Maybe she felt like this was her destiny—to be in charge of putting together an important event. It wasn't like it was just any party. It was in honor of those who helped others.

Who was I kidding? I tried really hard to see the positive in this particular encounter, but I just couldn't. An eternity in Hell for a fucking party was ridiculous. I couldn't tell her that, though. I had to stay professional. "Okay, Dotty. I'm assuming you've read the contract. You know that when your death occurs, your soul will be the property of Centaurus. It will be collected at the time of death and brought to the gates. If you choose to back out at this moment, you will be expected to pay a particular sum of money and—"

She interrupted my routine mantra. "Yes, I know, dear. I've read everything and understand, but I'm not backing out. I am a woman of my word."

I almost felt resentment toward Dotty, and I didn't even know her. She carried a confidence that I'd never seen before, and I was jealous. "Well, I guess we'll go ahead and get started then," I said as I began to prepare my tools.

"Oh, wonderful!" she shrieked. She slid the red silk robe down her shoulder. "Do you think we can put the Seal right here on my shoulder? I would love to show it off to the gals. Oh, goodness! They're going to feel like a bunch of old bitches when they see that I got a tattoo!"

I bit my lip and choked down a chuckle. "Sure."

The rest of the transaction went by smoothly. I didn't have to use any glimpses of Dotty's future to persuade her. It was tough to watch the old lady in so much pain during The Breakdown, but she bounced back pretty quickly, and soon after, acted as if nothing even happened.

We said our goodbyes and I started up my old car. As soon as I pulled out of the driveway, my phone buzzed in my pocket. It was a text message from work:

Last minute sale. Jessica Ford. 720 Fulton Avenue, Apt. 5C.

Shit! I was hoping to get home before midnight. I had a bottle of booze and a show on *Netflix* waiting for me to binge-watch.

Thankfully, Fulton Avenue was back near the city limits. It wasn't a neighborhood as gorgeous and affluent as Dotty's. As a matter of fact, it came damn near close to the crappy ambiance of my city. If the hobos and poor folks of Shitsburgh happened to get a tiny leg up on life, they would probably move there.

After circling the block several times, I finally found a spot nearly two blocks away from Jessica's apartment building. I realized before I got out of the car that I was seeing things more clearly. That wasn't good. I needed things to be foggy, so I decided to sit in my car for a few minutes to enjoy a cigarette and the rest of what was in my flask.

When I finally felt warm and fuzzy and flighty, I jogged to Jessica Ford's building. Nearly out of breath as a result of hotboxing a cigarette, I huffed up the five flights of stairs. The familiar sound of police sirens, babies crying, and adults fighting was muffled through the walls. The noise coupled with the rundown interior of the building was proof that this place wasn't that much different than where I lived.

I reached apartment 5C and knocked. About a minute later, someone answered.

"Jessica Ford?" I asked.

Her expression revealed suspicion, and she didn't open the door completely. Only her head was visible. "Hi. Yes, I'm Jessica. Are you—"

"Frankie. Yeah. Can I come in?" I asked in annoyance. She had to know I was on my way. I couldn't blame her that much, though. A woman living in these parts should take extra precautions when it came to safety.

She opened the door and gestured for me to enter. The smell of apples and cinnamon instantly hit my nostrils, replacing the odor of stale cigarettes and urine from the hallway. I peered around the small space, getting full visuals of the kitchen, bathroom, and living room/bedroom all in one view. It was a small studio apartment, but very clean. There didn't seem to be anything out of place. The kitchen counters were spotless and the main room seemed to have just been vacuumed by the evidence of fresh tracks on the carpet. I sat on the futon and what I was assuming to be her bed. She nervously came and sat next to me.

"I promise I don't bite." I grinned. People were usually a bit standoffish upon meeting me for the first time, so it wasn't a surprise that she was a bit hesitant. I didn't exactly offer any friendly cues, and my dark clothes and makeup usually made them wonder if I was up to no good. People and their stereotypical views.

Jessica attempted to smile, but the tension in her body didn't allow it to be authentic. There was an awkward silence and she turned away from me. I studied her for a moment to grasp what kind of person she was. She was completely different than me, maybe even my polar opposite. Her light brown hair was neatly pulled back into a ponytail. She wore jeans and a tank top, her arms and shoulders covered by a pale pink cardigan. She was exceptionally pretty, with a girl-next-door kind of vibe. Her makeup was au naturel, mostly nudes and a shimmery blush. As a woman who appeared to be in her early to mid-twenties, Jessica's features were soft and young, and she seemed as if she could be very sweet. She was probably exactly what I would have been if my soul was never sold.

She crossed then uncrossed her legs and fidgeted a bit before finally speaking. "I'm sorry. I'm just really nervous," she murmured.

"It's okay. Everyone usually is," I admitted. "Can you tell me why I'm here?"

She took a deep breath. "Yes. Um...well, I-I want to have a baby."

Okay, that wasn't what I'd expected to hear. "A baby?"

"Uh, yeah." She hesitated and drew back, most likely because of the expression on my face. I realized this and tried to keep my curiosity under control. "Is that...okay?" she asked doubtfully.

The truth was that this was a first for me. I'd sealed many souls for lots of reasons—some ridiculous, some at least a little understandable. But I had yet to come across someone who wanted to sell their soul to have a child.

I regained a professional composure. "Yeah, of course. Can you elaborate?" I definitely needed the details for the possibility of second thoughts.

"Well, my husband and I tried to have a baby for a couple of years. We finally got pregnant, but I lost her." Jessica's eyes clouded and her chest extended outward, as if trying to hold back any emotions that threatened to show. "I can't carry children," she informed me.

"I'm sorry to hear that." Truly, I was. I sometimes recollected on the plans Jacob and I had, especially lately. I knew I was young, but I felt the maternal extinct inside of me. Having a baby with him would have not only completed our dreams but completed me as a woman. Jessica's reasoning for not being able to bear children might have differed from mine, but I felt her pain.

"It's okay. I might never get over losing my daughter, but I'm ready to do what I have to do to have another child."

I glanced around the tiny apartment. "Does your husband know that you're doing this?"

She looked down at her hands and took a deep breath. "My husband...died in a car accident a year ago."

Are you kidding me? This poor woman! How is she even functioning right now? She lost her baby and her husband? I couldn't find the right words to respond.

"Please, don't feel bad for me," she said in a nearly demanding tone. "I've had enough of that in the past year. I'm just ready to move on. I've tried taking the adoption route, but no adoption agency will even give me a chance knowing I live here and have no husband. I lost everything when he died. He was no longer around to help pay the mortgage. Our house was foreclosed, and I had no choice but to rent this place on my low income. I've been working extra hours at the restaurant for months to make more money, but I still need a little more time before I can get a better place."

Well, that explained why such a clean, neatly dressed and well-composed young woman would be living in a shithole like this. I nodded in understanding. Her emotions were everywhere. A second ago she was holding back tears and now she was trying to convince me of her decision to sell her soul.

"I need this. I need to feel whole again. I need to know that I have that baby coming to me, the one I've always dreamed of having."

An overwhelming feeling of compassion fell over me, something I hadn't felt in a long time. I usually made it a point to detach myself from my clients. It wasn't smart to feel sadness or pity for why they were selling their souls. If I did, it would only make my job much harder because I knew what was coming to them. I knew that when their lives ended on Earth, I was the reason their souls were sent to an eternity of unhappiness and pain. I was the Sealer, the one sealing their fate. But my heart was aching for Jessica. She was hitting a nerve directly connected to my morals, and suddenly, I found myself doing something I had never done before.

"Are you sure you want to do this?" I asked, straight-faced and firm. I had never placed a client in a position to question the decision they were making to sell their soul. I was pretty sure it was against the rules.

She stared at me, puzzled. "Excuse me?"

I needed to explain myself. I didn't know this woman, and I feared she might report me. "I just wonder if maybe there are other options for you. I don't think you understand the repercussions of selling your soul. You experience a lot of pain and suffering in your afterlife. And you won't be able to be with your family when you die. You will go to a different place, far different from where they'll be." I had no idea why I was saying these things, but I couldn't control myself. Even if she did heed my warning and decide to change her mind, I would have to call the Henchmen and they'd be here in a second to take her soul to The Nothing. But at least she wouldn't be tortured in Hell.

It was either that, or I'd have to figure out a way to hide her away from them.

Her expression changed immediately. A sense of assurance and calmness replaced all the other emotions she had been showing me. "As long as I get my baby and my whole family ends up together when they die, it doesn't matter where I am, or where my soul is," she avowed confidently.

I knew then that I shouldn't push anymore. I sure as hell didn't want Dominic to find out that I was trying to persuade a client out of selling their soul. I had no idea what my own repercussions would be. And judging by her last comment, it seemed like she'd made up her mind. I understood completely. I might have done just about anything in this world to have a normal life. A life where I had the ability to love something I created. Alex and my mom crossed my mind. I thought about what they must have felt and gone through when they learned they couldn't have children.

I decided that I would do this in honor of them... and myself. "Okay, then." I reached into my bag for my tools. "Let's do this."

CHAPTER SEVEN

Whoa, Baby!

Jessica Ford's body visibly stiffened when I pulled the Seal out of my bag.

"Let's do this? Right now?" she asked with clear hesitation.

I placed the rod between us on the futon. "Yes. Are you not ready?" I asked. I could detect that I was being a bit snippy but I didn't know why. Maybe I was upset that she was making this choice. She seemed like she could be a smart girl—a girl who had more options than this. Or maybe I was jealous of her. She was going to get something I would never have.

Jessica swallowed hard. "I'm ready."

"Good. Where do you want it?" I was all business now.

She briefly scanned her own body before pointing to her ankle. "Here. I can cover it up with jeans and socks." She rolled up her pant leg. I wiped the spot with a sterile pad, then reached into the front pocket of my bag for the bite block. We were in a crowded apartment building, and while I would normally ask the client if he or she wanted it, I needed to insist that Jessica use it. Something told me she would not handle The Breakdown as well as Dotty. The chances of neighbors hearing her bellows of agony were high. Although, it might not have even mattered in these parts. There was already screaming and hollering coming through the walls in the hallway. "You need to bite down on this."

"Really?" she asked fearfully, pinching it between her fingertips as if it were some foreign object she'd never seen before. "Is it going to be that bad?"

"It's just a precaution." I wasn't going to tell her about all the pain she was about to experience. In fact, I decided against restraining her. I wasn't even going to mention it. The bite block scared her, and the restraints might push her toward calling the whole thing off.

I lifted the long iron rod and it illuminated. Jessica's eyes widened as she marveled at the glow. "It's beautiful," she breathed. If she only knew the immense discomfort she was about to endure, she wouldn't be saying that.

"Are you ready?"

She didn't say anything and gave me a blank stare.

"Jessica, I need you to grip down on the edge of this futon and tell me you're ready before that bite block goes in. If you move, it might be more painful. Are you ready?"

Her forehead wrinkled and her lips curled in. "Tell me it will be okay," she blurted.

"What?"

"Just tell me I'm making the right choice. Tell me I need to do this for the baby. Please," she begged.

Shit. I wished every client could be as easy as Dotty Swanson. It was enough that I had to do the actual sealing. That alone made me feel like the asshole who was sending them to Hell. But there was added guilt when I had to show them visions of what their future would hold and persuade them into selling their souls.

I positioned myself so that we were eye-to-eye. Clearing my mind of any of my own thoughts, I concentrated on forming mental pictures. "Look into my eyes, Jessica. You're going to be okay. In the next few weeks, you're going to come into some money, and you will pay to get artificially inseminated. You're going to find out that by some miracle, you were able to get pregnant this one time, and in nine months, you'll have a healthy baby with no complications. You will move out of this apartment and into a townhouse with a big backyard. It's where you'll watch your baby grow into an amazingly intelligent and beautiful person.

"Your child will be the love of your life, the only reason for living. You will be the caring mother you've always wanted to be. Can you see it? Can you see the love you'll have for each other?"

She didn't answer.

"Jessica? Can you see it?"

"No."

Damn it! What did she see?

Tears began welling in her eyes and she froze as if in shock. "I see...I see myself. Chained up. Naked." She began to shake. "They're whipping me. My skin is bleeding. It's...it's tearing me apart! My skin hurts!"

It was happening. The glitch. The glitch was showing her the future of her soul.

"They're beating me! They won't stop! I can't take the pain!" She tried to stand up, but I grabbed her shoulders and shoved her back down.

"Jessica, stop!"

She started wailing and flailing her arms about in my face. I threw my head back and dodged most of her slaps at the air, all except one. The palm of her hand collided perfectly with my right cheek. The sting rippled across my entire face. She kicked her feet up on the cushion of the futon, attempting to get away from me, but I sat down on her knees to hold them still. She continued to thrash her arms around until I was finally able to get a hold of her wrists, spreading her arms out wide and holding them in place on each side of her body. I was hovering over her, straddling her waist. We were both out of breath and huffing and puffing, but she wouldn't stop staring into my eyes.

"Please make it stop!" she cried out.

I realized then that I hadn't closed my eyes yet because I was busy trying not to get slapped again. The horrible vision of her tortured soul was hypnotizing her, and I had to close my eyes and start over.

"Jessica, it's okay. Shhh...it's okay." I brought my mouth down to her ear and changed the tone and volume of my voice to a near whisper. "It's okay. It's going to be okay," I said softly, and I realized I was also trying to calm myself down. My heart was racing, and I was a bit shaky. This was definitely a first. I never had to physically restrain a client with my own body before.

"It's going to be okay," I repeated a few more times.

Finally, after coaxing her heart and mine to a slow and steady beat, I could feel her muscles begin to loosen. I took a few breaths of my own before sitting up, purposely keeping my eyes away from hers. "Okay, I'm going to put some restraints on you before we start again. Don't be afraid. You've had to deal with worse. You can do this."

Jessica seemed to take my words of encouragement well and remained calm. I managed to get her to move to a chair with arms and attached her wrists to them with the restraints. She started to quietly weep. "I'm sorry. I just don't know if I can do this anymore."

I couldn't look at her just yet. "Jessica, you have to." I wished that I could tell her that if she didn't, then she would die. Either that, or just give her the damn Seal now that she was restrained. Quite honestly, I could have just done that. I was pissed at her; she fucking slapped me! But it wasn't the way I did things. I couldn't live with myself if I forced the Seal on a client. I had to get my concentration back, get the right glimpse of her future back.

I wanted a damn drink so bad!

"It's going to be okay." I focused hard on her future and her baby and gazed at her again. I bore deep into her blue-green eyes and repeated everything I said before. The money, the healthy baby, the townhouse. "Can you see it, Jessica?"

"Yes," she replied robotically, staring back into my eyes. "I'm ready now."

"Good."

I brought the bite block to her mouth, but she moved her head away from it. "Can I ask you a question first?" Jessica asked me.

"What?"

"Are you crying because I slapped you?"

I quickly took my gaze away from hers and wiped my cheeks. I *was* crying. Why the hell were tears streaming down my face? She hit me, but not hard enough for me to be crying like a little bitch over it. "I'm good. I'm starting now." I practically shoved the block between her teeth.

Embarrassed and pissed off that I got all emotional during an appointment for the first time ever, I hurriedly pressed the Seal of the Red Realm onto her ankle. She noticeably bit down hard on the bite block, squealing softly as her breathing grew heavier and heavier. I held the rod down securely in place for fifteen minutes, and the entire time, all I could think about was how crazy this transaction was...and how much I missed the baby I would never have.

The fifteen long minutes were finally up. Taking one last look at the sigil that now guaranteed Jessica a spot in the Red Realm, I packed my things. It didn't look right on her. Jessica's pale skin was inflamed and red, causing the scaly snakes and their pointy fangs to appear even crueler. It clashed with her innocence.

She walked me to her door. "I'm sorry I slapped you," she apologized shamefully.

I pulled out a cigarette and placed it between my lips. "No worries. It happens." Not really, but I didn't want to leave here making the girl think she did something terribly wrong.

She smiled slightly. "Thank you for not slapping me back."

"Next time, I will," I said before turning my back to her and heading toward the stairs. I heard a hushed chuckle, then the door shutting and several locks turning in place.

CHAPTER EIGHT

Secrets Never Stay Buried

I got back home at a little past midnight. Surprisingly, Alex was still awake and reading on the couch. "You're home late," she noted.

"Yeah, I know. Were you waiting up for me?" I asked with irritation. I knew the answer. It just bothered me that she still treated me like a child.

She took her reading glasses off and set the book down on the coffee table. "No, ma'am. I was just reading."

Yeah right. As much as I wanted to go to my room, take a couple of shots of delicious liquor, and fall asleep so I didn't have to think about anything anymore, something was gravitating me toward the empty spot on the couch next to my sister.

I pulled my jacket off, kicked my boots away from my feet, and went into the kitchen first to pour myself a cocktail. Alex called out, "Make one of those for me, too!"

Her request halted me for a beat—Alex almost never drank liquor—but then I proceeded to make her a drink, too. After stirring them with my pinky finger, I entered our tiny living room and plopped down next to her.

"Oh my! What happened to your face?" she asked, taking her cocktail.

"I got bitch-slapped."

"Why? Does it hurt?" She touched it gently. There was still a warm sting, and her cool skin felt nice against it.

"It doesn't hurt that bad. I didn't restrain a client. She hit me on accident."

"You didn't hit her back, did you?" she asked.

"I'm not an asshole, Alexandra."

She shrugged. "Well, sometimes you are." I gulped my vodka and rolled my eyes. She took a loud sip of hers. "Ahh! I haven't had alcohol in so long," she chirped.

"Why not?"

"I don't know. I was just never really into the whole getting-drunk thing. Not even when I was younger. Maybe I was just worried about becoming addicted. It's why I worry about you so much."

"You don't have to worry about me."

"Don't I, Frankie?" Alex asked thoughtfully. She knew I liked to indulge, but I didn't think Alex had a clue as to how often I *actually* drank. I tried to drink casually around her and hide the fact that I pretty much needed a taste every hour or so. She also didn't know about my flasks and other travel-sized bottles of liquor hidden in my bedroom and in my desk at work.

So, I had to shoot down her assumptions. "No, you don't have to worry about me. I'm fine. Just because I like to have a few drinks a day doesn't mean I'm an alcoholic."

"Well, I'm your sister. I'm worried. Besides, you're so different than you used to be," she said, pulling on the edge of my black shirt that read LEAVE ME ALONE.

"Just because I wear dark clothes doesn't mean I'm going to slit my wrists when the time is right. You're not going to find me in the bathtub soaking in my own blood. I hate my life, but I'm not going to waste it that way," I assured her. I'd thought about it many times, trust me. But there were two things that stopped me: I wasn't a coward and I had no desire to enter the Red Realm. I figured I was already in hell on Earth, but I could do without the flames and demonic entities breathing down my neck.

"I believe you. But why do you let the hate for your life control you?" she asked.

I took a sip to answer the question. "It's not that I hate my life. It's just...not going as I planned it."

"Frankie, I'm sorry to tell you this, but life can be unpredictable. It probably won't go the way you want it to about ninety percent of the time. It's simply up to you to move past the bad things that happen or dwell on the things you can't have. If you choose to move on and let things go, you're learning to grow and quite possibly open new doors. And some of those doors might eventually lead to what you wanted all along, only they will open at a different time and you'll have a different path. I know that I'm the reason why you're on this particular path, and you don't know how badly I feel about that every single day, but it's life now. We have to make the best of it."

"How can I make the best of it when I feel there's absolutely no chance of a better life? What if the only door I had was available before my soul was sold, but now it's closed forever?" I challenged her.

Alex could tell I was referring to a specific door. "What's going on?"

"Nothing," I exhaled sharply.

"Frankie, you can tell me anything. I'm always here for you," she offered.

I swallowed her words, and they hit hard in my stomach. I wanted to open up. I wanted so badly to confide in my sister, to allow her into my mind, but my war-torn heart kept telling me not to. I was afraid to let anyone in to see the person I was now.

The old me had dreams and ambitions and hope for happiness. Now, I felt like there was no use in having those things anymore. It was simply a waste of time if I couldn't get married or have children, if I couldn't share my hopes and dreams with someone else. To inspire them to keep hoping and dreaming, even when life was unfair. I was embarrassed to feel this way, to be this person. But maybe if I just told someone about my feelings, it would unload some of the weight...

What did I have to lose?

I swallowed another mouthful of my cocktail and settled deeper into the couch as the smooth heat traveled down my throat. I was mentally loosening myself up. "My client, the one that slapped me tonight..."

Alex gasped and covered her mouth as if to be shocked. "You killed her?"

"No! Stop it! She was nice, and young and pretty. She wanted a baby," I said flatly.

"Oh? She and her husband couldn't have children?" Alex asked curiously.

I stared straight out in front of me. "She and her husband had a baby, but the baby died. Then, the husband died. And now she wants another baby to raise on her own."

Alex was quiet.

"I tried talking her out of it. I actually tried giving her second thoughts," I admitted shamefully.

"Why did you do that? You know she would just have to die anyway if she backed out of the contract."

I finally turned toward my sister, and as soon as my eyes met hers, I could no longer cage my emotions.

They began to spill out, and through long, deep sobs, I attempted to explain. "Because, Alex! Because I didn't want her to give up a life to constantly think about what her eternity will be like. Instead of being grateful for even having a life and enjoying it with her new baby, she'll have nightmares and lingering thoughts in the back of her mind." I didn't know for sure if that would happen to her, but it was what happened to me. It was how I felt and what my dreams were like. "She'll be haunted by her decision to sell her soul. She'll constantly wonder what it'll be like in Hell. It'll weigh on her heart, knowing that she won't meet her family in Heaven when she dies. And I did this! I did it to her!"

I broke. I began to bawl, and I couldn't control it. It was a long overdue cry that my sister immediately understood needed to happen. She enveloped me in her arms. "There, there," she whispered into my ear. "It's going to be okay, Frankie."

I continued to weep into her shoulder. "I was so jealous of her. I hated her. Why can't I have a baby? Why can't I fall in love? I miss love so much." I felt like such a fraud. I was supposed to be thick-skinned. I was supposed to be a hard-ass and not care. But here I was, crying like some little sissy.

"We might not be able to have children, but we can still fall in love. We just have to be careful, that's all. We just have to remember that our job comes first. But we can balance it out if we really tried."

I sniffled, quieting down my sobs to hear what she was saying. "Our jobs will always be number one," Alex said. "But it shouldn't stop you from experiencing the love and affection that you deserve from someone. We all need love, Frankie. We all need someone and something to love in order to survive. It's what keeps us going. It's what life is about."

"Who do you love?" I mumbled.

She peeled me away from her and squeezed my shoulders. "You, silly." She smiled. "I love you. And it hurts me so much to see you this sad. I know you've been walking through this life like a zombie, and it kills me knowing that I'm the reason for your pain. But you have to at least try, Franklin."

She said my name. She only said my actual name when she was serious. When something truly meant something to her.

I nodded because I wanted Alex to know that her words were being heard, but simply doing that made me cry even more. I didn't know how to try anymore. I was afraid to search for the old Frankie, the one I'd buried so long ago. I worried that I would never find her again. Feared that she was lost forever. I had no idea how to find the aspiration for the happiness I once had. My life consisted of gloom and watching people suffer. The suffering was only for a short period of time, but it did something to me. I grew accustomed to it. There was no more compassion. No more empathy. And what was a person without compassion or empathy? What kind of person could watch someone's head fly off their body without so much as a scream or a whimper? What *asshole* could agree with murder?

Tonight, Jessica made me feel something I haven't felt in a while. I was jealous and sad, two emotions that I hadn't felt together since Daisy Clementine won Homecoming Queen by only two more votes than me. Maybe I did possess some of that humanity I thought I had lost. Maybe there were shreds of the real me somewhere left inside. I just needed to piece those shards back together again. I needed to desperately find her again. And I needed a reason to search for her.

Should I start caring again? Should I start making friends and being involved and doing that thing people called smiling? Maybe I should start searching for love. Maybe I should start dating.

I rested my head on Alex's chest and she stroked my hair. We sat silently for a moment, and I assumed we were both remembering our past.

Mom and Dad. I'd always adored them. I'd always believed that their relationship was a good footprint for how two people in love should be. They laughed together, cried together, supported each other, and even criticized one another in a constructive kind of way. They were always actively working to better themselves as a couple, even though they had been together for so long. They were comfortable enough with each other's presence that they could be their most real and authentic selves, no matter what that meant. No matter how serious or embarrassing or just plain silly it was.

Mom did things on a whim. Dad had to plan. Mom found positivity in the bad. Dad tried to fix what he could. There was always balance. There was always a harmonic union between the two of them.

"I want what Mom and Dad had," I muttered.

"You and me both. They were always so great together, especially after everything that happened."

"Everything that happened?" I sat up. "What do you mean? When Mom got sick?"

Alex leaned forward for her glass. "No. Years ago. When Mom and Dad had that falling out. Before you were born."

She said it as if I should have already known about this "falling out." But I didn't. "Alex, I don't know what you're talking about."

"What do you mean? It was huge! Mom and Dad almost got divorced. Mom left for a little bit and Dad had no idea where she was. Everyone thought it was the end and—" My dumbfounded expression must have stopped her. "Oh, Frankie. I'm sorry. I thought...I thought you knew."

"Mom left? For how long?" I asked carefully, afraid of what Alex's next words might be.

"Well...yeah. She left Dad. I was away at college, so I didn't know exactly what happened. They had a serious fight and Mom packed her bags and moved out. She was gone for a couple of months. When she came back, it wasn't long after that she found out she was pregnant with you."

My mom left my dad? The soulmates? The perfect couple? The people whose relationship should be used as a lesson in love? I had never heard this story. I didn't know that Mom and Dad could have ever broken so hard—hard enough to walk away from each other.

"You have no idea what happened?" I pressed. She had to know something.

But she shook her head. "No. Dad was a complete wreck when Mom left. He couldn't eat, couldn't sleep. He cried all the time. I had to leave school to care for him. Then, Mom just showed up one day. Out of nowhere. I went back to school, and when I came home for winter break just a couple of months later, it was as if nothing even happened. They were completely in love again, maybe even more so than before."

"And she was pregnant with me?" That seemed a little suspicious.

Alex glared at me. "Yes."

Did she sense the seed that was just planted inside my brain? She had to. She had to have the same thoughts. Mom was told she couldn't have kids because of some reproductive disorder. She and Dad tried for years and didn't succeed. Then she left and came back expecting a child?

Alex brushed the ends of my hair with her fingers. "Mom was the one who had problems conceiving," she reminded me. "Her pregnancy with you was what brought them back together. There was more than one reason why you were a miracle baby."

Alex smiled. I squinted. The wheels were turning in my head. Maybe it made sense, but it was still kind of funky. No way did I want to believe that my mom left my dad, much less became pregnant by another man. I couldn't even picture my mother *with* another man. It made me feel sick.

Alex wiped away what I assumed was the blackened mess of eyeliner and mascara smeared all over my cheeks. "Can I tell you a secret?" she asked in a hopeful whisper.

I nodded glumly.

"Now, this might upset you, but don't let it. You opened up to me and I feel like I owe you some honesty as well. So, promise me you won't get any sadder," she demanded, pointing a finger at me.

I nodded again, trying not to give away my eagerness to hear what this secret could be. I quickly tried to imagine what she could possibly tell me. Alex was not usually a keeper of secrets. And the secret she just revealed about my parents wasn't exactly a secret. She thought I'd already known about it. But Alex lived a pretty straightforward life before this one as a caring schoolteacher who happened to fall in love with and marry the wrong man. She worked overtime tutoring kids after school and volunteered at the soup kitchen on holidays. The only time she ever deceived anyone—the only story she ever told me about deceiving anyone—was when she had to hide from our parents the rose tattoo on her ankle that she got in college. And she could only hide it for a couple of weeks. So, what kind of secret could she have possibly been holding on to for all these years?

"I was pregnant," she uttered.

My heart dropped. "What?"

"When we signed the contract, I was pregnant with David's baby."

I was stunned. "What do you mean? How? I thought your womb was all fucked up."

"Frankie! Language," she shrieked. "And I thought so, too. But apparently, the doctors were wrong. Either that, or I had a miracle baby of my own."

"Why didn't you tell me?" I asked, a bit crushed that she hadn't.

"It all happened so fast. We got divorced, you got sick, I peed on a stick and tested positive. I took a few tests. I just couldn't believe it. But you were a miracle baby. And doctors are wrong all the time. But I didn't want to say anything. I didn't even know if I wanted to tell David and you were already going through enough."

"It would have made me happy, Alex," I said softly, squeezing her hand.

"Maybe," she responded. "But we had more important things to worry about."

I glanced away for a moment to put two and two together. "Wait, what happened? What happened to the baby?"

She reached for her cocktail and took a swig, then looked down at her glass. "Well, we aren't allowed to have children."

I shook my head in disbelief. "What?" Did I just hear her correctly? Was she insinuating that when we sold our souls, she lost the baby? Did they take the baby from her? "Alex, what are you saying?"

"I'm saying exactly what you're thinking, Frankie. I lost the baby when we got the Seal of the Red Realm," she explained. "They knew I was pregnant before I even said anything. They warned me of the consequences of working for them and—"

"And you still agreed!" I shouted. "How could you do that?" I was suddenly furious. How could she trade a baby for a life like this?

"Frankie, calm down," she soothed, gesturing for me to lower my voice. "We were going to die anyway. We were both sick and our chances of getting better were very slim. Did you forget that?"

I actually did forget. I sometimes forgot that if Alex hadn't sold our souls, I wouldn't be here at this moment. I'd be dead, not missing out on anything. Not being jealous of what other people had and what I couldn't have. But it was not easy to forget that I was alive now and would be for a very long time. An eternity, to be exact. To constantly long and wish for the things I couldn't have, like children and love.

As quickly as the anger came, it went away. I sat back and relaxed my shoulders. Alex took my hands into hers. "I need you to understand the point I'm trying to make. Yes, I was sad that my baby was going to be taken away from me, but the reality was that I just couldn't have it. No matter what. Soul-selling or not. So instead of dwelling on what I lost, I decided to focus on what I *did* have. And that's what helped me continue on with my life. With our lives."

"Did it hurt when they took the baby?"

"Not physically. I was only a couple of months along," she said. "It was like I woke up one day and wasn't pregnant anymore. But I did struggle with it mentally. I've always wanted a baby, you know that."

I felt absolutely awful for the amount of grief Alex had to experience on her own, and it was all hidden away from the world. "I'm sorry. I'm sorry that you had to go through that loss alone. I wish you would have told me."

"It's okay," she chirped encouragingly. "It's the past and I have you. That's all I need."

"You make me feel like a jerk when you say things like that. I'm crying and upset because I can't have love or a baby, and you're perfectly content with just me."

Alex brushed my matted hair away from my face. "Well, we are two totally different people, and that's

okay. I'm sweet and caring and you're a little selfish."
My jaw dropped until she grinned, and I knew she
was joking. I pushed her shoulder playfully. "But
don't think the love of a man isn't nice to have every
now and then, if you know what I mean," she added
with a wink. I performed a silent gag and she laughed
out loud.

Maybe there was a little truth in her comment.
Maybe I *was* selfish. Maybe I was so wrapped up in
my own self-pity and daily need to torment myself
that I was subconsciously pushing away anyone who
tried to get close to me. This idea suddenly made me
tired. "I'm going to get some sleep."

"Yeah," Alex agreed. "I've got an early day
tomorrow. And that really strong drink you made has
my head spinning."

I plucked at her forehead. "Then get some sleep,
drunkie." I chuckled to myself as I padded to my room,
mentally making a note to be more lighthearted with
Alex. I could actually feel my heart smiling, which was
something I hadn't felt in a very long time.

That night, I laid in bed and thought about what
Alex's baby would have looked like. I wondered if he
or she would have possessed any of Mom or Dad's
personality traits and talents. I wondered what Alex
would have named her baby, and what it would have
felt like to be an aunt.

I thought about Mom and Dad. About their fight.
What could it have been about? What could have been

so bad to have threatened their undeniable love for each other?

That suspicious infidelity seed threatened to grow, but I tried my hardest to stop it. If Alex was told her womb was no good for a baby and she ended up pregnant, then maybe it wasn't too far-fetched to believe the same happened to Mom.

As my body grew heavier against the mattress and my eyelids began to slowly shut, I thought about how much Alex and I have had to deal with. We had already lost so much, and I wondered...could Hell be any worse?

CHAPTER NINE

Are We Worthy?

I awoke with the cumbersome thoughts of the night before: Dotty's envy-worthy confidence, Jessica's desperate sadness, the glitch, my parent's almost-divorce, and Alex's heartbreaking revelation.

Sounds of plates clinking together in the kitchen resonated into my bedroom, and I briefly considered continuing the conversation from last night with my sister. The truth was that it did make me feel a tad bit better. But when I exited my room and got closer to her, I chickened out. I could feel the anxiety rising in my throat. Maybe the cocktail had a hand in my vulnerability. Sober Frankie still had things she couldn't quite truly discuss yet, like her ex-fiancé Jacob and Hank Hannigan's beheading.

Instead, I entered the kitchen and decided to ask her about something that had been nagging at me. "Alex, do you know what the Red Realm is like?"

I queried nonchalantly while pouring myself some cereal.

She continued placing the dishes in their rightful spots and spoke over her shoulder. "Um...well, I haven't been there myself." She chuckled. "But I've heard stories. Why?"

"I'm just curious," I responded with a mouthful of dry cereal. "I've heard stories, too. What have you heard?"

"That it's terrible. It's always hot and sad."

"Yeah, but what exactly happens down there? And what happens to people when they're sent to The Nothing? Like, if they back out of a deal? How do the Henchmen take their souls?" No one in the office had ever been to the Red Realm, that I knew of. And if they'd been there, they never really talked about it. This was one of the reasons why I still questioned its existence. As if it were taboo—like an unspeakable, company-wide understanding that it was not to be mentioned. We just sent souls there, no questions asked.

Alex finished dish duty and sat at the table with me. "If a client decides they want to back out of the agreement, they have to leave this world immediately," she explained.

"And move on to a floaty darkness," I clarified. "Yeah, I know. But what exactly happens there?"

"Nothing. Absolutely nothing. You're aware of the darkness, but it's like just sitting in a dark room all alone. Nothing to hear. Nothing to look at." In some ways, that almost sounded worse than Hell itself. Alex continued, "When we call the hotline, we inform them that the client has decided to back out, and then we leave as soon as the Henchmen get there."

I nodded in agreement.

"Well, I once stayed behind when the client changed his mind because I, too, was curious. I felt awful because he had no idea what was coming to him. I secretly went off to the bathroom and called the Henchmen. When there was a knock at the door, the man was confused as to who could be visiting him."

I was enthralled by this story seeing as how I had never heard it before. Alex never seemed to run into problems or much excitement when it came to work—that I knew of, anyway. This was the juiciest piece of gossip I'd ever heard from her. "So, what happened?" I asked, eager for more information.

But it seemed the answer wasn't as gory and scary as I thought it would be. "Nothing, really. The two Henchmen walked in, ordered my client to sit down on the couch, and he did so without a word. They said some kind of chant in another language and the client closed his eyes."

"That's it?" I asked, a little disappointed. Not that I necessarily wanted the client to experience a painful death, but I suppose I expected it to be more... terrifying. More... showstopping.

"That's pretty much it. My understanding is that they don't want to leave a mess because they take the body and dispose of it. You know all these disappearances and missing people you hear about sometimes? Well, a lot of those people sold their souls and backed out last minute. Don't even ask me what they do with the body. I don't know and I don't care to know," she said, waving it off.

"Did you even see his soul leaving his body?"

"No. I left right when he was pronounced dead. I've been told it takes a few minutes for the soul to kind of realize what to do, I guess. It was actually surprising to see how peaceful his death was," she admitted. "I suppose they save all the cruelty for the Red Realm."

The Red Realm was reserved for evil, malevolence, and darkness. There was really no need to execute the wicked practices of Hell on Earth. The physical ones, anyway. We definitely practiced manipulation.

Speaking of which, maybe the alcohol was still going strong in my veins because I decided to push my guard down a little further. "Do you have problems with your visions?"

Alex stood up and started filling an exercise bottle with water. "My visions? How so?"

"I mean, do you ever have issues showing clients their future? Like, do the visions ever...screw up?" I was nervous and starting to feel like I should not have brought it up. I just knew she was going to press me harder, maybe even go directly into blaming the alcohol for these glitches.

She glanced down at her watch and began packing a lunch bag. "Are you experiencing some problems with your visions? If you are, you should maybe see tech support."

I decided not to go into detail. "No, it's okay."

"Well, if it starts interfering with your work, then you definitely need to speak to someone," Alex advised. "It might even be wise to slow down on the alcohol, just until you figure out what it is."

I nodded, feeling my face flush with embarrassment. I quickly changed the subject. "So, what do you think the Red Realm is like?"

"My understanding of what happens there really depends on the devils. It's whatever they want. There really is no rhyme or reason to it, as long as they're able to do whatever pleases them and keeps them going. Whatever keeps them powerful." She slapped some peanut butter and jelly between two pieces of bread and wrapped it in cellophane.

"I've heard so many things."

"Me too," she concurred. "But they are devils, Frankie. Immoral malevolence is what they're made of. Let's just hope we never have to experience it firsthand." She grabbed her lunch kit and her jacket off the back of the door. "I gotta get on the road to meet my next client."

Dominic and Hank flashed through my mind. If she had to get to a client, I didn't want to hold her up. It was critical that she met quota from now on.

"Yeah, okay." Then, I grabbed her hand. "One more question. Do you believe we deserve to be who we are and do what we do?"

She stopped putting on her jacket. "What do you mean?"

I looked down at my fingers and began to fidget, feeling a bit self-conscious by my question. I peeked over at the leftover bottle of vodka from last night sitting on the counter and imagined my lips wrapped around its head, suckling on its spicy nectar. "Never mind."

"No, tell me."

I looked her in the eyes, and right then, decided to just let go. "I mean...if we didn't work for Centaurus. If we decided we didn't want to do this anymore and somehow didn't have to spend eternity in the Red Realm for quitting our jobs, do you think that we'd go to Heaven? Do you think they would accept us there?"

She didn't answer my question immediately, almost as if she was thinking of the right thing to say. "Well, I don't know much about Heaven. You know they don't really talk about that realm. But I think you would go there."

"Me? What about you?" I didn't understand. Why wouldn't she go to Heaven? The worst thing Alex had ever done was deface her body when she decided to get that tattoo of the rose on her ankle. And I really doubted getting ink would keep a person out of Heaven. Besides that, she was already pretty much an angel.

"Because I'm the one who made the deal. And behind your back, no less. But you, Frankie...Heaven would be gaining someone truly special." She glided her finger over my cheek, which thankfully wasn't bruised with Jessica Ford's handprint. "I have to go."

I was left sitting at the table, speechless at the fact that my sister didn't feel worthy enough to be accepted up there. It was true that what she did—making a deal with the devil in order to cheat death—was probably frowned upon by the heavens. But she did it with good in her heart.

I still struggled sometimes to even believe all of this existed. It could be true, or we could have just as easily been working for some crazy guy named Dominic who claimed that the Red Realm was real to scare us into doing his bidding. Who knew? But then again, there were many things in this world that we couldn't actually physically see but were real. Gravity, energy, and love were just to name a few. I hadn't seen Heaven or any of its occupants, but if Hell was real, why wouldn't Heaven be?

I'd heard around the office that there had been some kind of treaty made between Heaven and Hell. Kings and queens of neither realm were allowed to show their presence on Earth, which was why there were middlemen like Dominic to help build a bridge between humans and the supernatural. Although I had never met anyone who worked for Heaven, they were around somewhere. A world with only evil and no good would be constant, destructive chaos. I could only imagine if the devils ruled this world. It would be their playground and humans would be their toys. That treaty was saving us all.

These thoughts were giving me a headache. I was overthinking. My life seemed much simpler when I just didn't give a shit. But the events that had been taking place over the past few days seemed to have been screwing with the emotions I thought I had buried long ago.

I pushed my chair out and went straight to the bottle on the counter. It was definitely time for a drink.

Sipping on a morning cocktail helped squash the possibility of caring about the day. And when that warm fuzziness from the alcohol finally began to prickle my skin, I set down the glass and got dressed. My phone dinged and I knew it was work. I was due for a couple of days off but working at Centaurus and for Dominic meant that I was on-call twenty-four hours a day, no matter what.

I checked the notification bar, and sure enough, it was the *SoulCatcher* app.

1313 Elysium Drive

One soul. Male.

Please click here to download more information.

I hated this app. I hated technology. I would much rather be holding real paper in my hands with the client's information written in black ink. I followed the tedious instructions to sign into the employee login, confirmed that I was an ASR, downloaded the client's sale information, then clicked another folder to access it. Skimming through the contract, I learned that the client's last name was Lake, no first name listed, and he was selling his soul to Centaurus because he wanted to move on from his ex-girlfriend.

It was not uncommon to deal with clients selling their souls in return to forget about and move on from their exes. As a matter of fact, it was one of our bestsellers, and it irritated me. I didn't have the luxury of getting over Jacob with anyone's help. Granted, I didn't believe I would ever completely get over him, but I still had no choice but to move on with my life without him...and without help.

These folks were cheating, trying to bypass the late nights of crying, the consistent emptiness that lingered in their hearts, and the undeniable feeling of loneliness. They didn't want to go through the motions of that terrifying roller coaster, the one that left a person's emotions all over the place. One minute they were okay, and the next they were drowning in painful memories and continuously asking themselves why.

I paused for a moment, suddenly realizing that maybe I despised these clients because I was jealous. Why was I so jealous of everyone? Was this why I'd become so bitter, so detached?

My pondering was interrupted by another ding.

Please confirm client acceptance.

I rolled my eyes and clicked yes. I wasn't sure what was happening to me, but I needed to finish this damn drink and pull my shit together.

It was morning, but the hidden sun and heavy, dark clouds made it feel like dusk. I stopped in front of the shoe and cellphone repair store to light my cigarette. Reggie, the dark-skinned store owner with dreads, lifted his chin up at me, his usual greeting. I returned the gesture. I started to make a mental note to actually speak to him one day soon, but then I remembered I wasn't supposed to care about anything, so I immediately tossed that thought aside. I couldn't start caring. I needed to just stick to myself. Live this awful life alone because if I started caring, I would get hurt. If Hank Hannigan and I were friends, I might have been a wreck after seeing his death the other day. But I didn't cry. I didn't mourn him because I didn't care.

The truth was that life was filled with endless disappointment and loss. It was what my job had taught me over the years. My clients sold their souls because something had hurt them and/or something was missing from their lives, causing them to be unhappy enough to agree to live in torment for all eternity. I'd come to realize that if I didn't care, I would have less chance of becoming disappointed or unhappy or sad. It was only logical, right?

My sister was the only person I could ever love. And even then, I had to stay distant. Last night was the only exception. My vulnerability got the best of me, but I had to stop.

I started my junky car and headed to 1313 Elysium Drive. Surprisingly, this person lived within the city's vicinity. Not the usual clientele, but I was a little relieved that I didn't have to spend my day off traveling.

After a twenty-minute drive, I pulled up to a modest one-story home in what I considered to be one of the safer parts of town. And by safer, I meant there weren't homeless people sleeping on the sidewalks and groups of young adults gathered on the corners doing or dealing who knew what. But those things could easily be found just a block or two away from the subdivision. This area was where the senior folks resided, the ones living off their disability and social security checks and who'd been residents of the city for a long time. And the houses matched their owners—old.

I opened the chain-linked fence that wrapped around the tiny front yard, which was bare. No plants or garden accessories. Just faded green grass trying to hold on for its dear plant life. I walked up the four short steps to the front door, realizing then that it might have been a mobile home instead of an actual house. A stationary one, not on wheels.

Before I could knock, the door opened. Only the silhouette of a tall man was visible behind the mesh screen door between us. "Can I help you?" he asked, almost as if my visit was a surprise.

"Yes. I was notified to offer my services to a Mr. Lake," I said, using my professional voice. He didn't respond and just stared at me. I began to feel uncomfortable. "Sir?" I readied my keys in my hand, planning a quick escape, just in case this guy was some kind of freak with bad intentions.

Then, finally, he spoke. "Oh, I'm sorry. Yes. Please, come in." He opened the screen door, and suddenly, I was the one staring.

CHAPTER TEN

Greek Gods Do Exist

He was tall. Really tall. His stature towered over my five feet, seven inches. And he was big. Really big. His plain white T-shirt fit perfectly, hugging and defining the muscles jutting from his chest and arms. His physique was similar to one of those fake wrestlers on Monday nights, but not in that almost gross kind of a way with veins popping out everywhere. There was nothing gross about him. His hair was wavy and long, just past his shoulders, and highlighted with caramel and light brown strands. His trimmed beard encased his full lips, circling his mouth and running up the sides of his face. And his eyes were blue, as blue as the ocean in the Caribbean.

If Greek gods roamed the Earth in human form and walked among us, he would certainly be one. He was simply beautiful.

"Miss?" He was awaiting my entrance into his house. I came to my senses and stepped inside, hoping that we could both ignore my inappropriate ogling.

The interior of his home was bare. I imagined it was what a bachelor pad would look like. There was nothing hanging on the walls and had only the necessary furniture. I took a seat on his worn leather couch. He sat down on the chair across from me, leaning forward and resting his forearms on his knees.

We sat in silence for a few moments. He was examining me and I tried everything I could not to do the same to him. My eyes wandered around the room as I tried to understand what the hell was happening. I felt too shy to talk and too self-conscious to look at him.

But when the self-consciousness began morphing into embarrassment, I decided to clear my throat and speak up. "Mr. Lake, I understand you're making this transaction to move on from a recent relationship?" I couldn't help but wonder what idiot woman would ever give up a man so beautiful, but I supposed looks weren't everything. He could be a total jerk. Maybe his personality sucked. Maybe he wasn't romantic enough. Or he wasn't funny enough, or maybe he was too serious. After all, he hadn't smiled once since I came in and the air around him seemed dour.

"It's just Lake."

"I'm sorry?" I asked, confused.

"My first name is Lake. I don't have a last name."

"What kind of person doesn't have a last name?" I blurted with a sarcastic snort.

"An orphan."

I bit my lip, wishing I could crawl into a hole. "Oh. I...I'm sorry."

"It's okay," he replied. "I was found alongside a lake by some nuns who worked at a nearby orphanage when I was a baby. They named me Lake. I was never claimed, never had foster parents, never adopted, so that's why I don't have a last name."

I looked down at my hands, uneasy with the emotions this stranger was conjuring up inside of me. His short story ate at my heart, but it sounded so old school. Did things like that happen anymore these days?

I took a breath in. *Focus, Frankie. Just do your damn job.* "Well, I'm sorry to hear that. Now, can you tell me what happened? Why you want to forget and move on from this person?"

A sense of imposition washed over me, which was new considering I couldn't care less about my clients' lives. But there was no hesitation from him, and he answered directly. "I had a girlfriend. She and I had many differences, and we decided, mutually, to part ways."

"If you decided mutually, then why am I here? Are you having a hard time getting over her?" I asked curiously. I didn't usually grill my clients about the reasoning behind wanting to sell their souls, but it seemed I was on a roll lately. Jessica and Dotty were pretty interesting. However, this struck me as odd. There was only one reason why he would have been on the *SoulCatcher* app. Well, two reasons: to find love or to find sex. But he wasn't selling his soul for love, he was selling his soul to get over someone.

I had no idea what our sales associates did on their end. Obviously, their jobs were to persuade someone to give up their eternity. But what did it take to get there? I'd guess in a way they could be seen as counselors of sorts. I was sure they had to hear all about someone's love life in order to talk them into selling their souls. This was done without face-to-face contact, usually, so they couldn't use the slideshow technique. It could have been that maybe Lake changed his mind. He could have decided that getting over this girl was better than just finding love...or a booty call.

I studied the intoxicating glimmer in his eyes, and a noticeable longing seemed to be hidden somewhere behind them as he glanced back at me, as if they could still be sad over the whole breakup.

He finally answered. "Yes, I'm having a hard time moving on. I want to sell my soul because I can't stop thinking about her. She's on my mind constantly and it's hard to focus," he admitted. "We might have both agreed to our separation, but it doesn't make it any easier."

Jacob and I didn't both agree on a separation, and I knew what it felt like to want someone you couldn't be with. It was sheer torture.

"I love her," he stated. "I've loved her for a long time. I've watched her grow over the years into a beautiful woman. Life took a toll on her and she seemed to have lost herself somewhere along the way. I wanted to show her and make her believe that she was worth everything. More than she thought. And that she still had a light inside of her, a light that I could see. A light that made her eyes shimmer in the sun and glow with the reflection of the moon. She closed herself off from anything good and it swallowed her whole. If only she knew the fragments of her beautiful soul were still there.

"There isn't a moment, a second of my day when I don't desire to be near her. To hold her hand. To help her and guide her back to who she really is, because she truly is amazing. She is life."

I didn't know how long I had been staring at him. His words mesmerized me, and the deep compassion he had for this woman left me in complete awe.

"Miss?"

I heard him, but I couldn't step away from my thoughts at the moment. Jacob was by far the sweetest, gentlest guy I'd ever met. Granted, I didn't have a whole lot to compare him to, and I hadn't been romantic with anyone else since him, but every other man that I'd met just seemed like...any other man.

Nothing special about them. I could only hope and trust that when Jacob spoke to his friends about me, he said some very nice things, similar to what this Lake guy was saying.

His words were filled with endearment. His demeanor might be a bit more rigid and serious, but it was undeniable. He cared for her more than he cared for anything else in this world. And maybe his unyielding character was the pain revealing itself in its truest form. Maybe he was looser when he was happy, because clearly, he wasn't content without her.

"Miss?" he called out again.

I finally snapped out of it. "My name is Franklin, but most people call me Frankie." I had no idea why I felt compelled to tell him my true name, which I hated.

He nodded. "May I ask why you prefer Frankie?"

I hadn't explained this to anyone in a while. "My dad really wanted a baby boy. My parents chose not to learn the sex of the baby until I was born, and my dad was certain I was going to be his first-born son. So, he chose a name. When it turned out that I had girl parts, my parents decided to keep the name Franklin. But it's a boy's name. I figure Frankie sounds a little more unisex. And it's funny because my sister's name is Alexandra, but she's known as Alex. It sounds like we could be brothers."

"Franklin is a good name, regardless," he said softly. The blood began to rush to my cheeks and I quickly turned away from his gaze to hide it. "Did you know that in earlier times, the word *franklin* meant 'free man'?"

How ironic. "No, I didn't know that."

"Frankie, may I ask you another question?"

My head was still swimming in his heartfelt speech and the unrecognizable feelings he was stirring inside of me. His first impression made him seem standoffish. But as he spoke more and more, the atmosphere around us changed. Sitting in this room in front of him somehow began to make me feel safe and distant from everything. The world outside seemed far away, and there was only the mysterious familiarity of his presence. The more we spoke, the more comfortable I felt.

I gave him a slight smile to affirm that he may ask another question.

"Do you like doing this?" he asked plainly.

"Excuse me?"

"Do you like sealing people and guaranteeing their souls to an eternity in the Red Realm?" he reiterated. I was taken aback by his words. Normal every-day people didn't usually call Hell that. Although it was written in their contracts, they didn't even really understand that it was the proper name for Hell until their souls made it down there.

I was also a bit shocked by his question. For as long as I'd done this, I never had a client ask me anything personal about myself. No one cared to become friends, which really wasn't even professional behavior on my part, anyway. And as far as the opposite sex went and our sometimes-uncontrollable hormones, there was only the occasional flirtation by some men, and a woman or two. But any thoughts of hooking up with me would all be forgotten once that hot iron rod made contact with their skin.

And as I thought about Lake's question, I realized that he was being kind of nosy. It felt very personal. My mind was telling me it wasn't smart to share private details with a total stranger and it was definitely against the rules, but everything else inside of me felt tempted to do so. His dark eyebrows hung over his sapphire-tinted eyes, which seemed to be searching mine for an answer and showing a genuine interest in the next words to come out of my mouth.

It was on the tip of my tongue. I almost spit out that I hated the existence of my life. I hated my terrible job. The only reason I was doing it was because I didn't have a choice. I never had a choice. And if I attempted to quit or purposely tried to get fired, I'd have to spend eons in the Red Realm, and I wasn't ready for that. I didn't think I was, anyway.

But instead, I simply said, "It's just what I do. Now, are you ready to start?" He nodded in a disappointed kind of way and didn't say another word on the matter.

After going over his contract one last time, I pulled out an alcohol swab, a bite block, the restraints, and the iron rod and laid it all out on the rickety wooden coffee table between us. "Before I restrain you, can you tell me where you would like the Seal?"

He raised his shirt over his head. My breath hitched at the initial sight of his naked chest. I'd never seen anything like it in real life. The anatomy of this man was what you would think every man's should be, as if he were manufactured fresh that morning. Sheer perfection. I had to literally shake my head into reality.

With his eyes still on mine, he pointed to his pec, right where his heart was beating behind his perfect, tanned flesh and hard muscles. I grabbed the restraints and walked around the table toward him. He watched my every move. He was so tall; I didn't have to bend down much to where he sat. I strapped each wrist to the arms of the chair, then picked up the bite block. "Do you think you need this?"

His teeth were so pretty, I would hate for any of them to become chipped or cracked. But he shook his head. "No, I don't need it."

I took the swab and wiped his skin. Nerves threatened to force my hand to shake as I reached across his wide frame. His skin was flawless. Not a blemish, not even a mole. I wished he could touch me back, pull me close to his body, just to see what it felt like against mine. I hadn't felt a man's affectionate touch in so long. His embrace would probably make me feel small but protected, and at the same time, become aroused by the sexiness that oozed off him. I was so confused by what I was feeling and didn't know if I wanted to jump his bones or just have him hold me tight.

Once the area was sterilized, I picked up the brand and the entire rod instantly illuminated its tawny glow in my bare hand. Lake didn't seem to marvel or be interested at all, unlike my other clients who often asked why the rod wasn't burning me. I would usually shrug and plainly say it was magic in a joking tone. One client had even stupidly reached over and touched it. Needless to say, three of his fingers no longer had fingerprints.

But Lake just...watched me.

"Are you ready?" I asked.

"What happens if I decide I don't want to do this?"

Son of a bitch. I was hoping this wouldn't happen. It was always so much better for my morality when I didn't have to persuade the client into selling their soul. But for Lake, it was more than that for some reason. I was clearly attracted to him, and I had no desire to produce a slideshow of a happy life that I didn't even have a chance of being a part of. Dating a client would, for sure, land me an earlier spot in line to be tormented by the devils.

I decided to test his hesitation. "You seemed so sure about getting over your ex."

"I didn't say I wasn't. I just want to know what happens if I changed my mind."

This was certainly a first. It wasn't written in their contracts that they would meet their untimely death if they decided to change their minds, and we were not allowed to tell them either. It was the devils' own personal way of screwing with the living.

I was about ninety-five percent successful when it came to persuading my clients to give up their souls with my supernatural ability, even with the stupid glitch that showed them Hell sometimes. But as soon as they showed any signs of uncertainty or wavering, the highlights of their future began in my mind.

However, for some strange reason, I didn't want to compel Lake. I didn't want to lie about the dowry. I wanted him to know the truth. "They would come for you."

"Who would come for me?"

"The Henchmen. The devil's men. They would come take your soul now, and you would die this very moment," I explained in a near whisper. It suddenly felt like another set of ears was listening. I knew nothing about Lake, but I didn't want him to die. I didn't want the Henchmen to take him away to The Nothing. Not right now.

I gripped the rod tighter and its color brightened. Slowly, I inched it closer to his chest, but he spoke before I could reach his skin. "Don't."

"I have to," I mumbled, staring deeply into his eyes.

Our faces were inches apart and his warm breath kissed my lips. "No, you don't."

I cocked my head at him, trying to figure out why he would say that.

Then, at that very moment, there was a knock at the front door. It startled me and I turned toward it. "Who is that?" In the pit of my stomach, intuition nudged at me. Something didn't seem right.

Lake looked at the door then at me. "You have to go," he said in a quiet, stern tone.

"What do you mean? I have to seal you. If I don't, they'll have to come take your soul." I could hear in my voice that I was nearly begging for him to listen to me.

There were three more knocks, this time urgent. "You have to go now."

The front door nearly came off the hinges with more pounding. "Okay, okay. Let me just take the restraints off—"

He closed his fists into balls and flexed his biceps, and in one quick motion, pulled his arms up. The restraints broke away from his wrists and the chair, and I jumped out of his way as he stood up. Holy shit! Those restraints were heavy duty. They were like medical restraints, thick leather and sturdy straps.

The rapping at the front door continued. Lake picked up my bag, and I stuffed my things inside, hesitantly following his lead. His hand found the small of my back, and he gently but hastily shoved me in the direction of a door in the kitchen. He opened it to the backyard and pointed at the fence ahead. "There is an alley on the other side of that fence. Be careful when you climb over. Run and don't stop until you reach a cafe four blocks away. I will meet you there."

I resisted the push of his hand a bit, only because I was trying to decide whether or not he was serious. But all my senses were telling me to listen to him. To run like hell. So I did.

CHAPTER ELEVEN

All the Beautiful People

With my backpack secured on my back, I ran full speed to the chain-link fence. I jumped up and the toe of my combat boot hooked on. Thankfully, the fence wasn't too high, so I was able to swing my other foot onto the top, leaping over and landing onto the other side. The sound of glass breaking rang out from Lake's house. I turned around and peeked through the links of the fence but couldn't see anything happening inside. More glass and what sounded like furniture being tossed around a room echoed out of the back door. Groans and moans mixed in with the clattering, and that was when I took off.

I was scared. I had no idea what was happening back there. I ran as fast as I could, afraid that if I glanced behind me, someone would be on my tail. But as I ran down the alley, counting each street that I crossed, my worry for Lake rapidly grew. Who was on the other side of his front door? That noise was the sound of men fighting, that was for sure. Did the Henchmen show up without my call? How did they know? Was Lake fighting them off?

After reaching block three, I picked up my speed. My heart pounded with the eagerness to get to the cafe. My hope was that Lake would somehow already be in there waiting for me.

The old wooden sign that read *Gracie's Cafe* came into view. I swung the door open without slowing my pace and ran straight into someone on their way out. We collided, and the woman's fresh cup of steaming coffee crumbled between us both. The hot liquid splashed everywhere. "Shit! I'm sorry," I huffed.

She was not pleased. "Damn it! What the hell, lady?"

I reached into my bag and pulled out a loose five-dollar bill, stuffing it into the pocket of her jacket. "Here you go. I'm so sorry." I walked away as if nothing happened, raking over the entirety of the vintage-style cafe in search of a tall, muscular man with gorgeous long hair. Patrons eyed me suspiciously as I passed their tables down the aisle.

But there was no Lake.

I took a deep breath and plopped down at an empty table in the back. A bouncy girl wearing a tiny apron walked up with her notepad. "Hey! Can I get you something to drink?"

My eyes remained on the entrance. "No."

"Okay, well, we have some specials today and—"

"No," I repeated firmly. She left it at that and stomped back to the register. I pulled out my phone, but I doubted Lake would call me. The guy didn't even have my number. But there was one missed call from work. Crap. Should I call back? Lake backed out on his deal. He would be dead, and his soul would be in The Nothing right now if I had done what I was supposed to do. I always called the Henchmen when I had to. It was the rule. Although, there were times when I wondered if they already knew before I even called them. Did they *always* know?

No matter what, it was a direct order and a part of our job. What would happen to Lake now? More importantly, what would happen to me?

Ten minutes of watching the door and the windows slowly ticked by until, finally, the entrance bell chimed and there he was. The highlights of his hair were somehow still glowing even in the gloomy outdoor light. He didn't search for me, just marched straight toward the back of the cafe as if he already knew exactly where I was.

His stride was calm and smooth, and my pulse quickened with every step he took to get closer to me. I began to fidget when he approached the table and took a seat. I examined his face, but there was no evidence that any kind of tussle occurred. "Are you okay?"

"Yes," he confirmed. "Are you okay?"

"Yeah." I realized then that I still hadn't caught a decent breath since the run. "I just need to stop smoking."

"Frankie, we need to talk."

"No, *we* need to talk. What the hell happened back there? I heard fighting. Who were you fighting with? And I need to seal you, Lake. Do you understand what will happen if I don't? The Henchmen are going to come kill you." I made sure to lower my voice for the last part.

He didn't show any concern for what I'd just said. "I know. They were already there."

"What?"

"Three of them. They came for me."

I didn't understand. "But I didn't call them." My hunch about Dominic and his men already knowing everything was right. And how did Lake even know who the Henchmen were?

"It was a setup. I knew they were going to come for me. Listen, Frankie, there are many things that you don't know." He leaned in closer and his sweet, earthy scent reached my nose. "I need to explain some very important information to you, but we can't talk here."

I ignored his statements. "Wait, you set this whole thing up? What happened back there? What happened to the Henchmen?"

"I took care of them."

"How?" The devil's henchmen were all burly, all the same size as the office security guard, Boris. It wasn't surprising to me that Lake had "taken care of them," considering he was just as big, if not bigger, than they were. I was sure he could beat them out strength-wise...if they were normal humans. All of Centaurus' men had supernatural strength. They all had the ability to throw a man through a brick wall if they really wanted to. So how in the hell did he escape that?

"That really doesn't matter right now. We need to get some place safer and less public," he suggested.

I didn't listen and furrowed my brows at him. I wanted to know what he knew. "How do you know who the Henchmen are? Why did you say I didn't have to give you the Seal of the Red Realm?"

He inhaled and exhaled loudly. "Frankie, I can answer all your questions, but you have to come with me." He started to stand up, but I didn't move.

"Um...so, I'm just supposed to go with you? I don't even know you." I had already made up my mind to follow him, but I decided to be stubborn. Besides, I had no idea why everything inside me was drawn to him. I had no reason to trust this guy, but I did anyway, and I couldn't explain why.

I reached into the hidden pocket inside my jacket and pulled out a silver flask, unscrewing the top to pour the warm vodka down my throat, but Lake quickly snatched it out of my hand. "Hey!" I squealed, wiping dribble off my chin.

"You don't need this anymore," he chided. Anymore? What the fuck did he know? My phone vibrated and my work's number appeared across the screen. "You don't need to answer that, either," he said.

In that very moment, the entrance bell chimed and two beefy men wearing dark sunglasses appeared at the front of the cafe. Before their heads turned toward our table, Lake took my hand and pulled me up. We hurried down a hallway that led to restrooms and the kitchen area. He pushed through a swinging door, alarming the kitchen staff of our demanding presence. They stopped what they were doing and gaped at us in surprise. "Can I help you?" one of the workers asked.

Lake didn't pay him any mind and we continued to rush through until we found an open door leading outside, behind the cafe. We stepped out onto the sidewalk, but he didn't let go of my hand and we didn't stop. Cars honked at our indecency of not properly using the crosswalk as we dashed across the streets. Block after block, Lake didn't stop or let go of my hand. So much ran through my head as we practically jogged around the city. Who was this beautiful man and what did he know about me? Why did he agree to sell his soul and then back out of it as if it was his plan all along? And more importantly, why were my emotions all over the place for a complete stranger? Sure, any woman who laid eyes on him would instantly be attracted. I even caught a few ladies checking him out on the street. But my attraction to him felt like *more*. Running on the sidewalks with Lake felt...right. Holding his hand felt...natural, as if it was something we'd done before. As if I'd been touching his skin for years. It felt so completely comfortable.

I tried to catch up with Lake's pace, but his legs were too long and his gait was too wide. I simply followed as close behind as I could, ignoring all the curious looks as we passed by. I was sure it seemed as if this man was forcing me to go somewhere I didn't want to go. Stranger danger.

Every now and then Lake would glance back, almost as if to check on me. His hair whirled around his head in the cool wind, and every time we crossed an intersection, he tightened his grip around my hand. It hadn't occurred to me right away that we were heading in the direction of my apartment. This probably wasn't a good idea, considering Centaurus was only a few blocks away and I was running with a fugitive of The Nothing. Dominic had to know by now I was Lake's accomplice.

I stopped abruptly, nearly tripping over my own feet when he didn't slow down right away. "Wait!"

He turned around. "What is it?"

"We can't go this way," I said, panting. "My apartment is this way and they might be looking for us there."

He stepped closer to me. All frantic rushing suddenly stopped. Gazing down at me, he brushed my messy hair away from my face. "Do you trust me?"

I became lost in his soft, blue eyes. He didn't just look at me like any other ordinary person. He studied my face with intensity, as if he was searching for some part of me I didn't even know existed. Somehow, some way, his look was all I needed to believe he was trustworthy. Words were suddenly no longer available in the language department of my brain, so all I could do was nod to his question. He reached down and grabbed my hand again, and we continued on with our mission, whatever that was.

Crossing a few more major intersections, panic flowed through me when we reached The Hartley. I scanned the area, hoping not to see any big heads wearing sunglasses anywhere. Thankfully, there were none. To my surprise, we stopped right next door. Reggie, the Bob Marley look-alike, nodded at Lake as we entered. Lake returned the gesture. Did they know each other?

We approached the clerk's counter near the back of the store. Lake finally let go of my hand. I watched as he reached down behind the counter and moved an old dingy rug, revealing a hidden door in the floor which Lake pulled up. Intrigued and a bit skeptical, I took his awaiting hand. He pulled me close to the edge and I glanced down.

"So...I'm not going down there," I scoffed. There was a ladder, but the hole appeared endless and frighteningly too dark.

"Frankie," he simply said, reminding me to trust him.

I gave in almost immediately, but the fear didn't leave my body. He held my hand and grasped on to my hip, lowering me down gently until my feet were balanced on the rungs of the ladder. I began to climb down, and Lake held on to me until he could no longer reach. It felt like an eternity before my boots finally touched wet ground below. I glanced up, expecting to see Lake's large body halfway down, but no one was there.

"Lake!" I called up. My voice bounced off the rounded walls surrounding me. I peered behind my own shoulder at a dank tunnel leading to darkness, then glanced down at my feet standing in about two inches of stagnant water. I stepped closer to the reflection of the light on the floor from the opening above, afraid that if I stepped out into the shadows, something would snatch me away.

"Lake!" I called again, fear enveloping my body. There was only the sound of Reggie's weird Congo music blasting inside his store. There were no voices and there was no Lake. Anxiety began coursing through my veins at high speed. I shuddered at the blackness behind me, worried that at any minute I would feel strange fingers in my hair.

I placed my hands on the ladder and made the decision to ascend back up through the trap door. But before I could start my way up, Lake's body came crashing down. I was surprised at my own ability to dodge him, and thankful that he hadn't fallen on top of me. His body slammed into the ground, causing a hollow echo to travel down the tunnel. I quickly knelt down to his side. "Holy shit! Are you okay?"

A voice rang down from above. "Go! Get out of here! I'll take care of them," Reggie yelled down at us. He quickly shut the door and the illumination from the store was gone. Lake moaned, but I couldn't check his body for any wounds from his fall without any light.

"Are you okay, Lake? It's too dark. I can't see anything." I touched his body, feeling around blindly and finding his chest and his arms.

"I'm fine," he grunted and began to stand up. "Let's go."

He found my hand easily, as if he could see it, and pulled me through the dark and murky tunnel I was dreading all along. Our footsteps pounded below us as we ran, splashing dirty water up my legs. I closed my eyes, finding it much less scary when I wasn't searching for something I didn't want to see. This place was obviously a sewage system, judging by the disgusting odor and sounds of squealing rats. I wasn't sure if Lake knew where he was going, but we continued to run a straight path for a while.

We started to finally slow our pace, and I hesitantly opened my eyes. Still pretty dark and creepy. I decided to make conversation. "How do you know Reggie?"

"He's an old friend. I'll explain more later."

We stopped, and Lake's face was suddenly lit up. He handed me his phone. "Hold this up for me, please."

I held it up, revealing the end of the tunnel and a rather large, round steel door. Lake reached for the wheel in the center of it and turned it several different ways, as if entering some kind of combination to a lock. There was a click, and he pulled the seemingly heavy door open. I handed his phone back to him and he used it to help guide us the rest of the way.

We followed a slanted tunnel to another closed door where suddenly, there were sounds of muffled music and voices. Lake knocked five times before a small metal window slid open, revealing a set of bright blue eyes. Without a word, the window abruptly slid shut and the entire door opened. A very attractive man gestured for us to enter.

I wondered if we were truly at the right destination when we entered a room filled with people and blaring music. White strings of lights hung above our heads like twinkling stars. There was a long bar aligning the wall with bartenders and patrons awaiting their drinks. The bar top lit up brightly in white, just like the tabletops that were scattered around the room where people stood talking and drinking. I could no longer tell I was in a sewer. There was no putrid smell or gross water underneath my feet. It was all clean and nice, like I had just stepped into another dimension.

A deejay and his sound board were situated on a stage, dance music blasting from the enormous speakers on either side of him. People watched and swayed on the dance floor in front of him, lost in a trance of the electronic melody and the colorful strobe lights that followed their movements.

I peered over at Lake. "Where are we?" I asked in a raised voice. The music threatened to drown me out completely.

He didn't respond; instead, he pulled me toward a booth nestled in the corner and farther away from the booming of the bass. "Sit here. I'll be right back."

"Wait! Can I at least have a drink?"

"You don't need a drink," he replied.

"Look," I said sternly. "I've been running around the city with you for a couple of hours. Scary, giant guys who might not even have eyes are chasing us down and I have no idea what you know and what you don't know. I think I deserve a damn drink."

Lake visibly inhaled in annoyance and defeat. "Fine." He walked away, and a minute later, a waitress was at my table.

"What can I get for you, sweetie?" she asked in an intoxicating and sexy accent resembling a woman of European descent. I couldn't answer right away. She was the first person I'd seen up close and personal in this place, and she was stunning. Tall, pleasantly thin, and drop-dead gorgeous with big, blue doe-eyes and long blonde hair. Her glittery eyeshadow glimmered every time she blinked, and her full pink lips glistened. Her tiny white top and low-waisted white jeans revealed her perfectly flat tanned stomach, which sparkled in the lights from body glitter as she moved. I was completely lost in her beauty.

"Miss?"

I finally snapped out of it once I felt like I'd taken her all in. "Yeah. Sorry. I'll take a Screwdriver." She flashed a brilliant smile and turned toward the bar.

I took this opportunity to study the people surrounding me, watching their faces and their smiles as they laughed, examining their bodies and what they were wearing. They were all so beautiful. I was swimming in a sea filled with the most attractive men and women I had ever seen. They were of all shapes and sizes and colors, all features different from one another. Every single person was physically appealing. No one had a blemish. Not one strand of hair out of place. They were all happy, smiling and laughing and drinking and dancing. It almost seemed as though each and every one of them had a certain... glow. A beautiful shade of positive certainty mixed with shiny gold.

I suddenly became self-conscious.

The waitress brought my drink and Lake followed right behind her. I took a sip of my well-deserved alcoholic beverage. "Had to use the little boy's room?" I teased immaturely. I had no idea why I was being rude. It could quite possibly be my way of hiding the fact that all I wanted to do was stare at his sexy face.

He ignored my banter and scooted closer to me. "We really need to talk, Frankie. There are some things you need to know."

"You keep saying that. I'm here, so spit it out. What is this place, anyway?"

"It's a hideout. A place for my kind to converge."

"Your kind? What? Do you mean all the beautiful people in the world? Is there some kind of No Ugly People Allowed rule? I have not seen one unattractive person in here."

Lake didn't smile at my poor attempt at a joke. "What if I told you that you didn't have to work for the Red Realm anymore?"

"I'd laugh. I'd ask who the hell you were and what do you know? You're not telling me anything, Lake. Just fucking tell me," I demanded. This little game he was playing was starting to get on my last nerve. If it wasn't for the fact that I had this inexplicable feeling of trust and security around him, I would have ditched this man. At this point, Dominic was certainly looking for us both. He had to know by now that I was aiding in Lake's refusal to give in to the Henchmen that have already tried, and apparently failed, to kill him. I knew I was in trouble, which was why I was in no hurry to leave Lake's side. He was obviously strong enough to keep the Henchmen at bay.

"The profanity isn't needed here, Frankie," he said, and I was instantly embarrassed by his comment and felt everyone's beautiful eyes on me. "It's very possible for you to get away from Dominic, to get away from this life."

"Wait, how do you know Dominic?"

"Dominic and I have history. We have known each for a very long time. We were once partners."

"Partners? You know what Dominic is, right?" I was afraid to say any more. It seemed Lake knew more than I'd initially thought, but I wasn't going to reveal anything before he did.

"Yes, I know who Dominic is," he confirmed. "He works for Centaurus, but we were never partners in the Red Realm. We were partners in the White Realm."

"The White Realm? You mean Heaven?" No one ever really talked about Heaven at Centaurus. It was the first time I'd heard it called the White Realm, which made total predictable sense.

"Yes. We were paragons of virtue together."

I rolled my eyes and sucked on my straw. "Okay, I have no idea what that means."

"He was an angel from Heaven, like me," he said quietly and slowly, as if delivering very fragile news.

I appreciated his effort to reiterate this, but I needed to hear it again, and slower. "What did you say?"

CHAPTER TWELVE

I Can Fly!

I glanced down at the vodka and orange juice that hadn't been touched in fifteen minutes. The ice cubes were melting, watering down the alcohol that suddenly seemed like it wouldn't sit well in my stomach. Lake had just told me a story about Dominic, one that I was still trying my best to digest.

Many, many years ago, in Roman times, Dominic and Lake were captured and forced to become gladiators. They were slaves to a ruthless emperor who made them fight for their lives in the city they were taken to, far away from their families. Neither of them knew the other before the kidnapping but soon became friends after having to endure painful physical training and poor living conditions together. They fought endlessly with other gladiators and even animals like lions and tigers, living day by day as if it could have been their last.

After a couple of years, Lake and Dominic became VIP athletes, as it would seem they were the hardest to kill and the most fearless opponents. The people loved them and cheered them on at every event. The emperor basked in their glory, promising them riches if they continued to be the best. But this didn't stop the two men from hatching a plan to escape together.

On the day of their getaway, they were captured yet again. The emperor didn't want to lose the fame and fortune these two strong men brought with them. He decided to waive the consequences for desertion, which was execution. But Lake and Dominic were done with their life of fighting and killing and decided the only way out was to take their own lives.

They were judged by the Council of the NonAligned and their souls were risen to the White Realm, where they found each other again in paradise. It seemed they were destined to be friends, even in the afterlife. The people of the White Realm appreciated Lake and Dominic's strong and pure souls. They were good men who took care of their families but had the unfortunate luck of being forced to kill. The holy beings of the next world knew they were honorable men, and soon they became members of a counsel committed to finding ways to take down evil on Earth. When soul-selling became an issue, a group was formed. Lake, Dominic, and others were then formally named the Angels of Reform, a team of celestial beings whose job was to help people like...me.

"So, your job is to help the Sealers?" I asked.

"Basically, yes. The Sealers and all ASRs. We work to infiltrate and take down facilities like Centaurus, the places and evil beings that employ people like you. We have done this for centuries and have successfully taken down facilities all over the world." Lake's expression was so serious as he explained all of this to me, but I couldn't help getting lost in his eyes. His face was so stoically beautiful, but his eyes possessed a benevolence that was hard to ignore. It left a sense of comfort inside of me, creating a need to be closer to him.

"Take down?" I asked, leaning in closer to him.

"Take down as in destroy," he reiterated.

"How is that possible?"

"The portal into the Red Realm is located inside every soul-selling building. We destroy those portals, which gives access to and from the Red Realm, so that the facility is forced to close permanently. By doing this, we are cutting down the number of places on Earth to run such a business, minimizing the chances of a person becoming employed by the Red Realm and their whole operation."

"Are you destroying the kings and queens, too?"

"Unfortunately, no," he answered with obvious disappointment. "We do not have that capability... yet. The Angels of Reform's main mission is to end the soul-selling businesses on Earth."

"But when you destroy the facility, can't they just open a new business somewhere else? With a new portal?"

"Essentially, yes. It's part of the struggle we face in doing our jobs. But sometimes, when we destroy a soul-selling operation, the kings and queens become too weakened from the lack of souls in their region to restart it. Connecting with two worlds requires a lot of power, a lot of planning, a lot of construction to create a portal. And most just decide to deal with the souls who enter their realm naturally. Destroying the building in which they run the business cuts back the persuasion of mortals on Earth to sell their souls. Their souls don't belong in the Red Realm and our job is to stop it from happening."

"Well, what about the mortals? The people who aren't ASRs?" I asked. "The normal people who just decide to sell their souls for something?"

"Another group handles the mortals who sell their souls before they are deceased. Their souls, too, can be reformed and sent to the White Realm when they die. The Angels of Reform deal mostly with the immortals. We focus on preventing soul-selling from happening in the first place, on the employees who deal with the contracts and the sealing. Unfortunately, however, we cannot help the souls of the deceased, mortal or not. Once a person is dead before they were able to go through the reforming process, we cannot stop them from entering the Red Realm."

"Okay. Well, how do you reform us? Aren't we property of the Red Realm once we're sealed?" My neck tingled.

"Technically, yes. But the Seal of the Red Realm can be removed. It's a process—it requires incantation from the White Realm Elders, as well as time and patience. An ASR's soul is much easier to reform than a mortal. You are part of the supernatural society; therefore, your soul accepts the crossover process at a quicker rate."

I chuckled sarcastically and sat back in the booth. "Yeah, I have the supernatural ability to show people their futures and touch a hot iron rod."

Lake leaned in toward me. "You are unaware of your abilities, Frankie."

I turned away in frustration. Again, this man sounded like he knew more about me than he should. I watched all of the good-looking men and women dancing and talking and carrying on. "Is everyone here an angel?"

"At the moment, yes."

This was a nightclub. An angel nightclub. It was almost unbelievable, really. A little while ago, I wondered if angels even existed. And now, I was in the presence of at least fifty of the most gorgeous people I had ever seen in my life who have presumably hailed from Heaven.

The bass of the music vibrated through my body as I sat and watched the angelic beings smiling and laughing. They all seemed so happy, as if nothing bad had ever happened to them in their lives. As if there were no worries. As if the word pain wasn't even a part of their vocabulary.

"Is everyone here for the same reason you are?"

"Not all, but most are Angels of Reform," he answered.

With my attention turned back to Lake, and with a sour expression on my face, I decided to test his patience. "What if we don't want to be saved?"

He tensed up, but his eyes rested delicately on mine. "I told you to trust me, didn't I?"

"You did. And I'm not saying I don't. But a lot of my co-workers like what they do. They enjoy being ASRs and Sealers. They want to live forever on Earth. So, how do you expect to help those people who don't want to be helped?"

"The White Realm believes in free will. We are not here to force anyone into doing something they do not wish to do. However, it is our duty to try," he explained. "It is our job to rid this world of unnecessary evil."

"You can't get rid of evil, Lake. It's everywhere. The devils don't drive people to do bad things. We make those decisions ourselves." I understood that he was all about good and blah, blah, blah, but how the hell did he expect to stop evil?

"You're misunderstanding me, Frankie. You are correct, evil cannot be stopped. But Centaurus and other businesses like it are manipulating people, people who are good and don't deserve to have their souls tortured for all eternity." His eyes scanned the room, and suddenly, he seemed frustrated. "Let's go."

Lake wrapped his hand around mine and we both slid out of the booth. We moved through the crowd of beautiful bodies entranced by the electronic music. I watched each of them as if time had slowed down, as their arms reached above their heads and their bodies pulsated to the beat. They seemed so free, so careless, so happy, and in that moment, I just wanted to be where they were.

I stopped walking and pulled my hand out of Lake's grip. He immediately halted and turned around, brows furrowed in confusion. I ignored him and closed my eyes. Allowing myself to subconsciously feed on the energy of everyone around me, I lifted my arms high above my head. The music found my fingertips and flowed down from my hands, to my arms, to my body. My hips slowly began to follow the rhythm, and soon after, my legs and feet caught up. The melody got louder and filled my head completely. There was no longer any room for worry. There was no longer any room for the past or hurt or loss. There was only room for the now. This moment. The moment where I was the freest I had felt in years.

Memories of the giant mirror in the dance studio I trained at came rushing back to me. I moved as if I was watching myself in that mirror, and I hadn't lost it. It was there. The rhythm, the motions, the same floaty exhilaration of the music and my body meeting to become one was still there.

There were suddenly hands around my waist. My initial thought was that it was Lake, but when I glanced down at the arms and hands that were now enveloping my body from behind, I realized that these appendages were too delicate to belong to a man. The stranger's body hugged my back and I leaned into her. Our bodies found the same tempo and swayed together for a while before more hands came into view, this time from the front.

A stunningly handsome man with short but messy honey-tinted hair and a baby face glanced down at me and smiled. My knees weakened at the brilliance of all that he was, and within seconds, he was on the same cadence as the stranger and me. His fingers ran through my hair and down to my face, gently cupping it into his palms. The girl behind me continued to stroke my body with hers, a move that might have appeared sexual by someone simply watching us, but it felt friendly. There was an arousal forming inside of me, but not in a I-want-to-take-you-to-bed kind of way. It was more than that. It was on a spiritual level, one that far surpassed anything I had ever felt before. I felt comfortable, like I'd known these people my whole life.

Following the beat of the music, I turned my back toward the beautiful man to face the girl behind me.

To no surprise, her beauty was extraordinary. Long, big, golden curls framed her ebony face where her brown pie eyes and shimmery lips lived. She smiled at me, and I was instantly compelled to smile back. Her hands reached up and found my cheeks, where she then slid her baby soft fingers down to my neck. I instinctively lowered my head into my shoulder, fearful that she might catch sight of the Seal and run away or something. But her fingertips traced the brand and she simply smiled at me. I lifted my head up high, allowing her to touch me as much as she wanted.

The crowd seemed to be closing into our dancing space and the music seemed to have gotten louder. I shut my eyes again, totally and completely losing every ounce of myself. I handed my body over to these beautiful strangers, and I was perfectly okay with it. I knew that I was safe. I could understand with every fiber of my being that everything around me was protected by something so much bigger. There was a sense of wellbeing and familiarity and acceptance inside of me as I danced to the music and perfect strangers caressed my body.

The lights, the sounds, and the touching all melded together into one big ball of energy. Every single person on that dance floor became one. It felt as though I was floating on clouds, flying high above anything negative that could touch me. My body felt so weightless against a life that threatened my happiness on a daily basis. As if nothing could penetrate the invisible shield that guarded me from a world I suddenly didn't feel I belonged in.

I was so light. So weightless. Like a feather. Why did I feel like a feather?

I opened my eyes and looked down. We were floating! Our feet were floating above the dance floor! How was this even possible? My beautiful strangers and I were dancing in the air, high above the other beautiful strangers dancing below us. Was I dreaming? Was this even real?

I frantically searched my dance partner's eyes. "We're floating!" I yelled over the music.

She beamed back. "We're flying!"

As if on cue, large white wings appeared from behind her. They arched upward and out and shimmered in the strobe lights. They were about four feet tall and three feet wide, and she spread them out on either side of her as if to show them off. They fluttered slowly, each movement revealing new sparkles and feathers that I just wanted to reach out and touch.

I turned toward the beautifully stunning stranger-man dancing on my back. He, too, possessed his own wings. They were also white and shimmery, only his were taller and wider. I glanced down at my body, realizing then that my beautiful strangers had been holding me up this whole time. Their bodies were still moving with the music and carrying me simultaneously. But the strangest of all was that I didn't feel frightened or weirded out one bit. I felt weightless and free and almost even powerful. I was defying gravity. I was floating above the reality, leaving all my inhibitions on the dance floor below me.

My eyes closed again, and I just let it all go. We danced and moved and swayed for what felt like hours before my feet finally felt grounded again. I had no idea what time it was. No idea how long I had been there. I felt drunk with euphoria and had almost forgotten about Lake until our eyes met from across the room. He was leaning over a tall table, one hand in his pocket and the other holding a glass cup half full of something clear.

He stood up tall when I reached him. "I thought you were totally against alcohol?" I asked, pointing at his drink. I was out of breath and sweaty and thirsty, but not for liquor. I felt too high from the dancing, and I was surprisingly okay with it.

Thankfully, and exactly what a kind gentleman would do, Lake had a bottle of water waiting for me. I took it and guzzled it down.

"It's not alcohol," he said.

"Why not? Everyone else is drinking. Maybe it would loosen you up." I smiled playfully at him.

But he didn't smile back. "No one else is drinking. We don't drink alcohol or smoke or do drugs."

"Well, you have alcohol behind the bar because I ordered a drink," I countered.

"We keep it for our guests."

I glanced around at the crowd of jubilant dancers and people talking and smiling. "So everyone here is just high on life?"

"Yes." That was almost unbelievable. Who knew that people could be so naturally happy? "Did you have a good time?" he asked.

Embarrassment rushed the blood up to my cheeks. "Were you watching me?"

"Maybe."

"You saw me flying?"

"I did. But *you* weren't flying," he corrected. "Samuel and Ariel were."

"Well, thanks for bursting my bubble." Jerk.

"You're welcome." He smirked. "You are an excellent dancer, by the way."

"Oh. It's...nothing. I've just had a lot of years of practice." I was being modest. I knew I was a great dancer, but I always felt shy when people complimented me on it.

"You ready to go?"

I nodded and he grabbed my hand. We made our way back to the tunnel where we came from, and soon we were sloshing through murky water in the darkness again. "Can you fly?"

"Yes," Lake answered flatly.

"Can all angels fly?"

"Eventually."

"Does a bell have to ring?" I chuckled, hoping he would get my *It's a Wonderful Life* reference.

But he ignored it. "You will learn soon."

"What?"

"I will tell you everything you need to know soon. Let's just get back above ground."

I decided to refrain from asking any more questions. Instead, I turned my head and glanced behind me, hoping to see the glow seeping out of the angel nightclub. We were out of view of the round steel door by now, but I would never forget that feeling of flying. That sweet release of anything and everything negative in my life. I let go and loved myself again for a little bit, and it was amazing.

I twisted back to the darkness ahead of us and sadness fell over me. I didn't want to leave. I wanted to stay there forever.

CHAPTER THIRTEEN

Is This Real Life?

We headed back up the ladder into Reggie's store. It was dim and completely empty of patrons. The silence of the store strengthened the residual hum in my ears caused by the bumping bass of the music from the angel nightclub.

The storefront's metal gate was rolled down, blocking the view of the outside and my ability to tell what time of the day it could be. I reached down into my pocket for my phone. Three in the morning and ten missed calls from Alex. Great. She was probably having a conniption fit over the fact that she had not heard from me in hours.

"I need to call my sister," I whispered to Lake, cautious of who could be listening.

He shut the door in the floor and covered it back up with the old rug. "We still have much to talk about, Frankie."

"Okay, but she needs to know I'm not dead in a gutter somewhere."

"She's asleep." I turned toward the voice behind me. Reggie came strolling out of a back room.

"How do you know?" I asked skeptically.

"She was worried but fell asleep waiting for you to call," he said.

I peered over to Lake and searched his face for some kind of answer as to how and why Reggie would know anything about my sister. He read my puzzling eyes. "Reggie, could you please give us a little time to talk?"

"Yeah, sure thing."

Lake walked over to him and spoke in a low voice. "Did you take care of them?"

"Yeah. I called Micah for backup," Reggie replied.

"We'll reconvene in a few hours."

"Absolutely. Just make sure you lock up when you leave." He handed Lake the keys. "Have a nice night, Frankie."

As soon as he was out of the room, I began my twenty-one questions. "What's going on, Lake? How the hell does Reggie know anything about my sister? And I'll have to be at work soon. What am I going to tell Dominic about you? How am I going to explain any of this?"

"You won't."

I rolled my eyes and huffed to show him how irritated I was. The high from the angel nightclub was only temporary and already starting to wear off. "Why?"

"Reggie is an angel, too. He is your sister's Guide."

"My sister's what?" I asked, shaking my head in confusion. "My sister's Guide?"

"Yes. You might also know them as guardians."

I pulled out a cigarette. "Okay. I'm ready to hear everything. Start."

"You don't need to smoke."

"You don't need to tell me what to do. Now, go. Explain." I was beyond done at this point. Lake was still a stranger to me. The fact that I hadn't drank a drop of liquor in a couple of hours was starting to make me shake, and all I could think about was having to face Dominic at work and explaining why I didn't Seal my last client.

Lake leaned up against the counter. He was so beautiful, even in the dimness of the light. His wavy, highlighted hair, his ocean-colored eyes and strapping body... It was all too much for one man to have. It was almost unfair to the average male. It was almost unfair to me, having to keep my hormones in check.

Sex was certainly not an unfamiliar term to me. Jacob and I were like bunnies, dry-humping and actually humping each other every chance we could get—before school, after school, whenever our parents were out of town. The sexual attraction was strong, and I hadn't felt it since being with him. No other man had ever truly made me quiver with arousal. Except now. Except Lake. He stood in front of me and all I could think about was wrapping my legs around the width of his body.

I fiercely sucked the smoke down from my cigarette, trying hard to concentrate on his words and not on his ridiculous muscles that seemed to be begging me to touch them.

"Everyone has a Guide," he started. "But it's not what you see in the movies. The Guides only come to their protégé's aid whenever they need it."

"My sister needs him? Is she in trouble?"

"As soon as your sister started thinking about selling her soul, his presence and need to keep a watchful eye on her increased. Guides are trained to, without notice, guide until it is time for their protégé to enter the White Realm."

"How do they guide someone?" It was apparent now that angels had many supernatural abilities. Flying was probably the best, in my opinion, but I was curious to learn what else these angels could do.

"They have the ability to penetrate the subconscious, basically working as a second thought or intuition. They try to induce the good in a person, such as morality and making the right decisions. Ultimately, Guides leave it up to the individual to choose what they want to choose. When Alex sold her soul, Reggie was there. He pushed the virtuous thoughts as much as he could, but she chose to sell it anyway. Her determination to save you was much stronger. Reggie isn't an Angel of Reform, but he knew we were going to be sent here soon to infiltrate this region, which is why he stuck around. It could take decades or even centuries before a region is chosen. There are so many out there, and only so many of us. Reggie wanted to take advantage of this opportunity—one that doesn't come often—to help us through Alex's transformation. Until then, all he could do was open this store and be as close to her as he could."

I envisioned a tiny devil and a tiny angel whispering into each one of my sister's ears right before she sold our souls. If only she'd listened to tiny Reggie. "So, what if you reform guys weren't coming?"

"If her time to be reformed were yet to come, he would have had to move on. There are many mortals out there who are in need of a Guide, and he would have to be reassigned. Her human life and yours belong to the Red Realm. All of your decisions now revolve around doing what the king and queen want you to do. There is no longer a subconscious to try to preserve for the White Realm because your soul is now property of the Red Realm." Lake looked down at his feet as if to be saddened by this.

I glanced down at my own feet, heartbroken and horrified at the thought of my sister being tortured by Centaurus and Hysteria. I could barely even imagine it without feeling the anger build up inside me. And I suppose it would be a bit heartbreaking to Reggie and the angels, too. Reggie's sole purpose as a Guide was to help my sister get into the White Realm. To help her make the right decisions throughout her life in order to guarantee her spot there. But now that she'd gotten herself into the devil's grip, there was nothing he could do. She wasn't going to die, and if she somehow did, her place was waiting for her in the Red Realm. Unless she was reformed.

Lake continued. "It's the same for anyone who sells their soul or does something that denies admittance to the White Realm. They are no longer assigned a Guide. The Guide must move on to another protégé because they will no longer have the ability to help lead that soul into the White Realm."

"Do I have a Guide?" I was afraid to ask this question—more afraid of what the answer might be. My Guide probably gave up on me a long time ago, even if he or she knew about the reform guys coming. Taking on a drunk who curses too much? Fuck no!

Lake's eyes shifted away from mine for a moment, but then he met my gaze dead on. "No. Not anymore. He moved on."

I knew it. He didn't want to wait around for the Angels of Reform to come. I was too far gone. My soul was no longer pure. There was no hope for me.

I took a deep, dramatic drag of my cigarette. "Alexandra can still go to Heaven, right? That's your job. You're here to reform and Reggie can take her to the White Realm."

"And you can go, too. Just because you don't have a Guide doesn't mean you can't."

That didn't make me feel any better. I had no Guide. I was a shitbag. I lit another cigarette. "So what the fuck do we have to do?"

"Frankie," Lake seethed.

"Sorry!" I yelled and stood up. I was becoming enraged with the thought of my sister being harmed. "This is all so...crazy. I mean, Angels of Reform and Guides and Dominic and Centaurus and you. It's all so surreal. What if what I'm doing isn't even real? What if there really isn't a White or Red Realm? I have never seen it. Dominic could be some crazy-ass guy making me tattoo people just for kicks. And you could just be some ridiculously sexy man with nothing better to do than to mess around with my head. I don't know!"

"Frankie, this is real. And what you are saying and feeling is partially the reason why people think it's okay to do harm and evil and sell their souls. They don't believe an afterlife exists, but it is very much real. It has been real since the dawn of time."

"Well, then what is the White Realm like? What makes it so much better than just being here on Earth?" I asked.

"It's not that it's a better place. Our bodies, our physical selves only have the capability of existing for a certain amount of time. Our organs, our skin—all of our physical attributes age, become worn down over time," he explained. "Or it prematurely stops working as a result of illness or unnatural outside forces. When people die, their souls are welcomed into the White Realm as an extension of their lives here on Earth."

"Welcomed? But you have to be judged first?"

"Correct," he clarified. "By the Counsel of the NonAligned. The White Realm is a safe place. A place with no violence, no evil. A place for the good. We strive to keep it that way."

"And...my parents? Are they there?" It had been on my mind the entire time. I knew the answer. I just knew it.

"Yes," he confirmed. "They are in the White Realm."

I smiled and looked down at my hands, ignoring the sting that threatened to bring on the tears. I decided not to ask him anything else about my mom and dad. If I did, I wasn't sure if I could hide my longing for them—the pain that had replaced all else in their absence.

I walked closer to where he was standing. Suddenly, I felt I needed warmth. "What happens when you die?"

Lake adjusted himself from leaning against the counter. He stood up straighter and watched me inch closer to him. "What do you mean? Everyone dies differently, Frankie."

I turned my butt up against the counter so we were both facing the same way, determined to make our arms touch, at the very least. I had no idea what

I was trying to do, but there was something about the ambiance of the low light and my vulnerability to our conversation. I didn't know what was real and what wasn't, but touching Lake's arm felt very real. "What happens to your soul? Does it float out of you all ghost-like? Do you feel the same as if you were alive?"

He took hold of my eyes with his. "Your soul is your energy," he said softly. "Energy cannot be destroyed. Your body will decompose, but your soul is forever. Yes, you feel the same as when you were alive, only...lighter. There is no weight upon your shoulders. No apprehension. No fear. You are as pure and innocent as when you were born. You can still feel your limbs, your fingers, and your toes. You can still hear yourself talk. You can still think. Everything is the same, but different."

I gazed up at him in amazement, in awe of how much more perfect he seemed to be up close. "Can you still touch?" I breathed, leaning closer into his space. I watched his chest rise and fall gently, and my heart began to race.

What the hell was I doing? I hadn't been this close to someone in so long, and it felt so good. I had no idea if Lake was at all interested in me. He might not have even been attracted to me. Maybe he thought I was ugly, especially compared to what he was used to. I had nothing on all those beautiful angelic women at the angel nightclub. And what if he was dating one of them? Were angels even allowed to date? Did they have sex?

Lake adjusted himself again. I wasn't sure if I'd imagined it, but he might have taken a step away from me. I chose to ignore it and took a step toward him.

"Can you still...do things?" I asked in my sultriest voice. I wasn't used to making the first move or even flirting. Jacob and I flirted, but it was high school. We were kids and it was sweet. It was all giggles and nose bops and butterfly kisses. Sure we had lots of sex, but it was gentle and soft and slow, and most of the time we had no idea what we were doing.

But everything was different now. I was different now. I craved passion and heat. I had no idea if it had anything to do with living on the dark side, but my desires had matured with the sexual tension that lay between my legs. I wanted Lake to take me, to just lift me up on this counter, spread my legs, and ravage me. The idea of a beautiful stranger touching my body with his foreign hands thrilled me, stirred the erotic juices in all of my lady parts. Was he even capable of that? Would an angel be allowed to deliver such aggressiveness and dominance being that he was all about good and innocence?

I was about to find out.

He might have been talking, but I chose not to listen. I wasn't interested in what he had to say. My eyes slammed shut and I took a deep breath in before entering his personal space. Reaching up high with my lips, I opened my mouth slightly. The anticipation of meeting his parted lips made me dizzy with both fear and excitement. I realized, in that very moment, just how desperately I needed to feel his touch. I couldn't wait to kiss him. I couldn't wait to unravel myself inside his arms.

But that feeling never came. Instead, I was suddenly being physically rejected by a gentle push of my shoulders.

"Frankie," Lake breathed. I knew exactly what he meant by the way he said my name. But I didn't want to open my eyes. I didn't want to face rejection, so I kept my head down instead and walked over to where I'd left my pack of smokes.

"I'm sorry," I mumbled with a cigarette hanging off my lips. I flicked the lighter and inhaled as hard as I could.

"It's okay. I'm sorry," he apologized unnecessarily. "I just...this can't happen."

Son of a bitch. I needed some vodka. Like, now. "I get it. It's cool."

"We have a lot more to discuss and it's important that we stay focused."

How stupid was I? Of course this gorgeous angel man wanted nothing to do with a Sealer. With a mean-spirited, sad, smoky alcoholic who worked for the devil. He was everything I wasn't, everything I would never be. What the hell was I even thinking? "No, it's okay. Really. I was just having a moment. We can get back to what we were talking about. The Guides and dying, right?"

My eyes tingled. I wanted to die right then from disappointment and humiliation, but I held it together. I realized, in *that* very moment, that I was desperately alone.

CHAPTER FOURTEEN

Rejection and Vodka Go Well Together

Lake and I remained on our respective opposite ends of the space. Close enough to hear each other's lowered voices, but far enough to understand that there would only be talking. I was ready to drown myself in a bottle of vodka and pass out half naked in my bed, but according to Lake, there was much to discuss.

"You will have to return to work as if nothing has changed for the next couple of days," Lake insisted.

"What is Dominic going to do when he finds out I didn't give you the shaft?" I was trying to lighten the now awkward atmosphere that was threatening to choke me, but Lake's seriousness completely deflated my attempt.

"He will choose to ignore it. I know him. And he knows me. He now knows for sure that I'm here and what my plans are. He wants to play the game. He wants to fight."

"Like, a fistfight? I mean, isn't that childish?" Seriously? These men were over a thousand years old. Why did it have to come down to getting physical?

"No," Lake answered in a deadpan tone. "None of this is childish, Frankie. Far from it. Dominic and I have been enemies for a very long time. He has been waiting for this. For me to descend upon his region."

"Just to be clear, you wanted him to know, right? You set up the whole selling-your-soul deal?"

"Yes," he admitted. "I purposely used the *SoulCatcher* app and had you come to my house to finish the transaction. I knew the Henchmen would come if I declined the Seal of the Red Realm. Part of the reform and the destruction of the region is to get rid the bodyguards who protect the facility."

"So, there really wasn't a girlfriend," I stated. This was good news, but it disappointed me in a way. I wanted what he said about the fictional woman to be real. It was the best thing I'd heard in a long while.

Lake seemed pretty shameful of his deceit. "I do not have a girlfriend, but what I said was true. There is someone I feel this way about."

I bit my bottom lip, secretly hating whoever this girl was. "And did you get rid of them? The Henchmen?"

He nodded.

I stood up and crossed my arms over my chest, truly interested in knowing more about the Dominic/Lake feud. "What happened between you and Dominic? Weren't you guys besties before and after life? I mean, you went through a lot of shit together and became Angels of Reform. How did Dominic become evil? How did he end up working for the wrong team?"

Lake's eyes veered away from mine. "He chose a different path. He made a decision and did something that was unforgivable, thus resulting in his banishment from the White Realm." His words were intense and stern, as if it were coming from deep within.

"You're not going to tell me, are you?" I asked, disappointed.

"It's not important."

But it *was* important. I could tell. Lake and Dominic had major history together, and not just bad ones. I couldn't help picturing the two of them together in the White Realm, fighting evil crime side by side. This thought forced an image of Dominic to the forefront, and I realized now how I could definitely see an angel hidden underneath the menacing facade. And that splice of blonde that hung down over his forehead... I wondered if that could be a residual angel feature that just refused to let him go.

"Right now, you need to know that you will resume life as usual. Go home, go to work, engage with your sister," Lake said.

"How do you and your angel friends plan to take down Centaurus?" Every part of this situation made me feel like I was getting in the middle of a battle that I had no business getting in the middle of. It all felt bigger than me and I had absolutely no idea what Lake's plans were. Angels and demons fighting, supernatural powers, and centuries of grudges—it was all so crazy.

Before all of this, I was simply a young girl with rich parents, someone who wore pink dresses and loved dancing. All I wanted to do was make out with my boyfriend and braid my hair. Now, I just wanted to smoke and drink and wear leather jackets and dark eyeliner and live this screwed-up life that I hated.

I began thinking: did I really want to be reformed? Assuming that this was all real. That the White Realm and the Red Realm were real places. I didn't want to end up in the Red Realm, but did I really want to do the work to get out of it? Wouldn't it be easier to just live this life that I hated so much? I didn't want to be responsible for sending souls off to be tortured for all eternity, but I was torn between believing and doing and unhappiness and changing.

I bitched about my life daily, whether it was to my sister or internally, but now that there seemed to be a chance for something different, did I really want it? Besides, I didn't have a Guide anymore. He left me. What did that have to say about me? I didn't have someone to come save me from this hell. Save me from myself.

Goosebumps tingled my arms at the memory of Samuel and Ariel's magical touches as we floated together. Their beauty and radiance flashed in my mind. Could I be like them? They were so radiant and pure. Could I ever truly be accepted by the White Realm after ensuring all the people I have sealed a guaranteed spot in Hell?

I stubbed my cigarette butt out on the sole of my boot and placed it in the growing pile on the floor next to me. Lake could probably sense my sullen thoughts about whether or not I deserved to be saved, so I had to speak. "Well, what's going to happen?"

"Many centuries ago," he began, "there were wars between the Red and White Realms, causing problems for the human race."

"I don't remember reading about angels and demons roaming the Earth in history class," I quipped. Lake's rejection was still nagging at me and I couldn't help my bitterness.

He chose to humor my sarcasm. "It was not recorded. This was before your history books. No one but the White and Red Realms and a select few know of this information now." I lit another cigarette and Lake scowled but continued. "The devils fought to acquire as many souls as they could to fill the Red Realm, and the White Realm fought to stop it. Back then, the Red and White Realms had full-on capabilities of influencing humans. Finally, the Counsel of the NonAligned came up with a treaty, which read that no Elder from the White Realm and no king or queen from the Red Realm were allowed on Earth. Humans were now responsible for choosing their soul's own fate by the decisions they made on their own. Representatives from either realm were still allowed on Earth, to assist with particular duties such as escorting a soul to their respective eternities, which is why loopholes were eventually created. Each side had their own secret weapons, such as the subconscious forces of the Guides and the persuasion of the ASRs. But one thing had always remained a hard and fast rule: no entity from either realm is allowed to step foot into the other's plane."

"What would happen?" I asked.

"They would be destroyed."

"Destroyed how?"

"Vaporized," Lake said. "Their soul, their energy would cease to exist. It's one of the very few ways a soul can be eradicated."

Well, that was a sobering thought. I had an eerie feeling that his explanation was leading to something tragic. "You said the Angels of Reform need to destroy the portal. Why do I feel like what you are about to say is something really bad?" Images of the Centaurus building began flashing through my mind, and I tried to picture where the portal would be. I had never seen it before. Then again, I doubted there would be any big signs pointing to it.

"The portal doesn't lead directly past the gates into the Red Realm, so our Angels of Reform do not need to actually be there to destroy it. However, unfortunately, the power that is required to destroy the portal is too strong for an angel to withstand, thus resulting in the same outcome. It's...a sacrifice that one Angel of Reform must make for the sake of what we are set out to do." His eyes broke away from mine. Lake had been emotionless for most of this short time that I'd known him, but I could tell this particular subject had some kind of effect on him.

"That's sad. How do you decide who's going to die?" I asked.

"It's chosen by the Liberation Stone."

"The what?" Did he just say that a *rock* chooses who dies?

"It is much more detailed than it sounds," Lake replied. "The Liberation Stone is the key to destroying portals to the Red Realm. It holds the souls of the Great Elders, the beings who created the White Realm, which was formed long before the Red Realm came about."

"What happens to the rest of the building and the ASRs who work there?" I asked, curious about my co-workers. Not that I really cared about what happened to them. But my sister was one of them, and I cared about her.

"The portal is the only part of the building to get destroyed. Everything else stays intact," he said. "As I said before, the ASRs are allowed to make their own decision about being reformed. If they choose to, the process would begin, which is done with the help of other White Realm representatives like Samuel and Ariel. If not, then the ASRs move on, most of the time finding a different region to work for."

I yawned. Not because I was bored with his story. I wasn't. Not in the least bit. But I was exhausted from the day and this information dump. It was weighing me down. I needed some alcohol to take it all in.

"I will fill you in on the plans for destroying this region's portal soon. You should go get some rest," he suggested.

"In other words, I look like shit."

"Not even close to what I meant. It's been a long night. Your sister will be awake soon and you should let her know that you are okay. Let's get you home."

I didn't protest. I was tired. Really, really tired. Not to mention, I was still mortified. So much so, actually, that I considered declining Lake's offer to get me home and go on about my business as if I didn't even know who he was. The fact of the matter was, I *didn't* know this man. He was a perfect stranger. I only met him just a few hours ago, and yet, I still managed to throw myself at him like some stupid high school slut.

But even that and his dismissal of my poor attempt at seducing him still didn't change how I felt. I couldn't pinpoint what it was that had me drawn to him. Yes, it was attraction, but it was also more. It was the need to feel close to someone after years of no physical contact with the opposite sex. It was my vulnerability to the situation at hand, and the confusion of what I wanted my future to be. It was the longing for my past life. The familiarity of his closeness and the promise that he would keep me safe. It was his gorgeous long hair and his big hands. His tall, masculine body and authoritarian voice.

We exited Reggie's store into the early-morning dewy air. It was almost five in the morning now, but dark enough to still be night. The neighborhood bums were still asleep in their cardboard beds on the sidewalk and there were only just a couple of early work commuters waiting at the bus stop. Lake locked up the store behind him, just as Reggie had asked, and we walked the few steps it took to get over to my apartment building.

"You don't have to come up," I informed him.

"I just want to make sure you get in safe."

"I'm fine. Go. Go do...whatever it is you angels do." Honestly, I wanted to have a smoke in the hallway before stumbling into bed and Mr. Perfect didn't like my habit very much.

Lake stuck his hand in his pocket and pulled out a card. "If you need me, call me and go over to Reggie's. He can keep you safe until I arrive."

I took his card. "Seriously? You have a business card?" I sneered. His severe expression didn't budge. "Fine. I'll call you if I need you."

He nodded, and I turned for the entrance. I took one last glance at his gloriousness while opening the door, then lit a cigarette as I ascended the stairs.

"Frankie. Frankie, wake up."

I reluctantly pulled my eyelids open in response to the low voice and gentle shaking.

"Frankie, you're going to be late for work."

I was lying on my stomach, one leg hanging halfway off the bed. I could feel a draft of cool air colliding with my bare back.

"Jeez, Frankie. How do you manage to consume this much alcohol and still live to tell the tale?" Alex said.

I moaned at the clinking of empty bottles my sister was so obviously cleaning up. Every sound sent a series of jackhammering jolts to my brain. "And what is that on your back? You have two small red marks. Did you fall?"

"Alex, please...stop," I begged. I thought about moving, but my body wasn't having it.

"Where were you last night? I was so worried about you." Her question seeped into the one tiny part of my brain that seemed to be awake and working hard enough for me to understand her question. I couldn't answer right away, though. I was contemplating on what to tell her and what was even the truth. Did I have some kind of strange, drunken dream where I met the most gorgeous man to ever walk this planet?

I vaguely remember being whisked away to some underground angel dwelling where I got sexually charged in a nonsexual way with some very sexy strangers who claimed to be angels. And somehow, we were flying in the air while dancing to electronic music.

Somewhere in the middle of all of this, I learned some very interesting information about Dominic and the White and Red Realms. Then, I think I might have thrown myself at the gorgeous man, only to get rejected by him.

My mind struggled, but it wasn't long before I finally realized that it was definitely *not* a dream. It was all reality.

I curled up into a fetal position as the humiliation that I tried so hard to get rid of with booze came creeping back. "Ugh."

"Frankie, let's get you in the shower. You smell like you slept inside this bottle of vodka." Alex wasn't letting up. Her mission in life was to annoy the crap out of me, it seemed.

"Fine," I managed to mumble. I maneuvered my feet onto the ground but kept my body on the bed. I was afraid that if I stood up too quickly, the room would still be spinning and all of the contents of my stomach would come spewing out onto my sweat-stained sheets. Why did I drink so much? I remembered finishing my cigarette in the hallway before entering the apartment. I found my sister sound asleep on the couch, which was proof that she had been waiting up for me. I didn't believe she had ever slept in the living room before. Then, I quietly went into my bedroom. I recalled having a couple of cocktails while scrolling through my phone, but a couple must have turned into several.

I couldn't stop thinking about Lake and the angel nightclub and Dominic and the Red Realm and all the things wrong in my life. And I couldn't seem to stop missing the Guide that I didn't even know I had. I was trying to piece it all together, trying to understand how the fuck I got here. I was trying to determine whether or not I wanted to believe, whether or not I wanted to change who I was. No, I was not a fan of sealing the people who sold their souls. Nor was I comfortable with having a hand in ensuring that their souls were tortured for an eternity in the afterlife. But the thought of just accepting who I had become seemed so much easier. All I had to do was tattoo people on a daily basis and not care. How much simpler would it be to smoke and drink and forget about my past and live day to day, not having to worry about love and friends and nonsense? I hardly had to pay any bills!

There was a time when I wanted those things in my life, but I was different now. Everything was different now. The only drama I have experienced over the last three years was very recent. The whole Hank Hannigan beheading was definitely dramatic. Other than that, all I had to do was mind my own business and work.

I had no idea what Lake had planned in regard to taking down Centaurus, but Inebriated Frankie had apparently decided to help. He told me last night that the Sealers and ASRs had the choice to reform or not. I was taking that option into consideration and weighing my pros and cons carefully for myself. I wasn't sure if I was ready to give up my potty mouth and spiked orange juice.

As for my sister, I decided that she didn't have an option. I was going to make sure that she was no longer a Sealer. I was going to make sure Alex would go to the White Realm.

My body flinched when Alex playfully, but intently, smacked my ass.

"Ouch," I bellowed.

"Let's get that butt into gear, missy."

My heart ached at the similarity between my mom and Alex. I missed my mother greatly, but it was as if she were still around at times. Alex definitely inherited the matriarchal vibes. That mother instinct was engraved inside of her. She was born to be a parent, and I hated that she would never get that chance.

I took a deep breath, hoping to hold in any bile that might come up as I finally edged off the bed. I stood up and forced my feet to shuffle toward the bathroom. It had been a while since I was this drunk. I was a functioning alcoholic, so feeling this hungover meant that I definitely drank more than my body could handle. And for some strange reason, my back ached more than the rest of me. Dancing with the angels was the most exercise I'd gotten in a long time, so it made sense I'd be sore.

I concentrated as hard as I could on not vomiting. With my eyes closed, I stood under the showerhead, allowing the hot water to consume me and massage the back of my neck and drench my hair. But when I lowered my head, I noticed something near my feet. The water and dizziness from the hangover obscured my vision, so I bent down to pick it up.

Holding it carefully between my fingers, I stepped out of the falling water and placed the thing in the palm of my other hand. I wiped the water out of my eyes and stared down at it, squinting and forcing my eyes to focus. It was a...feather?

It was gray and sparkling. The quill was short, and the feathery part had gotten wet and separated. I wrinkled my forehead, confused by where this feather could have come from. Maybe it came off one of the angels at the angel nightclub. Maybe it belonged to Samuel or Ariel. I could have sworn their wings were white, but there were strobe lights everywhere. I could have been wrong.

I turned it over, and upon further inspection, found a tiny speck of red right at the base of the quill. Was it blood?

The faint sound of my phone ringing interrupted my thoughts. "Alex! Who is it?" I yelled out.

I poked my head around the shower curtain. Alex came in with my phone in her hand. "It's the office. Want me to answer?"

Shit. "No! No, I'll take it." My heart began to throb. I had been thinking about so many things that I completely spaced about coming up with some kind of story about the *SoulCatcher* app and Lake. Lake said that Dominic would play dumb, but I should have at least thought of a backup plan.

I decided to wing it and answered the phone. "Hello?"

"Frankie, this is Dominic's secretary, Raven. I was instructed to inform you that Dominic would like to see you as soon as possible." Raven's tone was both ominous and professional at the same time. She sounded like the fake voice that gave you directions on your cellphone.

The hot water streamed down my back. "Um... yeah. Sure. I'll be there soon."

"I will let him know. Goodbye."

I handed my phone back to Alex. "Everything okay?" she asked, worried.

"Yeah. Everything's fine. I gotta get ready."

Okay, so maybe there was more drama in my life than I wanted to admit. I mean, I could be losing my head today, and not in the figurative sense. More like...actual. My head could actually be removed from my body.

I looked down at the wet, gray feather still in my hand. "Where did you come from?" I asked it.

I think the more important question was, where's my vodka?

CHAPTER FIFTEEN

The Camera Never Lies

I squinted at the afternoon light as I exited The Hartley. Although there was no visible sun, the daytime gloom still stung my eyes. I could tell my body was angry with me. I was hungover and running on just a couple of hours of drunken sleep. Every step I took ached and that pain catapulted directly from my feet to my head.

I glanced over at Reggie's shop, which didn't have a name—something I had never noticed before. He was tending to a customer at the counter, but he met my gaze as if he could sense me walking by. I decided today would be the day that I finally stopped to talk to him.

When I approached the counter, the customer had just grabbed his bag and walked away. I peeked over my shoulder to ensure no one was standing behind me, then whispered, "Why didn't you tell me you were my sister's Guide?"

He licked his fingers and counted a wad of cash. "You didn't ask."

"How was I supposed to know—" My words were high-pitched, and I stopped myself. I didn't want to cause a scene. Reggie placed the money into the cash register, then met me on the other side of the counter. We walked toward the front of the store together.

"It isn't wise that we make ourselves known to anyone," he said.

"Well, does Alex know about you?"

"Not yet, but she will soon," he assured me. "Our protégés don't usually know of our presence, but these are different circumstances."

I watched him carefully. Reggie looked like someone who spent his days lounged on a beat-up couch getting high on weed and playing video games. An enormous dollar-sign pendant encrusted in diamonds (probably fake) hung off the gold rope chain around his neck. A joint rested on top of his right ear, for crap's sake! Granted, it looked freshly rolled and like it hadn't been lit, but still. He didn't look like he made the right life choices for himself, much less like he could guide someone else to make them.

We stepped outside the store. I lit a cigarette. "So you're going to help Alex get to the White Realm?"

Reggie smiled. He knew exactly what I was thinking. "That's the plan. And don't let my appearance fool you. I adapt to my surroundings."

Thank goodness. I didn't know Reggie all that well, but I was glad he wasn't what he looked like. Maybe I shouldn't have been so judgmental. I supposed I should have just appreciated the fact that he hadn't turned his back on my sister when he should have, according to the angel rules. It was comforting to know that he cared so much about the future of Alex's soul, regardless of how he looked. At least he stuck around, unlike *my* Guide.

I took a deep puff. "Are you also a gladiator from hundreds of years ago?"

"Oh, no." He chuckled. "I'm not *that* old...or brave. My human life ended in 1862. In the American Civil War."

"Your human life," I repeated thoughtfully. I hadn't really considered what that meant when Lake told me his and Dominic's story. They actually died at some point in their lives in order to become angels.

"Yes, my old life. The one I had before I traveled to the White Realm." He made it sound like it was just a road trip.

"Before you became an angel," I stated, trying to piece everything together.

He nodded. "When you arrive at the White Realm, you are thoroughly evaluated. Each angel is given a specific job, whatever the Elders feel is suitable for you, such as Guides and Angels of Reform. When you are selected for that job, you are trained for that particular position."

"Does that determine who can come back to Earth?" I asked, curious to know more about the White Realm rules. It felt like there was so much to learn.

"Pretty much," Reggie said. "It depends on what your job duties entail. Guides are required to be near their protégé most times. So, we must travel to Earth in order to operate more efficiently and effectively."

"What other kinds of angels need to travel back here?"

"Angels of Reform, of course. And Ushers," he said.

"Ushers?" Men in tuxedos opening doors at weddings came to mind.

"Angels who escort souls into the White Realm when a mortal dies," he explained.

"How does the whole reform thing work? Does it hurt?" Memories from The Breakdown came creeping back. That pain was unimaginable. It might have only lasted fifteen minutes, but it was the worst fifteen minutes of my life. I felt like I'd died—like someone tore my body into pieces and tried to weld it back together without any anesthetic. And that was just physically. Mentally and emotionally, it felt like loss, heartache, disappointment, and despair all rolled into one big pile of shit. I didn't know if I wanted to experience that again.

"Not at all," Reggie answered. I was relieved. "It isn't very complicated. It's just a process of ritualistic chants and spell casting."

Spell casting? Sometimes I didn't believe the world I lived in.

We were silent for a moment. My eyes wandered over to the two bums across the street. They seemed to be deep in conversation, one missing a shoe and the other grabbing his junk like he had to pee. It looked like one of them was holding a cellphone, which I found very odd.

"You aren't human anymore?" I questioned him. "You look human. Don't you look the same as you did when you died?"

Reggie also turned his attention toward the two bums, whose conversation seemed to be getting more intense pretty quickly. "A human is a being derived from Earth. Humans possess physical characteristics that make them human. We are humans when we live on Earth, but when we die, our physical bodies remain while our energy, our souls, move on to another plane. Souls are just called souls. And we are basically the same as we were in human form...only different."

One of the bums started to raise his voice then pointed in our direction. "Yeah, I know," I said, continuing our conversation. "Lake explained that to me, which is kind of vague, don't you think?" I took one last drag of my cigarette, then flicked it toward the street. "Anyway, I just thought maybe the soul form of ourselves would have a different name."

"No, they are just souls. It's a universal term."

The bum gestured a hand in our direction and shook his head. It would appear he was disagreeing with the other guy.

"Are they pointing at us?" I asked, alarmed and unable to ignore them anymore.

"It looks like it," Reggie replied. He stepped closer to me and we both watched them.

The heated conversation spilled over, and soon the bums began drawing a crowd. It was hard to hear exactly what they were saying. Their street slang mixed with the sounds of cars zooming past, talking pedestrians, and the music inside Reggie's store made it difficult to understand. But whatever it was, the reason seemed to be over something on the cellphone they both kept taking turns holding and staring at. It looked like they were playing a game of hot potato.

Then, the two hobos stepped off the sidewalk onto the street and began walking toward us. Traffic didn't slow down, and I held my breath when the one hobbling on a single shoe narrowly dodged the fender of a pickup truck. Reggie positioned himself in front of me as the two homeless men approached us. Reggie was much taller than me with a head full of thick dreads, so I peered around the side of his body to get a better view.

The men were still arguing. "That's her! That's her, man!" one bum yelled, holding the cellphone and pointing his dirty finger at me.

The other hobo, still grabbing at his genitals, yelled back, "No way, man! That ain't her! That ain't the same bitch!"

Reggie held up his hands. "Whoa, guys! What's going on?"

The one with the cellphone spoke first, slurring his words on account of a few missing teeth. I looked down at his one bare foot, filthy and full of sores. His tarnished toenails scraped the concrete and I nearly gagged. "Man, this dude sayin' this ain't her, but it is. That's her, man!" He held the phone up to Reggie's face. I kept my place behind him, worried that one of these homeless guys might accidentally spit on me. I was able to catch a glimpse of a blurred video playing on the screen of the phone. "Man, she's flyin'. That bitch has wings and shit!"

"Let me see this," Reggie said, snatching the phone away from the bum's gross hands. I cringed at the thought of Reggie getting sliced by one of his disgusting, long fingernails.

Reggie and I both watched the video on the phone. It was dark and grainy, but the big red letters on the roof of my apartment building was unmistakable. The shaky cameraman zoomed into The Hartley, where it looked as though a shadowy figure danced between the illuminated R and the T. I squinted at the tiny screen. I could tell the cellphone was an out-of-date model—most of the newer versions were practically like mini televisions. It was scratched up and chipped on the corners, and a giant gash right in the center of the glass display screwed up the pixels and quality of the video.

But I could see it. The silhouette of a person swaying and hanging off the letters of The Hartley sign. The movements were clumsy and uncoordinated, but definitely resembled dancing of some sort. I might have even observed a few pirouettes. The cameraman tried to zoom in some more, but it only muddied up the quality and made it difficult to identify anything.

"You don't know what you talking about, bro. Ain't nobody flyin'. You need to lay off that Ice," the other bum said. I wasn't educated on street slang, but I assumed Ice was a drug of some sort.

"Yo, I'm tellin' you. I saw that shit! I got that shit on video, man!"

"Shh!" Reggie hushed them. "Let us see."

After about a minute of extremely irritating amateur recording, the cameraman finally zoomed out and steadied the cellphone. The figure, which does seem like a female by her petite frame, looked like she twirled and spun a few more times around the letters before coming dangerously close to the edge of the building. I gasped, thankful when I saw there wasn't an accident. But she whirled around again, this time tripping over her own feet. She fell off the building headfirst as if she were sliding down a waterslide.

The cameraman mumbled, "Oh, damn," and followed her descent. But right before she hit the ground, a pair of gray shimmering wings shot out from her back!

"Replay that!" I yelped.

"I told you! I told you, man! Them was wings!" the bum shouted aggressively.

Reggie backed the video up by a few seconds, then pressed play. The woman fell off the side of building headfirst but right before she smashed into the pavement below, a set of large, grayish-colored (I could be wrong because it was dark) glittery wings shot out from behind her. They flapped once, forcing her entire body to jolt and boomerang away from the ground in just enough time. The cameraman caught the wings flap two more times, propelling the girl upward toward the top of the building.

Then, the screen turned black.

I yelled at the phone. "What happened?"

Reggie took the device away, pressed a few things, then handed it back to the bums. "Here you go."

The shoeless bum gaped down at it. "Hey, where'd it go? What'd you do, man?"

"I don't know." Reggie shrugged. "Something happened and the video got deleted. I think you need a new phone, brother."

"Yo, that shit is fucked up," the other bum said.

"Man, don't you fix cellphones?"

"You got a hundred dollars?" Reggie countered.

The homeless man smacked his lips. "Man, I ain't got a hundred dollars." He turned to his homeless friend. "Loan me a hundred dollars."

As they debated over who might have a hundred dollars to spare, Reggie gently pushed me toward the inside of his store. Once we were a few yards away from the dueling hobos, he spoke. "I had to delete the video."

"Why?"

"Because it was you."

"What?"

"That was you in the video," he said.

"That wasn't me," I chided, holding my hand to my chest as if offended. "I think I would know if I fell off a building, grew wings, and started to fly."

"Maybe not if you were really drunk."

I glared at him. The man had a point.

CHAPTER SIXTEEN

Misconstrued

I didn't know what bothered me more: the fact that Reggie knew that I was drunk last night, or that my back suddenly tingled and itched something wicked. Particularly over my shoulder blades. How could that have been me? I didn't remember flying. Sure, I flew in the angel nightclub, but I wasn't *actually* flying. Samuel and Ariel were. They just carried me.

"Reggie, how could that be me? I can't fly," I said.

He looked away from me for a moment, then turned back. "I think you should talk to Lake."

"I can't right now. I have to go to Centaurus. Dominic wants to see me."

"Then go to Centaurus. As soon as you leave there, call Lake," Reggie insisted. I had a weird feeling. Reggie wasn't telling me something, and I knew it. I looked down at my phone. I didn't have time to question him.

"I've got to go. I'll talk to you later."

He nodded. "Be careful."

I hurried out, sticking my hand in the front pocket of my jeans. It was still there, the little gray feather I found in the shower. The bums were still out on the sidewalk in front of the store. I tried my best not to make eye contact.

"Yo, what would you do if you could fly?" I heard one bum ask as I strode past.

"Man, I would fly right out of Shitsburgh, back to when I was a kid."

"You dumbass! You don't time travel with wings!"

"Shut up! You would prob'ly crash! If I had wings, I would..."

I couldn't hear the last bit of their conversation over the rumbling and screeching of the train on the tracks above us, but I decided they would both crash— probably into each other.

As I continued to walk toward Centaurus, worry over what Dominic might do to me forced an involuntary urgency in my pace. There were only about ten minutes left to try to make sense of what happened last night before I reached my destination. To try to remember dancing on the roof of my apartment building around The Hartley sign. But I couldn't. I was just too drunk. I couldn't recall any feelings of free falling off a building. My back ached now, but I couldn't remember any pain last night, pain related to large wings breaking through my skin and protruding out of my shoulder blades. There had to be some kind of crazy mix-up because I think I would have remembered that, drunk or not.

Also, there was the question of why? Angels had wings, but I wasn't an angel. I was a Sealer. There was no literature in the contract about ASRs developing wings over time. No one in the office had ever mentioned anything about flying. So how could this be possible?

Empty thoughts filled my head space while I walked. Nothing in particular, just a kind of daze over what was happening. And before I knew it, I was back at the front doors of my workplace. I had to forget about my so-called "wings" for now, which was hard to do because the gray feather was burning a hole in my pocket and I wanted answers. But I needed to focus on this meeting with Dominic instead. There could be a slight chance that I might die today.

Boris stood in his usual spot. "Good day, Frankie." Even with his sunglasses on, I was too weary to make eye contact with him.

"Hey," I muttered.

He reached over to open the door. "Dominic is waiting for you. He would like you to head straight down to his office."

My eyes widened with concern. If Boris was telling me this, then Dominic wanted to be sure he saw me right away.

I entered Centaurus. An extremely pale receptionist with jet-black hair and smoky eyes lifted her head from whatever it was that she was doing behind the front desk.

"Hi, Frankie. Dominic would like to see you now. Please enter the elevator and go directly to his office." She smiled at me and I shuddered. Her grin was creepy—creepy like one of those antique, twelve-inch tall porcelain dolls dressed like a tiny woman from the Civil War era. She must be new because I had never seen this employee in my life. So how the fuck did she know who I was?

Concern quickly manifested into fear. Dominic had apparently told everyone in the office that he was summoning me. Did he want to make sure I was stopped before trying to turn around to leave? Did he want to make sure no one was allowed to let me out?

I entered the elevator and pushed the thirteenth button. It illuminated red and the doors shut, leaving me with the sounds of an electric guitar from Pink Floyd's *Run Like Hell*.

Oh, to hell with these damn songs!

Thankfully, the doors opened right as the next song with the word *hell* in the title started. My heart palpitated as I approached Dominic's secretary. Raven watched my every stride with a maniacal grin.

"Hello, Frankie. Dominic is waiting. Please," she insisted, gesturing with her hand for me to enter as if she was some kind of showroom floor model. I took a deep breath in and turned the knob.

Dominic wasn't looking out of his window of nothingness, which was now covered by floor-to-ceiling curtains. Instead, he stood at his desk, facing me. Like he was waiting for me. I shut the door behind me as silently as I could. Honestly, I was afraid to make any kind of noise. Even the sound of my own jeans rubbing together while I walked scared me.

He watched me intently. I couldn't quite place his expression. It was stony. Foreboding. Unease roiled in the pit of my stomach. I recalled the minacious glare he gave Hank Hannigan before rendering his demise and mentally compared it to this moment. But it wasn't the same. The nefarious glint was there, as it always was, but there was no concentrated determination to end a life. This didn't make me feel any less worried. It just made me wonder what he could be planning in his thousand-year-old brain.

I glanced over at the flames dancing in the fireplace, fighting my hardest not to remember Hank Hannigan's last moments. But I was unsuccessful.

I took a seat in front of Dominic's desk before he finally smiled and spoke. "How are you, Franklin?" he asked brightly, moving over to his chair.

"I'm okay," I answered quickly.

"Good. How are those clients coming along?"

"They're coming along."

He looked down at some paperwork. "I see that you are meeting your quota this week, which is very good. You never disappoint, Franklin. I appreciate your hard work."

I didn't realize that I hadn't replied as quickly as I wanted to until there was a deafening silence in his over-sized office. A million things were running through my head at the same time that I was just trying to maintain my composure. I still had no idea what I was supposed to say if he mentioned Lake. Or the angel nightclub. Was I supposed to lie? What would happen to me if I did lie and he knew I lied?

He cleared his throat. "Uh, usually, if a compliment is given, the receiver replies with an expression of gratitude, whether it be a thank you or a simple nod of the head. It's considered rude, in my opinion, to ignore someone who is going out of their way to be nice." His weird accent made his words sound excessively polite, but there was a patronizing undertone.

My stomach turned. "I'm sorry. Thank you. Thank you for the compliment. I try to work as hard as I can."

Holy shit. This meeting was killing my nerves and my mental capacity to handle such an unpredictable encounter. I had no earthly idea what this man was going to say next, and I was fraught with anxiety. I hadn't drunk enough before I came here, and even if I did, the thoughts of sprouting wings would have definitely sobered me up. It was difficult not to keep questioning where the wings could have even come from. I didn't feel like a hunchback. There was no noticeable bulge underneath my clothing. Where did they go?

The small vodka-filled flask in the inside pocket

of my jacket was burning a hole through my shirt. I could almost hear it begging me to take a swig.

He tilted his head. "Is your mind preoccupied with something, Franklin? Is there something going on that you would like to discuss?"

"No, not at all. I had a late night." *There you go, Frankie. Pull it together.*

"Oh, I see," he said. His tone brightened. "Did you go to a party? Did you hang out with some friends and play in a little snow?" He brushed his index finger across his nostril and winked.

"I, uh...I don't do drugs." It wasn't surprising that he'd assumed it. Many of the Centaurus employees did drugs. We were immortal. We could do whatever we wanted.

"But you drink, right? You like to drink alcohol."

My chair suddenly felt uncomfortable and I repositioned myself. I knew I was an alcoholic. I knew I enjoyed drinking more than the average person. But I had never openly admitted it. Out loud, in person. Alex would always passively complain about it but had never actually sat me down and tried to discuss it fully. Maybe she felt like I did about it—embarrassed. Maybe she worried that I would respond negatively to her attempt at an intervention.

She was probably right. I would probably raise my voice and leave the room because the truth was...the truth was that it was all I had in this world that helped me forget the pain I carried every day. It helped to ease the constant strain on my heart from the grief of losing my old life and the unhappiness from leading the life I had now. And, I actually liked drinking. I liked the action of it. Holding a cool glass in my hands or feeling that flask against my body, as if it were some kind of security blanket. I liked the sound of the ice cubes clanking together as I swished the mixture. I liked unscrewing the metal top of my shiny, silver, pocket-sized decanter. I liked how it didn't matter if my liquor was shaken or neat, it always coated my throat with the same warm and tingly sensation. It was my friend, and it never disappointed me.

It also helped, greatly, that I didn't have to worry about harming my body. I was fine because I was immortal, and I could never die of an alcohol-induced disease. Well, that was according to Dominic, of course. He could be lying about the whole immortality deal and I could be on the verge of needing a liver transplant.

Either way, I was aware of my alcoholism. It was time for me to own up to it. "Yes. I like to drink."

"Would you like to see something, Franklin?" Dominic asked.

I hesitated a tad but nodded. I didn't know how much my stomach could handle witnessing another decapitation, considering I was hungover and all, but I supposed I would just have to swallow down the bile if I had to.

Dominic opened the drawer of his desk and pulled out a tiny remote control. "I think you will really find this interesting," he declared and stepped away from his desk. "Come, Franklin. Come stand next to me," he insisted in a friendly tone.

I left the safety of my chair to stand next to him. We turned toward the window wall sheathed in curtains. With a click of a button, the drapes began to move to opposite ends of the wall. It reminded me of the stage curtain at my high school, sliding slowly to reveal the opening scene of a play performed by the drama department. I knew what to expect then. I knew I was going to see pimple-faced, mediocre actors and poorly constructed backdrops. But this was far from high school. I grounded myself for what Dominic was about to reveal to me.

To my surprise, however, the window exposed nothing. I furrowed my brows in confusion and glanced over at Dominic. This was the closest I had ever been to him, and it was the first time I was able to truly see his physical features.

I always envisioned demons and entities deriving from the Red Realm to be disgusting and ugly. I even assumed that, as part of punishment and torture, any soul sent off to Hell automatically lost any beauty they possessed when they were alive and were made to resemble the worst versions of themselves. For instance, I might turn into some dirty, disheveled mess with tangled hair who wore vomit-stained wife beaters. I imagined this was what really bad alcoholics looked like. Filthy and smelly with yellow skin and awful posture.

But Dominic simply did not possess a gross or disgusting bone in his body. There was no evidence on his skin that he'd been working for devilish monsters for a really long time. As a matter of fact, he was just as flawless as Lake, only his features were darker and more mysterious. He was neat and tight in his buttoned suit jacket and glossy loafers. He was business in a can, but the illegal kind. The kind of businessman who drove expensive cars and lived in an elaborate house but didn't pay taxes.

He didn't look away from the windows. "Just give it a moment."

I turned back toward the darkness, and just a few seconds later, spotted a small flicker of orange. I thought maybe it was the reflection of the flames from the fireplace, but after squinting to focus, I realized it was at a distance and seemed to be getting bigger. The orange light was growing, illuminating everything in its path as it increased in size. At a length that began yards and yards away from us, the light started coming closer. Gray walls and arches were unveiled, along with what seemed to be some kind of road or pathway that glowed from the lava-like substance flowing through its cracks.

The ball of red-yellow hue intensified, causing my arm to reflexively shield my eyes from its gleam. When I thought it was safe, I removed my arm and opened my eyes again. With the spherical glare gone, I was now able to see what appeared to be an enormous set of doors. It was still at a distance, but from what I could tell, it was grand. Easily the most gigantic piece of architecture I could have ever dreamed up. Above it sat a stone sculpture of Centaurus and Hysteria. Below them and in front of the baroque-style doors, I spotted what almost resembled a line of ants. I all but forced my eyes to cross in an attempt to really understand what I was looking at.

"What is this?"

"The gates," Dominic said.

I stepped closer to the window, careful not to touch it. Who knew if I would just so happen to fall through.

With the better view, it now seemed that Dominic and I were standing above a row of ants, a perspective similar to having box seats at a football game. "Those are people?"

I could feel Dominic step next to me. "Souls. They are souls waiting to enter the gates of the Red Realm and the region that belongs to our great ruler, Centaurus." I couldn't see how far back the line reached, but I imagined it was long. "Their eternity is awaiting them."

Sympathy washed over me and a sense of sorrow forced my head down and my eyes to shut. I didn't want to see any of those souls. I didn't want to watch them waiting to enter an eternity of anguish.

Dominic's cool breath chilled my ear. "It's not as bad as you think," he whispered. "Those souls might be entering the gates of unknown evil, but most of them are deserving of it."

I turned to confront his statement. "How so?"

"Well, according to our consensus, eighty-five percent of those souls awaiting entrance earned their spots by carrying out evil on Earth. It was their choice. They decided on their own, or maybe with the help of drug addiction or a fucked-up childhood, to murder or lie or cheat. It is the Counsel of the NonAligned who decide whether or not they are to be banished to the Red Realm."

"But the other fifteen percent?" I said bitterly. "It's us. We decide. We send them there." I trembled at the volume and steely tone of my own voice. I was challenging Dominic like some kind of idiot. Did I have a death wish?

He didn't play on my rigidness, though. "Do you ever wonder what kind of person would even consider selling their soul to the devil? Do you wonder what a person such as that might be capable of? They are self-centered. They are selfish. They only care about what they want and how it will benefit them. Mass murderers are also selfish people. So are adulterers and liars. If people don't sell their souls, then what do you think they will do? Thus, aren't we simply thinning out the crowd? Aren't we basically aiding in the decision-making process for the Counsel of the NonAligned?"

I allowed his unconventional views to seep into my brain for a moment. It actually did seem to make some kind of warped sense. There were times when I questioned what kind of people we were dealing with. There must have been some hint of corruption in their hearts if they were willing to do business with the devil.

Did this mean my sister was corrupt? Was there something hidden inside of her—something rotten?

I refused to believe so. She had to be one of the few exceptions.

Dominic grinned and sucked air into his chest as if silently boasting a win. "You understand."

"It doesn't mean I like it," I hissed.

Dominic inched closer to my face. "Don't you?"

I stood tall and tried to match his confidence. His sultry eyes threatened to weaken my knees. "Don't you like the power?" he asked, leaning in just a bit closer. "Don't you crave the potential to control someone's eternity?"

"No."

"Ah, you see, I would have believed differently." He brushed the length of my arm with the back of his hand. "You traipse around here in your leather jacket and domineering demeanor as if no one should dare speak to you. You drink and smoke excessively, knowing damn well that nothing, not even a little bit of emphysema, can touch you or take you out. You treat your clients coldly, as if you are too good to be dealing with their problems. I've even seen you engage with your sister in the same manner."

His last words stung. Everything he said was true, but it wasn't because I enjoyed being a Sealer. He had me all fucked up. He was mistaking my unhappiness for arrogance. "It's the opposite, actually. I—"

He swept his thumb across my bottom lip, stopping me in my tracks. "I admire your unwavering strength. You handle this job as if you have been an employee of the Red Realm for centuries. It takes a certain kind of courage, a certain kind of grit and conviction to be a woman like you. It takes a certain kind of beauty and allure." My breathing slowed and I couldn't move. "Women like you become goddesses of the Red Realm." I couldn't speak. "Women like you reign over regions."

My heart pounded so hard, I was sure he could either feel or hear it. I froze, hesitant to move away from him in trepidation of what he might do. His hand was so close to my throat. With just a squeeze, I could end up like Hank Hannigan. Dominic could drain the life right out of me in this very moment.

"Are you afraid, Franklin?" he asked in a deep, hushed pitch.

There was something inside me that didn't want to give in. There was something inside me that didn't want to show him the trembling of my core. "No," I lied, returning his whisper.

He opened his hand and cradled my face. "Good. You shouldn't be. We are the same, Franklin. You and I are the same." His gaze shifted from my eyes to my mouth, and before I could think another thought, his lips were on mine.

CHAPTER SEVENTEEN

Tease

His tongue crowded my mouth, slithering expertly around mine while his hands cradled my head with a gentle force. I was too shocked to figure out what to do with my own hands. I wasn't at all prepared for this kiss. It was the last thing on my mind to ever happen. But I couldn't stop it.

I wanted to. I wanted to stop kissing my boss. There was no way in hell this was a good idea, and the thought of how many other of my co-workers he'd made out with in this very office, maybe in this very spot, made me feel cheap and used.

But I still couldn't stop it. Those hormones that reared their horny heads before I got rejected by Lake were back, and this time with a vengeance. Dominic was nourishing me in all the ways my body had been desiring. He was awakening parts of me that had been asleep for a long time, and I couldn't stop. I didn't want to stop.

I wrapped my arms around his neck, and he moved his hands to my ass. He didn't waste any time. Within a second, I was lifted up off the floor and practically tossed onto the top of his desk. His right arm found its way under my left leg, spreading it open and making it easier for him to push himself into me. I could feel the hardness through his slacks, which only aroused me even more.

While I was almost certain there was nothing really special about me, it was still flattering in some way. Dominic was so sexy that I couldn't believe he'd want to have anything to do with me. I didn't consider myself in his league at all. As a matter of fact, I had no idea why this was even happening.

We kissed and touched each other for a couple of minutes before Dominic began to tear off my jacket. Once that was thrown to the floor and out of the way, he skipped my shirt altogether and moved straight to the goods. He unbuttoned and unzipped my jeans but didn't remove them. Instead, he shoved his hand down, and suddenly, I was flushed with ecstasy. My chest caved in as I exhaled and threw my head back. His fingers were magical, working their way around my sex as if he could see exactly what he was doing.

I moaned and groaned, and my breathing grew heavier and faster. I was already almost there. Already at the brink. So ready for the intense explosion of fulfillment. It was coming. His fingers were circling and moving and thrusting. He was doing everything so perfectly and I was so close.

And then, he stopped.

I lifted my head back up to glare at him. Inside, I was screaming. How could he just stop? I was on the edge, about to climax my brains out, and he just stopped!

Dominic pulled his hand out of my jeans and stepped away. He brought his fingers to his mouth and sucked on each one as if he were just eating a plate of messy barbecue ribs. He raised an eyebrow and grinned mischievously at me. "You taste really good."

I immediately felt self-conscious and began buttoning my jeans. I didn't know what to say and I was afraid that if I did say something, it would not be kind.

"Forgive me, Franklin, but I have a lot of work to tend to."

I slid off his desk and reached down for my jacket. The door to his office was all I could think about. It was only a few feet away but felt like it would take decades to get to it. I wanted to run out of there as fast as I could, possibly into a bathroom to finish what the bastard started.

He adjusted the sleeves of his jacket and the knot of his tie. "I trust that we will continue this in the near future." I didn't want to look at him, but he stepped closer and pulled my chin up. "I would *like* to continue this in the near future," he whispered, all throaty and raspy.

The truth was, I also wanted to continue this. Badly. Very, very badly. The asshole left me hanging, but my private parts throbbed in anticipation to feel his fingers again.

I simply nodded.

Dominic smiled. "Now, please, have a seat."

Son of a bitch. He wasn't done.

I sat down and he walked around his desk to do the same. Everything was business again. "You are probably wondering why I showed you the gates to the Red Realm." He leaned forward. "I would like to promote you, Franklin."

"Promote me?"

"Yes. Did you think I called you up here just to ravage you?" He chuckled. "Aside from having a dark and compelling charisma, which I find very arousing, I wasn't kidding when I said that I admire you. You have the potential to be a leader and to become a very powerful asset to this region. I would like to utilize your abilities and your potential by offering you a promotion. I believe that you are very capable of learning how to apply your work ethic to this particular job position, and I believe you would excel at it."

I felt a tad uneasy. "What's the job?"

"I would like you to become our newest CA."

"CA?"

"I realize that this is very different from being a Sealer. Most of your job will consist of sitting behind a desk. You won't be dealing with the clients on a one-on-one basis as you do now. But something tells me that you will be okay with that."

I looked down at my hands. I knew Dominic was aware of how much I didn't enjoy being a Sealer, and I felt ashamed for it in some ways. This wasn't necessarily the best job in the world. But...I did have a life. I was breathing and living, something I would have lost the ability to do if Alex didn't sell our souls three years ago while I was on my death bed.

A CA was a contract auditor. Their job was to make sure that the clients received what they sold their souls for. They checked in on the client's life after they are sealed, ensuring that Centaurus was living up to his part of the deal and the contract. I wasn't completely up to speed on the details of a CA's job duties, such as what were to happen if the client wasn't getting what they asked for in exchange for their soul. All I knew was that CAs didn't get paid much more than the Sealers, which didn't really matter to me.

With that said, not having to travel would definitely be a plus. Not to mention, I wouldn't have to seal anyone anymore. I wouldn't have to watch someone's painful journey through The Breakdown. Instead, I would be ensuring that the client didn't have to undergo such an awful experience for nothing.

Although an eternity of torture and misery awaited them in the Red Realm, at least their life on Earth would be happy. And I would have a hand in that.

This could actually be a good thing. "Will I still be in the same department as the Sealers?" I asked out of curiosity. Our building had many different departments and I didn't mind having to move from mine, but it would have been nice to continue working closer to my sister.

"Well, you would have to move out of the department you are in now," Dominic stated.

"To what floor?"

"No floor."

"I'm sorry?"

"You see, while CAs normally work on the eighth floor of this building, I will need you to work somewhere else," he said.

"And where will that be?"

"The Red Realm."

I shook my head in disbelief. "You want me to work in the Red Realm?" I was suddenly afraid. Very afraid. I was about two seconds away from hauling ass out of Dominic's office. I only knew of souls entering the Red Realm—dead people's souls. I didn't know any other co-workers or living people to have entered Hell and come out to talk about it. So what did this mean? Did this mean that I was going to have to die? Did this mean that Dominic was going to kill me right here, right now?

He must have sensed my sudden panic. "Don't be alarmed, Franklin," he insisted. "I understand how you'd believe working in the Red Realm to be frightening. But I can assure you that there's nothing to be afraid of."

"How would I get into the Red Realm without dying? I thought only souls were allowed there."

"I visit all the time and I'm not dead, am I?" he noted. Quite honestly, I wasn't even too sure of that. "As long as you have the Seal of the Red Realm, you are allowed to enter. It's a requirement that employees who work there also live there. They feel that it's better than living here on Earth, anyway. Many of the Red Realm employees are Afflictionists and work in the torment department and pain chambers and have no desire to travel between dimensions. They work very long hours. I'll have to admit, working there was pretty fun. So I see the interest in it. I certainly will not be surprised if you decided to change departments one day."

My stomach churned with a sick feeling. How could anyone have fun while inflicting pain on someone else? There was no way in hell I was ever going to be an Afflictionist.

"Why can't I work in this building with the other CAs?"

"CAs are required to report to me in the event that a client is not receiving their settlement. I, then, report it to Centaurus and Hysteria and we all work together to guarantee our clients get what they paid for," Dominic explained. "But, after much discussion with Centaurus and Hysteria, we decided it would be best to cut the middleman and just have the CAs report directly to them. We feel it would be more effective and beneficial to our clients and the quality of service we provide them. You won't be alone. The other CAs will be moving into the Red Realm as well."

Dominic seemed very thrilled about this. I, on the other hand, was undeniably against it. The word was out of my mouth before I could stop myself. "No."

"No?" he asked, eyebrows raised.

"I can't leave my sister," I stated plainly.

"Franklin, we understand that you have a sister and you two are very close. We have taken this into consideration, which is why we will be allowing you to come visit Alexandra."

"Allowing?" *Holy shit! Shut up, Frankie.*

He immediately released a boisterous laugh, then came to lean against the desk directly in front of me. "You see what I mean? You have a fire in you, Franklin! You have a way about you that deserves to be seen. Centaurus and Hysteria need to know you personally. They need to see what I see, a woman with the potential to manage and maybe even run an entire department on her own."

I eyed him with skepticism. Now he was suggesting that I become a manager? I didn't understand what was happening. Before this day, all I did was my job.

I have only ever been a Sealer for this company. I minded my own business, kept to myself, and met with Dominic once a month just to discuss my work, nothing more. And now, I was suddenly one of his best employees? Now, he was offering for me to work *with* the king and queen, to possibly one day become some kind of boss?

Last night flashed through my mind. The club, Ariel and Samuel, Lake, the flying... Dominic had to know something. This couldn't all be happening out of the blue. And I wasn't stupid. I knew wholeheartedly that I was no longer just a normal human being living a normal human life. His comment about "allowing" me to see Alex was no surprise. They owned us. They were in control of our lives. But permanently living in the Red Realm scared the crap out of me. What did that mean? I had to wonder what it meant for my soul. If I had any reservations about one day becoming full-on evil, completely and totally on the side of the devil, well...living there would certainly put me straight over the edge.

"I sense that you have some hesitation. Tell me, what's got your panties in a bunch?" He bit his bottom lip and half-smiled at me. I knew he meant it as a joke because of what we just did, but that smolder in his eyes nearly compelled me to jump out of my chair and onto his tongue.

I decided to be candid with him. I mean, he did just taste me, for fuck's sake. "Dominic, I don't know if I want to live in Hell. I have no idea what it's like there, and to be honest, it's kind of scary. I don't understand why I can't just be a CA and live here with my sister. I'm all she has. And the job sounds very interesting and I'm very interested in doing it, but I'm not interested in living in the Red Realm."

Okay, I wasn't being completely honest. I wasn't going to mention anything about the angel nightclub and Lake. The whole night before was still fresh in my mind, even with the hangover still slightly looming over me (this meeting managed to remedy it for the most part). I didn't forget that Lake wanted me to join his team of angel reformists. He somehow wanted me to help take down Centaurus. If I moved to the Red Realm, I probably wouldn't be able to assist with the plan, which was another reason I couldn't relocate there.

Although a part of me didn't quite believe that Centaurus could be taken down completely, I still had plans to help. But it wasn't for myself. I had decided once and for all that it would be my mission to get Alex into the White Realm, where she belonged. If this "take down" could do that, then I was in. As for myself, it really didn't matter what happened to me. My heart was probably no longer pure enough and my soul too corrupt for any place other than the Red Realm to accept me. Lake kind of proved it when he informed me that I no longer had a Guide. And Dominic pretty much confirmed those feelings earlier in this meeting when he said I was cold. Maybe I was better off in Hell. I might be able to help Lake with his plan and still live there. The portal might be destroyed, hindering anyone from traveling to and from this particular region, but what if I was already on the other side? And knowing now that I didn't have to die definitely altered my view of it all.

But I couldn't go while my sister was still here. I had to help Lake get her to the White Realm, which meant there was no way I could move away from her yet.

Dominic's smolder and the playfulness in his eyes changed. He looked down and inhaled deeply, almost as if his patience was suddenly running low. "Franklin, I don't think you understand."

I could sense the air around us shift. I cut him off, bravely, to help change the direction this conversation seemed to be going. "I'm not interested in living in the Red Realm at the moment," I clarified. "Maybe... maybe just give me a little time. You know, with my sister, to get things in order?"

I stood up, realizing right then that it was going to take more than hoping Dominic would show some compassion. He was practically a devil himself. I had never met Centaurus and Hysteria, but I was almost certain compassion wasn't a known characteristic of theirs, or any boss from Hell for that matter.

Stepping forward and reaching out for Dominic's hand, I spoke in a softer, more seductive tone.

"Besides, I was really hoping that we could finish what we started." Okay, this was me being really honest. I wanted him. Plain and simple.

Without a word, he kissed me. Our tongues met again, this time with less urgency and more fervor. His hands moved up and he buried his fingers in my hair. He maneuvered my head delicately from side to side, following the fluidity of our mouths closing into one another.

Dominic's lips then parted from mine, his hand gently pushing my head to the left. My skin tingled as his tongue glided over it. I closed my eyes and my breath hitched when he finally reached the nape of my neck. He kissed and licked up and down and all around. I tilted my head until it just couldn't tilt anymore. If he were a vampire, it would have been the perfect opportunity to bite. To drink the warm blood from my veins. I was his prey, and that thought excited me to the core.

He pulled me close to him and squeezed my ass. His mouth glided up from my collarbone to my earlobe and sucked. As he licked and kissed, my hips swayed into his body. All of the nerves connected to my female parts pulsated with sexual need. I was damn near close to pushing him down on his own desk and tearing his clothes off with my teeth.

But then...he stopped. Again. With his lips lightly brushing against my ear, he whispered, "You don't have a choice. You are going to the Red Realm. Either you go now, or your sister dies."

CHAPTER EIGHTEEN

The Apartment Guest

It was as if someone had punched me right in the gut. My lungs deflated and I forgot to breathe for the moment it took to comprehend what Dominic had just whispered into my ear.

I pulled away from him and we locked eyes. "I trust that you understand, Franklin. This is simply business."

Threatening to kill my sister was business? I mean, I guess it was. I *did* work for the underworld. But I didn't understand. I didn't understand why this was all happening. Why he demanded that I take this promotion and live in the Red Realm. It had to be some kind of punishment. He had to know about last night, and this was the consequence for having been with Lake and his angel buddies.

However, Dominic showed no evidence of knowing about my escapade at the angel nightclub, or about my meeting with Lake. If he knew, he wasn't letting on that he knew. And I wasn't going to say anything about it. Dominic was too unpredictable. One minute he was beheading poor Hank Hannigan, and the next his fingers were down my pants. There was no telling what he was going to do, especially if he had any idea I had plans to help take down his region.

If my sister died, she was going to the Red Realm. And that was not an option. No way. Not happening.

I didn't know what this meant for Lake's plan to take down Centaurus and reform Alex, but it was either this or the possibility of not even being able to help my sister find residency in the White Realm because she would be dead, and Lake said they cannot reform the dead. I had to give in.

"Okay," I said, straight-faced and firm. I didn't want him to know how scared I truly was. I didn't want him to know that inside I was full of panic and fear, completely freaking out about the fact that I was literally going to Hell and this meant that I was probably going to end up playing for the team of evil.

I was afraid. I was afraid of what I would see, of how I would feel. But somehow, in some twisted kind of way, I felt calm about it all. I was a strange mixture of cool and terrified. Maybe it was meant to be. Maybe this had been my destiny all along.

I didn't want Dominic to suspect anything, whether I was truly okay with it or not. I managed to bury all other feelings about my past life and Jacob and the fact that I missed my parents dearly, so hiding the worry and concern for my wellbeing and the future of my morality should be a piece of cake. Right?

He kissed my cheek. "Lovely. Just lovely. And you know what? As a token of my appreciation for your cooperation with this arrangement, I am going to promote your sister as well."

Fuck.

"Raven has been drowning in paperwork and is in desperate need of some help. The poor thing needs an assistant of her own. I would love to have Alexandra here, in this office, with us. She can stop being a Sealer and start right away. How does that sound?"

"She would be here with you?"

"Oh, yes. She will remain in here, in the Centaurus building. Right here, in this very office. I will see her every day."

In other words, Alex would be under Dominic's watchful eye. Double fuck. I wasn't sure how to feel about this and I didn't know if this would make it harder for Lake and Reggie to reform her.

Dominic's motives were still unclear, but I had to take this as some kind of win. It meant Alex would not be going to the Red Realm, and that I could somehow still help her get to the White Realm.

I nodded and forced a smile, acknowledging that I was okay with it.

"Very well. It's decided. Now, let's get you settled. I will have someone escort you to the gates. I have an assistant who is awaiting your arrival on the other side, and he will show you to your living quarters."

"Um...you want me to go...now?" Was he serious? He might have practically forced me to live in the Red Realm, but there was no way he was going to make me leave without at least letting my sister know.

Dominic walked back behind his desk. "I'm afraid so. Entering the Red Realm is not simple. There is a ton of paperwork to be filed and the journey can be quite lengthy."

"Dominic, I cannot leave without at least telling my sister goodbye." I wanted to scream at him, but I kept my voice steady and low. I was learning as I spoke to him that it was critical to watch what I said and how I said it.

He sat down with an exasperated exhale. He steepled his fingers together and leaned back into his chair, glaring at me from across the desk. It felt like I'd pissed him off, and my heart rate shot up exponentially as I awaited his next words. He seemed to be thinking really hard. Was he actually considering this, or was he just contemplating how he wanted to rip my head off my body without leaving too much of a bloody mess?

Then, finally, he spoke. "Fine. You can go see your sister. But you will go with Boris."

The main reason to go back to The Hartley was to see Alex and inform her of this meeting, but it was also to contact Lake. We had to discuss so much and figure out how to get Alex reformed now that she was going to be working so close to Dominic. I wanted to believe that I could somehow get away with it, but it was proving to be impossible. Lake was definitely right. Dominic knew. He knew and he was throwing some curve balls—trying to screw up a plan that he knew was in the works. He was probably sending Boris with me to make sure that I didn't meet with any angels.

I pursed my lips, fighting any urge I had to come up with some kind of lie that might persuade Dominic to allow me some alone time. I didn't want to push it with him, though. I would just have to accept this. Damn it! I really just wanted to go on about my business. Help Alex get to the White Realm and figure out what I was going to do with myself.

And to make this fucked-up situation even more fucked up, all I could think about was screwing Dominic. I wondered if that was even going to happen.

This was a fleeting thought, of course. Our meeting was wrapping up and I had more important things to worry about.

"Thank you, Dominic, for allowing me to see my sister before I go."

"Oh, no. Thank *you*, darling." Dominic smiled a glamorous smile. I stood up and hesitated for a moment, pretending to adjust my jacket and glance at my seat to see if I'd forgotten something. I didn't. I didn't have anything to forget. I was simply stalling to see if maybe he had anything else to say. Anything about what had happened between us or what I should expect in the future.

But he didn't say anything. He picked up a pen and looked down at a piece of paper on his desk, almost as though our meeting didn't even happen. As if I wasn't even standing there. Like he didn't even just tease my poor, deprived lady bit into thinking she was going to get some long overdue release.

I shook the embarrassment away and headed out of his office. I wasn't being completely selfish and clueless. I knew what living in the Red Realm meant. I knew that it meant I was leaving my sister. Sure, Dominic claimed that he would allow me to come back to see Alex, but would he really? Would he really allow me to come and go whenever I wanted? There had to be stipulations.

But what if he and I were involved?

If he had motives, so did I. Yes, I wanted to have sex. I'd been floating around the office on a cloud of I-don't-give-a-shit for a long time, but that didn't mean I didn't have...needs. My sister was right; the love of a man would be nice every now and then— the physical love of a man—and I haven't had it in a while. Being around Lake awakened a part of me that had been lost, but Dominic found it and pulled that part right out of me. He made me ache. He made my insides throb, even as I walked away from his office and to my desk to collect my things.

I pulled open the drawer that housed my sad little banana nut muffin and nearly empty silver flask. I didn't bother saying goodbye to any of my co-workers. I was sure they wouldn't miss me. With all the dirty looks and rude responses I'd given them over the past few years, I was sure they'd be happy to see me leave. Keeping my head held high and my eyes focused only on what was in front of me, I managed to avoid contact with anyone and made my way upstairs to meet Boris.

I ignored the obnoxious elevator music—*Heaven and Hell* by Black Sabbath—and allowed my thoughts to venture back to Dominic and our dry humping... and his otherworldly fingers. If he and I became something, maybe it could give me some kind of leverage. Maybe I could somehow convince Dominic to grant me more visitation rights. Maybe I could convince him to allow me to live between both worlds. If my mission was to get Alex out of this hellhole and up to the White Realm, I had to know what Lake's plans were. Learning all the details could really be helpful to my own plans.

The elevator doors opened to Boris' blacked-out sunglasses and beefy frame. Great. I needed to figure out how I was going to meet up with Lake while Boris was up my ass.

"Hello, Frankie. Are you ready to head over to your apartment?" He was surprisingly upbeat and happy for someone who was a supernatural being from the Red Realm. His physical appearance and job title just didn't fit his bright attitude.

"Yeah, let's go."

On our way out of the Centaurus building, the new receptionist and I locked eyes. She watched us both intently as we walked from the elevator to the exit. Her head was slightly tilted, her wide smile never faltering, her eyes never blinking. She was the definition of creepy. I sincerely hoped that not everyone in the Red Realm was like that.

Boris and I walked back to my apartment together in silence. I smoked two whole cigarettes back to back, then lit a third and purposely stopped in front of Reggie's store to put it out halfway on a lamppost as if saving it for later. I peeped inside in hopes of spotting Lake's glorious caramel-colored mane, but only found Reggie checking out a patron at the counter. His eyes moved from me, to Boris, then back at me. I couldn't read his expression. I couldn't tell what he was thinking. He had an expert poker face.

We headed up the stairs and I unlocked my apartment door. It felt awkward knowing Boris was behind me, watching my every move. But I could tell he was keeping a little distance from me, like he felt just as awkward as I did.

I opened the door, prompting Alex to turn away from whatever she was doing at the kitchen table. "Hi, Frankie. And...Boris?"

"Hello, Alexandra," he said, bending slightly under the frame of the door. Boris was a very large man.

"Boris, you can have a seat there," I said, pointing to a tiny, wooden chair by the kitchen table. He looked at it dubiously, and I knew for a fact he was trying to figure out how he could sit on it without having it break apart underneath his weight.

"I'll stand."

"Okay, I'm going to talk to my sister for a moment."

"Can I get you anything to drink?" Alex asked. Of course she had to be polite. I rolled my eyes. We had no time for hospitality.

"I'm okay. Thank you," he said.

I took Alex's hand and led her into the living room. Our apartment was teeny tiny, and I worried that our voices could be heard from any vantage point. I brought my finger up to my mouth as I guided her to the couch, indicating for her to keep a low voice. "Alex, I have something to tell you. I don't want you to freak out."

"Are you okay?" she asked fearfully.

"I'm okay," I responded with a steady pitch. "I had a meeting with Dominic. I don't want you to panic, but he wants me to move to the Red Realm."

"The Red—" Her volume shot up, but she caught herself and lowered her voice. "The Red Realm? Right now?"

"It's too risky to explain," I whispered.

She leaned over and pretended to move something on the coffee table to get closer to my ear. "I know about Lake."

"What?"

Her eyes flickered to my bedroom and then to Boris. I turned to see that he was looking down at his phone. I knew the Henchmen had supernatural abilities, such as super strength. I knew they spoke different languages and were capable of sending souls to another dimension. But I wasn't sure of what other supernatural skills they possessed. Superhuman hearing could have been one of them. I simply furrowed my brows at her.

"Why don't you get your things from your bedroom and I'll get Boris some coffee and a slice of that fabulous cake we got from the bakery," she said audibly enough for Boris to look up from his phone. Her eyes widened. I wasn't completely sure what she was trying to tell me, but I knew whatever it was, a clue had to be in my bedroom.

We stood up at the same time. "How about it, Boris? Care for something sweet?" Alex walked over to the fridge and pulled out the cake, leaving Boris with no other option than to agree.

"That sounds nice. Thank you." He looked at me.

"I'm going to grab a small suitcase."

"Just keep it light, Frankie. We can't transfer much over to the other realm."

"Okay," I replied innocently and almost childishly. I reached my bedroom door and turned the knob, careful not to open it too wide. I didn't know what Alex wanted me to see and I didn't want Boris to see whatever it was. I nonchalantly slid through the small opening as if I did it all the time and shut the door quietly behind me.

And there he was, standing in the window. The only sunshine I'd seen in three years seemed to be beaming directly down on him through the glass, illuminating all of his beautifully angelic features.

"Lake?"

CHAPTER NINETEEN

Chosen One

Lake brought his finger up to his mouth, and I knew he wanted me to stay quiet. I hurried over to him and whispered, "Lake, what are you doing here? Boris is right outside the door. If he knows you're here—"

He grabbed my hand and pulled me into my tragically small, wannabe walk-in closet and slid the pocket door shut. The darkness swallowed us whole. I wondered how Lake was even able to breathe in this tight space. I could feel him hunched over and almost every part of our bodies was touching. The sting of rejection came flooding back, and I was suddenly uncomfortable to be so close to him, but not so much so that I didn't enjoy being able to feel his muscles and all their glory.

I tried to maneuver myself but stopped when I realized there was no point—the closet wasn't going to get any bigger. "Why are we in here?"

"Just in case," he huffed. His breath smelled like flowers.

I glanced up at him. "I have to go to the Red Realm."

"I know."

"You know? How do you know?"

"I felt you earlier."

"Huh?" Thankfully, it was dark, and Lake probably couldn't see the color of my cheeks. His strong voice filled the air and hugged me when he said those words. My mind could not stay out of the gutter. How could it? I was dealing with so many good-looking men...and I was horny as shit! "What do you mean?" I whispered loudly. Suddenly, *I* couldn't breathe in this tight space.

"I felt your fear. I don't have time to explain how, but Dominic is sending you away because he knows I'm here. He knows you and I are conspiring to do something."

Lake was right all along, and I could see every monkey wrench Dominic had thrown pretty clearly. It hurt to think that his seduction was most probably a conniving tactic, but it honestly didn't turn me off. It didn't stop my sexual need for him. It didn't stop the mental pictures of our naked bodies writhing on the floor in front of the fireplace in his office.

"If he knows, then what are we doing?" I asked. "He'll stop us. He might even kill me."

"He won't kill you," Lake confirmed. "He knows it wouldn't be wise. And you have become too valuable to him now that he knows you and I have been in contact. Just play along. He doesn't know exactly what we are going to do or what we have planned. Just do whatever he wants you to do."

Ha! Whatever he wants me to do? And if Lake knew what *I* wanted Dominic to do, he would probably call this whole thing off. Or not. At this point, I was pretty sure Lake could give two shits about what was happening between my legs.

"I know you are afraid of going to the Red Realm, but this will actually help us. The kings and queens do not know how we destroy their portals. Normally, the portal is an elevator that leads down to the gates. It's the bridge between Earth and the Red Realm. When our sacrificial angels are chosen, they disguise themselves and strategically infiltrate their way to the portal. Once they are there, The Liberation Stone is activated and the portal is destroyed, as well as the angel."

"What happens to The Liberation Stone?"

"It always finds its way back to the White Realm. On its own."

He moved, and it seemed like he was reaching into the pocket of his jeans. I couldn't see it, but I could hear what sounded like the slight clang of metal—like chain mail. Then, his hands were on either side of my head, and as soon as I felt the weight of something on my chest, my tiny closet illuminated. A bright, white beam of light shot out from whatever was hanging around my neck, and it made sense why he wanted to be in the closet.

It was super intense, almost blinding even. I squinted and winced, until it finally calmed down and I was able to actually see again. It was still gleaming, but more of a soft glow with sparkly little wisps dancing in the air all around us.

"I knew it," Lake breathed. I could now see him as if we were standing outside with the afternoon sun hovering above our heads. And he looked disappointed.

"You knew what? What is this? The Liberation Stone?" I glanced down at it. It was exactly that—a stone. Encased in a gold frame and hanging from a necklace, the round, rose-colored rock speckled with gold flakes rested square in the center of my chest. I touched its rough and raw surface and it felt warm in my fingertips.

"They chose you. The Great Elders have chosen *you* to destroy this region's portal."

"Me? But I'm not an angel. And isn't it a sacrifice? Won't I evaporate or some shit like that?" Give me a fucking break. I was ready to help Lake, but I definitely wasn't ready to die over all of this. "No. No way. I'm sorry, but I'm not losing my life over this." I grabbed on the necklace and tried to pull it up and over my head, but it wouldn't fit. Somehow, it got smaller. Odd, because Lake had no problem putting it on me.

When I realized there was no chance of it coming off that way, I ran my fingers up and down the length of the chain, searching for a clasp. There wasn't one. "Lake get this off me," I demanded. I was getting pissed.

"I can't. It won't come off until the mission is accomplished. It's a defense mechanism. The stone is spelled with a safeguard against evil. It's what keeps you and the stone protected."

"Right, because protecting me means killing me," I snapped.

"I'm not sure. I'm not sure what will happen," Lake admitted. He seemed to be trying to understand something going on inside his head.

I was growing impatient. This thing felt like it was choking me, and I started to fidget with it again. "What do you mean? You *just* told me that this thing kills angels. And not only that, I'm not an angel. You said that the Great Elders choose an angel and I'm definitely not an angel." I was panicking. My mouth was dry. The flask inside my jacket pocket was empty. Now that I could see, I stood on my tiptoes and reached up to find the shoebox. When I pulled it down, I heard the sound of liquid swooshing inside. I couldn't wait to taste its contents.

"Does this have to do with the wings?" I asked, twisting the top off and taking a swig of vodka from the flask.

"The wings?" Lake asked, confused.

"Yeah. Reggie and I saw a video of me flying last night. I had wings, but I don't remember." I bit my bottom lip and glanced down at the bottle of booze in my hand, knowing exactly why I didn't remember.

"I don't understand. This has never happened before, so we don't know how it works." Lake spoke low, as if having a conversation with himself.

I swallowed another gulp and wiped the dribble of alcohol that escaped my mouth. "Great. You don't know anything, either." I remembered the feather and dug into my pocket to retrieve it. "And look. It's gray. Samuel and Ariel's wings are stark white. So this means it had to have come from me, right?"

The light from The Liberation Stone had been steadily dimming, but we could still see. Lake picked it up gingerly from my palm and examined it.

"Why is it gray?" I asked. "Is it because I'm a Sealer? Do people from the Red Realm even have wings?"

"ASRs and Sealers don't usually have the capability to fly. Wings might be awarded to them in the Red Realm, or beings derived from there might have been created with them, but that isn't the case for you."

The sound of Alex's voice found its way into our tiny space. The door to my bedroom creaked open and Alex's words flowed through the cracks. "Frankie, you about ready in here? I'm gonna give you a hand while Boris finishes his cake and coffee." I could tell she was being fake.

As soon as I heard the bedroom door close, I popped out of the closet. I didn't think I could take another minute standing so close to Lake without once and for all making out with his face against his will. Crazy shit was happening, but he was still hot.

Alex looked up at Lake, then at me. Her quizzical expression confirmed that the wheels in her brain were turning. I was almost certain she thought something was going on between Lake and me.

"What's going on?" she asked, smirking. "Are you two…"

"What? Me and Lake?" I sneered involuntarily. If only she knew that he basically rebuffed my advances in disgust last night. Okay, maybe he didn't rebuff in disgust, but he might as well have.

"No!" I shouted, then huffed when I remembered I had to be quiet. "Nothing is going on. We were hiding from Boris. Speaking of which, why aren't you out there distracting him?"

"I had to come see what was going on and make sure you didn't leave me." She pointed at the window with the fire escape.

Admittedly, that would not have been a bad idea—sneaking out with Lake and getting the hell out of dodge. But I just couldn't do that to her, and it kind of hurt that she'd think I would.

"I would never do that."

"What's that around your neck?" she asked, running her fingertip over the stone.

"Alex, there is so much I have to tell you."

"I already know some things," she said.

"You do?" I was relieved. I didn't know if I had enough time to explain it all to her, but she certainly deserved to know as much as I did. I didn't want to keep things from my sister. I didn't want to repeat her mistakes—the ones that I had very recently decided to forgive.

I peered over at Lake. "Did you tell her everything?"

She grabbed my hands. "I know who Lake is. I know about Reggie and about reforming, and I'm ready. You and I are going to be reformed and get the fuck out of here."

Whoa! Language! Alex never cursed.

I smiled and raised a disbelieving eyebrow at her. She seemed different. Alex was sometimes almost meek. She didn't have a sassy attitude problem like me. I'd never seen her upset over something that wasn't of high importance. She was a lot like our mom—always finding the positive in situations. She didn't break rules or go against them. She just followed what she was supposed to do. But right now, she was showing certitude. Boldness. Some fucking gall! And I liked it. I was so happy that she wanted to be reformed. I was happy that she knew exactly what she wanted. That she wasn't toying with the idea of trying to stay away from evil and dancing with her demons at the same time. But I didn't know how to tell her that apparently, Lake had plans for me to die.

"Alex, I don't know about this," I said.

Lake interrupted. "Listen, we need to stall Boris a little while longer. I need to contact the Elders to discuss The Liberation Stone and the wings."

Alex peered at me curiously. "What wings?"

I shrugged and began to speak, but Lake cut me off. "I need to find out a few things before you go."

"Can't we wait until I come back to visit my sister? Why are we in such a rush?" Centaurus had been around forever. What was a few more days? I was almost tempted to ask him if there could be any other way to help Alex get to the White Realm because...well...I wasn't into this whole dying thing. I supposed it all boiled down to if I was willing to die for my sister.

"Time works differently in the Red Realm," he explained. "The longer we wait, the more people will be manipulated and persuaded into selling their souls. We also don't want to risk Centaurus, Hysteria, Dominic, or any other being from the Red Realm finding out about our plan. The Liberation Stone holds great power and it's the only one in its existence. It doesn't only tear down portals, it does many things for the White Realm. If they know about it, we don't know what they would do to try to destroy it. Keeping it and our plans hidden is how we have been able to succeed in the past. So if we have a chance, we must take it right away. Do you understand?"

I suddenly felt like a child being scolded for taking a cookie out of the cookie jar without asking.

"Yes. But doesn't Dominic know about the stone? He was an Angel of Reform, right?"

"It wasn't until after Dominic's departure that we learned how The Liberation Stone would play a role in succeeding in the destruction of each region's portal. We were only in the beginning stages when he..." Lake trailed off. He didn't want to reveal whatever it was that Dominic did to get banned from the White Realm. "He knows nothing of The Liberation Stone or how we do things now," he rasped and narrowed his eyes at me. "It's the reason why Dominic won't kill you. He's just trying to learn what you know, learn how the Angels of Reform do what they do, all while keeping you away."

That comment made it feel like Lake somehow knew more than he was letting on. Did he know that Dominic and I had a quick tryst in his office? Was he trying to tell me that Dominic had no genuine feelings of attraction toward me?

I glanced down, worried that Lake would read my thoughts.

He continued. "Regardless of what Dominic knows or doesn't, we need to find out more about your connection to the stone before it's activated. I have some ideas, but I need to have a discussion with the council in the White Realm. It will take me a couple of days before I can get some answers. In the time it takes you to get to the portal for your journey to the Red Realm, I will have already communicated with the Council to ask them to hold off on the activation. It should buy me a couple of days, but I'll need you to be back by then. Persuade Dominic to allow you to come back for a visit."

"How does time work in the Red Realm?" Alex asked.

"And what if I can't make it back in a couple of days?" I added.

Lake's eyes bored into mine. "You'll have to."

The sound of a fork clinking with a glass plate came from the kitchen, then heavy footsteps outside my bedroom door. "Frankie? Alex? We have to get going soon."

Alex knew what to do. "She's changing, Boris! Please don't come in here unless you want to see some really small boobies!" she sang.

I slapped her arm and hissed at her. At the corner of my eye, I could have sworn I saw Lake's lip curl up into a slight smile, but I was too embarrassed to turn toward him. He was probably looking at my tiny tits. Alex shrugged and went back out into the kitchen to continue distracting Boris.

I started to actually pack a suitcase, grabbing pretty much the only thing I wanted. The only thing that held any importance to me—my hidden bottles of vodka around the room. Alex might have known I had a lovely fascination with vodka, but she didn't need to find these guys while I was gone. She didn't need to know the full extent of my addiction.

Lake didn't seem very pleased. "Why do you need all of those?"

"Dominic said he is going to promote Alex and that she will be working in his office," I said, changing the subject. "How are you going to protect her?"

"Reggie and I will have plans set for that. Don't worry."

"You didn't tell her about the sacrifice, did you?"

"No." He inched closer to me, took hold of my arm and spun me around, causing me to misstep and ram my face straight into his chest. I bounced right off his muscular pecs. He gently grabbed my shoulders and pulled me at a distance. I glanced up at him and bit my bottom lip. He smelled so delicious.

"I won't let anything happen to you," he muttered deeply. "I won't let you die this way."

"But it's how it's done."

His enormous hand cupped my cheek, his thumb grazing my skin. "I told you to trust me. We will figure it out."

"Why is this happening? Why was I chosen? I'm not an angel."

He didn't say anything for what felt like too long, and then simply repeated, "We'll figure it out."

I searched his eyes for truth and I found it. It was there, staring back at me. His kind and humble soul. He wore his righteousness and devout loyalty to being a good man on his sleeve. His eyes were opened wide and soft, a world away from Dominic's, whose eyes were narrow and mysteriously dangerous—always hungry for something.

Lake gazed at me as if he knew me. As if he knew all of my deepest secrets. As if he finally found something he had been desperately searching an eternity for. He made me feel like I could pour my heart out to him completely, right then and there. I wanted to show him how terrified I was of going to Hell, but how strangely right it felt. I wanted to tell him that I truly didn't want this task. I wanted to ask him to please care for my sister and get her up to the White Realm without me somehow, someway.

He pulled my shirt away from my neck and lowered the stone inside. I heaved a long drawn-out breath when his skin brushed mine. My eyes met his lips and the courage started to build inside of me. I closed my eyes and leaned up, ready to finally taste an angel. Hoping that I could somehow translate everything I wanted to say into a kiss. But his hands dropped to his sides and there was suddenly a big void of air between us.

I opened my eyes. Really? Rejection number two. Check.

He turned away from me, and I rolled my tongue against my cheek. *You dirty bastard.*

I started packing again, aggressively throwing things into my suitcase to show my irritation.

"The souls of the Great Elders inside the stone normally activate it when they feel they are ready. Like I said, I will buy you a little bit of time."

I scoffed loudly. "I sincerely hope so, because I don't want to die."

He turned back around and squinted at me. I wasn't sure if it was disappointment in his stare or not, but I suddenly felt guilty. Was I being selfish?

"Frankie! Boris is ready!" Alex called out. I could tell in her voice that she was growing desperate— probably running out of ways to keep Boris occupied.

"You should go," Lake said.

I zipped my bag shut.

"I'll be waiting for you to get back."

"Frankie!" Alex yelled again.

Lake and I both looked at the door then back at each other. "You have to go now," he insisted.

I was pretty pissed about having been rejected by the same man twice in less than twenty-four hours, but his face was too divine. I couldn't help but want to suck on his bottom lip. Lake was still a stranger to me, but there was an undeniable connection between us, whether he wanted to admit it or not. I didn't know what was going to happen in a couple of days, but just in case, for some reason, I never saw him again...

I tiptoed and reached up, placing a quick peck on his cheek. His whole body visibly stiffened for a moment, then relaxed.

"I'll see you soon," he said before climbing out of my window. I placed a hand on The Liberation Stone resting on my chest underneath my shirt. It felt heavy, like it was weighing me down with expectation and responsibility. What if Lake came back and said I have no choice? Either Alex wouldn't be reformed, or I'd die for good. I didn't want to evaporate into thin air. I wanted to live. Whether it was here on Earth or in the Red Realm. Did that make me a selfish person? If I didn't activate the stone at all, this region's portal would remain and Alex would just stay here, living on Earth. How bad could that be?

I didn't have to die to live in the Red Realm and that was the beauty of it. No one had to die. I knew Lake said this was for the good of everyone, not just my sister and me. But did I really give a shit about anyone else but the people who meant something to me? Let's be honest, everyone in this world ultimately only cared about themselves and their own.

Alex opened the door with Boris standing directly behind her. "It's time, Frankie."

"I know." I walked up to my sister and wrapped my arms around her neck. "It's going to be okay, Alex," I assured her. "I'm going to be okay."

She pulled my body into hers tightly. "I know you will be, Frankie. You're strong. Stronger than me. Mom and Dad would be proud of you." She pulled me at arm's length and smiled. "And Jacob. Jacob would be proud of the woman you have become."

I squeezed my eyes shut, forcing the tears to retreat back. If Alex knew what being chosen by The Liberation Stone meant, she would never allow it to happen. She would beg Lake to find another way.

I hugged her again for about another minute, then let go. I didn't want to drag it out any longer, as much as I truly wanted to.

"I'll see you really soon," I said.

I had to pretend to be that strong, arrogant, bitchy person everyone thought I was. I had to keep that I-don't-give-a-shit facade up in order to even walk out of this apartment. Otherwise, I would only want to lock myself in my bedroom and soak my fears and worries in a bottle of booze, praying to finally choke on it and die so that I didn't have to *choose* whether or not I wanted to die.

CHAPTER TWENTY

The Journey

Boris and I walked back to Centaurus with only the sounds of Shitsburgh's streets weaving through our out-of-sync walk together, the city busy with panhandlers and the honks of traffic speckled with cars probably older than I was. Boris carried my suitcase for me. In the meantime, I chain-smoked nearly a whole pack of cigarettes, which should have granted me a medal of some sort considering the short distance between The Hartley and the office. I didn't peek into Reggie's store this time. I was too worried that Boris might pick up on something and question me.

Boris wasn't necessarily threatening in his demeanor, only in his physical attributes. In the three years that I'd worked for Centaurus, he had never made me feel frightened for my safety. Actually, it was quite the opposite. Walking next to him made me feel as though I had my very own personal bodyguard. But he was one of the Henchmen. The Henchmen were known for being murderers, essentially. It was their duty to kill the clients who decided to back out of selling their souls and send them off to The Nothing.

Alex did mention that her client's death wasn't as cruel as one would imagine. So maybe the Henchmen weren't as menacing as Dominic. Maybe they were just big old oafs who were actually cuddly and sweet outside of the office, but just doing their jobs.

I glanced over at him. He looked like he was barely even holding my bag, using only his fingertips. "Is it too heavy?" I asked, attempting some kind of playful banter.

"Not even a little bit."

"Oh. I thought maybe my britches might have been weighing you down. Slowing your stride a bit."

"Not your britches, but probably the three bottles of vodka you have stuffed in here."

I tried to hide my chagrin and chose to play on his accurate assumption. "Wanna take a few swigs before we get into work?"

"Nah. I'm good." He pulled something up from his jacket pocket, just enough for me to recognize it was his very own flask. "I've got some whiskey."

I half-smiled at the way his Scottish accent made the sentence sound like a question. "I knew I liked you, Boris."

When we reached Centaurus, Boris opened the door and ushered me in. The creepy porcelain receptionist wasn't there anymore, and for some reason, I got an eerie feeling that she might not have been there in the first place. Like she wasn't even real. A figment of my imagination. A ghost.

Instead of using the elevator that I normally used to get to my cubicle, Boris escorted me around to the other side. It didn't make any sense. It was the same elevator, it seemed, only we were entering through the backside, which I had no idea even existed.

Boris must have noticed my confusion. "It's the only way to the gates." How incredibly annoying. The portal was hiding in plain sight this whole time.

I nodded, fighting the urge to touch The Liberation Stone under my shirt.

Boris pulled out a card and waved it over the metal panel near the door, causing it to open. Once we stepped inside, he did the same on another panel that should have had round numbers to push but had none. As soon as the doors slid shut, all four walls illuminated bright neon red. A robotic but feminine voice came over the intercom somewhere above our heads. "Please state your identification number and destination."

"81074600. The gates."

"Thank you."

I hadn't the slightest clue what this whole experience was going to be like. This was a first for me. I'd never even heard stories about the journey to the Red Realm. Dominic said that it was lengthy, but it couldn't be that bad if the Henchmen were coming and going every day. Also, it couldn't be that far from Dominic's office. I saw it for myself from his window. Honestly, I had no perception of where Hell could be. In a normal human's mind, it was underneath us— below our feet. But where was below our feet? Under the dirt and rocks that made up the Earth? In my supernatural brain, and because of the fact that it was called the Red *Realm,* I figured that it was in another dimension. On another plane. But what did that even mean?

I worried what my body was going to feel like if I had to travel between realities. There had to be some kind of science involved. Something maybe similar to when an astronaut ventured off into outer space.

The elevator began to move, and it was as if someone had slowly poured a jar of nervous butterflies into my stomach. I guess I was going to find out soon what it felt like. Thankfully, there was no stupid elevator music about Hell. That would have definitely added some nausea to the itinerary.

I glanced over at Boris, who seemed perfectly casual. When it was clear that the speed of the elevator had begun to increase, he didn't falter. He stood perfectly still in an awkward elevator pose, the one where you're not sure what to do with your arms or your eyes—look straight ahead at the shiny, reflective doors or at the numbers counting up or down? But there were no numbers to look at. No indication of what floor was coming next. The elevator was going down for sure, down past my cubicle floor, past Dominic's office. That much I knew because I could somehow feel it. I could feel my body descending farther and farther away from anything that felt familiar to me. A sense of sorrow pulled on the nerves in my face. My forehead scrunched up and wrinkled involuntarily, a clear sign of worry and stress. The corners of my lips turned downward on their own, into an uncontrolled frown. I crossed my arms around my body, frightened by the unknown manipulation that was being forced upon me.

I tried to think of something good, anything, like Jacob's kiss, Mom's exuberant laugh, my sister and my dad. But my most profound fears were pooling around those cherished memories, drowning them out. Everything I had ever been afraid of since I could remember flashed before my eyes. The silver elevator door became a mirror, my reflection staring back at me. As the red lights began to flicker, my image changed with each flick.

Spiders crawling all over my face.

Flick.

Gunshot wound to the head.

Flick.

Hair falling out in patches.

Flick.

Skin and bones.

Flick.

Missing legs.

Flick.

Tube down my throat.

Flick.

I coughed and gagged and grabbed at my throat, realizing simultaneously that I was doing this in real life. But just as quickly as it began, it stopped. I couldn't see myself anymore. It was completely dark now, no red neon lights, and the sound of the elevator skimming down the mechanical wires went away. Boris had disappeared, it seemed, and I wondered if the elevator even stopped because the movement in my stomach was no longer there.

I had never, ever been afraid of the dark, even as a child. I never had any issues walking through the house in the middle of the night without any lights on, using the memory and familiarity of my daily routines to help guide me to the bathroom or to the refrigerator for a midnight snack. But this darkness was different. It was suffocating, surrounding me, violating me. I closed my eyes, hoping that could somehow protect me. Somehow keep me safe inside a bubble shaped as myself. But it didn't help. It made me feel even more lost, more lonely. As if I had never known a single person in my entire life. I was completely abandoned. Desolated in the middle of a vast nothingness. I couldn't remember what a face looked like, what I looked like. I didn't know anyone. I had no one. No one knew me. No one loved me.

It was the most vulnerable I'd ever felt. The most uncertainty I'd ever experienced. Unclear of whether I was awake or asleep. Alive or dead. Did I have limbs? Was I breathing? Was this real or not? I didn't know. I couldn't be sure of what to believe—how to believe what I wasn't seeing.

I thought I might be sick. Everywhere. Things coming out of every orifice in my body. I was suddenly aware of things happening again, and I was sweating profusely. The temperature had risen. The red neon lights came back on, but Boris was definitely missing. I scanned around me, but he wasn't there, and I panicked. I didn't want to feel any more alone than I already did.

My hand flung up and collided harshly with my chest. I was running out of air fast and desperate to grab onto any that might seep out so that I could swallow it back up. I was hyperventilating, losing control of my focus. I stumbled into each of the four metal walls, hoping that maybe one of them would pop open and provide a gust of cool, refreshing air into my lungs. My vision tunneled, leaving me dizzy with fear and loss and anxiety. A ringing in my ears grew louder, and I tried to shield my eardrums by tilting my head into my shoulder. The abrupt deprivation of air and hope and sense of existence threatened to kill me. It was out to get me; I was sure of it. I needed out. I needed to breathe. I needed to wake up.

My heart pounded hard and fast. It felt unnatural. The friction from the thumping was going to cause a spark and my insides were going to combust. I inhaled and exhaled, coughed, gagged, opened and closed my eyes, pulled on my hair, wiped the sweat from my armpits, paced the width of the elevator floor back and forth a million times. I just wanted out. I didn't want to live anymore and considered clawing at my own wrists to find my veins and pull.

Then, again, it all stopped. I could breathe. I could see. I was calm.

There was a tap on my shoulder. I turned around, but there was no one.

Another tap.

I turned. No one. Just me and the glowing crimson walls.

I positioned myself straight forward again, holding a stillness in place. Someone was there. Someone was breathing down my neck. The unseen presence was strong, and I could feel it invading my space.

Another tap, and I turned as fast as I could to catch the culprit.

And there she was. Her beautiful fresh face was glowing. Her deep brown hair was long and gorgeous. Her green eyes sparkled, and she smiled at me.

My knees nearly buckled, but I managed to keep standing. "Mom?" She was inches away from me. All I had to do was reach out my hand to touch her skin. "Mom? Is that you?"

It *was* her. It was totally her. I was suddenly brought back to our lake house, watching her hands glide over the canvas effortlessly. It was like magic, as if the brilliant colors of the thick paint poured freely from her fingertips. The afternoon sun shined brightly through the windows and kissed her skin in all the right places, making her glow. She was a vision.

"Mom, please," I whimpered. I was a child again.

She didn't say anything. She squinted at me as if she couldn't recognize who I was. Her smile faded and changed into something I had never seen before. Her body shrunk right in front of me, like a wilting flower, and her skin transformed. She was now old and wrinkled and deformed. One side of her body drooped down toward the floor. Her lips parted and started moving, but only the left side had enough strength. "Frankie," she moaned in a strained, ghostly tone.

I began to weep at the flashback of her in the hospital. She'd been very sick, the cancer causing complications like pneumonia and stroke. She fell into a coma and didn't wake up again, but I would never forget the sight of my mother, who was usually so infectiously upbeat and funny and honest. The color of her skin had turned a sickening pallor. She looked so defeated, so tired even though she was asleep.

Somehow, this was worse. The red glare from the walls cast a haunting shadow upon her, something that just didn't fit. It didn't belong to her. My heart broke all over again. I wanted to hold her, but I was too afraid. I didn't want to touch her. She was scaring me to my very core.

But I'd missed her. I missed her so badly. My heart couldn't take it anymore.

I stretched out my arms and bravely lunged forward, suddenly frantic for our skin to make contact. I expected to embrace and fold her fragile body into mine, to try to shield her away from the ominous red shade, but instead I fell to my knees onto the ground. She faded into a cloud of smoke that slowly dissipated all around me.

"Moooom!" I cried out, surprised at the desperation and despair that escaped my own throat.

My body jolted from the intensity of my cries as I rested forward on my knees, but I was still somehow able to feel another tap on my shoulder. A shot of hope pinged through me. She was back!

I stood up and whirled around, ready to take her all in no matter how awful and frightening she looked. But it wasn't her.

His dark spiky hair. His full pink lips and hairless face. His skin, so much more milky than mine. His football jersey. It was all the same as when I'd last seen him.

Jacob. My Jacob.

Tears filled my eyes, and he was blurry for only a moment until I blinked. Jacob was real. He was there. He stood still, staring at me. I stared back, unable to move. Unable to breathe. Petrified to do either because then he might change or vanish into the stifling air that surrounded us. Bursts of bright, vivid images replayed across his eyes, as if he were the one hypnotizing me—using supernatural abilities to convince me of what I was seeing. But he didn't have to persuade me because I was there, too.

We are underneath the weeping willow tree, its frilly, lush leaves dangling all around us, swaying ever so slightly with the light breeze from the lake. It echoes a swooshing sound into our ears, lulling our calm spirits. My back is leaning up against the large trunk. Jacob is holding his weight with one hand next to my head, the other caressing my cheek.

He's forcing a mousy coyness out of me, as if we have only just met and I am trying to hold his attention with my novice allure. Although, at this point, we've already seen each other naked about twenty times, so there's no reason to be reserved. But there's something about the proximity of his face to mine—something about his half-smile and soft skin and the smell of his minty breath from his favorite wintergreen gum. His eyes are open wide, and he's allowing me to take a peek inside, deeper than he would allow anyone else to.

"You are so beautiful."

"Am not," I respond bashfully, lowering my gaze away from his.

"Are too! You are the most beautiful girl I've ever seen. The most beautiful girl in the world."

"You haven't seen all of the girls in the world, so how can you say that?"

"Don't need to."

"And why is that?"

"Because you're the only one that matters."

I bite my bottom lip, unsure of how to match his words. He is definitely the most beautiful boy that matters to me.

He moves my hair behind my ear. "You know that sometimes when we're napping together, I watch you sleep?"

"No, you don't," I say, pushing his shoulder playfully.

"Yes, I do. I watch you. I watch your eyes twitch. And I like when your mouth opens a little bit."

I drop my mouth open right then, completely surprised and a bit embarrassed by this admission. "Do I snore?" I ask in horror, hoping that he says no.

"No. You never snore. But you do make these tiny little noises. It's like moaning, but short and quick. Not like when we're...you know." The tops of his ears turn pink, and I smirk at his ability to remain innocent when I know he's a big horny hornball.

He continues. "I wonder what you're dreaming about. I wonder if I'm in any of your dreams." I briefly try remembering any of my dreams, but I can't on the spot. I don't want to lie to him and say he is because I don't know for sure, so I just tilt my head at his charming curiosity.

"But then I realize that I don't care," Jacob says. "I just want to watch you dream all the time. I just want to be that close to you all the time."

My heart begins to race. For some reason, I'm filled with a nervous excitement. I'm not sure where he is going with this. It isn't the first time Jacob has said sweet things to me, but I can feel the atmosphere shift around us. It's more mature. More...sophisticated than our daily flirtation and puppy love infatuation with one another.

"Frankie, will you marry me?" he blurts out.

"What?" I'm in complete shock. "Jacob," I mumble.

He rubs the back of his neck. I regret my reaction, because now he might be wondering why he just asked me something like that, but he's looking me right in the eyes. "I know we're young. I know it sounds crazy. But we both want the same things. I have so much fun with you, and I want to do everything with you. We're graduating soon and we're going to the same college. It just makes sense to me."

"Our parents will freak out," I say.

"We don't have to tell them right now. Besides," he says, taking my right hand, "I don't have a ring. We can tell them once I save up enough from working at my dad's shop to buy you a ring."

I look down at my hand in his. I don't have the heart to tell him the ring should go on my left hand and not my right.

"I love you, Frankie. I love watching you dream. I want to do it forever because...because you're the girl of my dreams."

In that moment, a swift wind sweeps loose strands of my hair across my face. Before I can do it myself, Jacob swipes my forehead to clear my face. I look up at him and we kiss. It's a different kind of a kiss than usual. It's all lips. No tongue.

He pulls away. "Will you marry me, Frankie? Please?"

There's a part of my brain that thinks we are wildly too adolescent to be having this kind of conversation. I wonder for a moment if he'll still feel this way in a couple of years, let alone a couple of months. I'm young and naive, but I know that we still have so much growing to do, with each other and ourselves. Feelings change. People change. Situations change.

But he's Jacob, and I love him. I love laughing with him. And kissing him. And hugging him. I love being near him. It's as simple as that. So why not? Why not marry him?

I grin slowly. "Yes. I will marry you."

He smiles back and we kiss again, this time hard and fast and with our tongues all over the place. Then, we run hand in hand to the dock and jump into the lake together.

Tears streamed down my cheeks like an open faucet. My chest caved in deeper and deeper with every exhale. Jacob stood inches away from me, staring at me. I wanted him to hold me, to swipe the hair off my forehead and ask me to marry him again.

But he wouldn't move. He just stared.

Was this even real? He looked real, but was he really here? How could he be here with me?

I decided to do it. I decided to reach out and touch him. I had to. I had to feel his face, to feel close to him again. I'd missed him so much.

I raised my fingers up to his face, but just as I did, his head snapped back violently. The back of his head touched his spine, then jolted back up and to the side where it hung, hovering over his shoulder. Bones protruded out of the other side of his neck, breaking through his skin and instantly forming black and blue bruises. His expression contorted into a painful grimace.

He began to walk forward in quick, jerky motions. I moved back with every step he took toward me, completely horrified. It wasn't him. It wasn't my Jacob. His neck was broken. His eyes were hollowing out. Every time he moved, his skin changed. It was changing colors. Aging. Sloughing off. He was decaying.

I kept stepping away from him. "No," I sobbed. "Please, Jacob. No."

He wouldn't stop. He kept coming at me. His face melting. His lips falling off his face. I refused to look but could hear pieces of his body hitting the ground. Blood splattering.

The red neon lights began to flicker again. On and off. On and off. I stepped back a few more times before the heels of my feet hit the wall. I pressed my body up against it as much as I could, willing myself to become invisible and fade into it like some kind of apparition. I couldn't look at him anymore. My stomach churned with sick. I turned my head away from him and slammed my eyes shut. "No! Please! Stop it!" I yelled forcefully.

A puff of his minty breath coated my nostrils and his old familiar voice breathed, "Frankie."

A twinge of hope crept up to my eyes, forcing them to pop open and turn back to face him, but he was gone.

CHAPTER TWENTY-ONE

Sssalutation

I guess the Elders decided not to activate The Liberation Stone. This was unfortunate. I would have preferred to have been disintegrated into thin air rather than going through whatever the crap that was.

"Frankie."

Someone was nudging me, but I didn't want to move. I didn't want to look up. I didn't have the strength to, completely exhausted by everything that had just happened. From everything that I'd just seen. And quite honestly, I didn't know if I could handle another visitor from my past.

"Frankie, everything is okay."

No, it's not.

"It's time to get up."

No, it's not.

"We've arrived."

At some point, after witnessing Jacob's decomposition right before my eyes, I'd shrunken down into a fetal position and placed my face into the palms of my hands. It didn't feel any safer, just necessary.

I could tell by the Scottish accent that it was Boris speaking to me, but I still couldn't be too sure. A few minutes ago, he had disappeared and wasn't even in the elevator with me. Now, somehow, he was back and trying to lift me up by my elbow. "There you go. I've got you."

I allowed him to carry my weight as I staggered to my feet, feeling a bit dizzy and disoriented. I fought to roll my eyes at the red neon walls. I wanted to get out of this elevator ASAP. "Are we here?"

"Yes, we've made it to the In Between. The hard part is over."

I shot him a dirty look. "That's an understatement." I couldn't help but feel a sense of betrayal from him. Like he could have warned me ahead of time about the horrors of this damn elevator.

"I know," he said. It was only two words, but they sounded sincere.

"That was fucking terrible."

"It can be quite vexing."

"Vexing? Um...that shit was traumatizing!" I huffed.

"People usually complain about The Nothing."

"Did we go to The Nothing?" I didn't remember making any stops along the way.

"We pass through it for a brief moment before we reach our stop," he said. That would probably explain those awful feelings of loneliness and despair, right before seeing my mother's gruesome ghost.

"Where did you go?" I asked him.

"Nowhere. I was standing next to you the whole time," Boris said, as if he's had to answer this question many times before.

I wanted to yell at him. Why the hell didn't he help me?

"Are you okay?" he asked. He seemed to be genuinely interested in my wellbeing.

"I'm fine. That was just rough. Does that happen every time?"

"It's different for everyone." I could tell he didn't want to tell me the truth, which was that the journey to the Red Realm fucking sucked every time.

"What about you?" I asked, curious to learn what kind of awful nightmares came to life for him.

"It doesn't happen to me."

"You don't see dead people or creepy shit like that?"

"I am a spawn of the Red Realm. I was created by King Centaurus and Queen Hysteria. I have no human emotion tethering me to a human past," he explained.

"So, you have no irrational fears or loved ones to miss," I reiterated, in simpler terms.

"Right."

This saddened me a bit about Boris, and I wondered if all the Henchmen were completely supernatural. He was never human like Lake and Dominic were thousands of years ago. Did this mean he wasn't capable of normal emotions? His cheery attitude confused me. All the other Henchmen seemed deadpan and programmed, unlike Boris. Maybe he secretly wanted to be a real man, like the robot from the movie *Bicentennial Man.*

Ugh. All of the thinking and emotional distress made me thirsty. "Can you hand me my suitcase?"

He wheeled it next to me. I unzipped the side pocket to pull out a pint of vodka. One twist and the top shot off the bottle and onto the floor. I didn't care. I poured a long swig into my mouth, opening my throat wide and barely using my own muscles to swallow. I just let it flow freely as it burned and soothed my esophagus all at the same time.

I almost belched a theatrical *ahhh* to prove just how perfect it tasted, but held back and replaced it with a modest, girly burp. It was exactly what I needed to get myself together. Seeing Jacob and my dead mother took a lot out of me—a weakness that I'd managed to keep under control all these years. But that needed to change pronto. If for some reason the whole take-down and reforming didn't pan out, I couldn't start a life in the Red Realm as some kind of pansy ass, especially if I was going to be working with the king and queen. I needed to forget about Mom and Jacob. I had to keep my head in the game. Cut all the emotional crap and figure this shit out.

"I'm ready now," I said.

Boris waved his card over the metal panel and the elevator doors slid open.

It was just as it looked from Dominic's window, only now it was at eye level. We stepped out of the elevator onto the rocky ground. I side-swiped my boot away from the cracks, worried that the flowy, bright orange lava-like substance might burn a hole through the rubber sole.

"It won't hurt you," Boris informed me.

I scanned my surroundings as we walked deeper into the vast space. It definitely felt like we were underground, but more like a basement in an aged home that had been completely remodeled. It was stuffy and dirty and smoky, but yet, strangely beautiful in its architecture. Detailed carvings of numbers and words I couldn't read, mixed in gold and gray and black hues, covered the stone walls and ceilings. I assumed it was all in another language. Columns with torches aligned aisles that seemed never-ending. Dramatic arches curved high above us and tall chiseled statues of devilish creatures with wings and clawed feet watched our every move. Literally. I could have sworn I saw some eye movement.

"This is called the In Between?"

"Yes. It's the sector between the portal and the gates, where souls wait to be inducted into either The Nothing or the Red Realm," he explained.

When I felt I'd taken it all in and my curiosity had peaked, I was finally able to focus on what we were walking into. The line that I'd seen from Dominic's office. The souls. The seemingly endless train of souls.

I had never seen a soul before. When the Henchmen collected souls and escorted them to the Red Realm or The Nothing, it was done discreetly and, apparently, through the backside of the elevator that all the regular employees of Centaurus used. None of us, or at least me, had ever seen a soul up close and personal.

But before we could reach the line and I could get my first look, a horse and buggy pulled up next to us and came to a halt. A—no shit—horse and buggy.

The convertible carriage had no doors and two rows of seats. The back was empty and the driver sat in the front—a person wearing a black fitted suit with a long tailcoat and an almost comically tall top hat. He sat high and faced forward, holding onto a frayed, ratted rope in each hand, which connected to two horses whose manes were made of fire. It was mesmerizing, the way the amber flames danced gracefully from their heads down to their backs. But their bodies were gaunt and bloodied, chunks of skin and meat missing, revealing rib cages and innards. These horses were heartbreakingly repulsive and terrifying, and I struggled to understand how they were even alive. But they neighed and galloped in place, clearly containing their desire to trot off.

Boris put my bag into the buggy, then turned and offered me his hand for support. I took it, hoisting myself up and taking a seat behind the driver, whose face I had yet to see. Boris was so tall he barely had to step up, and so heavy that the buggy bounced when he took a seat next to me.

"Evening, Borisss," the driver greeted with an exaggerated, accented hiss.

"Hello, Ziggy."

"To the gatesss?" Ziggy's voice was high-pitched, and he emphasized his s's just like I'd imagined a snake would if it could talk. His words ended at the tip of his tongue and between his teeth, and it kind of hurt my ears.

"Yes," Boris answered.

"Did you enjoy the ride down?"

"Yes. Same as usual," Boris replied with an exasperated exhale, as if bored with Ziggy's attempt at small talk.

Ziggy finally turned around. His big eyes slanted vertically, red glowing around jet black corneas. His cheekbones arched high on his face and two pointy yellow fangs underneath his top lip curved downward. I wondered if he could pierce his own skinny chin if he wasn't careful.

His emerald green skin looked wet and scaly, and there was a distinct black zig-zag pattern running down the middle of his reptilian face. "And how about you? Did you have a niccce ride?"

I recoiled in disgust, worried that the long forked tongue that kept darting in and out of his mouth could somehow reach me. He awaited a response and I simply nodded. I wasn't about to have a conversation with this weird snake man.

"Let's go, Ziggy," Boris insisted. "We've got to be somewhere soon." He must have felt me shifting uncomfortably in my seat next to him.

"Yesss, sssir." Ziggy promptly turned around and pulled on the reins. The burning horses' whinny echoed loudly, and we started moving fast, right in between the lines of souls. We zoomed past them, the sounds of their voices a sea of hushed whispers. I studied each of them as we whizzed past. They were like flashes. It was as if they were partially invisible. They looked like normal people, all shapes and sizes, all different colors. But there was something different about them. Something off. Something sad. Something...sobering in their faces.

They were anxious. Shocked. Reluctant to believe they were even standing in a line leading to the gates of Hell. They didn't want to be there. Worried about the horrors that lay ahead. They had no idea that Hell was real. No idea what they were getting themselves into when they committed their crimes, sold their souls, did whatever it was that landed them a reservation. At least, this was what it seemed like they were feeling by the look on their faces. Some of their expressions were frozen in a state of trauma. Some were crying profusely. Some were visibly trembling. Hands over their eyes, over their ears. But they all had one thing in common. They were all missing something. Life. They all seemed drained of any life. Pale. Lacking vitality and essence. They were just...there. Just souls. Dim and dull and sad.

We reached the front of the line in no time and stopped at what reminded me of a toll booth. My attention had instantly been drawn to the colossal doors that stood boldly in front of us. The souls were taking turns at the toll, then being escorted by a large guard wearing a black armored suit to the gate. He held a leash in his hand that restrained a bulldog-like creature with two heads, each mouth sporting a vicious grin. The gates to the Red Realm opened then closed once the soul was on the other side. The sound of the textured metal engraved with words and patterns coming apart and meeting again echoed all around us.

A commotion forced my eyes back down to the toll booth. Several guards rushed over to someone—a soul. The soul hollered and flailed, but the guards lifted him up by his arms and carried him to what resembled some kind of well. Then, without warning or hesitation, they threw him in. His screams bounced off the walls all the way down, until he hit what I assumed to be the bottom. I touched The Liberation Stone through my shirt as I remembered its promise to protect me.

"Did he just...die?" I whispered toward Boris. I hadn't realized how silly my question was until after I asked it. He was a soul—already dead.

"That is another entry into The Nothing."

"Why did they throw him down there?"

"Don't know. He might not have the Seal of the Red Realm. Or it's his punishment for something he did."

I felt awful for him. I didn't know if he would be banished to The Nothing for an eternity, because even a few minutes there was enough to drive someone mad. I had wanted to rip myself apart just passing through it.

The horses trotted up to the toll booth where a person shrouded in a black robe stood behind a counter. Tall stacks of papers piled high all around him. He looked up at us, and I realized then that it wasn't a person. It was a...skeleton? He didn't have a face. The inside of the hood was empty, but white bony fingers poked through the edge of the sleeves and the robe hung off his body as if it were ten sizes too big.

Ziggy doffed his hat to the cloaked skeleton and the gates opened. My heart began to pound in anticipation of what was on the other side. This was it. I was about to enter the Red Realm.

CHAPTER TWENTY-TWO

Can't Say No to Free Booze

The sound of the gates of the Red Realm slamming shut behind us reverberated as we approached a man standing near a podium. He was dressed in a crimson-colored suit, complete with a vest and a little black handkerchief stuffed neatly into the front pocket of his blazer. It was a little too much considering the temperature had risen quite a bit between here and the other side of the gates. Nevertheless, he looked like a well-groomed, fashionable man from the neck down, but his face was a different story because...he had no face. It was black smoke in the shape of a head, wisps of it curling and evaporating high into the air above him. There were eyes, a mouth, and a nose, but it was all just dark vapors in constant motion.

The man clutched a clipboard, and as Boris and I stepped off the buggy, it almost gave me the feeling that we were about to be seated at our table in a fancy restaurant.

"Hello, welcome to the Red Realm, Frankie." The man's voice was surprisingly normal, with just a hint of an echo, which I assumed was because of the fact that he was made out of smoke. It kind of sounded like he was underwater.

"Hi," I greeted him back.

"I'm Alcazar, I'll be getting you settled in."

"Frankie, I have to go," Boris interrupted.

"Yeah, okay. Thanks for bringing me here."

"If you need anything from me, just have Alcazar shoot me a message."

I couldn't think of a reason to need Boris, but I smiled and nodded at him. Unexpectedly, Boris leaned in close and wrapped his enormous biceps around my body, locking my arms in place. He pulled me in close to him, and because I couldn't move my arms, the hug felt really forced and strange. He lowered himself down to my height, which practically doubled him over.

Then his warm, breathy whisper filled my ear. "If you need *anything* at all, I'm your man." He pushed me away and stepped back onto the buggy. Ziggy smiled and his tongue slithered in and out of his mouth a few times before he waved goodbye.

"I bid you a good night, Frankie. Sssee you sssoon." He pulled on the reins and the two fiery horses simultaneously released a loud, sickly whinny before rearing up and trotting off. After about twenty feet, the carriage lifted up off the ground and flew into the air, which was when I finally noticed the backdrop.

Alcazar and I were standing on a cliff, overlooking an entire city in the distance. A whole city, complete with buildings and roads and even rivers.

"Is that where we're going?" I asked Alcazar, pointing ahead of us.

"Yes. This is the City of Centaurus."

"It's less...Hell-like than I pictured." It was true, but rather refreshing. Everything else seemed so cliché. The symbols and colors at the Centaurus office had led me to believe that the Red Realm was going to look like all the pictures hanging on the walls. I imagined fire and brimstone and cloaked demons everywhere. But it just looked like a mirage in the desert from a distance.

Alcazar chuckled. "Everyone says that at first." At first? "Now, let's get you to your new home."

I hadn't noticed it before, but a very sleek and shiny black sports car was parked right near the edge of the cliff. Alcazar climbed into the driver seat, and I settled into the passenger side. He started the car and the engine roared to life. We backed out of the parking spot and began down a long stretch of road leading to the city. I stared out of the window at the sky, which was tinted in shades of red and orange. It reminded me of a sunset, only I couldn't see an actual sun from my position. The hue cast an amber glow on everything, as if the entire city was in the shadows of a raging fire burning somewhere close.

Alcazar let go of the steering wheel and grabbed his paperwork. "Okay, let's go over a few things, shall we?"

"Um...aren't you going to drive?" I asked, reaching behind my shoulder in search of a seatbelt, but there wasn't one.

"Oh, it's fine. It's on autopilot," he said, waving his hand dismissively over the steering wheel as it gently moved on its own. "So, you're going to be a CA. We'll get you checked into work tomorrow. Tonight, let's get you acquainted with your new living quarters."

The car purred as it drove us down an empty, narrow road. Black sand resembling charcoal on either side of the street surrounded us as the distance of the city steadily grew closer.

"This might be a stupid question, but is it... nighttime?" I asked.

"It's not a stupid question at all, dear. The time difference between dimensions is kind of tricky and hard to get used to. Also, it's a little hard to tell what time of day it is when it always looks like this. But to answer your question in time, like in hours and minutes, I can't because there is no time here."

No time?

"It will feel kind of wonky at first, but you'll get used to the no-clock thing," Alcazar added.

I shot him a look of disbelief. "No clock?" This made me nervous. How was I supposed to know what time it was and how long I was here? And what about

Lake and the take-down? He was expecting me back at a certain time. I would somehow have to keep track of time myself.

Alcazar flipped through his papers, smoky fingers somehow gripping onto the sheets. He didn't even look up at me and answered my question as if he had to answer it a thousand times a day. "Time is an illusion on Earth. Humans rely on it for everything. But in other dimensions, it's pointless. No one cares about it."

Fuck. What did I get myself into?

"Okay, your roommate's name is Lilith," he continued. "She doesn't like the smell of flowers or the color yellow. She hates puppies and cupcakes and refuses to say thank you for anything. But she's my cousin, so I'm sure you'll get along great with her."

Lilith hates puppies? How could I get along with anyone who hated puppies? I might have been all dark and sulky, but there was no way I could ever hate a sweet, innocent creature like that.

"You and Lilith are related?" I queried Alcazar.

"She doesn't look like me, if that's what you're asking."

My face burned with embarrassment. "Oh, I wasn't...I didn't mean to..."

"Don't worry about it. I don't expect humans to have an open mind. You all are notoriously judgmental," he declared.

The sporty car suddenly began to jerk and vibrate, and my body shook with it. I peered out of the windshield, realizing then that the smooth, open road we had been coasting on had turned into white rocky terrain. "What is that?"

"Bones."

"Like skeletal bones?" I gawked.

"Yup. We're passing the dumping grounds."

Dumping grounds for what? It didn't make much sense. I didn't think that souls had actual body parts. But maybe they did because they still looked like humans. Maybe. I didn't know. This was all so fucking confusing.

"Do you have any preferences for food and drinks?" Alcazar asked me.

Drinks. The need for alcohol instantly hit the back of my throat. It was hard to tell how much time had passed since I had my last taste, but the craving came on strong. My suitcase rested at my feet and I could almost see my bottles of vodka through my bag, the liquid swooshing with every movement of the vehicle. I wanted to reach down and retrieve it but pulling out a bottle of liquor didn't seem like the appropriate thing to do on my first day here.

Alcazar raised his misty eyeballs up at me, awaiting a response. "Well?"

"I, uh...I guess it's whatever you—"

"We can get whatever you want. Anything. Pizza, chips, steak, lobster, alcohol, cocaine, heroin, dildos, whips, chains... Whatever you're into, we've got," he said nonchalantly. He ran down the list of food and drugs and porn props as if it were all ingredients in a Caesar salad. I couldn't help blushing from the last items he rattled off, as the thought of Dominic's fingers made my nipples harden and my lady part palpitate.

I shifted in my seat. "Um...I would love some vodka."

Alcazar jotted *vodka* down on his paper. "We'll make sure you are stocked up."

"Grey Goose," I requested, but it was practically a murmur. It did not feel right asking him for this.

"How about Belvedere and Crystal Head?"

Holy shit! I would never buy those brands. Not that I couldn't afford it—the liquor store down the street from The Hartley sold Belvedere for forty-five dollars a pop. But that was forty-five dollars multiplied by six bottles a week. The twelve-dollar bottles of Skol got me plenty drunk enough to forget the cheap-ass taste.

"Yeah, that sounds good," I responded bashfully.

We were now approaching the city. Buildings taller than my eye could see towered over us. They were all glistening in golden colors and it was almost hard to tell if they were on fire or not. Our car zoomed down the streets, now sharply cutting corners as it navigated us to our destination. The population increased, and a mixture of people, souls, and creatures came into view. It honestly resembled any other crowded city on Earth, except this one had flying dragons and giant one-eyed monsters with horns walking around, minding their own business. Part of me was expecting to see unusual things. After all, I had become a supernatural being three years ago. Between that and the constant alcohol flowing through my veins, it was easy to accept the abnormal. But another part of me was trembling in fear. I was in Hell. Who wouldn't be freaking out right now?

But I didn't want to show it. I had to try to remain as an emotionless bitch who didn't care. Or at least, I had to *act* like it now that I was in the Red Realm. At least until Lake figured out what to do about The Liberation Stone and how to save Alex.

We crossed a bridge high above a river of red liquid rushing through. I presumed it was blood, given the fact that I *was* in Hell and all.

After about ten more minutes of Alcazar asking me questions, like what kind of car I wanted to drive and how much money I would like to start out with in my bank account, we finally reached my new home. A nice single-family house would have been lovely seeing as how I was really tired of sharing a wall with strangers, but this building looked nothing like The Hartley. The entire front facade was gleaming in neon reds. There wasn't a single window on any of the many floors, which I found a little odd and alarming. Claustrophobia already started to creep up my skin at the thought of being in close quarters with a perfect stranger who hated puppies.

But those feelings subsided as soon as we entered the building and a burst of cool air hit my face. The high-end decor certainly changed any thoughts that might have been leaning more toward wishing I didn't have to stay here. A beautifully large vintage-looking chandelier hanging above our heads in the lobby immediately demanded my attention.

"It's real gold encrusted in painite gemstones," Alcazar informed me, like I was supposed to know what painite was.

The black and white lobby furniture didn't look very comfortable to sit in, but it also didn't even look like furniture. The unique shapes scattered around the room reminded me of sculptured art. The walls were covered in a maroon velvety wallpaper and my boots clanked against the lustrous marble floor.

Alcazar watched as I admired the opulence. "I take it you've never seen anything like this before?" he asked with a sassy tone as he eyed me up and down. I would imagine that Alcazar viewed me as a grungy low life. The way I carried myself might have aided in that, what with the unkempt hair and black clothes and dark makeup and all. But he might not have been aware of the fact that my dad was a successful doctor and bestselling author, and my mother was a well-paid artist. While we didn't live in a gigantic mansion or brag about our wealth, I had been to a party or two in my past life at some of my parents' friend's houses—friends who were renowned physicians and famous artists who actually did enjoy flaunting their money.

Over the past three years, I had to endure living in filth surrounded by hobos who walked around with shit stains on their torn-up clothes. Now, it seemed I would be living in an upscale high-rise. So far, this journey to the Red Realm was turning out okay. But I didn't want to lose sight of my main mission. The Liberation Stone hung around my neck for a reason, and I needed to keep Alex and Lake at the forefront of my mind, no matter how enticingly amazing my new home seemed.

Alcazar led us to the elevator, and I hesitated before entering, flashes of my horrifying journey here still fresh on my nerves.

"Don't worry, this elevator is normal," he insisted.

I half-smiled and stepped inside, relieved to see a large panel of round numbers. When the doors closed, there was no red flickering light. Even better, there was no music about Hell softly playing over the speakers. It was also nice to note that the direction we were headed was up, not down. Although, we were already *down* in the Red Realm, so I guess that little detail didn't matter much here.

The elevator doors finally slid open on floor fifty-five and I followed Alcazar's smoky head down the hall. We stopped at the very end in front of a purple door and a big box on the floor.

"Oh good, they already sent your provisions."

"My provisions?" I asked, peeking into the half-opened box.

"Your vodka." He bent down and opened the lid enough for me to see what looked like about twenty tall, skinny bottles of Belvedere and glass skulls filled with Crystal Head vodka. My mouth watered.

"Those are all for me?"

"Lilith doesn't drink," Alcazar said. "She prefers a less sloppy kind of high. So, yeah, this is all yours."

That felt like a dig, but I chose to ignore it. I was beginning to get the feeling that Alcazar had a pretty brazen attitude, and I wasn't quite sure how to handle it yet. Part of me wanted to curse him out, because he didn't fucking know me. But the other part of me was kind of scared of what he was capable of. The man was made out of smoke!

Alcazar unlocked the door with a keycard, then turned and handed it to me. He swung the door open and we walked inside. "Lilith!" he called out.

As he moved through the apartment in search of his cousin, my eyes widened and my jaw dropped open at the view in front of me. The entire back wall along the living room was one big seamless window. It had to be over ten feet high and twenty feet wide. And as I stepped closer to get a better look at the scenery it was offering, I couldn't believe what I was seeing. It was stunning in the most eerily beautiful way. An ocean of red, surrounded by fiery cliffs went on for miles and miles, its crimson water meeting the coral-colored sky and creating an infinite edge effect. Massive dragons circled the sky high above the sea, their iridescent wings flapping slowly as their mouths breathed long streaks of fire.

"Frankie, this is Lilith," Alcazar said behind me. I turned to find him standing next to his cousin.

"Hey," Lilith greeted.

"Hi," was all I could manage to say because her beauty stole all my words.

CHAPTER TWENTY-THREE

Girl Crush

When I was in high school, before my soul was sold and I started working as a Sealer, my life was pretty cut and dry. There was nothing complicated about it. My parents were completely in love and had great jobs. I had no idea my mother and father were on the verge of divorcing before I was born. They never even hinted to it or showed any signs of ever having marital issues. No awkwardness. No residual aftereffects of the whole ordeal, that I could tell.

My sister was older and had her own life. There was a little bit of drama surrounding her separation from David, but he didn't put up a fight. He knew and completely understood why Alex was leaving him—the gambling just got too out of control and he admitted to it. As for me, I went to school, maintained good grades, danced, hung out with my equally popular girlfriends, and spent the rest of my free time making out with my boyfriend, Jacob. And in this pretty normal teenage life, my appearance was also pretty simple. When I wasn't in my cheerleading or dancing attire, I was wearing my school uniform—plaid skirt no higher than just above the knee and a starched button-down oxford shirt with our school logo sewn onto the breast pocket. Whenever I was out with my friends at the mall or with Jacob on a date, my go-to outfits consisted of trendy overalls and brightly colored skirts and crop tops and ribbons tied into my caramel-colored hair.

My taste was girl-next-door back then, completely different than what I preferred now in my Sealer days. Raven hair. Black eyeliner and eye shadow that created a constant shadow around my eyeballs and made my pupils more of a gray than their natural blue color. My black clothes matched my chipped black fingernails. I was aware of how melodramatic it made me look, but I didn't give a shit. The circumstances that befell my past brought the darkness to the surface, and my current situation only fueled it, forcing it to leak out of my pores.

But Lilith... Lilith was an entirely different story.

Her darkness was clearly ingrained into her, as if she was born with it. She was mysterious and sexy. Devious-looking. And she carried it as if she'd been all of those things for hundreds of years. The woman standing before me was the epitome of a *woman*. Her shiny, black hair was parted on top her head, half tucked behind her ear, the other half draping the side of her face, its thick, perfect curls partially hiding her right eye and cheek. The beautiful mane pooled right at the top of her large breasts, which were practically spilling over her blouse. An ebony-colored jewel pendant hung off a gold chain around her neck and rested just on top her cleavage, nearly buried in its crevice. Her leopard-print spaghetti-strap top revealed her colorful arm tattoos, which covered both her arms in a kind of sticker sleeve pattern. The skin-tight blouse led to a skin-tight pencil skirt, which accentuated her voluptuous curves and hugged her waist as if it were a second skin.

My gaze flowed from her red pointy-toed heels back up to her pouty, crimson lips and mystifying eyes, colors that were even more striking against her porcelain skin. I was staring at a real-life pinup girl. The only difference between her and one of those mesmerizing models from the 1940s was the fact that Lilith had horns. Two of them. On her forehead, each one above her eyes. They were very small, in a shade similar to red wine, and the texture kind of reminded me of an elephant's trunk. Each horn curved out of her flesh and up, twisting into a kind of curlicue. Honestly, it only seemed to add on to the sexiness.

Lilith sat down on the couch, spreading her arms across the back and crossing her legs, one knee over the other. "I've never had a human roommate before," she said, voice thick and sultry.

"She's a Sealer," Alcazar said tartly, eyeing me up and down again. What the fuck was his problem?

Lilith raised her eyebrows at me, then turned her attention to Alcazar. "We still on for tonight?"

"Um...yeah! I've got to get back to the office to finish up some things. Text me when you're ready. Frankie, you should get some sleep. You've got an early day at your new job tomorrow." Alcazar wrote something down on his clipboard before turning on his heel to exit the apartment, his stride fierce with a bit of a hip sway.

I took the handle of my suitcase. "So, where is my room?"

"You're fucking him, aren't you?"

"Excuse me?" I sputtered. "Alcazar?" I shook my head. "No, I-I—"

"Dominic. You're fucking Dominic. That has to be the reason why he set you up in The Croft."

"The Croft?"

Lilith rolled her eyes. "This building. It's called The Croft."

"I'm not fucking him." After I said this, my eyes immediately wandered away from hers. I didn't want her to somehow read my thoughts, which were tainted with images of Dominic and me rolling around naked on his desk. Legs intertwined. His fingers inside of me. Our tongues licking and tasting one another.

I cleared my throat.

Lilith narrowed her yellow eyes, the heavy wing of noir eyeliner making her look like a cat. "Sit," she demanded.

"I think I'd rather go unpack."

"Sit down," she said again, this time a little more aggressively. I might have cursed her out, but I didn't have nearly enough vodka in me, and judging by the fact that her horns were now glowing as if little lightbulbs had suddenly switched on inside of them, I was afraid of what she might do to me if I didn't obey her.

I exhaled and took my seat on a purple ottoman, then reached inside my suitcase and pulled out my bottle of liquor. At this point, I really didn't care what Lilith thought about it. I needed it. *A lot* of it.

She fiddled with her gold bracelets for a beat before cocking her head at me and smiling seductively. "You're really hot. I can see why Dominic wants to have sex with you."

"We are not having sex," I retorted.

"Fine. But Dominic doesn't put just anyone in this building. You have to earn your spot here. And human Sealers aren't necessarily considered hot commodity in this business. So how did you do it?"

Honestly, I had no idea how I did it. This was just where Alcazar brought me. But judging by Lilith's disapproving expression, I clearly didn't belong here.

I wrapped my lips around the head of the bottle and took a big swig, slightly coughing from the briny tang. After wiping my mouth with the back of my hand, I decided to match her brash attitude instead of doing what I really wanted, which was to contact Dominic myself to ask why he sent me to live here. "And what did *you* do to get a spot here? Fuck Centaurus?" I said stupidly.

Lilith's horns brightened. "I worked my ass off to live here. There are tons of other Centaureans who have put in just as much time and effort and blood and body parts and still can't get a spot in The Croft. And yet, here you are."

"You don't know anything about me. I've been working for Centaurus for three years."

"I've been working for Centaurus for three *hundred* years."

I was over this cockfight. "What's so good about The Croft, anyway?"

"The view, for one," Lilith responded, gesturing toward the window wall. "And second, you really have no idea what this place is, do you? You surface dwellers think just because we are employees, we don't get treated like the souls who are banished to the Red Realm? More than half of the Centaurean population live in squalor. They work endlessly, with barely any time off. They are issued rations for everything. The Croft is the only place in the City of Centaurus that has air conditioning, clean water, and showers that don't require having to deposit money in order to use them. There are hundreds of Centaureans who have waited hundreds of years to be in your shoes right now."

Shamefully, I glanced down at my bottle of booze. The past three years had been my own personal torture. Having to issue the Seal of the Red Realm to people who sold their souls and locking their fate into eternal damnation made me feel dirty and guilty and shitty on every kind of level. I hated having to do it. But I never really thought about what other employees had to do, or whether or not they felt tortured about having to do it. My co-workers on Earth did their jobs with smiles on their faces. Could it have been fake smiles? Sure. But it would be hard to fake it. This job wasn't like waiting tables at some seedy diner in the middle of nowhere, when you'd fake giving a shit about what your customers wanted to eat until your shift was over. Being an ASR stayed with you long after your shift was over. Long into every minute of every day, regardless of where you were, what you were doing, who you were with. It became a lifestyle. Something that grew inside of you like a cancer, poking and prodding its way into your every nerve.

Lilith continued her lecture. "And that box of alcohol out there, that's child's play." Her long and pointy manicured fingernails dove into her blouse and pulled out a small, clear baggy out of her bosom. She held it up in front of her face, revealing some kind of green, glittery powder. "This is the shit you should be asking for."

"I don't do hard drugs." I sniffed, wrinkling my nose to show that I wasn't interested in whatever that substance was. Lilith opened the baggy and dipped her pinky nail inside, scooping some of the stuff that kind of resembled cake-decorating sugar. She stuck her nail into her mouth and sucked, her eyes simultaneously rolling back. After it seemed like she'd had her fill, she licked her lips, then ran her tongue over her top teeth. This move aroused something inside of me, and I stood up when I realized that Lilith was turning me on.

"Where's my room?" I asked sternly.

Lilith pressed her red lips together, and then pointed. "Second door on the right down the hall."

I couldn't get out of that living room fast enough.

The rest of the apartment resembled many other high-end places I'd been to over the years. Homes of clients who were selling their souls to become more rich or more famous or whatever ridiculous selfish reason to sell their souls for. Black and white and red furniture pieces, track lighting, and abstract paintings were just a few of the plush touches that showcased the difference between The Croft and The Hartley, which had brown rickety, half-broken furniture, old yellow lighting that made everyone look jaundice, and deep cracks in the wall—if that was what you'd consider some sort of art.

I entered my room and was thrilled to see that the window wall carried over. Not that I necessarily enjoyed watching scary dragons fly through a fiery sky above an ocean full of blood, but having a view of something definitely relieved that feeling of claustrophobia I thought I'd have to deal with. My bed looked like it was king-sized, and I had my own bathroom, which was a plus. It looked like it might have taken Lilith hours to get ready in the morning.

After setting my suitcase on the bed and guzzling down a little more liquor, I found my phone. My heart dropped when I noticed I had no bars. There were no messages, no missed calls, and absolutely no service. How the hell was I supposed to keep in touch with Alex and Lake while I was down here?

Lilith was standing by the kitchen island, surrounded by needles and threads and fruits like oranges and bananas, when I barged in almost out of breath and held my phone out. "Do you know why my phone isn't working?"

"You're in the Red Realm," she deadpanned, refusing to take her eyes away from the needle and banana in her hands. She was sewing the fruit. "Did you expect that your phone would work here?"

"Well...yeah."

She threaded the needle through the peel and raised her arm up into the air, pulling the length of the black string up with it, then came back down and carefully weaved the needle through again like some kind of surgeon. "I've never been to Earth, but I'm told that we have pretty much the same shit you all have, with the exception of a few things. And one of those things is the Earthling cellphone service. We have our own down here. FireLink."

"So how do I get that?"

"You'll have to register for one at work tomorrow. They will tell you all about it."

The tension in my body relaxed just a smidge, but it was only because I got an answer to my question. I was still concerned about how I would be able to contact my sister and Lake. This just meant that I would have to try to get permission to visit Alex sooner rather than later.

Still concentrating on threading the banana peel, Lilith asked in a low voice, "Is there a reason why you need your phone so badly?"

"Oh...I was just curious," I said, then smiled as innocently as I could. She raised her eyebrows and bit her bottom lip. "What are you doing, anyway?" I asked, attempting to change the subject.

"Practicing my suturing technique," she said in a near whisper.

"Are you a doctor?"

Lilith giggled. "We don't have doctors here. But I've heard about them. They help the sick. I guess you can say I do the same. After all, aren't the sick souls the ones exiled to the Red Realm?"

"How do you help them?" I asked, dreading how curious I was being.

"I guess you can say it's a kind of behavioral therapy. I like to use physical reinforcement. For example, a soul that's banished to the Red Realm for being a compulsive liar should probably have their mouths sewn shut."

I ran my fingers through my hair and shifted on my feet uncomfortably because on Earth that might have been some kind of passing comment that someone would say out of anger or something. No one would ever actually sew a person's mouth shut. But this was the Red Realm, so chances were that it probably really happened.

Lilith must have sensed my discomfort because she finally looked up and glared at me as if I were an idiot. "I do more than sew mouths shut. I'm an Afflictionist. I do whatever the fuck I want to do. As long as it promotes torture and pain."

No words would come to mind, and we stared at each other for another moment before I could finally come up with some kind of excuse to the leave the room. "Okay, well I'm going to wash up and get some sleep." But as soon as I turned toward my bedroom, her voice purred behind me.

"You should come out with us. It would be fun."

I didn't turn around. "Yeah, I'll think about it," I called out over my shoulder before entering my room. My heart raced inside my chest. I needed more alcohol.

My roommate was an Afflictionist? A no-shit Afflictionist? Someone whose sole purpose was to torment souls. Maybe some of those souls deserved it. But I knew for a fact that at least fifteen percent of those souls might have been persuaded into signing their eternity away. And how many of those were souls that I've actually sealed myself? I might have sent them here. Sent them to Lilith to get their mouths sewn shut.

I brought my hand up to my chest, all of a sudden feeling the need to touch The Liberation Stone. I gently picked it up out of my shirt and observed it. The gold flecks embedded into the pink rock sparkled, and when I squeezed it, warmth emitted into my palm. It was hard to believe that this thing was going to destroy an entire portal that led into another dimension. That somehow, there were elders living inside of it. And for some reason, they chose me to do it. It didn't make any sense. I wasn't an angel. Apparently, I had wings, but there had to be another explanation for that.

The idea of just saving my sister and choosing to live in the Red Realm seemed a little crazy at first, I'd have to admit. But if this place, The Croft, was going to be my home, then it didn't seem too crazy. According to Lilith, it was the best place to be. And I could learn to live with an Afflictionist. After all, I wasn't going to be one myself. My job was going to be fulfilling in a positive way. Making sure people got what they sold their souls for sounded a billion times better than sealing someone. The idea of it already lifted at least a months' worth of guilt for what I'd done so far in this career.

There had to be a way around the whole sacrificing deal. I trusted Lake. I trusted that he would find a way. For now, I just needed to keep my head low and do my job. Keep track of the time and ask Dominic if I can go back to visit Alex soon.

I dropped the chain back down into my T-shirt, reached over for my bottle of booze, and poured some into my mouth as I gazed at the infernal view of my new home out of the floor-to-ceiling window.

About three hours passed—I only assumed because the fucking time was all different here—when there was a knock at my door.

"Come in," I slurred. I was sprawled out on the bed, one Crystal Head bottle down from the provisions Alcazar had gotten for me. Lilith opened my door, her body-hugging sequin dress immediately catching my eye. The shiny disks reflected the orange-red glow from outside my window and made her look like she was covered in embers.

"You ready to go party?"

"Maybe I shouldn't go. It's already late and I have to be up in a few hours," I sputtered, sitting up and hiccupping in between.

"Oh, please." Lilith stepped in and snatched the bottle of Grey Goose I had just popped open out of my limp hands. "This shit is trashy. Here, take a taste of this and it'll straighten you up." She threw the baggy filled with emerald, glittery powder on my lap.

"I told you...I don't do drugs."

"Just do it," she ordered. "I promise you this isn't that filthy bullshit you tellurians get addicted to."

I glanced down at the baggy, then back up at Lilith, who was now spinning in circles. There were three Liliths staring at me—six horns and three pairs of seductive, bedroom eyes—waiting for me to dip my finger into this tiny bag and suck the contents into my mouth. It was hard for me to keep my head still because it seemed to be moving in orbit with Lilith. I loved drinking, but I hated being this drunk. It made me feel stupid.

Lilith did this drug earlier and it didn't look like she felt stupid about it. Maybe I should just give it a try. Lake wasn't here to judge me or give me disappointing glares. And Alex was nowhere near to make me question what I was doing or make me feel guilty for enjoying the occasional cocktail. If I did it this one time, they would never even know.

My eyelids were heavy, but I managed to keep them open while I fumbled with the baggy. When the drug was finally accessible, I licked my index finger and stuck it inside, wiggling it around the powder while the granules adhered to my skin. Then, without even thinking twice about it, I brought my finger to my mouth and sucked. Almost instantly, my impaired brain came back to life. Everything came back into perspective perfectly, as if I was never even intoxicated in the first place. My skin flushed with heat before it gradually cooled off, and everything around me just kind of went into slow motion. The muscles in my face loosened and my entire body tingled with delightfully pleasant pinpricks. I inhaled deeply, closed my eyes, and fell back into the bed, into a state of euphoric bliss.

CHAPTER TWENTY-FOUR

My Personal Drug Dealer

Whoever said drugs were bad clearly never had demon dust. According to Lilith, demon dust was the ground-up bits of fallen former kings and queens. Initially, I thought the kings and queens of the Red Realm could never die. However, on very rare occasions—like every thousand years or so—a king or queen might be eradicated by a rival. Apparently, not all kings and queens got along. Each region was its own, and sometimes there could be bad blood. I asked Lilith what could cause entire regions to fight each other, but she said there was no way of telling. It could be for a number of reasons and that anything could piss off a king and queen.

Whatever the case might have been, I was truly grateful that a king and queen died every now and then because this shit was a million times better than liquor. Alcohol always took so much work. If you were a functioning drunk like me, that meant that you'd have to consume quite a bit of it in order to feel any inebriation. And it took a while to get there. One thing drinking had going for it was that once the liquor started to take effect, the outcome was always the same: floaty, lightheadedness with a warm and cozy vibration coursing all throughout the body. But it came with a price: loss of coordination, clouded judgment, and annoying hangovers that required even more liquor to correct.

Demon dust had none of those repercussions. When that sweet green powder collided with my taste buds, it was instant. An instant connection with every molecule in my body. Instant gratifying sensation that left me alert, awake, and aware, but chill, calm, and collected at the same time. The reason for its potent effect was because it was composed of strong, powerful entities, and the remnants of their almighty nature induced a pretty fucking amazing high. And since the death of a king and queen happened so rarely, demon dust was in extremely high demand. Everyone wanted it, but not just anyone could get it. Only the privileged tenants who lived in The Croft.

The next couple of days—or it could have been a couple more since I still wasn't used to the no-time situation—had surprisingly gone by smoothly for being a newcomer to the Red Realm. And a human one at that. I learned that not every creature on this plane really cared for our species. There were some horrifying glares by a few Cyclopes and moans and groans in a language I didn't understand by some demonic gargoyles as I walked past, but nothing that truly frightened me. The demon dust Lilith had provided me with might have aided in my confidence and fearlessness. I now had my very own baggy and a taste an hour really did the trick.

I had begun a routine of waking up to start my day—again, not sure when was morning and when was night—and using my new expensive ride to get me to and from work, which was about one blood river and two enormous flaming goblin head statues away from The Croft. Alcazar gifted me with a sporty car that resembled some of the ones we had on Earth, but it had a different name. As a matter of fact, everything in the Red Realm was strangely different, but the same. The contrast was kind of like night and day, but the similarity was equal to Chinese knockoffs. They looked the same...but were they? It was like this whole dimension was one big ripped-off flea market trying to sell counterfeit goods.

For example, our cellphones. On Earth, I couldn't afford the most expensive phone with a sleek design and ridiculously high-powered camera. Mine was pretty basic. As long as I had unlimited Internet data and text message capability, I was happy. But the FireLink cellphones might as well have been the first generation of flip phones. They were clunky and the reception was horrible and there was no camera. Even seasoned residents of the single luxurious apartment building in the Red Realm didn't have anything better. It was either this or nothing at all.

Thankfully, I didn't have to take pictures. Taking selfies was never really something I did pre-ASR days and we were actually prohibited from snapping any kind of photos in the City of Centaurus. It was a law. Also, my phone was only used to communicate with Lilith and Alcazar. That could change over time if I made friends, but judging by the interaction between me and my co-workers, that might not ever happen. While there were a handful of CAs who were also human, they were only interested in doing their jobs. Just like every other ghoul and monster and human I'd come in contact with. Every being in my department only cared about one thing: working. There was no gossip, no shit-talking. No lunchroom to convene and ask about the weather or whatever bullshit sports team won the finals the night before. It was simply a bunch of ghouls and monsters and other humans working at their desks, quietly minding their own business. It was simply perfect.

Speaking of my department, the Contract Auditors shared an office with recruitment and other administrative services, like what Alcazar did. He was an ambassador for the City of Centaurus and part of the welcoming committee. My job as a CA was easy. All I had to do was look through a shimmering glass hole in the wall and spy on people who had sold their souls to make sure they were receiving their end of the deal. The mirror thing was pretty magical...and snazzy. I'd say the name of the client out loud from my list and a slightly pixelated image of the person would appear. I'd study them, decide whether or not they were getting 'paid,' then move on to the next client. If they weren't receiving their compensation for giving up their souls, I was to make a note of it and place that note into a bin. My supervisor would then sort through those names and make certain that the humans began getting what they were owed. And unlike my last job, I was happy to report that there was no glitchy weirdness going on.

It had only been a few days, I think, but so far it was a million times better than having to actually seal someone. I didn't have to speak to the clients directly, and I didn't have to feel like an asshole for doing my job. If you asked me, the Red Realm was shaping up to be not as bad as I'd thought.

I still wondered why Dominic stuck me in The Croft, and it was clear that everyone else wondered the same thing. Granted, I hadn't met even half of its residents—The Croft had over one hundred floors— but the few that I had met did not even try to hide their opinion of me. It was written all over their faces. And my attempt at trying to find out why I was living in air-conditioned extravagance in the sky while the majority of Centaureans lived in soot and overpopulated living quarters that only had one bathroom to every fifty beings had failed. Every time I called Dominic's office, Raven would inform me that he was either out or too busy to take my call. Fucking men. Of course he'd tease me, make me believe he wanted me just to get inside my pants, then turn around and ignore me. It was the first time any guy had ever done that to me. I'd heard stories from my girlfriends in high school before. But usually those stories involved the girls being used for sex, and Dominic didn't even get off.

Jacob would have never done anything like that to me.

My hope was that when I called Dominic's office, my sister might answer the phone since she was now supposed to be one of his secretaries, but I guess she wasn't promoted to that particular job duty just yet. I also didn't forget that I had to ask permission to go back to visit Alex, which was still my number-one priority.

Well, aside from just getting acquainted with my new life, I had to be on everyone's good side before I could ask for something like that.

The topic of my winning-the-dream-home lottery had been something Lilith and Alcazar couldn't stop debating over the past couple of nights I accompanied them to the nightclub called Pandemonium on the first floor of The Croft. And tonight was no different.

"All I'm saying is there has to be some legitimate reason why Dominic would have placed her in The

Croft," Lilith said before licking the demon dust off her manicured pinky nail. Her eyes rolled and she did that fascinating tongue-curling-over-her-teeth thing that made me question my sexuality. Alcazar sat close to her in the purple velvety booth, his smoky vapors wafting off his head as if it were dancing to the heavy bass of music pounding out of the speakers above us. What was it about supernatural beings and their love for EDM?

"Maybe they were having sex," Alcazar said to Lilith.

"For the millionth time, we did not fuck!" I shouted from across the table as I focused on opening my own baggy of demon dust. It was my turn to have a taste.

"But you wish you did," Lilith blurted.

"Of course! Who wouldn't want to have sex with Dominic?" Alcazar chimed in. "He's hotter than the lava rainstorms during eruption season." His comment wasn't at all surprising, considering Alcazar preferred other creatures of the male variety.

I rolled my eyes out of irritation, tired of being reminded of the fact that Dominic ghosted me. "Whatever. I would like to think that I earned my spot at The Croft. Either way, I'm here and I'm not going anywhere," I said, glancing down at my chest and fighting the urge to rub The Liberation Stone underneath my shirt. Something that I had been doing every day like it was some kind of magic lamp.

The idea that Lake would float out of a rock like a genie was preposterous, but rubbing it somehow made me feel less homesick. I wondered what he was doing and whether or not he had figured out this whole sacrificing-myself-to-blow-up-the-portal-to-The-Red-Realm thing. If it was bad down here, I might have been in a hurry to get answers, but there was no rush. Especially if it meant that I was expected to kill myself. And especially now that I had this green powdery dust that just made the time here so much more...interestingly bearable. Besides, I trusted that he and Reggie were keeping a watchful eye on my sister.

The Liberation Stone hadn't been seen by anyone yet. Since the Great Elders inside of it refused to let me take it off, I made sure to keep it tucked inside my shirt. Out of anyone's view. Lake mentioned that no one in the Red Realm knew about the stone, or should know about the stone, and I wasn't going to be the one who screwed that up.

The dance floor was filling up, and I watched as the monsters and supernatural Centaureans moved to the music. As wonderfully unattached but emotionally in-tuned as demon dust made me feel, it was still kind of difficult to accept the fact that I was surrounded by evil beings. To a normal, every-day human on Earth, what I saw on a regular basis now might have been the stuff of nightmares. And it turned out that some of those paintings in Dominic's office were pretty accurate. There were lizard-looking freaks with scaly skin and sharp teeth and giant beasts made out of molten rock walking around like it was completely ordinary.

Red and violet strobe lights cast an ominous haze all over everything. It was a stark contrast to what the angel nightclub on Earth looked like, which was bright and full of sparkly silver specks of light reflecting off everyone's perfect, flawless skin. In the Red Realm, there was no such thing as flawless. There was something out of place on everything.

"Oh, hey. I forgot to give you this," Lilith said as she reached inside her bosom and pulled out a baggy filled with green dust. She slid it across the table toward me.

"How much do I owe you?"

"Don't worry about it. It's on me," she insisted.

I eyed her curiously. This wasn't the first time Lilith refused to let me pay for my drugs. As a matter of fact, I haven't had to pay for it since I got here. It was a bit troubling. On Earth, there was no way a dealer would give away drugs without some kind of payment, whether it be monetary or not. And I wondered when I was going to have to pay up. But as I glared at the small packet of demon dust in the palm of my hand, my heart racing over the idea of its particles meeting *my* particles inside my mouth and sending jolts of blissfully electric vibrations to my brain, having to pay a tab one day didn't matter. There was a box full of very good vodka upstairs in my bedroom that might be able to do the same if I drank enough of it, but that was peasant shit compared to this.

"Thanks," I said, stuffing the baggy into the pocket of my leather jacket to accompany the other one that was nearly empty. I must admit, Lilith knew exactly when to replenish my druggie needs. I took a peek at my FireLink phone for the time but remembered there was no time. Mentally noting that I'd have to stop that habit, I decided it was time for sleep. "I'm going upstairs to bed."

"Don't be a fucking downer, Frankie," Lilith snapped.

"I'm tired," I lied. Really, I just wanted to eat some more demon dust and lie in bed to enjoy the high in peace.

"Just stay until the seventh sun comes up."

"You know you want to," Alcazar added.

There was no nighttime in the City of Centaurus, but seven suns rose and set throughout the day, which was one of the reasons for the constant red-orange glow and sweltering weather. And when all seven suns were high in the sky, the heat emitting off each one was enough for a regular human to combust internally. Thankfully, I wasn't a regular human. It was still hot, but not enough to kill me.

The seventh sun wasn't due to come up for what I would have equated as another hour, I think, and as much as I would rather be alone at the moment, appeasing Lilith and Alcazar seemed to be a better plan. "Fine, I'll stay," I said, giving in to them. After all, Lilith did provide me with demon dust. And Alcazar's gray, vaporous body was fun to look at on the stuff.

I pulled out the almost-empty baggy and finished it off, leaning my head back against the cushion of the booth and allowing the robotic sounds of EDM pump through me.

CHAPTER TWENTY-FIVE

BIRTH

We are lying in Jacob's bed, the soft duvet wrapped around my naked body. Jacob is in his boxers and he's lying on his back, staring up at the ceiling, ankles crossed. I'm watching him, just like I always find myself doing whenever he's shirtless. He has such a nice body, and while my girlfriends always talk about checking out a guy's butt, I appreciate the upper portion—defined pecs, washboard abs, muscular back. Jacob's got all that going on.

The room smells like jasmine, a sweet and rich fragrant note that Jacob's mom favors. His parents are out of town, which means we are taking advantage of their ultra-comfy king-sized bed. I don't even care that his parents probably had sex in the same spot this morning. All that matters is that Jacob and I are together.

"You know what we are?" he asks, his eyes still trained on the ceiling, but I know he's directing his question at me. His hand blindly wanders to my hip and squeezes.

"What are we?" I give in to what feels like a game.

"A circle."

"A circle?"

"Yeah. Look," he says, then reaches over to the nightstand to grab a pen and pad. He places it on his lap and starts to draw a semicircle. "This is you," he informs me as he points to one end. Then he points the tip of the pen to the other end. "This is me." He draws a crescent to connect the ends, forming a full circle. "This is us together."

Wow. This has to be one of the corniest things he's done yet. I'm quiet because I'm trying to swallow the laugh that's fighting to escape my throat. But I fail and snort loudly instead. Jacob whips his head at me. "What? It's true! You complete me."

"Did you watch that Jimmy Maguire movie again? You need to stop watching your mom's Rom-Coms. What would your teammates think about that?" I tease.

Jacob turns on his side to finally meet my eyes. He smiles and moves my hair behind my shoulder. "First of all, it's Jerry Maguire. Second, it's about sports. And third, I like those movies. They remind me of us."

"You're such a girl," I sing.

"Am not! You're a girl!" He reaches his hands out and I know right where they are going.

"No!" I beg and start to giggle even before his fingers poke at my sides and tickle my ribs. Jacob gets up and straddles my body. He buries his face into my neck and playfully swats my arms away as I try to guard myself from him. But he wins and makes me laugh so hard I nearly pee on myself. We giggle and play for a few more minutes until happy tears are forced out of our eyes. Then, the laughing turns into kissing and the kissing turns into touching and...

"Frankie!"

I snapped out of my daydream and back into reality, which was Alcazar standing in front of me in a cobalt, slim-fit suit.

"What did you say?" I asked groggily. The demon dust effects were wearing off and that mixed with the Jacob nostalgia was making everything foggy. I didn't even remember coming into the living room and sitting on the couch.

"Lilith wants you to meet her at work," he said.

"Why?"

"Not sure. Something about Dominic and paperwork. I think you have to finish signing some contracts to be her roommate. She has everything you need."

"Why don't you have it?" I queried curiously, wondering why a participant of the welcoming committee wouldn't have those documents for me.

Alcazar rolled his smoky eyes. "Not my problem. I have other things to do. Later." He turned on his designer shoes' heels and waltzed out of the apartment door, leaving behind a trail of vapors from his head when he slammed it shut. This wasn't good. Lilith was an Afflictionist and worked two buildings away from mine in the torment department. I had yet to go anywhere near that place, and I really had no fucking desire to.

So far, my time here had been decent. With the exception of having to get used to living in close proximity to terrifying monsters and demons, the Red Realm actually seemed like a better place to live than Earth. I didn't have my sister, but I did have a rewarding job, a new home in a lavish apartment, a semi-friendly and super sexy roommate, and a constant flow of possibly the best drug I would ever have. There was no hiding it, either. I was free to eat as much demon dust as I wanted, without Alex hoping that I didn't turn into a crackhead.

But over the past few days, I hadn't once asked Lilith about her job and what it was like. I didn't want to know. The idea of sealing someone's soul into an eternity of pain and torture...tortured and caused *me* pain. Guilt deepened in my own soul with every Seal, with every sizzle of the client's skin against my blazing hot rod. It wasn't my choice. It wasn't my choice to live in the Red Realm either, but it was necessary in order to save Alex. And if I could, I was going to steer clear from having to actually *see* the souls that I have sealed.

However, now I was being summoned to the one place I had been avoiding and dreading to go anywhere near. Why couldn't Lilith just bring the damn paperwork back to The Croft and have me sign it here?

I frantically reached inside my leather jacket in search of the little plastic baggy. Demon dust would definitely take the edge off before I stepped foot into that place.

The large neon sign above the entrance blinked bright red words that read MERCY. I entered the building, immediately freaked out and taken aback by what I saw. A cluster of clowns with big, jubilant smiles painted across their faces giggled as they blew up balloon animals. Across the room, there was a sign that said PET ME with an arrow pointing down at a kennel full of tiny kittens meowing sweetly. The sugary aroma of freshly baked chocolate chip cookies forced my gaze to the source, which was to a woman wearing a pink chef toque pulling a tray of perfectly browned and round desserts out of an oven. In another corner, what I assumed to be a mother and her child were playing peek-a-boo, the baby's genuinely infectious laugh filling my ears. The room was bestrewn with confetti and colorful streamers, and piñatas hung from the ceiling. Taylor Swift's peppy singing voice played over speakers that reverberated off the walls.

Behind all of the weird shit happening, I spotted a door. There was no way to tell where this door would lead me, but anything had to be better than this creepy-ass freak show. No one seemed to even notice me as I bravely stalked past them. However, the strangeness only continued when I entered another room. More clowns and kittens and babies were scattered about, along with a buffet table filled with assorted candies, a comedian telling jokes on a stage, and the smell of freshly cut grass. What the fuck was happening?

Thankfully, Lilith's perfectly pale skin and curvaceous body appeared through a different door at the back of the room, and I hurried over to her.

"Follow me," she instructed, and I trailed close behind her as she went back to where she came from. She brought me to a hallway that looked like it went on for miles and miles, aligned with doors all the way as far as my eye could see.

"What was all that about?" I asked, giving Lilith an exasperated sigh. As bizarre as that was, just that little bit of time in those two rooms started to conjure up some kind of happiness from deep down in my stomach, which made me feel uncomfortable. It could have possibly been because I hadn't seen things like that—pure and innocent and normal—since before becoming an ASR.

Lilith's stilettos clanked against the marble floor of the hallway, her black curls bouncing with every step. I wasn't looking, but I imagined her hips swaying as she moved, all provocatively. If I was a lesbian, I might have tried to sleep with Lilith. Honestly, I didn't even think I had to be into girls to do it.

"It's a front," she finally answered. "King Centaurus and Queen Hysteria enjoy mind games."

"How so?"

"When a person dies and their energy transitions into soul form, they tend to become disoriented for a while. The king and queen like to play on this. Make them feel like they are someplace good instead of evil for a little while. It's actually pretty fun when they realize this is the Red Realm and they are about to be tortured for all eternity."

"So the souls really believe they are in the White Realm because they see clowns and kittens?" I ask skeptically, disbelieving that the souls failed to understand where they were going when they died. The journey to the gates was horrible, and I was pretty sure they'd be able to tell by the fiery sky and bloody rivers that they were in the underworld.

Lilith stopped and cocked her head, knitting her brows together and squinting at me as if thinking on something. "Careful what you say around here. The king and queen don't like to talk about the other realm." She licked her plump lips. "Anyway, how did those two rooms make you feel?" she asked.

I thought about it for a second, choosing not to answer her and to ignore the subtle warning she'd just handed me. I also didn't want to admit that all those things back there made me want to smile and snicker like a giddy little girl. Instead, I changed the subject when I noticed a portrait of Dominic's face hanging on the wall we'd just passed.

"Was that Dominic?" I asked.

"Yup. There are pictures of him all over this building. He was the best Afflictionist to have ever worked here in the past thousands of years."

I bit my lip, guilt-stricken by the fact that I wanted to sleep with an expert torturer. I cleared my throat in hopes of forgetting the way Dominic's bulge felt against my jeans when he rubbed himself against my sex. "Where do these all go?" I asked, pointing at each labeled metal door we walked past.

"Each door leads to a pain chamber. A soul's placement is determined by the circumstances surrounding their judgment," she explained.

"You mean, why they were sentenced to the Red Realm in the first place?"

"Yes. Most of the time. But sometimes it's just a matter of what the Afflictionists feel like doing that day." Lilith gestured to the door beside us labeled EXTRACTION. She dug into the cleavage of her breast and retrieved a keycard, then swiped it through a slot near the door. A tiny green light appeared, and the entire metal door shimmered into glass, its transparency allowing us to see what was on the other side. My eyes widened and my heart began to race when I realized what I was looking at.

A tall creature with long, hairy arms, wearing nothing but a lacy ballerina tutu covered in splotches of red, towered over a soul—a man—sitting in a chair. The monster's legs were skinny and bent backwards, his knees inverted. Its feet looked like they belonged to a Sasquatch and a single horn protruded out of its head, the spiked end menacingly pointing upward as if it were ready to impale something. Its face was shrouded in a red leathery mask, only its glowing yellow eyes visible. And if I wasn't mistaken, it looked as though the creature was wearing purple costume wings.

It hovered over the man whose hands were tied behind the chair. The monster's claws were pulling the man's hair with one hand and gripping onto some sort of clamp object in the other. Blood dripped from the man's mouth all over his naked body.

"Can they see us? What is he doing?" Right when I asked Lilith the question, the creature forced the clamp past the man's lips and jammed it into his mouth. The man hollered and cried out in gargled agony as his tooth was yanked out of his gums. I cringed, feeling the man's tormented pain from my toes to my head.

"They can't see us," Lilith said, undisturbed by what was happening in front of us. "And that soul was sentenced to the Red Realm because he committed crimes of embezzlement."

I shot her a look. "He's getting his teeth pulled for stealing?"

Lilith rolled her eyes. "He stole a lot. So he gets his teeth stolen from him. And look! Tanglefang dressed like a tooth fairy today. He's so much fun," she said and grinned admiringly at the monster.

"What happens when Tanglefang runs out of teeth to pull?"

"It starts over. His teeth just come back and Tanglefang pulls again," she explained.

My own teeth and gums started to throb. "For how long?" Surely, this couldn't happen for all eternity. Didn't the monster have anything else to do?

"For however long the soul is sentenced to that particular type of torture. Once that's done, the soul goes to work doing various things like construction or being servants to the king and queen." She swiped her card again and the glass shimmered back to a silvery metal door, blocking our view of Tanglefang and the man.

We moved down the hall to the next door labeled STONING. Lilith swiped her card and the metal did a magical sparkle into glass again before revealing another man—this one a lot older-looking than the last. His nude body was suspended in the air, arms and legs spread apart by chains. Black and blue welts covered every inch of his skin, some of them bloody divots. On the far end of the room, a shadowy figure stood next to a large barrel filled with what looked like rocks. It picked one up and threw the rock with a high, supernatural velocity straight at the man's face. The rock slammed into him, smashing his eye and splitting his nose in half.

"Oh! Bullseye! Way to go, Smokevein!" Lilith cheered. The shadow picked up another rock, threw it again and crushed the man's forehead, leaving behind a gash deep enough to expose the man's brain. Blood immediately rushed out as if a water pipe had suddenly burst. "Wow! Two in a row! She's got a really good arm."

"What did he do?"

"Racist." Lilith swiped her card and the window closed. I finally exhaled the breath I had been holding and silently hoped she wouldn't swipe her card at the next door labeled INSANGUINATION. Thankfully, we bypassed it when she began to walk down the hallway again. "You get the point. There are millions of rooms and every single one is different."

How many fucking ways could someone possibly be tortured? I felt sick to my stomach. Although these souls might have deserved to spend time in the pain chambers, how many of them didn't? How many of these souls might have been placed here for simply selling their souls and not doing something horrible? How many of them were here because *I* sealed them?

We continued to walk side by side for about a minute or so before Lilith stopped at another door.

This one had a sign that read BIRTH, and I swallowed hard. Birth didn't sound all that bad, but in the Red Realm, it could be something downright terrifying.

She swiped her keycard and the metal turned to glass. A naked and blindfolded pregnant woman appeared on an examining table. Her body was strapped down and her legs were spread wide open, her feet chained to stirrups. She was trying her best to thrash and get free, but the restraints were limiting her movements. All it seemed she could do was scream in terror. Surprisingly, a very normal, human-looking man dressed in surgical attire—a green gown, surgical mask, and cap—sat on a stool at her feet. It became apparent to me what was happening. The surgeon's hands were elbow-deep inside of the woman's womb. Red liquid spilled out of her as if he were dipping his hands into a bucket full of blood, causing it to overflow. I could see the outlines of his fingers moving through her pregnant belly, almost like he was reorganizing her organs.

I averted my eyes, peering down at my boots instead.

"Don't tell me you can't handle this," Lilith commented. "Bladesnare is an expert obstetrician and surgeon. It's like an art."

I gaped at Lilith. "Is he...is he aborting a baby?" I asked, barely able to choke the words out.

"Hell no! Bladesnare is doing something much more special. He's *delivering* a baby. And how timely! You're here to witness the birth of your niece."

"My what?" I glanced back over at the woman. It was hard to tell what she looked like because I couldn't directly see her face and half her head was concealed by a piece of white cloth. But her hair was familiar. Her body too. And her screams...they did sound like... like it could have been...

My body crashed into the glass door like a magnet and my eyes darted to the woman's ankles, desperately searching for one thing that would prove her identity. And when I spotted it, the rose tattoo, all of the air expelled out of my lungs and I could no longer breathe. It was her. It was Alex.

CHAPTER TWENTY-SIX

The Sexy Mole

It couldn't be. It couldn't be my sister. How was this possible? Alex was in the Red Realm, and if she was here being tortured, that meant that she was dead. My sister was dead!

"You seem surprised," Lilith said, amazement in her own tone.

"What the fuck!" I turned to her and yelled. "Why is my fucking sister in there?"

"Um...because she's dead." She said it like I was supposed to already know this. But I didn't. I didn't understand why a demon man had his hands inside of Alex, pulling her organs out of her body and about to deliver a baby. A baby!?

I twisted back around and started banging my fists against the translucent door. "Alex! Alex, please," I cried out, hoping by some miracle that she would be able to hear me. And for a split second, I thought maybe she did when she stopped wailing in agony and slightly tilted her head in my direction. The blindfold covered her eyes, but I could imagine them searching for my voice. Did she actually hear me?

She couldn't. Alex turned her attention back to what was happening to her and began screaming again. The evil doctor continued excavating the inside of her stomach, stopping only to scoop out pieces of my sister's insides and place them gingerly on top of a metal tray next to him as if her organs were valuable and he could sell them for a lot of money if he kept them in mint condition. They *were* valuable, but not to him. He was just some lunatic Red Realm employee doing his job. My sister didn't mean anything to him. Her liver and kidneys and other parts I couldn't name, all slippery and covered in blood laying on that tray next to him, didn't mean a damn thing to him.

And then, when I thought Bladesnare had removed everything he possibly could from my sister's body, I realized he wasn't done. His hands and arms dove into her stomach and dug around some more before he slowly withdrew them back out, cradling one last large organ in his palms. Only this organ was thrashing its stubby arms and legs and expelling a high-pitched, blood-curdling shriek out of its fang-filled mouth. Its skin was covered in warts and dripped green ooze down to the floor, and three crimson spikes protruded out of its skull.

My sister had just given birth to a demon baby.

"Aww, look how adorable!" Lilith gushed. "She's probably going to give birth to about a few hundred more. I'll be sure to round up the cigars!"

"Alex!" I tried getting her attention again.

"She can't hear you," Lilith mocked behind me. "You're wasting your time." I swung around and reached up for Lilith's neck, wrapping my hand around her throat in one quick motion.

"What the fuck did you do?" I seethed.

She put her hands up as if to surrender, but the horns coming out of her forehead told a different story. They were angry, aggressively glowing in my face. "I didn't do anything to your sister," she hissed.

I inspected her black pupils, desperate for some kind of truth. Then it occurred to me. "You brought me here on purpose. You wanted me to see Alex like this," I said, squeezing her neck tighter. But my grip didn't seem to have any effect on her. Before I could stop her, Lilith reached for the chain of The Liberation Stone and pulled it out of my T-shirt.

"Why don't you explain what this is?"

Stunned, I released my hold on her and snatched the chain out of her fingernails. Shit! "This is nothing," I insisted.

"Oh, it's something. And the king and queen want to know what it is."

Anxiety and panic began to build inside my chest. An instinct like something was about to happen produced nauseating knots in my stomach, and I briefly wished I either had a gallon of vodka to guzzle down or a big wad of demon dust to chew on. Something was telling me to run away, but before I could take a step in the direction of where we came from, Lilith pushed me. I lost my footing and tumbled to the ground, my left cheek slamming into the unforgiving marble. My head hit the floor so hard, my teeth shook and sent vibrations to my brain. My eyes lost focus and I had to blink several times to regain my vision. Blood instantly pooled around my mouth.

A moan somehow managed to make it past my lips. Lilith's red heels meeting the marble floor sounded like explosions in my ear. She stepped close to my head and shoved the point of her stiletto into my ribs, forcing me to turn over on my back. She bent down near my aching head.

"I knew there was something off about that fucking thing around your neck. You tried your damnedest to hide it. But I'm not stupid. Dominic will be pleased to know that I figured it out. And now you'll have to answer to the king and queen."

"Wait," I said, wincing from the pain of moving my busted mouth. "I'm not—

"Shut up," Lilith growled. She lifted a small bottle and tapped it with her index finger, sending a stream of orange particles toward my face. I moved my head away, but a strong odor of burning rubber mixed with feces coated my nostrils. I gagged and fought to bite back the bile rising in my throat. But not even two seconds later, I was out.

CHAPTER TWENTY-SEVEN

King and Queen

A constant crackling sound slowly built inside my ears until it forced my eyes open. The orange sky was above me, rouge streaking it haphazardly like some kid went to town with a red crayon. The air was hot and stale and humid, somehow warmer than anywhere else I'd been in the Red Realm. I usually only wore my leather jacket in the air-conditioned loft at The Croft, but I stupidly decided to go full Goth today and cover myself in all black, which was a bad choice. Now my arms and legs felt like they were melting right through the fabric of my clothes.

Dragons circled overhead, resembling hungry vultures waiting to chow down on something that just died. That idea made the vision of Alex's pregnant belly and her organs being yanked out of her start to trickle back. And that creature that came out of her. My poor sister. I never thought I would see her pregnant, let alone dead.

I slammed my eyes shut and sucked my lips inside my mouth, gritting my teeth down into my skin until it hurt. The tears mixed with sweat began sliding down the side of my face as I pictured Alex's mouth contorted into a distressing grimace and the horrifying cries that ejected from her throat. Those screams came from deep within her, and I had never heard anything like it before.

It was my fault. I left her. I left her behind to fend for herself. How could I have expected my sweet sister to live in our crazy world alone without me? She had a big heart and a forgiving nature. I was the tough asshole with the shitty attitude and hopeless outlook on life. She needed me to protect her. But I didn't. I agreed to come here without even putting up a fight. I was blinded by Dominic's seduction, which was a waste because he didn't even care. There was no telling what he got out of burying his fingers inside of me, but he did, and I was stupid enough to believe he might actually want me.

But how did this happen? It had only been a few days since I left her in Dominic's questionably charming hands. Granted, the time here had been a slightly blurred drug-induced combination of working and hanging out at Pandemonium all night with Lilith and Alcazar, but I hadn't been gone long. I didn't know how long Alex had been here; Dominic must have killed her and sent her soul to the Red Realm soon after he shipped me away.

"That's enough!" The baritone of a male voice boomed and reverberated out into the salmon-colored sky. The echo startled me, and I flinched. "Acidhag, get her up."

Heavy footsteps pounded toward me until I was suddenly swung up high off the ground like I was on some kind of pendulum and placed onto my feet. Acidhag was a giant monster with bubbling vomit-colored skin and three eyes. At this point, none of these monsters really surprised me anymore. Each and every single being on this plane was different than the next, and I was getting used to the diversity.

Acidhag stepped out of the way, revealing something I was definitely *not* used to seeing.

"Employee 99012977, state your name," King Centaurus demanded sternly. There was no assuming he was the king. It was completely obvious who he was by the uncanny resemblance to all of the enormous statues scattered around the city that honored his half-man, half-horse appearance. He seemed to be the only monster around who had hoofs for feet and a torso of a male model. Also, he was wearing a crown made of fucking flames.

"State your name, human!"

"Frankie," I whispered, but didn't mean to. My throat was filled with grief and the muscles in my neck were struggling to choke down emotions from seeing my sister in such a terrible state. I immediately lowered my head because I knew this might piss him off, but I honestly didn't have the strength to speak louder.

"Speak up!" King Centaurus ordered.

"Maybe the Tongue Slayer has already gotten to her," someone said. My eyes drew up to the source of this beguilingly harmonic female voice. A woman wearing a lacy black veil that covered her face sat in a throne next to King Centaurus. It had to be Queen Hysteria, and the only reason I knew that was because of the tall, brown horns that twisted off the top of her head. They belonged to the same woman in all of the grim, moody portraits of her and King Centaurus in Dominic's office.

"State your name," King Centaurus repeated.

I finally cleared my throat, realizing then that this was truly the King and Queen of this region, and if I didn't answer, they could probably kill me right this second. But...would that be a bad thing?

"Frankie!" I said.

"Frankie, you have been accused of treason. How do you plea?"

How do I plea? Was I on trial? Was this some kind of court? I glanced around at my surroundings. No jury. No pews behind me filled with curious onlookers. We were completely alone and seemed to be on an edge of a cliff. The King and Queen were facing me, the red-orange sky open and wide behind them, dragons flapping their large, dinosaur-like wings in the smoke clouds. The whooshing sound of blood ocean waves crashed below us, and we were high above the rest of the city. The tops of the fiery buildings were clearly visible. I had never been afraid of heights, but now I definitely was when I considered how easy it would be for Acidhag to push me right of this mountain.

"How do you plea?" King Centaurus said again. His voice was husky and authoritarian—like a high school principal.

"I...I don't know what you mean," I said shamefully.

"She's an idiot," Queen Hysteria said, then started cackling loudly. I squinted and covered my ears in an attempt to shield my hearing, but her sharp laughs stabbed at my eardrums even through my hands.

King Centaurus did not look amused. As a matter of fact, his handsome face showed the complete opposite expression: annoyed. He shifted his weight between all four horse legs before speaking. "You have something around your neck. Something that is not of this plane. I do not know who gave it to you, or what it does, but it does not belong here. And neither do you."

Fuck. It didn't sound like he knew about The Liberation Stone and what it did, but he knew something wasn't right about this necklace. That bitch Lilith must have tattled on me. Lake didn't tell me what to do if they found out. But for some reason, that didn't matter. Something was starting to bubble up inside of me and I was about ready to belch it out. It was rising from my stomach, to my chest, up my throat, and forming words into my mouth. I couldn't stop it, and before I knew it, those words had slipped off my tongue. "You killed my fucking sister, you assholes!"

Queen Hysteria stopped laughing and King Centaurus just stared blankly at me. My bones rattled inside my body. Acidhag made some kind of gurgling sound at the both of them. It might have been talking. I didn't know because I was too busy having an out-of-body experience.

The silence from the king and queen lasted for far too long before King Centaurus finally spoke. "What is around your neck?"

"Wouldn't you like to fucking know?" Mother of crap! *Why am I saying these things!* Booze or demon dust or even heroine would be perfect right about now. I glanced down at the pocket of my jacket, remembering that I still had the little baggy of drugs. But as soon as I reached inside to retrieve the demon dust, long elegant fingers gripped my wrist and squeezed. My eyes shot up to Queen Hysteria standing in front of me. She was tall—supermodel tall—and her thick horns added several inches to her height. The thought of yanking my arm away from her crossed my mind, but before I made a decision that could possibly end my life in a single moment, she let me go.

The queen removed her black veil and let it slide down onto the floor. My breath hitched at her beauty. Even Lilith, the first woman to have ever made me consider playing for the other team, didn't have anything on Queen Hysteria. Her pupils were scarlet and glowing, cheekbones high up on her face and pointy as if the bone was going to pierce right through her blanched skin at any second. She had a long, slender neck bejeweled by a necklace made of hundreds of black diamonds that sparkled when her chest rose and fell with every breath she took. She reached up and traced my jawline with a fingernail, licking her black lips and staring at my mouth like she wanted to taste me.

Suddenly, out of nowhere, her face morphed into someone different. I stared at her, stunned, until I realized she looked like someone I'd seen before. The creepy porcelain receptionist from work back on Earth! It was her. It was Queen Hysteria. But it couldn't be possible. Lake said the rulers of the Red Realm were not allowed on Earth because of the treaty.

An instant later, her face changed back to the queen. "You are very sexy, Frankie," she said.

I didn't respond. Between the revelation I'd just had and the way she touched me, I couldn't find the right words. The tip of her fingernail moved from my jawline to my chin and down my neck, where she gently wrapped her slim fingers around my throat.

She leaned down and lightly pressed her supple lips against mine, leaving behind a sensuous sensation. The soft kiss left me spellbound, until I felt her mouth part and her teeth puncture my bottom lip. Instantly, the coppery tinge of my own blood coated my tongue, and I tried to pull away from her, but the queen snatched my chin and twisted my head, her warm breath spreading over the side of my face like silk sheets conforming to my skin as she whispered into my ear, "You taste just like your sister."

Before I could think another thought, my hands balled into fists and slammed right into her chest. Queen Hysteria didn't even budge, but her eyes widened and her lips turned up into an unhinged grin before she opened her mouth and released some more deafening cackles—a noise that sounded like a cross between The Wicked Witch of the West and a schizophrenic lunatic trying to unsuccessfully *sound* like an evil witch.

My next move was going to determine my fate, but I wasn't scared. This bitch had something to do with Alex's death and I wanted her to know how pissed off I was. So I continued ramming my fists into her chest, punching as hard as I could. The queen still made no move until I decided to aim for her face. She didn't like this very much because she caught my wrist midair before my knuckles could make contact with her cheek. The obnoxious giggles stopped, and suddenly, she was serious.

"You can't hurt me, you stupid human."

"You killed my sister!" I yelled at her. It was kind of a statement, kind of a question. It didn't matter. Someone did it, and if Queen Hysteria was on Earth, it could have been her.

The queen bent my wrist back and my body instantaneously gave in to the pain, curling on its own and buckling at the knees. My mouth opened but nothing came out.

"And it was so much fun," she said, smiling. She twisted and pushed and pulled on my wrist some more, my body following in the direction she was manipulating my bones, until there was a loud crack. A yell finally burst out of my lungs, the echo of my own tormented voice surprising me as it rang out all around us.

Queen Hysteria had just broken my arm!

With my focus on the pain emitting from my arm, the queen took advantage and reached for the necklace. But right as she snatched The Liberation Stone into her hands and attempted to yank it free from my neck, a bright, white light shot out from the rock. We both squinted away from its intensity until it died down a second later, right before an explosion of electricity surged out from the stone in her hand. The bolt collided with Queen Hysteria's chest and she instantaneously flew back a few feet away, landing on her ass right at King Centaurus' hoofs. For a second, the ache of my broken bones stopped when I saw the king and queen's faces. They were clearly stunned—completely surprised by what just happened. And I was convinced that I was about to die.

CHAPTER TWENTY-EIGHT

The End Is Near

Queen Hysteria crouched down on her hands and knees, breathing heavily and staring at me. I blinked twice and shook my head, taking a few steps back. And when I blinked again, she was standing inches away from me. She reached for my forearm and lifted it up, my broken bones crunching underneath my skin and in between her fingertips as she pressed down deeper and deeper. The queen was enraged— lips receded and teeth bared. The bolt of lightning that emitted out of The Liberation Stone had clearly hurt her. The skin on her chest was no longer perfectly pale and blemish-free. It was now marred by a dark shadow the size of my palm, spidering out into the rest of her chest like angry black veins. I tried to get out of her grip, attempted to pull away and use my other hand to scratch and claw at her, but the queen was too strong. She simply watched me struggle and cry. She didn't do anything. It was almost like she was still trying to figure out what had just happened to her.

"Hysteria!"

It took her a few moments, but she let go after King Centaurus called out to her. She then flashed back to the seat next to him. My legs finally gave out and I crumpled to the ground, cradling my injured arm.

"We don't have time for this nonsense. My inclination is that the necklace belongs to another realm. I don't know who you are or what you are doing in my region, but I am banishing you. You have two options, human. We cut off your head and remove that necklace to dispose of it, or we send you to The Nothing, where you will live for eternity. It's your decision."

Oh, well...I was so glad I had such an awesome fucking choice to make. Quite honestly, I would much rather chop my own head off instead of having to live in The Nothing for all eternity. If it felt anything like it did in the elevator, dying was definitely the more humane choice.

"Can't I gut her open with a rusty blade and force-feed her intestines down her sister's nose?" Queen Hysteria was pouting as if she were a teenage girl begging her daddy for a new car. "I think maybe I'll leave some chunks. I wouldn't want it to slide down so easily."

King Centaurus turned to his wife. "We have other important engagements to tend to, my darling queen. And we must get rid of whoever this treasonous human is right now. If you want, we can have Acidhag retrieve her sister after we are finished with our other meetings and you can afflict her however you please then."

"No! Wait!" I cried out. I was well aware that it probably didn't matter how much I pleaded, the king and queen were going to do what they wanted. As expected, the queen narrowed her eyes at me and grinned mischievously, my begging clearly adding fuel to her desire for inflicting misery upon souls. Specifically, Alex at the moment.

"I have a better idea," Queen Hysteria said, switching her attention to her fingernails as if she was bored with this whole thing. "Give her back to Dominic. He's the nitwit who sent her down here. Perhaps he can force some information out of her about that hideous necklace."

"Dominic is already busy running my business. It is not his duty to be involved with affliction anymore."

"This isn't about affliction! That human is here for a reason and we must find out why. If she stays, she might somehow use that thing around her neck against us. We cannot risk it. Send her back to Earth where she will be far away from our realm and Dominic can deal with her."

The King didn't reply right away. Instead, his eyes fell toward the floor like he was in deep contemplation.

It was strange how in that moment, they reminded me so much of an old married couple. Like my mom and dad when they were having a "heated" discussion over how to punish me because I broke curfew by an hour. It didn't happen often, but every now and then Jacob and I would get carried away and lose track of time in the backseat of his Jeep after a movie theater date. Something told me his wife would win. My mom always did, anyway.

King Centaurus glared at me, pressed his lips into a hard line, then spoke. "You will report back to Dominic at the Centaurus office on Earth until further notice. Acidhag, escort Employee 99012977 back to the gates. A Henchman will be waiting there to take over."

The ground trembled and shook under my ass as Acidhag sauntered over to me. Afraid that he might place his slimy monster hand on my broken arm, I rushed to get to my feet. "Don't touch me," I huffed.

The monster started to walk, but I stayed put and faced the king and queen. "What can I do?"

"Excuse me?" the king asked, cocking his head.

"What can I do to stop you from torturing my sister?" My sweet, sweet Alexandra. I would do anything to stop the mad doctor and Queen Bitchface from causing her soul any more agony. Whether or not she was being judged for selling her soul in the first place, she just didn't deserve to be here. Alex sold her soul and mine to *save* us. She did it out of love, and I forgave her for making the decision for me. The Red Realm had no business torturing her, playing on her weaknesses that way. She deserved to be in the White Realm. I needed to get her there somehow.

"There is nothing you can do. Your sister has already been sentenced," King Centaurus responded, lifting his chin. Acidhag wrapped his large claw around my bad arm. I winced and moaned, but it didn't interrupt my petition to stop what they were doing to Alex.

A part of me knew the king was right. Lake informed me of this as well. Once a soul reached the Red Realm, the Angels of Reform or any other angels couldn't help them. But I had to try. "I will let you kill me. I will let you cut my head off. Send me to The Nothing. I'll do anything. Please."

The King and Queen exchanged looks. Then Queen Hysteria asked, "Tell us what is around that scrawny little neck of yours!"

I fought the urge to explain exactly what The Liberation Stone was. It physically pained me to swallow it down, the words stabbing the tissue of my esophagus as if I'd eaten a box of nails. But the fact was that if I traded information about Lake, the Great Elders, and the White Realm for my sister's clemency, then the whole plan to destroy this region would be ruined. How many other souls would it endanger? How many other humans? Not to mention, Lake and Reggie and all of those other angels at the angel nightclub. Besides, if my sister were here, she'd tell me to save everyone else before her.

Defeat filled my mouth with a sour taste in the spit I choked back. "No."

"Very well. The decision is made. Acidhag, show her to the gates."

Acidhag jerked my damaged arm toward him and I didn't fight against his grip. I didn't make a sound from the pain that shot through my shattered bones and inflamed nerves as he led me away from King Centaurus and Queen Hysteria. Not one single noise while he loaded me into Ziggy's carriage parked just a few feet away, waiting for us. The thought of asking to be allowed to retrieve my things from The Croft crossed my mind, but that idea frittered away when the flaming-horse duo drawing our buggy rode right past it. There was a pack of cigarettes in my back pocket and about a gram of demon dust left over in my jacket. That was enough to get me from the gates and through the portal, and being drugged out should definitely help lessen the hallucinations from the journey in the elevator. Or...at least I hoped so. It might even intensify it. Regardless, it would hold me over until I got to the other side. I'd be leaving behind the box full of fancy liquor Alcazar provided me with, but there was plenty of cheap, mediocre alcohol hidden back at my apartment at The Hartley. Unless Alex found those bottles and disposed of them, which still didn't matter because there was a liquor store on the corner where I could buy some more. It was also where I could find Shaky Joe, the old one-legged crackhead who either twitched and trembled from years of smoking dope or from undiagnosed Parkinson's disease. Either way, I would be able to score some pretty inexpensive drugs from him—maybe even in exchange for jewelry or my cellphone instead of money. Because I won't need them.

I won't need anything anymore after I find a way to get rid of this stupid thing around my neck and give it back to Lake. I figured out what my next move was going to be. I was going to kill myself. Either by a drug overdose or alcohol poisoning. I hadn't made up my mind yet. Or maybe the Great Elders would decide it was time to activate The Liberation Stone once I got inside that elevator/portal. That would be preferable. It would take less time. Less chance of getting physically ill, because I hated being physically ill. And better yet, *all* of me would evaporate into thin air. My body and my soul. I would be gone, completely. Ceasing to exist in any form.

Wouldn't it be better that way?

For seventeen years, I had lived a charmed life. It was so quintessential—the doting parents, the smart and caring big sister. Beautiful house on the lake. Student of a privately-owned school. Girlfriend of the star quarterback. Just a rich girl with loads of friends, aspiring to become a dancer in a prestigious dance company. I had it all planned out, and Jacob would be my center. The boy who made me feel like the luckiest girl.

But it all seemed so distant now. Plans and dreams and expectations that weren't in my reach anymore. Those things were so far out there, I couldn't possibly see them if I tried. It was almost fascinating in a way— the idea that I once believed I could live a normal life. Did a normal life even exist? Those Rom-Coms that Jacob used to watch with all the feel-good vibes and endings that always resulted in the main characters living happily ever after had to have come from somewhere. It had to have been modeled by real life. Or was it some kind of cruel joke Hollywood played on all of us? To make us believe we had a chance at happiness? That we didn't have to work so hard for it, or that it couldn't be taken away at any minute of any day at any point in our lives. None of those movies ever showed what life would be like if that happiness was taken away permanently. Gone forever, never to return. What then? What would be the use of living anymore?

It made me wonder why anyone wanted to live in the first place. At the risk of sounding philosophical or too deep, it really made me question what our purpose as humans was. Well, not myself in particular because I was immortal and supernatural. I couldn't just die. A bullet wouldn't kill me. Not even getting hit by a car. I'd just get right back up. It was up to Dominic or the superior beings of the Red Realm to dispose of the

ASRs. But humans weren't supernatural or immortal. Without warning, without any reason, a human being's life could be snuffed away in an instant. Like simply blowing out the flame of a candle. Poof. Gone. As if it didn't happen. But it did happen because evidence of a charred wick would be left behind as proof.

But humans? They could die and leave no mark at all. It wasn't enough that their lives were so fragile, threatened daily by pretty much anything from disease to man-made machinery to weather, but humans ran the risk of dying and leaving no legacy. If they weren't famous or well-known in some way, they would merely be lumped away with the billions of people who have died and been forgotten.

My sister Alexandra was gone. My parents were gone. The love of my life...gone. I had nothing left to live for. Absolutely no reason to continue this fucked-up life. All I wanted to do now was end it. End the pain and hurt and loneliness. Sever those few ties left to the love and contentment I once felt long ago. There was no sense in holding on to it any longer if there wasn't any chance of feeling it again. It was exhausting, holding on to hope. I just wanted to let it all go for good.

At some point during my self-loathing, Acidhag handed me off to Boris, and Boris led me through the gates, past all the poor souls who were unaware of the monsters lurking on the other side, waiting to torment them forever. One look at those soul's faces—

translucent and lost and lifeless—gave me enough reason to ingest the last of my demon dust and chain-smoke five cigarettes before reaching the last dreadful leg of the journey back to Earth. My heart pounded at the thought that maybe the Great Elders were ready to activate The Liberation Stone. Even though I was ready to commit suicide, it was still a scary prospect. I'd be lying if I said I wasn't a little scared. It was the end of life. Death.

But as we started the ascension to Earth and passed through The Nothing, and I suffered the same psychological delusions of seeing dead people despite being under the influence of demon dust—this time my mom, Jacob, and my dad—the stone around my neck did nothing. Part of me hoped to see Alex. I wanted the opportunity to ask her if she was okay. If she was upset with me for leaving her behind. If she hated me. But Alex didn't make an appearance in my delusions.

Boris and I exited the elevator and entered the lobby of Centaurus. My eyes darted to the front desk, expecting to see Queen Hysteria disguised as the creepy receptionist glaring back at me, but there was no one there. I wondered how often the queen broke the treaty agreement and hung out on Earth, and who else knew about it. And if I told on her, what kind of trouble it would get her into?

The dark sky and lack of people seen walking the sidewalks outside the windows confirmed that it was nighttime. I knew that some time had passed since I was gone. But between there being no time in the Red Realm, all the demon dust I had ingested, and what had just happened with the king and queen, I lost track of trying to keep up with the time on Earth. I couldn't remember what day of the week I'd left or figure out how many days exactly I'd been gone. The demon dust was definitely mostly responsible for influencing my ability to recall times and dates. The drug was superlative in giving me a clean and intense high, but it was still a drug. There was still of sense of hazy reality associated with it.

Boris walked to the normal elevator that led to the offices and workspace below us and pushed the down arrow. He was ready to take me to Dominic, but I wasn't ready to go. I had to find Lake first.

"Do you think I could go to The Hartley?" I asked behind him. The chances of Boris allowing me to go back to my apartment were slim. And doing it alone was a long shot. "I won't be long. It's been a really bad day, I'm pretty sure my forearm is broken, and I know I've got some painkillers in my medicine cabinet. I just want to try to take a shower and take some pills before having to answer to Dominic." The demon dust I'd eaten before the elevator journey was still running its course through my nervous system, continuing to diminish the excruciating ache from a bone fracture. But Boris needed to think I was still in pain, and if I was lucky, he'd be a little sympathetic about it.

He twisted toward me, my reflection in the black lenses of his glasses obstructing any view of the expression in his eyes. I couldn't read what he was thinking or about to say.

"I'm sorry, but my orders are to take you straight to Dominic."

I threw my head back dramatically. "Please, Boris. I'll only be thirty minutes, forty-five tops."

He exhaled and glanced down at his watch. "Fine. We can go." He stepped forward but I held a hand out.

"Um...do you think I can have this time alone?"

"Frankie, I can't allow that," he said.

"Yes, you can," I countered. "I just lost my sister. Chances are, Dominic is going to torture me until he kills me. All I want is just a little time to grieve my sister's death. Please." Begging was starting to get old, and I told myself this would be the last time. No more pleading. My life was my life, and I was going to do whatever the hell I wanted with it from here on out.

Apparently, Boris could sense how strongly I felt about having alone time and granted me permission. "You have forty-five minutes. Don't make me come find you."

I fought the urge to hug him, even though he might actually appreciate it considering the weird hug he'd given me before. Instead, I shot him a forced smile before rushing out of the Centaurus building and onto the streets of Shitsburgh. I bolted in the direction of The Hartley, but I had no intention of going to my apartment building.

Reggie's store. The angel nightclub. Lake had to be at either one of those locations.

CHAPTER TWENTY-NINE

No, Not Her Heart

It was no surprise to see Reggie's store locked up, the metal grate rolled down to keep any potential burglars away. After all, it was the middle of the night. But it was pretty shocking to see a sign that said FOR LEASE.

I didn't have a normal Earthling phone. Just the stupid FireLink cellphone the Red Realm provided me with upon my arrival, which would not be able to make any calls in this dimension. But that wouldn't matter, anyway. Apparently, this wasn't Reggie's store anymore, and I wasn't sure who to call to help me get inside. I slammed my palms against the alloy wall separating me from the sewage tunnel that would lead me to the angel nightclub. A thick bang bounced back, echoing into the empty streets behind me, and the stupid sudden fit of rage sent a violent vibration through my injured arm. I winced and cradled it into my chest until the screaming pain began to die down a little. It felt almost exactly how a stubbed toe would feel—intense and serious at first, then tolerable. Only, there were clearly at least a couple of broken bones, so the pain didn't subside that much.

The sound of a glass bottle rolling on concrete took my attention, and I turned to find a Shitsburgh hooker and what I assumed to be her pimp standing under a blinking streetlamp on the corner. The yellow light shined down on the Lady of the Night, who was barely covered by a slinky, hot pink dress that looked more like a lingerie number. She cowered over in her clear, stripper-style stilettos with her arms folded over her size DD breasts, clearly in need of a chair to rest her feet. She was visibly shaking from lack of protection from the frigid air, but the man next to her looked nice and warm in his shiny leather jacket. He glared down at his cellphone as he leaned against the brick building, one leg kicked up behind him. I was suddenly reminded of Boyz to Men and their 90's fashion.

If I couldn't get to Reggie and inside his store, then I would have to find Lake another way. I could go back to his little house where we first met, but it would appear my slightly drug-addled state was preventing me from remembering his address at the moment. Besides, I didn't have any transportation.

Right as I considered stalking over to the corner store and loading up on some alcohol to drink the night away at The Hartley, a familiar voice crept up behind me.

"Welcome back."

I twisted around to Reggie approaching me. "You're here," I pointed out before rushing over to give him a one-armed hug. This was definitely an unusual move on my part, but I truly was relieved to see a human I knew from Earth. Well...he wasn't human. Or from Earth. But you get the damn picture. Although, I was a bit surprised to see that Reggie didn't look like the Rastafarian that I had left. His fat dreads were gone, replaced with a nearly shaved head. There was no colorful Baja hoodie or gaudy diamond encrusted pendant with some random, insignificant symbol hanging around his neck. Instead, he was wearing just plain old jeans and a white T-shirt with a bomber jacket, a lot like something Lake would wear. He also didn't smell like twenty pounds of weed, but more like a newly opened bottle of rose-scented body wash.

Either way, he was far different from a fucking one-eyed monster with scaly reptile skin.

Reggie bent down and returned a hug. "It's good to see you, Frankie."

His embrace comforted me and the loneliness that I had been feeling since I got back here, but I pulled away not a second later, realizing something. "You're still here. My sister is... Shouldn't you be gone? Moved on to another protégé?"

He disregarded my questions. "You're hurt?" he asked, grazing my arm gently with his fingertips. I held it close to my body, like it was hanging from an invisible sling.

"It's not bad," I lied. "Just sprained, I think. You didn't answer me. Why are you still here?"

His brows hung low, the muscles in his face falling into a sullen frown. "I did leave. Right after Alexandra died." He was hurting over her death. I could feel it. "But it's been months, Frankie."

"Months?" I asked, confused by what he meant. "Months since what?"

"Since she died. You've been gone for over seven months," he said, sounding surprised that I didn't already know this.

The words coming out of Reggie's mouth actually stung, causing my temples to tingle from shame. Seven months? I left my sister for seven months without so much as a single peep from me? She might not have known I was even alive. Dominic may have updated her on my status down there, but I truly doubted it. The former Afflictionist probably enjoyed watching Alex squirm and worry about her little sister.

I felt awful for not even trying to check in with Alex. In my defense, I was high pretty much every moment of the day while I was there. My brain was under a clouded influence, causing the hours and days in the Red Realm to blend and make me lose track. But that really wasn't a defense, was it? That was only me being an asshole, choosing to be selfish and allow my self-pity to win above all else. My sister might have died not knowing what happened to me, and it was my fault.

"There is no time in the Red Realm. Didn't they tell you that?"

"Yeah, but..." I trailed off, opting not to admit to my narcissistic tendencies and the fact that I chose demon dust over blood. I was embarrassed to even be standing in front of this angel man.

The curiosity was eating at me, and I had to ask. "How did it happen, Reggie? How did they kill her? You and Lake were supposed to be watching over her." I regretted my last words because it sounded as if I might have been blaming Reggie and Lake for my sister's death. I wasn't. I knew damn well they wouldn't have let it happen if they could have helped it.

Reggie's eyes drifted away from mine and down to his feet, then back up at my face. "We didn't... It was out of our control. The queen of the Red Realm. She murdered her at Centaurus."

"Murdered her? How? What did she do to Alex?" My pulse rose. That bitch, Queen Hysteria. I should have done something to her. Punched her in the face. Gouged her eyes out with my thumbs. Anything! I might have died doing it, but at least I'd be avenging my sister in some way.

"You don't want to know, Frankie."

I needed nicotine. "But Lake said it was against the rules for the kings and queens of the Red Realm to cross over to this dimension," I said, sticking the butt of a cigarette between my lips. "How could the queen have murdered Alex?"

"Unfortunately, the kings and queens have found loopholes around the treaty set in place by the Council of the NonAligned. But it does take much power to do so, and not all kings and queens have the ability. This region in particular is pretty strong, and the queen does take advantage of that sometimes."

It felt like I was sucking the gray smoke from my cigarette down into my stomach and it was making me nauseous. This region was powerful because King Centaurus and Queen Hysteria were feeding on so many souls, and I had something to do with that. It made me feel sick that I directly contributed to Alex's murder. If I didn't seal people, there would be less souls. Less strength to garner in order to cross over to this plane.

A dense silence filled the space between Reggie and me for a good minute before I couldn't stand it any longer. "How did she die, Reggie?"

Reggie folded his lips in and shook his head in disapproval, but I didn't break eye contact and raised my eyebrows as high as they'd go. I wasn't going to let up. As much as it would kill me to hear about how Queen Hysteria ended Alex's life on Earth, I just had to know.

"She ripped her heart out of her chest."

My legs gave out and I stumbled forward into Reggie's arms. Her heart? The queen ripped Alex's heart out of her chest? Alex's good, sweet, selfless heart?

"Are you okay?" Reggie asked as he held me steady. I was dizzy with despair, finding it hard to accept my sister's fate.

"We have to get her back."

"We can't. Her soul is now property of the Red Realm. We have tried to help those who have entered the Red Realm unwillingly, but once they do, their souls are property of the king and queen. It's the same in the White Realm, unless they are banished."

"There has to be a way!" I insisted loudly. The prostitute and her John peered over in our direction, but it seemed we weren't interesting enough to hold their attention. It made sense. We probably just looked like one of the many other Shitsburgh resident couples airing out their dirty laundry, not giving a shit who was around. But Reggie did care because he gently grasped the elbow of my good arm and pulled me toward his old store.

"Frankie, I'm sorry," he said in a low voice. "There is nothing we can do for Alex now. But you still have The Liberation Stone. The Great Elders have chosen you to stop this region's business of soul-selling. You might not be able to save your sister, but you'll be able to save so many others."

Tears stung the corners of my eyes, but I refused to give up. "That's fucking bullshit!"

Reggie pursed his lips, and I was afraid that I might have offended this angel with my profanities. "We have to get you back to the portal. The Great Elders will be ready to activate the stone soon. I can feel it."

"I'm not going back to Centaurus without speaking to Lake," I said defiantly. The need to see him tugged on my insides and I couldn't exactly explain why. Besides, Lake had seven months to retrieve all the answers he was looking for about why I was chosen and what would happen to me when the portal was activated. At this point, it didn't matter if I lived or died, but I deserved to at least know.

Thankfully, Reggie didn't protest to my demand. "Then let's go." He reached inside the front pocket of his jeans and pulled out a ring of keys. "I'm surprised Lake hasn't been here already, anyway. He should have been able to feel you crossing over to this plane earlier."

Again with the *feeling* me stuff.

"He should be down in the hideaway with the others," he said.

Reggie pulled up the metal grate and unlocked the door of the storefront.

"This place is still yours?" I asked.

"For now. A new Guide was just assigned someone right down the street. They'll be taking over soon."

Duh, I thought, catching a glimpse of the hooker on her knees, head bobbing back and forth in front of the whoremonger's groin as we stepped inside the building.

CHAPTER THIRTY

The Good Ones Always Die

The store was empty. No shoe racks. No cellphone repair area. No reggae Congo music blaring from blown-out speakers. Nothing. There was only a slight musky odor of patchouli in the air and the old clerk's counter left behind.

"Do you know the Guide who will be taking over?" I asked, trying to make small talk.

I followed Reggie to the counter and watched as he moved the ratty hemp rug and opened the hatch. "We all know each other. This place is one of two entrances to the hideaway, so it must stay within our community."

"Then why the for-lease sign?"

"We've got to at least pretend to blend in."

There were so many questions circling my brain: How long had this place been here? Who was the Guide assigned to? Would it remain a cellphone repair/shoe store? Where was the other entrance? Now that I'd seen the inner workings of the Red Realm, my curiosity for how the White Realm functioned was rising. And, shamefully, I wondered if the White Realm had any kind of narcotic that one might be able to try. I had a sneaking suspicion that the answer was no, but the thought of a drug made by beautiful, benevolent celestial beings piqued my interest. It would probably elicit a phenomenal high.

But I chose to keep those particular questions to myself as we sloshed through the murky sewage water and down the dank tunnel. It was dark as shit and I couldn't see a thing, but Reggie had become my eyes while I kept my head down and followed close behind him. My hand rested on his back and the feel of his muscles flexing with each movement made me curious about something.

"What does it feel like...when your wings come out?" I asked.

"Freeing," Reggie said.

"I mean, physically. How do they even come out? And where do they go? I don't feel them inside of me."

"You won't. Do you feel your fingers and your toes when you aren't thinking about it? Your wings are a part of your body. They simply eject and retract on their own," he explained. But this was only leading to more questions.

"So, there's nothing in particular that makes them come out?"

"They know when to," Reggie said plainly.

Basically, my wings had a mind of their own. Interesting. It could explain why they came out when I fell off The Hartley and nearly met my untimely death. I was clearly drunk off my ass and had no clue I even had wings to begin with. They must have felt I was in danger or something and saved my life.

Hmm... These wings were all right.

It wasn't long before we reached the round steel door. Reggie turned the wheel in the middle, entering the combination. The door opened, and we made our way to the next one. But I could tell something was different already. There was no muffled music pulsating through the tunnel walls. And when Reggie delivered the special sequence of knocks, the bouncer guy didn't slide the small, rectangular door open. Nothing happened. It was completely quiet.

"There's something wrong," Reggie said, then pushed on the metal door. It wasn't latched and easily swung open.

Horror. Carnage. Blood. Bodies. Death.

Strobe lights flickered beams of colorful rays haphazardly around the large room. The flickers were delayed, illuminating random portions of the space every few seconds. The eerie sound of what used to be electronic music now skipped and screeched, sending chills down the back of my neck. Lifeless bodies sprinkled the dance floor and cocktail area, scarlet blood splattered all over the floor and walls and tables and chairs. Thick pools of it outlined each person—I assumed wherever the most extensive and critical injury had occurred. They all lay in different positions, arms and legs either sprawled out or closed together or twisted in an unnatural manner. It was hard to tell exactly what had happened here, but there was no mistaking that this was a massacre.

Reggie immediately rushed over to the closest angel. I recognized her as the beautiful, doe-eyed cocktail waitress with luscious blonde hair. But she now lay on her back, eyes wide open and no longer encompassing gentleness and innocence. Instead, they were fixed into an empty stare. Coagulated blood was smeared across her lips and trailed down the side of her cheek, accumulating in a puddle of it behind her head and back. One of the waitress's arms was missing and her legs were spread open, placed into a rather...compromising position. She had no bottoms, and my mind immediately floated off to dark places.

Reggie approached her side. His eyes remained on her face the entire time, choosing not to discuss the fact that she was half naked, clearly trying to respect the woman even in death. He simply analyzed her head very carefully.

Still cradling my arm to my chest and trying to forget about the pain of my broken bones, I just stood there, watching and taking it all in. The smell permeating the air was a nauseating mixture of rotting flesh and dried blood. Broken glass and furniture littered every square inch of the place, making it look worlds away from the lively nightclub filled with happy, dancing angels and fast, upbeat music. I couldn't tell off-hand, but it looked like everyone who was here that night I came with Lake—easily about a fifty people—was dead.

"What happened?" I asked breathlessly.

Reggie moved on to the next dead body, assessing and examining wounds, but never touching anyone. "The Red Realm," he answered matter-of-factly. He didn't seem as upset as you'd imagine someone to be after seeing such bloodshed. Maybe there was a deeper seriousness to his facial expression—more of like a concentrated focus as he moved from person to person and assessed them. But there were no tears for his fellow angel friends.

To be honest, I wasn't sure what I was feeling myself. I didn't feel like crying over these people that I didn't know. My life was suddenly overflowing with death and despair, and an overall numbness was beginning to replace what little bit of compassion I'd managed to hold on to after selling my soul.

But Alexandra was the only thing keeping that characteristic intact, and she was no longer here with me.

"What do you mean 'the Red Realm'?" I asked.

"They did this. King Centaurus, Dominic, and the Henchmen," Reggie clarified.

"How did they even find this place?"

"Don't know. One of the angels might have been followed or something. This has happened in the past. Sometimes, employees of the Red Realm find our hideaways."

If this has happened in the past, then it explained Reggie's poker face. I wondered how many times before.

"But this doesn't mean they're dead. Their souls are back in the White Realm," I stated, believing that angels were supernatural, and they couldn't be *completely* dead. Maybe their physical bodies were deceased, but their souls had to go back to the White Realm. Like Lake said—all energy had to go somewhere.

"Come see," Reggie instructed. He crouched down next to two bodies, one of which clearly suffered a painful death. His leg was bent backwards and looked like he had bled profusely from a pelvic wound. I cautiously stepped over three bodies to where Reggie was to get a closer look. That was when I saw her. And that was when I felt like I'd been punched in the gut.

Ariel, my gorgeous dance partner from the only night Lake and I hung out in here, lay dead on the floor in front of us. The memories of that natural high I had on the dance floor with Ariel and Samuel came streaming back. I was reminded of the weightlessness of flying and the overall profound sense of security and familiarity with people who radiated goodness. This made my heart sink, and suddenly, an overwhelming feeling of loss made my eyes water. I didn't know how I knew, but she was definitely gone, and this hurt me deeply.

Ariel didn't look like most of the corpses. There weren't copious amounts of blood or obvious wounds that could have ended her life. But her wings had been expelled. The feathery appendages were clearly broken, bent and cracked in random spots. The plumes that I remembered to be stark white and glittery—magnificently hypnotizing—were now dull and somehow colorless despite them still being white. I pictured seeing them flutter effortlessly, the movement of the feathers resembling a flag blowing softly in the wind. But not anymore. Now, they were stiff and loose pieces of frayed plumage covered her entire body as if someone crumpled them into a closed fist and threw them on top of her.

Reggie pointed to one of Ariel's wings, then poked at it. As soon as his index finger made contact, the wing shriveled up like moisture being sucked out of a sponge and turned to dust. This created a kind of domino effect and the other wing changed, followed by her entire body. Within a blink of the eye, Ariel had transformed into a pile of ash. Reggie looked up at me.

"This is how we know an angel is truly gone. Her physical body and soul are destroyed. And the only thing that could destroy a soul is something supernatural. We don't know exactly how this is done, but it was definitely by someone from the Red Realm. We believe that they might have an amulet or stone similar to The Liberation Stone. We've just never seen it."

Anger. Anger started building inside of me as I peered around the room full of fucking dead angels. Why? Why would anyone kill an angel? Or better yet, *how* could someone do this? Morally, I mean. You had to be completely heartless to want to eradicate these kindhearted souls.

I wasn't in the Red Realm long enough to know how or what was used to kill these angels but learning about these two realms was insane! It made me feel so insignificant. So trivial compared to what was happening. The Red Realm and the White Realm had been at war for eons, and I couldn't even wrap my head around all of the things that must have occurred in that time. And what was even more crazy was that there was an entire world full of oblivious humans who hadn't a clue the Red Realm or White Realm even really existed.

The sight of Ariel's wings deteriorating right before my eyes created a strangely familiar tingle on my back near my shoulder blades. It itched, but I ignored it.

"Well, where's Lake?" I asked, scouring the room for a large, broad-shouldered man with beautifully long hair. I needed to find him, but I was afraid to. If Lake was killed, a man that I barely knew but somehow felt so connected to, I might lose what little sanity I had left.

Reggie seemed pretty concerned too, and we both scanned the room full of blood and death and destruction in search of our Angel of Reform friend. My heart pounded at the idea of seeing him. Of course, I was frightened to witness his strong body in such a vulnerable state if he was dead. But the anticipation of seeing Lake alive and well after what felt like years made me nervous. My weird connection to him was strong—not just the undeniable attraction I had to him—and I wished that I could understand where it came from.

Reggie moved toward one side of the angel nightclub and I moved to the other. It was difficult, but I somehow managed to keep my eyes away from what rigor mortis looked like in real life and stay focused on dodging body parts and puddles of angel fluids. I didn't want to touch anything. It was safe to assume there weren't going to be any detectives coming to investigate the crime scene—not human detectives, anyway. But I didn't want to be responsible for turning an angel into powder.

Fuck. I needed a cigarette.

Right as I made the decision to light one up, Reggie called out to me. "Frankie, over here!"

I rushed to where he stood, relief washing over me from head to toe when I realized he'd found Lake. "Don't touch him!" I said, not mentally prepared to watch this beautiful man disintegrate into nothing.

Lake was sitting upright, his back against the wall and his upper body slumped to one side. Long legs stretched straight out in front of him, and his arms just lay helplessly at his sides. His jeans and boots were intact, thankfully, but his plain white T-shirt was torn and speckled with blood. His caramel-colored hair hung over his face like a curtain, keeping us from examining him for any wounds or injuries.

"He isn't dead," Reggie informed me.

"How do you know?"

"I can feel it," he said.

Son of a bitch. Why couldn't I feel the things these angels could feel? Oh right, because I worked for the devil and had evil embedded into my soul. And I was an asshole.

Reggie pushed Lake's hair to the side, and there he was. Perfectly perfect. Not a scratch on his magically flawless angel face. Even in this incoherent state, he still gave off a luminous glow. It was captivating, and I felt like I could watch him sleep for hours.

But as soon as Reggie gently shook his shoulder, Lake's eyelids fluttered open. "Lake, can you hear me?"

Lake moaned and winced.

"It's okay, Lake. Frankie and I are here to help you. Can you tell us what happened?"

"Fran-kie?" Lake asked, his eyes sluggishly widening. I leaned down to his level.

"Yes. I'm here. Are you okay?"

Lake attempted to lift his arm, but it seemed to be too heavy for him. His usually strapping physique was now fragile and weak, and I didn't like it one bit.

"My-my..." he muttered and tried to lean forward. Reggie knew exactly what Lake was talking about and helped him get his back off the wall. When he analyzed Lake's backside, his face fell.

"They took his wings."

"His what?" I asked, stunned. I heard what Reggie said, I just couldn't believe it. And when I leaned over to see it for myself, it made it all too real. Lake's T-shirt was ripped away at the shoulder blades, revealing deep, wide crevices in his back. The edges of his flesh around the holes were jagged and coagulated chunks of blood only slightly hid the layers of meat and skin that made up that part of his back. It was clear that his wings had been yanked right out of him, and it looked so painful. "What does this mean?"

"I have to get Lake to the White Realm. When an angel's wings are taken from them, it's only a matter of time before their entire body and soul turns to dust. It's a slow-acting spell the Red Realm casts on an angel, specifically when they want them to suffer," Reggie explained.

"Can he be saved?" I asked frantically.

"Only sometimes. But no matter what, it requires the Elders to cast a counteracting incantation, which is why we need to get him there quickly."

"Why would they do this to him?" It didn't make sense. Why didn't they just kill him like the rest of the angels?

"Dominic," Lake murmured.

When he said that, it clicked. Lake and Dominic were long-time rivals. Besties turned enemies. And as sexy and irresistible as Dominic was, he had to pay. He took my sister away from me, or at least allowed Queen Hysteria to, and now he was threatening the only good people left in my life. I felt like such a jerk for spending as much time as I did in the Red Realm and not making more of an effort to help Lake with the plan to destroy the region. But now I was ready. I was ready to do what I had to do.

I stood up and lit the cigarette that I'd been holding on to. Both Reggie and Lake glanced up at me. Reggie sensed that I was anxious. "What are you doing?"

"I'm going to kill Dominic," I declared after taking a long puff.

Lake moved his legs and tried to lean his body forward as leverage to help get himself up, but Reggie rested a hand on his shoulder. "You can't go, brother."

"She can't go alone," Lake huffed.

"She shouldn't go at all. But if she must, I'll go with her," Reggie said.

"You can't defeat him."

Lake hadn't told me much about each angel's role, but I'd learned enough to know that Reggie was not equipped to fight and defeat a being from the Red Realm. The White Realm had chosen specific souls as warriors to defend its dimension, and these warriors had special abilities to aid in that, such as strength and flying.

"Fellas, we don't have time to argue. I'll go alone," I said.

Lake clearly wasn't giving up so easily. He shuffled to his feet, but not without Reggie's help. "Frankie, you can't do this on your own," Reggie said as he held most of Lake's weight. "Dominic will kill you within a matter of seconds."

"Then who's going to fight him, huh?" My patience was growing thin.

"When I get Lake to the White Realm, I will request that the Elders send Mercenary Angels. But it isn't guaranteed. The White Realm does not usually seek revenge."

"This isn't about revenge, Reggie!" I yelled. "This is about a bunch of assholes taking things from us. Taking people from us." Remorse for screaming at an angel quickly set in, but it felt necessary to get my point across.

Lake's eyebrows furrowed, and I wasn't completely sure whether it was anger or worry or pain that did it. But he looked straight into my eyes and said, "Let's go get him."

CHAPTER THIRTY-ONE

Just Wingin' It

Lake's body felt like it weighed a ton, but I was somehow managing to carry most of it on my uninjured arm. He leaned his burly frame against me as we rushed down the sidewalk leading us to the Centaurus building. It was now daylight outside, the early morning sun peeking through the narrow alleyways between the buildings. It was unusual. I couldn't remember the last time I'd seen sunlight in Shitsburgh. I had grown so accustomed to the gloom that the bright rays felt intrusive and unwanted.

Although Reggie and I protested, Lake insisted that Reggie get back to the White Realm to inform the Elders of what was happening, and to request the assistance of the Mercenary Angels. He claimed this was his and Dominic's fight, and even though he knew there was only limited time before this spell would disintegrate him, he seemed to believe he would have time to kick Dominic's ass and get back to the White Realm to be saved. Deep down, I think he didn't care whether or not he died, as long as he got the chance to end the feud between him and Dominic once and for all.

I still had The Liberation Stone, and the plan was that while Dominic and Lake were settling the score, I would figure out a way to get inside of that elevator. I wasn't all that excited about it. Yes, I wanted to get rid of Dominic and the stupid portal, but we still didn't know what would happen to me once the Great Elders activated the stone. Lake traveled to the White Realm while I was gone to figure it out, but no one seemed to have any answers. Apparently, there has never been a chosen one like me before.

My nerves felt jumpy as the idea of facing Dominic sunk in. Lake and I barreled through the doors of my place of employment—soon to be former—and I couldn't stop thinking about how all this was going to go down. How the fuck were two gimpy-ass people going to fight a strong, evil Red Realm prince who'd been named one of the best Afflictionists to have ever worked there? My arm was broken, and I hadn't a lick of any intoxicants coursing through my veins to give me the strength and balls I might need to do this. And Lake was way worse than me. Although he still looked like a Norse god, his limping and moaning with every step wasn't too promising. The ratted T-shirt hanging off his body was a serious tease, revealing just little bits of his perfectly sculpted chest and abs. But I couldn't think about that at the moment. Now, we had to figure out how we were going to get past the Henchmen. I was sure Dominic would have Boris and a few others waiting for us, just to be a dick and throw a wrench into our plans. He wouldn't make it easy to get to his office.

But to our surprise, there was no one in the lobby of the Centaurus building. A sigh of relief escaped me, but the tiny victory was short-lived. Dominic wouldn't make it this simple.

We reached the normal elevator, and the thought of being so close to the portal elevator irritated me. All I needed was a damn keycard to get inside.

I helped Lake into the regular elevator and headed down to floor thirteen. As soon as the doors slid closed, *Twisted Sister* and their heavy metal guitar notes started telling us we were gonna burn in Hell.

Not tonight, 80's-hair band. Not tonight.

The doors slid open to Dominic's floor, and I was sure there'd be some Henchmen waiting for us, but the room was completely empty. No Henchmen. No Raven sitting at the receptionist's desk. We stepped onto the blood-colored carpet and began staggering toward Dominic's ornate wooden office doors. I was shocked when Lake reached for the handle and swung open the door. It seemed like he might have gained some strength between our walk from the building's entrance to Dominic's office, which was a really good thing. We needed as much combined energy as we could possibly get if the plan was to fight and win.

The curtains to the large window wall in Dominic's office were wide open and the glass perfectly clear, revealing the In Between and all of those helpless souls waiting in the impossibly long line below us. The fireplace was going strong, glowing embers dancing away from the tall flames and disappearing into the air.

"Are you okay?" Lake finally said, and I realized then that he hadn't said a word to me this entire time. It was okay. I didn't notice on account of trying to figure out how the fuck we were going to get out of this alive.

"I'm fine."

"Of course she's fine," Dominic's deeply distinguished voice called out before he swiveled his chair around to face us, reminding me of the classic evil villain from those old retro cartoons. His sexiness caught me off guard. I'd forgotten how arousing even his eyes could be, and I was suddenly thirsty for his brand of seduction. My gaze lingered on his fingers and a familiar throb nearly forced me to cross my legs. How could he make me feel this way when I was so mad, I wanted to kill him?

"Dominic, don't drag this out. You know what has to be done," Lake said, then coughed. That wasn't good showing on his part.

"Look at you, brother. You're a mess. You know as well as I do this won't end well."

I've always loved when men called each other 'brother,' even when they really weren't related. It was a masculine term of endearment that I very much admired. It made it seem like, though Lake might have hated Dominic for whatever reason, there was still some semblance of amiability toward someone he was once very close to. Then again, it might not have meant a single thing and Dominic was about ready to throw Lake into the hungry flames of his fireplace.

Lake let go of me to stand on his own. "You know I can fight you, even without my wings."

Dominic stood up. "You brought this upon yourself, Lake. You chose to be my enemy. I offered you a place here with me."

"And you betrayed the White Realm," Lake said. "I could never form an alliance with you."

"Oh, *I* betrayed the White Realm?" Dominic chuckled sarcastically. "All I did was kill one of our own. I didn't mean to murder him. You know as well as I do it was an accident. I didn't know my strength when I became a warrior. And the guilt of what I'd done weighed heavy upon my soul. But the Elders didn't forgive me. They banished me, sent me away for a mistake. Unlike you. They forgave you. Shit, they even promoted you."

I didn't understand. It sounded like Dominic was insinuating that Lake did something just as bad as he did, which was completely insane because I couldn't think of anything that would be just as bad as murdering someone in the White Realm. "Lake, what is he talking about?"

Dominic stepped around his desk toward us. "You didn't tell her?" he asked Lake.

"I haven't had the time," Lake said, gritting his teeth.

"Tell me what?"

Lake's eyes met mine, eyebrows raised up high in an apologetic furrow. "It wasn't the right time."

"Now, this is awkward," Dominic interjected. "Here, let me do the honors. Frankie," he said, his hand gesturing to me, then Lake. "Meet your father."

My stomach twisted into a knot. "My what?"

Lake grasped onto my hand. "I was going to tell you, eventually."

I hastily pulled out of his grip. "How is this even possible? You're an angel."

"Hence, the betrayal part," Dominic said. "Angels are not supposed to fuck humans." His words made me flinch when I realized he was talking about my beloved mother.

Lake stepped in front of me, blocking Dominic and his boorishness. "For those couple of months that your mother left your father, her Guide lost track of her. I offered to help find her, as sometimes angels help one another if they are in need, no matter what their job title. And when I did find her, she had almost made a poor choice that could have affected many people. Guides are only supposed to induce virtuous thoughts and allow a protégé to choose his or her own path, but I stepped in and stopped her completely."

"What did she almost do?" I asked, angry tears threatening to erupt from my eyes. There were different levels of rage forming inside of me as Lake spoke, but most had to do with the fact that Alex wasn't here to help me make sense of all this.

"She was very depressed about the fight she and your father had, which had to do with the fact that she could no longer have children. It was why she felt she needed to leave him. This left her very emotionally vulnerable and mentally distraught, and she wanted to end her own life."

"Ah, but you made sure she didn't, and you gave it to her good," Dominic said while making a crude gesture.

Lake ignored him. "You must know that I cared deeply for her. It wasn't just sex."

"Please don't talk about my mother like that," I said to both Lake and Dominic, fighting the urge to slap them.

"Things happened," he continued. "I didn't even know I could procreate. And because I was supernatural, it's the only reason why your mother was able to get pregnant with you."

"Why didn't she tell me? She let me grow up thinking my father was my father. I called him *Dad*."

To be honest, there were times when I felt different than the rest of my family. My physical features weren't the same as some of theirs. But I had no idea it was because I was a bastard child of an angel. Suddenly, the anger shifted to my mother and the fact that she cheated on her husband. "Did my da-...my... did he know?" I wasn't even sure what to call him now.

"He'll always be your father, Frankie. And he knew. He knew everything about me."

Not what I expected to hear. "Did my sister know?"

"Your mother and father decided not to tell anyone else. In fact, it was because of them that the Elders decided not to banish me. They made a plea for me and asked that the White Realm forgive me for my indiscretions. In return, they were to keep our secret and the knowledge of the White Realm to themselves."

"If you cared about my mother, why didn't you stay with her?" I asked. Part of me knew the answer to this. I assumed it was a no-no for angels and humans to have a relationship.

"Your mother and father are soulmates. They belong together in this life and the next. And they were thrilled about having you. They felt it was a miracle. A blessing for them."

Lake's words comforted me, filling my unanswered questions with a temporary sense of calm. Flashes of my mom and dad flickered through my mind. The angry tears turned to longing, and they were now too heavy to keep locked in the corners of my eyes. I missed them so much.

"Are you seriously believing the shit that is coming out of this man's mouth?" Dominic asked, folding his arms across his chest. "Lake fucked your mother. He's your damn dad and you had no idea. You actually wanted to fuck him, too. Did you think I didn't know?"

I turned away from Lake and wiped my eyes. Dominic was right. I wanted to kiss my own dad, and now I felt sick. Disgusted with myself. How could I have looked at my father that way?

"Don't listen to him, Frankie. You didn't know I was your father. And I'm also your Guide. I became your Guide when you were born, and I've been with you this whole time. I wish I could have stopped Alexandra from selling yours and her soul, but we cannot *force* a protégé to do anything. Everything is ultimately their decision."

"Now, tell me, how the hell does that happen? You fuck her mother, which is against the rules, and then you become her daughter's Guide? Were the Elders drunk when they allowed this?"

"I thought you said I didn't have a Guide," I reminded him. But Lake didn't look pleased with himself.

"Although the Elders weren't very happy with it, they allowed me to become your Guide at your mother's request. She didn't trust anyone else because I was your biological father. I hadn't told you because it still wasn't the time. I had to keep it from you for a little while longer. At least until I spoke with the Elders."

"And you were going to let the Great Elders kill me for good?" I asked, betrayal hitting me hard.

Lake shook his head vehemently. "No. I wasn't going to let that happen."

"So...I'm an angel? Is this why I have glitches?"

Lake studied my words. "Glitches?"

"And my wings. Is this why I have wings?"

"Wings don't normally reveal themselves until a soul reaches the White Realm. But it seems to be different with you. You are both human and angel, which is something that doesn't happen." Lake explained. "What I did with your mother has happened before, but it's usually against our rules. It is very, very rare and has never resulted in conceiving a baby. In the time that you were gone, I was able to discuss what your fate and what your wings meant with the Elders. According to them, it's something completely special. They have never seen it before either. They feel that maybe you have started a new lineage. We don't necessarily know what this means. Maybe it means that eventually we don't have to keep our existence a secret. Who knows? But it is something that the Elders are open to exploring."

"Is this why they chose me?" I asked, whispering it to him to prevent Dominic from hearing me. He still didn't know what exactly destroyed the portals.

"We aren't sure," he said.

"You know," Dominic interrupted again. "I can totally understand the obsession you have with these women. If Frankie's mother tasted anything like she does, I would have definitely put a baby inside of her."

The tears were now replaced with a fresh layer of humiliation, and I turned away from...my dad. There was a distinct possibility that Lake probably already knew about Dominic and me, but it was still embarrassing.

It seemed Lake had just about enough of Dominic's bullshit and finally broke away from our extremely uncomfortable conversation. He twisted back to Dominic, giving him all his attention. "We both made mistakes, and you know as well as I do that I begged the Elders to allow you to stay. They were willing to work something out with you, but you'd already decided not to come back."

Dominic stepped away from his desk, jutting his chest out as if to be claiming the spot he stood in. "I was banished from the White Realm, but I found my place. I was born to be an Afflictionist, not some pansy angel like you."

"You knew it was a matter of time before we descended upon your region, Dominic."

"Oh, I knew. But I'm not going down without a fight."

Lake glanced down at his feet, then back up into Dominic's eyes. "Let me help you. Maybe I can talk to the Elders. Frankie is breathing new life into our kind. Maybe they will allow you to atone for your mistakes."

Dominic laughed, long and hard. "Atone for my mistakes?" he repeated in between breaths. His laughing didn't stop, and I backed up into the wall farthest from where he and Lake stood. He seemed to be unhinging right before our eyes—like some kind of crazy person. My heart pounded with anticipation of what he was going to do next. Lake didn't move and just watched, waiting.

But it wasn't long before Dominic's laughs morphed into a thundering roar as he hunched forward and back up again. Then, giant black wings exploded out of his back, ripping his blazer and shirt right off his body into pieces. The wings stretched out wide on either side of him before curling into his body. Dominic's feathers were mesmerizing—charcoal black with an iridescent purple sheen with every movement. It looked like his wings were alive and had a mind of their own. And he was now naked from the waist up. Son of a bitch, I was right... Dominic's body was absolutely superb.

I nestled myself into the corner of the room and squatted on my haunches. Lake turned to take stock of where I was. But when he twisted his head back around, Dominic surprised him with a right hook to the mouth.

"No!" I yelled but thought twice about moving. This was their fight. I had no business being in the middle of it. Besides, what the fuck could I possibly do to stop it? My arm was still broken as hell.

Lake only stumbled slightly, which made me proud considering he was low on fuel. The back of his T-shirt was ripped to shreds, revealing the deep, dark wounds where his wings once were. I'd imagine by this point his own wings would have erupted out of him, but they were gone now. Would he ever get new ones?

That tingling itch was back, and I winced and rubbed my back against the wall to try to scratch at my shoulder blades.

"This is ridiculous, Lake. How the hell are you going to defeat me without your wings?"

Lake lifted his foot up and rammed it against Dominic's stomach, sending a forceful push through Dominic's body and causing it to slam against the window wall behind him. His wings pinged off the glass, but his left one quickly bounced off and swung into Lake. The wing flicked Lake clear across the room, his body gliding through the air before meeting the wall next to the fireplace. Lake slid down, leaving behind cracked sheetrock in his wake.

"Give it up, brother. You can't do this without your wings," Dominic yelled at him.

Lake took a breath on all fours before rising to his feet. "I don't need them to defeat you, Dominic," he huffed.

"Oh yeah? Then how do you expect to win this?" Dominic lifted his hand and flung it toward the fireplace, ordering angry flames to shoot out at Lake. Fireballs landed on Lake's face and arms, and he quickly swiped at his skin to put them out.

In that very moment, my chest began to glow. I glanced down at my shirt as The Liberation Stone pulsed a bright pink hue underneath the fabric. My eyes darted to Lake.

"It's happening," he said.

"What's happening?" Dominic asked, his attention immediately drawn to the bright light emitting from me. I stood up, my back tight against the wall. "Tell me what's happening," Dominic demanded.

Lake said that the Great Elders would activate the stone inside of the elevator portal, but I must have been close enough to it for them to believe I was on it. So now it was time. It was time to get my ass to that portal before Dominic killed Lake. We didn't know what would happen to me, if I would vanish into thin air forever once The Liberation Stone destroyed the region's portal. But none of that mattered anymore. Alex was stuck in the Red Realm forever, and I had nothing else to live for. If I had to leave this world for good, then I might as well go out with a bang. It was what Alexandra would have wanted me to do.

The door out of Dominic's office was just a few feet away from me...

"Is that it?" Dominic asked, his eyes fixated on the rock around my neck. "Is that what destroys the portals?" He began to move toward me, his hands held out in front of him as if he were ready to snatch the chain from around my neck. "Lilith told me she suspected it. And the king and queen had a feeling about it, too."

I wanted Dominic to touch it. I knew what The Liberation Stone could do after it knocked Queen Hysteria Bitch on her ass. So I wasn't at all afraid. But, apparently, Lake wasn't going to wait because he lunged at Dominic before he could get to me, crashing into his side. They both tumbled onto the floor, and Dominic's wing collided with the window wall on the way down, busting it open. Pieces of glass shattered all over both of them. The breathable atmosphere in the office was immediately replaced with the hot, stagnant air outside of that window.

"Frankie!" Lake hollered from the floor as he held onto Dominic. "Go! Now!"

Right as Lake yelled at me, a terrible ache shot through my shoulder blades, forcing me to falter. Suddenly, my leather jacket felt full and needed to get off my body. I removed it as fast as I could, wincing at the burning sensation—like something clawing its nails through the layers of my skin. Trying my hardest to ignore it, I reached for the door and swung it open. But before I could cross the threshold into the lobby, something burst out of my backside. The pressure of it pulled me back a little, but I was able to keep my footing. And when I finally glanced over my shoulders, there were my gray, glittery wings. The weight distribution felt a little strange, but there was no denying the unmistakable power these wings surged through me. They flapped once as I stood still, then flapped again when my feet started moving. This combination launched me forward and I was down the stretch of crimson-colored carpet to the elevator in a blink of an eye.

My wings slightly curled inward when I entered the elevator but fit just fine once I was completely inside. I jammed my finger into the number one over and over again and waited for the doors to shut. And just as they were sliding toward each other, I saw Dominic hoist Lake into the air, then toss him through the broken window wall.

"Lake!" I cried out. Dominic spun around and glared at me. His fierce wings expanded wide at his sides before they flapped, lifting his entire body off the ground. He flew from his office into the waiting area, but right as he reached the elevator, the doors finally closed.

CHAPTER THIRTY-TWO

One Last Puff

I thought long and hard about finding the speakers within the inner workings of the elevator to stop Black Sabbath from singing about Heaven and Hell. But as the red digital number on the panel slowly ticked backwards, the words from the high-pitched rock and roller were kind of making me think.

If only these words were true. Maybe this was all some crazy-ass dream. Maybe Alex never actually sold our souls, and I just succumbed to the cancer that was eating away at my stomach. This could all be part of my afterlife. I could be in another dimension, different from Earth and The Red and White Realm. How far-fetched would that be? Quite frankly, it'd be more believable than running around the streets of this horrible place called Shitsburgh—that I wasn't even sure could be found on a map—with a bunch of unrealistically beautiful angels and demon

Henchmen. Oh, and let's not forget the fact that I now had ash-colored wings—couldn't even get pretty ones—growing out of my back, and that my real father was a thousand-year-old former gladiator angel who, up until just a few minutes ago, I wanted to fuck. Sure, this life wasn't fake at all.

I glanced down at the tip of my wing, which curved inward close to my body. A sense of warmth and security filled the space between myself and my new appendages, something that resembled snuggling with my favorite blanket fresh out of the dryer when I was a kid. Or a tender hug from Jacob. The kind where he'd gently squeeze me into the crook of his neck and a clean whiff of his aquatic cologne filled me with a heady excitement that usually led to sweet sex. My fingertips grazed a gray feather, and I was surprised at how silky it felt against my skin. Even a bit of a girly, teenage thrill sent butterflies to my stomach when the light caught glittery gleams of silver burrowed between the plumage. My curiosity followed the curvature of the wing, my head trying to twist in an unnatural manner in an attempt to get a better look at my back now that I had these things. I was glad that my shirt didn't shred into pieces when they popped out like it did for Dominic. But I was still able to feel a cool draft where the wings punctured holes into the fabric.

As if the wings knew I was trying to take a better look at them, they spread out wider. It was extremely strange. I didn't exactly feel myself make them do it, like moving my arms or my legs, but there seemed to be some control on my part. I wondered how the hell I would be able to shove them back under my skin and into my shoulder blades.

There was no time to inspect my new wings and explore their capabilities. The elevator doors slid open, and just around the backside of this elevator was the portal to the Red Realm. The Great Elders must have known as much because as soon as I stepped out, the pink glow from the stone on my chest brightened. The view ahead of me was still an empty lobby. But right as I was about to round the corner, the ground shook and exploded open. Literally fucking blew up like a geyser. Chunks of the floor flew high up into the air, followed by Dominic and his massive black wings. My wings immediately formed a protective shield over my head, blocking the raining debris from giving me a concussion.

When it sounded like the coast was clear, and I was sure my brains weren't going to get smashed in, I slowly emerged from my cover. My eyes shot up to Dominic floating in midair, his wings moving in slow, long waves. It was interesting—Dominic's appearance didn't match his age. He looked so much younger than thousands of years old. But the way his wings moved told a different story. Somehow, they exuded a level of prestige that only an angel who had been around thousands of years could have.

The muscles in his bare chest flexed with every movement, and his body didn't look like it was just hanging there. It was flying *with* his wings—upright and strong. Although he was now only wearing his suit slacks, he continued to give off that suave businessman vibe.

And still very much sexy, if not even more so because of his gorgeous pinions.

"Franklin!" Dominic's voice boomed off the walls of the destroyed lobby of the Centaurus building. "You are not getting on that elevator. Hand over the stone. Now!"

"I can't," I called out. "It won't come off my neck." I mean, it was the truth. The fucker wouldn't come off even if I agreed to just hand it over to him. But Dominic did not look amused by this.

"You expect me to believe that? Are you going to make me remove it from your neck myself?"

"You could try." I chuckled at the memory of Queen Hysteria touching The Liberation Stone. She had to be much stronger than Dominic, and if the Great Elders managed to give her one good, I could only imagine what they could do to Dominic.

It didn't take long to find out, either. Dominic clearly thought I was bluffing because as soon as I'd said that, he flew directly at me. Directly at The Liberation Stone. But before he could even lay a hand on the rock, a deep pink blast of light collided with Dominic's right wing. A plume of dark feathers instantaneously burst into the air and Dominic's body flipped backward. His other wing didn't see it coming and didn't flap quick enough to pick up the slack, causing his flight to falter. He crashed into the rubble of the smashed-up ground, but swiftly recovered and barely took any damage from the fall. But his wing did from the Great Elders. There was a clear bald spot at the cusp, and now it seemed to be flying differently.

"Aargh!" Dominic hollered. "You won't be able to defeat me! I am far much stronger than you'll ever be."

I shook my head. "But it's not me you have to worry about. This stone will kick your ass."

"That stone is a joke, as are you. I knew from the moment you started working here that something was off with you. And then I found out who your true father was. I sent you to the City of Centaurus on purpose. Lilith drugged you on my orders. Everything was set in place purposely because I knew it would draw Lake to me. He'd come looking for you eventually. And I've wanted to kill him for a long time."

The image of Dominic throwing Lake out into the In Between came back. I wasn't sure if the fall would kill him, but the fact that he wasn't getting treatment for the loss of his wings and that Red Realm spell would.

"You should have stayed in the Red Realm, Franklin," Dominic continued. "You're a fucked-up addict. All Lilith had to do was keep feeding you demon dust. If she didn't show you your sister, you'd still be there. You'd still be working for nothing."

"Working for nothing?" I asked.

Dominic released a devious chuckle. "Did you seriously think your job as a CA was meaningful? All of those people you called to check up on to make sure they got what they paid for? It was all fake."

"What do you mean?"

"This is all fake!" Dominic hollered, spreading his arms out wide as if speaking to the building itself. "The devils do not make deals. We do not give anyone anything for their souls. No one gets what they ask for."

I couldn't believe what I was hearing. The guilt of the past three years had just multiplied. "But what about me and Alex? We didn't die. We sold our souls to stay alive, and we didn't die."

"The only exception. We must procure employees to do our bidding, after all."

Losing my sister was devastating. Not knowing what happened to Lake was fucking with my head. But learning this was...a crushing blow. The only thing that had kept me from falling over the edge the past three years was the idea that every person I had sealed was at least getting something that would make them happy. But it turned out that I was sealing their fate to an eternity of torture for nothing. Nothing!

Rage began to build in the pits of my stomach. I didn't know what to say to Dominic's revelation. Alex was in the forefront of it all. "Why did Lilith show me Alex?"

Dominic rolled his eyes. "Lilith is an asshole who felt threatened by you. But her actions didn't ruin my plan. Lake is lying dead as we speak."

I chose not to believe that and questioned him more about Alex instead. "Why did you have to let Queen Hysteria kill Alex?"

"The Queen was looking for something to do. Every time she comes to visit Earth, she takes a soul herself. I figured I wouldn't be losing much if I let her have Alexandra. Besides, your sister's work performance had been lacking. She would have been dead sooner rather than later, anyway. She's where she deserves to be," Dominic said, his voice sounding a bit stronger since he was hit with The Liberation Stone. But his last words infuriated me. Alex didn't deserve to be punished the way she was.

A jolt of fury started at my feet, rising up through my legs and my torso, to my back. My wings expanded, then flapped once, the inertia from their movement lifting me off the ground. It shot my body up about ten feet in the air, and when they flapped again, set me just at the same height as Dominic. That wonderful weightless feeling I had felt with Samuel and Ariel at the angel nightclub came back, but it was even better knowing that I was flying on my own.

Dominic and I were now face to face, hovering over the giant hole in the floor that led all the way down to the thirteenth floor. I hadn't a single clue what I or my wings could do, but I felt pretty confident about The Liberation Stone and its ability to protect me.

"You realize that all I have to do is rip your head off and the stone is mine, right?" Dominic asked calmly. I glanced down at my feet, then back up at him with only my eyes.

"You could try," I said, then smirked. As if those words were on cue, my right wing curved inward, practically blanketing my body, then swung away from me all in one rapid motion. The momentum carried my body with it as it vigorously struck Dominic, causing him to twist and somersault in the air like he was some kind of Olympic gymnast. I couldn't even believe what I'd just done, but I certainly didn't display the dubiety of my own actions. Instead, I did a power pose—fists at my hips, chest jutted out, wings spread broadly on either side of me. Resolute in my fight plan. A vigilante fucking superhero. My broken arm hurt to no end, but I was fighting through the pain.

Dominic righted himself before launching straight at me. His wings thrust him forward, but my own wings waved high then low, heaving me over just in time to dodge him. This made me smile, but it was immediately replaced with a worrisome grimace when Dominic quickly looped back over *me*. There was an eerie moment of silence when I lifted my head to meet his gaze while he stared at me in an upside-down position. Everything seemed like it was happening in slow motion, but I didn't have time to evade a collision. He came down on me, our bodies crashing into one another, with so much force that it shook the contents of my stomach and I was instantly nauseated. My head jerked from whiplash, and for a brief moment, I thought stars were actually twinkling around me until I realized that the twinkles were the lights flashing from each floor. Dominic's force rocketed us back down the hole in the ground, down the multiple floors that led to his office on the thirteenth floor.

This was bad. This was really fucking bad. He was pushing me farther and farther away from the portal.

Our bodies slammed into the crimson carpet. Each and every one of my bones felt like they had cracked, but Dominic was undeterred by the fall. As we lay on our backs, he immediately reached over to me in an attempt to grab hold of The Liberation Stone. I wanted to call a timeout and ask that he gives me a second to catch my damn breath—and maybe smoke a cigarette or two—but there was no chance of that happening.

I erratically slapped Dominic's hands away from me, hoping that somehow this might be enough to stop him. But it wasn't, of course. He worked his legs over me and straddled my body, pinning my arms down on either side of my head. The fractured bone in my arm screamed at me and an involuntary groan escaped my mouth.

Why wasn't this stupid stone doing anything now when I needed it the most?

His hands moved to my neck, and *my* hands instinctively attempted to pull them off me. But he slowly applied pressure to my throat, cutting my airway little by little. I gasped and fought to catch a breath while my legs thrashed beneath him. I could feel my wings trying to push my body away from the ground, but the heft of Dominic's solid muscle wouldn't allow it. Hank Hannigan's last moments came to mind. His head falling off his body. The blood spilling over the stump left behind. Dominic was about to squeeze my head off to take The Liberation Stone.

And right when I felt just about ready to give up, some kind of crazy energy metabolized within my exhausted limbs and found its way through my hands. I dug my fingers into the divots between the knuckles of Dominic's closed fist. Remarkably, I managed to get him to release his grip from my neck and interlace our fingers together. My strength was now matching his, and I was successfully guiding his arms away from me. Albeit, my muscles were shaking almost uncontrollably. But so were his, it seemed. We were at a draw. A power struggle. A race to see just who was going to be the first to cave. Dominic cocked his head at me, and I wondered if that glint in his eye was surprise or intrigue. But I didn't know how much longer I could hold him off. If I stopped fighting and let go, he would have the opportunity to finish me off. Remove my head and steal The Liberation Stone. Which, by the way, had to come alive soon. It just had to. Any other time someone tried to touch it, it got pissed off and retaliated. I was desperate now for the Great Elders to help me. They couldn't let me die here. I had to get to the elevator to destroy the portal. If I didn't do it, then who the fuck would?

Finally, the light. The light from the stone that had been steadily glowing right on my chest finally did something. It brightened. Dominic squinted at its intensity, which consequently lessened his grasp around my esophagus. I took advantage of this and shoved him off me with all my might, exhaling and inhaling deeply for the full breaths of air properly circulating in and out of my lungs. I couldn't believe it, but the radiance of The Liberation Stone was forcing Dominic to retreat. He stood up to his feet, cowering away from the beam that only seemed to be getting stronger. I stood up with him, mindfully following his every move with my bust. I didn't want the Great Elders to break contact with Dominic.

The rosy-hued beacon of light grew and grew, until a fireball the size of a cantaloupe shot out from The Liberation Stone and hit Dominic square in the stomach. He sailed across the room, crashing into the Gothic portrait of King Centaurus and Queen Hysteria before landing on the ground. The ruined picture dropped right on top of him as he lay sprawled out on the ground.

This was my chance. I couldn't waste any time wondering if that blow killed Dominic. I glanced up at the seemingly endless hole leading to the lobby where the elevator portal was. Live electrical wires dangled from the broken ceilings of each floor, blue currents erratically dancing out of the severed cables. Metal rebar stuck out all over the place. The only way to quickly get away from Dominic and up to the portal was to fly through.

I glanced over to each one of my gray wings. It still wasn't known exactly how they were controlled, but I mentally imagined them starting to flap, lifting my feet inch by inch off the ground until I was completely in flight. Not sure if this was the reason or if it helped in some way, but soon I could feel my body levitating while my wings fluttered.

The first half of the journey was scary. Trying to dodge getting stabbed by rebar or electrocuted by the wires fucked with my ability to focus on my aerial journey through the hole, but once I was past the fifth floor, all was good. I soared straight through, reaching the lobby of the Centaurus building and planting my feet directly in front of the elevator.

"FRANKLIN!"

Dominic's voice rumbled through the ground and the walls, shaking everything around me. I dashed around the normal elevator to the portal to the Red Realm elevator, and with every step, the brilliance of The Liberation Stone was enhanced. I was worried that the Great Elders were actually going to blind me and prevent me from reaching the portal.

But it didn't stop me because...Boris did. He was standing at the portal elevator, both feet planted firmly on the ground right in front of the closed door, hands balled into fists at his sides.

We stood face to face, a completely unfair stalemate. He was a giant compared to me, and I knew his supernatural strength could overpower me if I tried to break past him, even with my wings. Besides, the elevator door was shut. I didn't have a keycard.

But he did.

"Boris, please," I said, attempting to calmly talk my way out of this. "I don't know what this will mean for you, but I need to get inside that portal. This whole operation is fake. It's all fake. Please. The Red Realm is only going to continue to take from innocent people."

Boris didn't say anything. Instead, he lifted his dark sunglasses off his head, finally revealing what was behind them. And it was nothing. He had no eyeballs. Only two deep, black holes in his head. He reached inside of his jacket, and I braced myself, expecting him to pull out some supernatural laser gun to shoot right at my forehead.

But there was no gun. Instead, Boris pulled out the keycard. And without a word, he swiped it over the metal panel on the elevator door, prompting it to slide open. I rushed inside and turned to face him.

"I won't need this anymore," he said, handing me the keycard. I took it from him.

Dumbfounded, I stared at him. "Why?" was all I could say.

Boris shrugged. "It just feels right, Frankie. That's all."

The feeling that Boris was somehow different had always been there, and I was grateful that there was obviously some ounce of goodness beneath the evil. Maybe he had a glitch of his own. Maybe everyone had a piece of both the light and the dark in them. I knew I did.

Boris hurried out of the lobby and out of the building, climbing through the rubble and bypassing Dominic on the way out. Had Dominic seen him, he would have destroyed Boris. There was no telling where Boris was going or what he was thinking, but there was no time to find out.

"Franklin!" Dominic's voice rang out again. The Liberation Stone was still blazing, and the rough surface of the pink rock rubbed warmly against my skin. I exhaled an exasperated breath. I was tired.

My wings relaxed and rested on my back while I reached inside my back pocket, pulling out a pack of smokes. The hard box was now smashed and soft, and the one cigarette left was wrinkled but still smokable. I lit the end and sucked on the cotton filter, the scorched paper slowly transforming into ash. The toxic fumes filled my lungs with a satisfying burn, and I silently wished I had some vodka to accompany this magnificently well-deserved moment.

I had no idea what was about to happen. By the way The Liberation Stone continued to shine brightly and now that I was in the portal where the Great Elders wanted me to be in order for them to destroy it, these were probably my last moments. Alex was gone. Lake was probably dead. This whole place was completely fake. There was nothing else to live for. I hoped that my life would at least flash in front of my eyes before there was no longer any evidence that I even existed in the first place. Before my soul was gone forever. I wanted to see my mom one more time. And my dad, even though we weren't biologically related. I didn't care. He was my real dad.

I wanted to see Alex and apologize to her for letting her down when she needed me the most. All these years, she fought to try to restore the old me and I resisted. She stood by me through all the bitchiness and sarcasm and bad moods. Alex never even came in between me and my addictions. She just let me indulge and truly tried to accept me for who I had become. I needed to tell her how sorry I was.

And Jacob. I wished I could finally say goodbye to Jacob. If not for myself, but to give him the closure that he probably needed to once and for all move on from me.

"Franklin!" Dominic said once again, appearing in the shadows of the portal elevator. Soot covered his body. His wings looked ratty and worn, feathers missing from random spots. He held on to his stomach, where I could clearly see a large black-and-blue bruise he was trying to cover up with his forearm. "You're dead!"

He dove forward at me, his free hand stretched out in front of him and his fingers curling in anticipation of grabbing onto The Liberation Stone. I dropped my cigarette and spread my arms out, my wings following suit. Lifting my chin up to the air, I welcomed death.

Right as Dominic's fingertips landed on my chest, the light from the stone enveloped us both, and everything turned white.

CHAPTER THIRTY-THREE

Welcome to the Right Realm

The radiance around me dimmed, and I was able to see clearly again. Sitting before me at a long, glass table were three silhouettes of what looked to be the shapes of people. However, I couldn't tell if they were actual people because they were all shrouded in a light blue hooded cape, the glossy fabric hanging low and hiding their faces. The entire room was white. Not a vibrant or stark white. More of a muted white. As if there wasn't any color at all, if that made sense. I glanced around, searching for something to tell me where I was, but there was nothing but me and the three beings in front of me. The one in the middle spoke first.

"Franklin Shepherd," the being said. I couldn't quite tell if it was a male or female, but the voice had a beautiful harmonic ring to it that somehow sent a calming chill down my spine. "You are standing before the Counsel of the NonAligned to receive judgment for your time spent on Earth as a human being."

"I am?" I asked, surprised. It was pretty interesting that after having heard so little about them, the representatives who chose which souls went where in the afterlife, they were now sitting in front of me. Though, I would have to say, their appearance was a tad bit underwhelming. I wasn't sure what I imagined them to look like—really old men wearing curly white wigs and matte black judicial robes, maybe? But their faces weren't visible, and I started to wonder if they even *had* faces.

I also didn't expect this. My understanding was that once the Great Elders chose me to destroy the portal, I was done for. Dead forever. No soul. No nothing. "I thought I was supposed to die."

"That is correct. Your human body is no longer actively existing in the Earth dimension."

"So...I *am* dead," I stated, an overwhelming sense of loss suddenly flushing me. The desire to grieve my death was strong. I tried to remember dying, tried to recall seeing my life flash before my eyes, but there wasn't any of that. Only the really bright light and Dominic reaching out to touch me. The idea of dying before was scary, even with the times I thought about taking my own life, but now that it had actually happened, I was strangely okay with it.

I glanced down at my chest, remembering that sharp, blinding beam shooting out of The Liberation

Stone, but the necklace was no longer there. The stone was gone, as if it were never there to begin with. And so was the thirst and hunger for self-medication. The underlying craving to remedy my sorrows with alcohol and cigarettes and demon dust had dissolved.

The silhouette in the middle continued, "Under normal circumstances, an angel who is chosen and sacrifices their soul for the greater good of humankind relinquishes the right for their energy to move on to another plane. It is impossible for an entity to survive such power released by the Great Elders in order to eradicate a portal to the Red Realm. However, it seems your kind was able to withstand it."

"My kind?" I asked.

"That is correct. Your kind. You are of angel lineage. And while on very rare occasions a human and an angel have mated, an offspring has never been conceived. In addition to this, you also have the Seal of the Red Realm, which bonds you directly to the underworld and lends you some of its supernatural abilities. We are fairly certain that this is the reason why you were able to survive the intense energy discharged by the Great Elders. Therefore, establishing another *kind* is under further investigation."

"Okay... So, what does this mean?"

The cloaked figure on the right decided to answer. "You were successfully able to destroy the portal to the Red Realm and survive, a deed that has never been achieved over the many centuries since The Angels of

Reform began their quest to end the business of soul sealing. We would like to explore this further, as you might quite possibly not only be able to save the souls of humans heedlessly selling their souls, but the souls of the angels as well."

"You want me to be an Angel of Reform?" Okay, they didn't clearly ask that, but it sounded like they might have been hinting to it.

"That is something to be discussed amongst the Elders of the White Realm," the middle silhouette explained. "The Council of the NonAligned is only here to render a decision on a soul's final destination."

"In accordance with the White Realm Scrolls of Reformation, a soul who has received the Seal of the Red Realm must be required to undergo reform and rehabilitation before he or she can enter the White Realm," the left figure continued. "However, because you have already demonstrated your character through sacrifice, and survived, we would like to offer you a place on that plane."

Were they serious? They were offering me a spot in Heaven? How was this possible? I was a terrible person. I cursed like a sailor, and drank, and smoked cigarettes. I had considered living in the Red Realm amongst other evil beings, choosing to eventually accept the wicked things they did. I left my sister alone because all I cared about was myself. And yet, they were still willing to allow me to be a part of the good team?

"Of course," I said. "I'll...I'll do what I have to."

"Very well," the middle being said.

"What about my sister Alex? Can we go get her?" In the depths of my weird, new *kind* of a soul, I knew the answer to this. But hearing it from the three beings who ultimately decided someone's fate might give me closure.

Who was I kidding? I would miss my sister for all eternity.

"Alexandra Shepherd's soul cannot be saved."

My eyes fell toward my feet as the agonizing loss punched me in the gut all over again, and I struggled to keep my composure. My poor, sweet sister. She never deserved this.

"However..."

My gaze shot up and my heart fluttered. Hope? Could there be hope?

"Because of these new findings and upon learning your abilities, we will also investigate the possibility of recovering and reforming souls that are property of the Red Realm, dependent upon the circumstances of which these souls were sent to the Red Realm in the first place. It is important that we evaluate these souls thoroughly to determine if they are, in fact, worthy of reform and allowed into the White Realm. It would seem that nothing is impossible at this point."

I felt like I could finally take a deep, full breath, something I hadn't done since seeing my sister's tortured soul. Alex was worthy. She was a good person in her human life. There wasn't an evil bone in her body, and she didn't deserve to spend her eternity that way.

And then I thought of Lake. Could he really be dead? "What about Lake? Is he gone?"

"We are here to discuss *your* eternity," the figure on the right insisted.

"But I need to know if... I need to know if he's gone," I said, holding back my emotions the best I could. He lied to me about being my biological father, and there was still a hint of anger leftover about that. But he was still my father. The connection that I kept feeling before I found out the truth was still there. It explained why it was there in the first place and, if anything, only created a deeper, unspoken bond between us. I might have lusted after him at first, but those thoughts were far behind me now. There was no way I could ever look at him that way again.

The beings paused for a beat before the one in the middle answered. I braced myself for the bad news. Dominic threw Lake out of the glass window and into the In Between, which had to be a long way down. He was already in bad shape from losing his wings. I knew he was a supernatural being from another realm, but the loss of his feathery appendages was already enough to kill him. "Lake has suffered a great amount of injury due to his fall. In addition, the removal of an angel's wings carries a high mortality rate when nothing is done to reverse the spell."

My heart sank and my eyes dropped to the floor. He was gone.

"But it would seem that he was recovered in time."

A pang of hope forced my gaze back up at the three hooded figures at the table. "He what? How? He was thrown into the In Between. How did he get out? The portal imploded."

"The In Between can only be reached through the portal leading to the Red Realm," the being explained. "It's essentially an unofficial extension to The Gates."

"What are you saying?" I asked, confused and trying to understand.

"The window in which Lake was thrown out of could not lead to the In Between. The window itself was an illusion. A magical looking glass that reflected the happenings of the Red Realm in real time. Lake was actually thrown into another part of the building, where he was later found by the Guide Angel Reggie and Mercenary Angels sent down from the White Realm to help clear up the aftermath left behind."

"So, Lake is okay?"

"It is not completely known for certain at this time, but steps are being taken in an attempt to rectify the matter."

This answer was better than what I'd originally imagined, which was that Lake was dead.

Dominic. That bastard. He intended to kill Lake. I didn't know why, but for some reason there had been a tinge of doubt that Dominic hated Lake that badly. After all, they had so much history together. But I was wrong. And in my opinion, Dominic needed to rot in Hell for what he did.

"What happened to Dominic?" I asked, refusing to hide the animosity in my tone. Lake had explained what would happen to the angel sacrificing themselves and the ASRs who worked in the building once the portal was destroyed. The process of reform would begin for them, if that was what they chose. But he never told me what would happen to Dominic. He wasn't physically inside the portal with me, but the radiation of The Liberation stone still reached him, and I hoped that it swallowed him whole and reduced him to shit.

None of the veiled beings moved. I couldn't see their faces, if they even had one, but I imagined a stoically indifferent expression glaring back at me from each of them. I briefly wondered if I could be wrong, and there was some kind of emotion for Lake underneath each cover. Sure, they were the Council of the NonAligned and their job was to remain neutral, but who wouldn't want to be on the good team?

"Dominic was banished to The Nothing by King Centaurus and Queen Hysteria, a punishment bestowed upon him for his rote incompetence."

I pressed my lips into a hard line, fighting the urge to smile. The Nothing was worse than dying, in my opinion. It was where he belonged.

"Franklin Shepherd, please sign this document," the shrouded figure on the left said. It was so strange that they all had the same exact, non-gender voice. It was also strange that there was paperwork to sign.

It wasn't until I started moving that I remembered the extra weight on my back was from my wings. I glanced on either side of my shoulders at the gray, bird-like appendages, all silky and glittery. My fondness for them rose by the minute.

My eyes drifted down to the rest of my body. I was still covered in grit and small pieces of sediment from the wreckage of the Centaurus building, and my clothes were torn, showing evidence that I had been in a fight. As soon as I looked at my arm, the pain from the fractured bones came back and I immediately cradled it by the elbow. I made my way over to the glass table, which I soon realized wasn't glass at all. The long, flat surface twinkled and waves of cloudy clusters moved in fluid motions all across it. Various colored dots, large and small, speckled random areas, some spread apart and some bundled closely together. I was reminded of the pictures of our galaxy in my science textbooks from school and mentally compared the two. This table was live footage of the universe.

One of the hooded silhouettes noticed that I was slightly hypnotized by the beautiful cosmos right at my fingertips. "Please sign."

I signed the single piece of paper, which contained

nothing more than an x and a line for which to write my name over. Then, I stepped back. "Now what?"

"Franklin Shepherd," the being in the middle began. "The Counsel of the NonAligned hereby grant you admission to the White Realm, wherein your soul will spend eternity with fellow residents of the White Realm under the rules of the Elders. An Usher will escort you to Passage Gardens, the entrance to the White Realm."

Shuttering memories of the portal and the journey to the Red Realm surged back. I doubted getting to the White Realm would be anything like that, but I just had to ask. "What will it be like? How long will it take?"

"The journey to the White Realm will take approximately seventy-five years in Earth time. However, as you know, other dimensions do know follow a timetable, as time does not exist."

"Seventy-five years!" I said, stunned. An image of Alcazar flashed back, and his explanation of how other dimensions didn't necessarily follow the same time rules as Earth did. *Time is an illusion.* But it didn't take me long to get used to having no time in the Red Realm. As a matter of fact, it was kind of liberating. A timeless eternity in Heaven certainly didn't sound bad at all.

"I can assure you that it will not feel like seventy-five years," the being said. "And you will not be aware of the travel. It will all be over in a flash."

That was a relief.

The genderless NonAligned person in the middle spoke one last time. "Upon arrival, a representative from the Franklin Shepherd welcoming committee will greet you and give you a tour of your new home for all of eternity. It was nice meeting you, Franklin. Safe travels."

"Wait. The Franklin Shepherd what—

"Frankie."

A distant, familiar sound called to me. The guy's voice echoed right into my ear, pulsating high and low,

"Frankie, open your eyes."

I opened my eyes. Immediately, the sparkling lake lined with tall, leafy trees surrounding it took my attention. And it looked very familiar.

My gaze wandered up to the pastel blue sky dabbed with puffy white clouds. They looked unbelievably fluffy, like the creamy goodness of a marshmallowy dessert. To my right, a long wooden pier led out to the water. My eyes followed the length of it in the opposite direction, where it began at the bottom of a hill. A flagstone path trailed the grassy hillside, a walkway leading directly to a big, two-story cottage. *My* two-story cottage. Or rather, my parent's lake house!

"Frankie."

He whispered softly again, this time a fresh and

cool breath wafting through my hair and caressing the skin on my cheek. I turned to my left and there he was, the dangling branches of the weeping willow tree swaying gracefully in the lakefront breeze all around him. "Jacob?"

"Yes, Frankie. It's me. Welcome to the White Realm."

ACKNOWLEDGEMENTS

Special thanks to my editor, Precy Larkins. I am always so terrified to get your feedback, but incredibly grateful to even have you in the first place.

To my cover designer, Murphy Rae, who just has to be the best in the business. And to my formatter, Elaine York, for adding the perfect touch.

A very gracious thank you to my super talented tattoo artist, Richard L. Nagy (Midcity Voodoux Tattoo) for his one-of-a-kind contribution to this book—I might actually get the Seal of the Red Realm tattooed on me at some point.

As always, a thousand kisses to my husband for constantly believing in me.

And finally, to my support system: My parents, Alexis and Vito Sparacino, Juan Quintana; my beautiful sister, Ariana Sparacino; my brother, Pee-wee; and the best besties anyone could ever ask for—Emily Vix Ocampo, Megan Patin, Mary Dias D'Antonio, Morgan LaCombe Young, Will Avelar,

Rolando Gonzalez, and Edgardo Osorio. I might not have been able to finish this story if it wasn't for your overwhelming love and encouragement. You all gave me the strength I needed to fight...and so many reasons to live.

ABOUT THE AUTHOR

J.Q. Davis is from New Orleans, Louisiana. She has a bachelor's degree in healthcare but chooses to pursue her dreams of being a writer. Her husband is a retired Marine (23 years!) who works with surgical robots. They don't have kids but spoil their pups as if they were real little girls.

Her other interests include reading, watching true crime shows, and reading some more. She is also a video gamer and might spend too much time playing The Sims.

She is excited to continue this journey through writing and hopes that her readers enjoy her books.

Follow J.Q. Davis on:
Twitter: @JoJoQD (https://twitter.com/JoJoQD)
Instagram: @authorj.q.davis
Facebook: @authorj.q.davis
Website: www.jqdavis.com

ALSO⊙ BY J.Q. DAVIS